BY GARLAND ROARK

Star in the Rigging:

A NOVEL OF THE TEXAS NAVY

DOUBLEDAY & COMPANY, INC.
GARDEN CITY, NEW YORK, 1954

DISCARD

LIBRARY OF CONGRESS CATALOG CARD NUMBER: 54-7316

COPYRIGHT, 1954, BY GARLAND ROARK
ALL RIGHTS RESERVED
PRINTED IN THE UNITED STATES AT
THE COUNTRY LIFE PRESS, GARDEN CITY, N.Y., FIRST EDITION

FOR MISS VIRGIE SANDERS

Foreword

Late in the year of 1835 a little navy was launched by the grace of God, American credit, and private purse; sponsored by a province that had not yet declared its independence; and sent to sea almost before the ink was dry on the paper that legislated it.

Several months later the Texas naval flag fluttered bravely over the waters of the Gulf of Mexico; a single white star in union blue complemented by thirteen prolonged stripes alternating red and white. It was rather shrewdly designed and was often called the ensign of pirates. Under it and for it cannon fired on the roll of schooners-of-war and men sailed, sometimes without pay or reward, and often as not victims of politics in the land they served. They were good men and bad, adventurers every one, gambling their all for a just cause, their hopes kept alive by the star flying the main.

This is the story of one of the forgotten men who helped make Texas free, a commander of the tiny fleet that sailed without tradition or security, that ran the winds down, and fought and blockaded with unsurpassed audacity.

In writing this novel, I have endeavored to portray the true cause of the Texas Revolution. History has so played down the maritime side of the struggle that the heroes of the four Texan war vessels of 1836 remain unsung, unremembered. While holding close to history, I have exercised a novelist's privilege by drawing on the imagination

7

in depicting the lives, loves, passions, cruelties, triumphs, and disappointments that existed at the time. Finally, in order to escape the criticism of historians, I should perhaps catalogue certain historical discrepancies effected for the sake of fiction. However, the admission of such should suffice.

In acknowledging sources of information, I cannot fail to thank my friend Jim Dan Hill for his help, as well as for my greatest source of information, his *The Texas Navy*. Great appreciation is due Miss Virgie Sanders of Nacogdoches, Texas, for the use of her private collection of historical papers, also Miss Mildred Wyatt, Librarian, The Stephen F. Austin State Teachers College, Nacogdoches, and her staff, as well as the entire staff of the Rosenberg Library, Galveston, Texas; the Houston Public Library, Houston; and the University of Texas Extension Loan Library, Austin, Texas. Particular thanks are due to all persons living or dead who have published or contributed to *The Texas State Historical Quarterly*, of which the issues from 1904 have been of vast help to me. Other sources include: *Romantic Flags of Texas*, Mamie (Wynne) Cox; *History of Texas*, Ralph W. Steen; *The Isle and City of Galveston* (manuscript), Charles Waldo Hayes; *The French Quarter*, Herbert Asbury; *The History of Texas*, Eugene Barker; *Laws of Texas*, Gammel; *Official Correspondence of the Texas Revolution*, compiled by William Campbell Binkley; *Handbook of Texas*, Walter Prescott Webb and H. Bailey Carroll; *Life of General Santa Anna*, Clarence R. Wharton.

Garland Roark

NACOGDOCHES, TEXAS
DECEMBER 11, 1953

Contents

Book Three: THE EAGLE'S TALON—1835–1836

Book Four: STAR IN THE RIGGING—1836

Book One

UNDER THE MEXICAN EAGLE—1832

Chapter One

THE EMBARGO

On a morning in early January of 1832, Captain Jeremiah H. Brown got out of bed and moved to a window of the American Hotel in Velasco. There was a searching restlessness in his face as his eyes narrowed in study of cloud formations above the fairway to the Gulf of Mexico.

For two days the elements had battled for control of the Texas coast, a norther versus a warm Gulf wind. The weather was a prankster that kept wild geese, sharks, and seamen guessing. Even now the upper clouds moved southward above the prevailing wind off the sea. In the Captain's favor, the lower breeze came in steady. It chased yesterday's chill air inland with a promise to hold fair and balmy. He could fling sail to the wind today.

Anticipating an easy run out past Velasco Bar, Captain Brown ran an eye over the scene of town, wharf, and river.

Wagons creaked under loads of lumber, hides, and cotton to waiting ships. Slaves sang and sweated over cargoes to and from New Orleans as boats from upriver Brazoria and San Felipe de Austin stood by to take on supplies. The trapper in buckskin, farmer in homespun, store clerk, river boatman, bandy-legged sailor, and saloonkeeper, all were close to one another in common pride and common hopes.

Oblivious to the usual riverbank industry, the wide Brazos flowed serenely past sand bars and shoals to merge its fresh water with salt. Eddies formed in the current and banks were awash by the turn of the tide. Atop the fort the Mexican flag stood straight in the breeze, its eagle, serpent, and cactus plainly etched in the center field of white. Under the banner, cannon placed *en barbette* gazed grim and silent over the Velasco approach. Circling the outer wall and surrounding moat, hungry gulls dipped and screamed at the Mexican garrison of two hundred and fifty convict soldiers before banking in graceful motion toward the wake of an inbound sloop.

Captain Brown's face grew quizzical as the craft held his attention. Soon his gaze shifted to his schooner *Sabine*.

She was chockablock with Texan goods ranging from tobacco to peltry. Her masts glistened under varnish not two days dry, and the mainsail in harbor furl failed to reveal signs of age. With deck holystoned, hull solid black, and bulwarks a fresh white, she belied her age. But she didn't belong to him. The schooner he dreamed of was longer and roomier. The *Sabine's* cabins were so small that passengers had to sleep on deck. Many complained, since passage to New Orleans cost fifteen dollars. Despite her failings, she was seaworthy. And now, gleaming in the morning sun, she seemed as anxious as he to hoist sail and away.

The pleasing aroma of coffee lifted from the dining hall window below him. He dressed carefully, as was his habit in port. The light filtering through the window shone on long brown hair combed back from his forehead. It hung thick at the neck after the fashion of the time. A new cap shadowed a lean, rugged face so reddened by sun and sea wind that the blue of his eyes in contrast seemed bluer.

He made his way downstairs to a table set with ham steak, red-eye gravy, and wild honey. His long mouth spread in a grin as the hotel-keeper's niece moved to his table near the window and flashed him a vivid smile.

"Good morning, Polly."

"Late as usual, Jerry Brown," she said. "Why, the gravy is sleepy."

"Warm it up, girl." He glanced up and down her slender but mature figure, carefully noting and avoiding the sharp look in her brown eyes. "Has the *Commandante* made further advances?"

He suppressed a chuckle when she colored beyond the kitchen flush of her cheeks.

"He has not! And you know it. Lieutenant Pacho——"

"Why I thought you called him Juan, Polly."

He knew what to expect. When Polly Merchant struck such a pose, hands on hips, red mouth tightening into a line, one could expect to be set on his course right off. He pinched her cheek, which did nothing to suppress her look of indignation.

"Brazos thunder and damnation, Jerry Brown! One fine day I'll forget I'm a lady and lay you to the decks with a ham platter."

Fixing his glance on the cleft of her bosom, he said, "And after spanking you, I'll ask the sailmaker for a flying jib to raise your neckline."

As a hand lifted instinctively to cover the divide, she said incredulously, "Flying jib?" Then she whirled and left him.

Watching her go, he said under his breath, "That made her take notice, all right." He thought her pretty by any standard. Though taller than average, her curves were in the right places. For several years she had shown a marked interest in him, which she tried to hide with such talk as he had just heard. A man didn't have to be conceited to recognize admiration in a woman's eyes, as he had seen in Polly's when she measured his six feet and wide shoulders as if to say she liked big men.

Everyone liked Polly. Everyone teased her; simply because she was quick to retaliate. They were making a spitfire out of her. And he was as guilty as the rest. He was thinking she needed a brush with polite society, which she wasn't getting waiting tables in a frontier hotel.

She returned with a pot of coffee. Pouring his cup full, she said, "What are you looking at now?"

"You. You're growing up, girl."

"Well, I'll be damned! Does a girl have to be an old woman before she's grown?"

"Now that depends. In Mexico a woman might have five children by the time she's eighteen."

"I'm nineteen."

"Eighteen." He didn't look up. "Pass the biscuits."

"Nineteen." She placed them just beyond his reach.

He glanced up with mock amazement. "Then you could be the mother of six."

"For the right man, yes. But they wouldn't be webfooted little schoonermen." Suddenly she leaned forward and focused her eyes on something beyond the window. "Jerry, look! A Mexican sloop is dropping anchor near the fort."

Jeremiah stood for a better view. "Which could mean it's Colonel Renegade's ship." When she questioned the word "Renegade," he said, "Colonel Bradburn, head of the Mexican garrisons in Texas. Since he's an American, like Fisher his superior, we call him 'Renegade.'"

A troubled expression crossed his face as he thought of the recent quiet of the customs collectors. Ships had entered and departed from Texan ports for months without paying port or tonnage fees once imposed on vessels of foreign registry. Since Texan-owned ships retained their American registry, Mexico said they must be taxed.

Jeremiah reached for his cap. "What shall I fetch you from New Orleans?"

"I dare you to take me with you," she said, excitement brisk in her eyes.

"On your nineteenth birthday." He pinched her dimpled chin. "It's a promise."

"Coon oil!" she flung after him.

At the door, Jeremiah stopped suddenly and stared. A woman he had never seen before was entering the dining hall. She was dressed in lavender taffeta, cut low at the neck. Her hair flowing from a matching bonnet was like spun gold. When the bluest eyes he had ever seen lifted to examine him intently, he smiled and bowed. Her glance dropped and she made her way to a table.

His next sensation was like a bee sting on the arm. Polly had pinched him. She was saying in low tones, "Grinning like your face was made out of melted tallow! You're supposed to sail. Remember?"

He paused long enough to hear the woman ask if there was a ship leaving for New Orleans. Polly replied glibly, she didn't know of one. It was just as well, he decided. The *Sabine* couldn't accommodate another passenger, not even one as pretty as the stranger.

Aboard ship, all was ready for embarkation. The mate looked at the sheets and felt of the wind as he waited for the order to loose mooring lines. Slaves stopped their work on the wharf. Polly waved from the hotel entrance. Passengers on deck eyed the mainsail and the captain at the helm as Velasco paused to witness the departure of the *Sabine*.

Jeremiah was ready to give the order to raise sail when the *Commandante* of the garrison stepped up the gangplank, braid and brass buttons gleaming. After executing a bow from the waist with all the flourish of his race, he greeted Captain Brown politely and asked his indulgence a moment.

"A proclamation has just arrived from Colonel Bradburn of Anáhuac."

Jeremiah nodded. "All right, Lieutenant, let's hear what His Exalted Highness has to say."

Lieutenant Pacho struck his heels together in military fashion and translated the order:

" 'As of the date affixed any and all vessels of foreign registry departing for sea on the Texas coast, from garrisoned ports of entry, shall and must henceforth, according to the stipulations set forth in the Tariff of 1827, be obliged to pay a tonnage fee of $2.12½.' "

Jeremiah smiled. This had been tried before. The law remained as elastic as the port officials' instincts for trading it out with shippers.

"That is not all, Capitan Brown. Before I can allow your ship or any other in port to sail, such clearance must be issued at the chief customs office in Anáhuac by Colonel Bradburn."

"Say that again, Lieutenant." When the *Commandante* obliged with a reading of the profusely worded order, Jeremiah glared at him. "Do you mean to say I must go a hundred miles to Anáhuac for clearance papers?"

"That is correct, Capitan Brown."

"By a suffering gull! There are no land communications with Anáhuac. And since the embargo prevents intercourse by water, what the hell do you suggest?"

"Strict compliance with the order. Perhaps it does impose a burden. But," he shrugged, "I must enforce it."

"All the way, Lieutenant?"

Jeremiah studied the genial receiver for some indication that he might entertain an offer. Lieutenant Pacho grinned noncommittally before bowing and taking his leave.

Alone, Jeremiah glanced at the wheel in his hand, then frowned out over the river. Here he was with cargo aboard and passengers waiting for the *Sabine* to make sail, and an utterly impossible order staring him in the face: All the way to Anáhuac for clearance papers! Why this was ridiculous; actually worse than forcing an overland trip from New York to Philadelphia, since the Eastern cities were connected by roads.

His eyes thinned to slits of blue as he trained them on the fort and guns that guaranteed Bradburn's order.

2

Jeremiah stood grave and silent, a man thwarted by something he could neither understand nor control. Anger came in waves, only to fall away in half-formulated schemes of defiance which he knew were foreign to his nature.

Like his father, he was a man of peace.

He was thinking of his parent then, placing the wiser man in his shoes in an effort to exact sane judgment out of what evoked only resentment. He saw the elder Brown through the eyes of his youth and manhood and knew him to be one his sons admired more than any other. George Brown was honest, fearless, exacting, but fair, and his knowledge of men and the times had been, and was now, informed by the teachings of the Holy Bible. He had instilled in his two boys a profound respect for laws laid down in heaven and on earth, no matter what the errors of the latter.

But even George Brown could be pushed too far.

Standing the *Sabine's* deck, Jeremiah remembered also his mother's faith in the future and in her sons. The years following her death seemed a void that ended with the great panic of 1819, which turned the eyes of many Americans westward. Land laws in 1820 provided for public lands in eighty-acre blocks at $1.25 per acre, cash, while in Spanish Texas land was free. Money was scarce, and the will to pioneer was strong. Late in 1821 the Browns migrated to New Orleans and boarded Stephen F. Austin's ship *Lively*, loaded with seeds, tools, supplies, and a few colonists for the mouth of the Colorado River in the province of Texas. The *Lively* landed by mistake at the mouth of the Brazos at a time when Mexico was winning her independence from Spain. Due to the uncertainty of land grants at the time, the brothers Jeremiah and William returned to New Orleans to await the outcome of war. They took berths on sailing ships. In 1824

William returned to Texas, where he and his father applied for grants.

Meeting the requirements, evidence of good character, loyalty to Mexico, and acceptance of the Catholic faith, William received his league of land on the Brazos River, their parent his league and labor of land. They settled down to farm, trade, and fight thieving Tonkawa Indians while Jeremiah sailed aboard a schooner plying between the Brazos and New Orleans. The Browns pooled their resources and won over the wilderness, though without Jeremiah's sailing pay they might have failed. It seemed at first they had given up everything man had struggled to create over the centuries just to endure the hardships necessary to establish these things all over again; and in a setting where formal education appeared to be of less value than true aim and a hand at the plow.

In Jeremiah's mind was more than resentment against Bradburn's order. His very roots were threatened. Only the year before he had secured a grant of land. By borrowing and straining his resources he had bought slaves to tend the land. Later in the year his brother William had gone to sea again in order to help pay for tools and slaves. They sailed and left to landsmen the unending task of establishing social and cultural standards after the American pattern, helping in their way by bringing to a new country the trade and supplies essential to its existence and growth. No matter the water they placed between them and this frontier, their roots had been anchored in Texas as had their hopes and aspirations.

The future of the Gulf Coast was promising. Shipping was less competitive than in older ports. And his personal ambition to own a schooner, not just any craft, but one likely to astonish his fellow Texans by its size and accommodations, might soon be realized. Credit was available, though he had decided to wait until his private capital assured him a comfortable equity in a craft.

Thus he reviewed the past, right up to the present. And where the present joined the future he felt the threat which had fallen so suddenly over all that Texans had gained by land and sea. The security of trade hung in the balance.

Turning to the deck, Jeremiah said to the mate, "John, sailing is postponed indefinitely."

Upon learning all that had transpired, John Bailey smothered an oath and broke the news to passengers and crew.

Jeremiah studied his mate in half detachment. A stocky, powerful man for all his fifty years, John Bailey had sailed the pirate seas under Lafitte's Captain Dominique You and fought in the Battle of New Orleans, where he gained the proud scar on his right cheek. And again he was ready to fight. If his captain failed to rise to the occasion, he might sulk for a week or so.

Jeremiah put Bailey out of mind and went below, wondering what shipowner Edwin Waller would have to say about the order that would paralyze trade.

Long before the shipowner returned from upriver Brazoria that morning, the town of Velasco buzzed with excitement. Small groups gathered on wharves, about wagons, and in front of stores to discuss the situation. Jeremiah decided to stay aboard ship if only to avoid the maze of questions he could not answer.

The citizens found a leader in William H. Wharton. An amiable and spirited man, he was bitter on the subject of Mexican tyranny, as he called it, and an ardent advocate of the overthrow of the Mexican President, Bustamante.

Next Edwin Waller arrived. Being the owner of the *Sabine*, he withheld opinions and sent for Jeremiah. A Virginian of thirty-two, slight of stature, he had migrated to Texas in 1831 for his health. But so instilled in him were the principles of justice which Virginia had battled for in the cause of American freedom, he was quick to burn under the injustice of Bradburn's order.

Walking the floor of his small office, he said, "Jeremiah, they can't do this to us."

"Seems they are, Ed. Looks like Lieutenant Pacho's palm needs greasing."

"Not one penny for pirates."

"It's a long way by horse and foot to Anáhuac. And you forget we're loaded for New Orleans."

"Yes," he replied, staring at his captain. "Jeremiah, the trouble with you is you're too damn peaceful."

Jeremiah took no exception to the truth. He watched Waller depart, knowing his better judgment would take him straightway to the *Commandante*. What would follow depended on the Mexican's willingness to settle the matter for a consideration. Waller returned a little later with Wharton, who had gone with him to the fort. Both sat down and looked at Jeremiah.

"I offered him fifty dollars to lift the embargo," Waller said. "He wanted one hundred."

"Did you trade?"

"Hell, no!" Wharton exclaimed. "It's blackmail. To trade with him is to set a precedent for future extortion. Every ship in port would have to pay from now on. Jerry, it's a matter of principle."

"And fifty dollars." Jeremiah smiled.

Wharton flinched. "Well—at first it was. Until Edwin spoke to Lieutenant Pacho with a damn sight more emphasis than deference."

Jeremiah could well imagine.

"Jeremiah," Waller said, "as you know, I came to Texas for my health. I placed you in command of the *Sabine* for good business reasons. We've made money out of her, you and I. Well, I'd like to stay in Texas, but I can't stay healthy under such conditions as this."

Jeremiah realized that Waller was leading up to something: Either his captain was about to be cashiered or given an opportunity to buy the *Sabine* here and now. Certainly there was nothing warlike in his voice or demeanor to indicate what he said next:

"Jeremiah, I want you to run the blockade."

Chapter Two

SCHOONER OF DEFIANCE

Jeremiah could not check a laugh. The proposition struck so suddenly that he was caught unprepared. His hand raised in a mock gesture of defense.

"I'm serious," Waller said.

He was not a big man physically, though he radiated strength of purpose as he sat there proposing the first real Texan act of defiance against Mexico. Actually, he amazed Jeremiah, who said nothing of what he was thinking, that the battery would blow his ship out of the water, that both owner and captain would be sent to Matamoros to face a firing squad or, worse, to rot in a Mexican dungeon. He said slowly:

"Trouble leads to trouble, Ed. Wouldn't it be better to abide by the order and file a protest with General Teran?"

"What does it take to get you riled, Jerry? Can't you see this for what it is?"

Jeremiah got to his feet. "Teran stopped it once. He's Austin's friend, so he'll do it again."

Words were useless. He was getting nowhere with Waller and Wharton and they were not convincing him. He left them and walked slowly toward the schooner.

The *Sabine* lay against her moorings when she should be heeling on a good beam wind under San Luis Pass. There was a bracing lift in the Gulf breeze, and though the urge to run for the deep stream was strong in him, so was good judgment. The duty of the big brown muzzles lying over the outer wall of the fort was to cough fire and heavy shot. One shot placed just right could splinter mast or hull as well as a mortal's bones. Then again a ship might run without damage.

Squinting against the glare of the river, he measured the distance to the bore of the guns against wind velocity and slant. Then helm over and schooner a good five or six points off the wind before the first shot. After that—well, all depended on the skill of Bustamante's gunners.

The devil with it! Why take the risk in defiance to orders Texans must live with?

A commotion up the street drew his attention. The dust kicked up was from the feet of Waller, Wharton, and fat Dr. Robinson. They were marching toward the *Sabine,* and bringing up the rear in his sly old way was Captain Fuller. It was as plain as the red nose on his face that he desired someone else to be the initial target so he could slip to sea under big sail and small risk.

When Stephen F. Austin came out of the hotel and joined the group moving to the *Sabine,* Jeremiah breathed a sigh of relief.

Austin was not disposed to quarrel. First a colonizer, then invested with enough authority by the Mexican Government to turn most men into autocrats, he held Texas in the hollow of his hand with wisdom, honesty, tolerance, and loyalty to his own people as well as to Mexico. He was the man Mexico held responsible for the conduct of Texans, and the man Texans looked to for land grants, surveys, settlement of disputes, and the general welfare of the colony. His labors for just and fair laws before the Mexican Congress, at his own expense, were known to all. Only Austin of them all knew how to deal in politics the Mexican way.

Jeremiah knew him well, admired and loved him. Watching him then, he wondered if he would ever meet a smarter, more honest, fearless, or placid man than the little *empresario* who was listening patiently to Waller and Wharton.

Soon Austin was leading them toward the fort. A half hour later they boarded the *Sabine.* Austin's thin, sensitive face seemed more grave than usual.

"Gentlemen," he exhorted, "as you know, I declared myself. I regard Bradburn's order as utterly impracticable and advised him to let the ships go, only to identify myself with the opposition. This will prove embarrassing in my correspondence with General Teran. However——" He looked away and then at Jeremiah. "I appreciate your position, Jerry. At the request of William and Edwin, I will set you straight on the law."

There was more to this than met the eye, he said. And since Jeremiah believed in upholding the law, he felt it his duty to explain the difference between Mexican statutes and Bradburn's order. After that, the choice of obeying the true order of the government or the unreasonable deviation from it was the captain's. He proceeded to read the decree of September 1823 that specified: " 'All goods of every class, national or foreign, that be introduced into the province of Texas for the consumption of its inhabitants be free of duty.' " The period was for seven years, to expire in October of 1830.

Austin went on. "The Mexican tariff law of 1827 conflicted with the seven-year law, and General Teran decided the 1823 law still held. Then article 12 of the decree of April 6, 1830 extended the exemption four more years.

"That's the law. There isn't any other."

He let this sink home before saying, "Colonel Bradburn's mandate is therefore an open contradiction of Mexican legislation now in effect."

Jeremiah knew he was right. While he had not been in total ignorance of these decrees, the result had been the same. The attitude in the past had been an abidance by Mexican inconsistencies in order to avoid interruption of trade.

Austin's hand fell on Jeremiah's shoulder. "Given a few days, I may be able to present our case favorably to General Teran."

"They've broken their own laws," Wharton protested.

Waller added, "And forced an embargo that would shock the Mexican Congress."

Looking at Waller and Wharton, their eyes probing him as though he were some last hope in a lost cause, Jeremiah found it difficult wholly to exclude personal aims and ambitions in favor of open defiance. To sacrifice a clean past and promising future by one act seemed idiotic to say the least. With sentiment and good judgment at odds, he was wishing that the *Sabine* lay far out to sea. But she wasn't at sea, and his eyes were opened to the truth.

Resentment was quick once more. The absurd order was a personal affront to men who refused to give up one shred of their freedom.

On the other hand, why should the responsibility of initial defiance to Mexico fall to his lot? He had a feeling that he was being pushed into something from which there was no return; of being severed from the quiet, tolerant, and patient man the colonists knew him to be. He was wondering if such transformation were possible in any man when Waller said impatiently:

"Well?"

Jeremiah took in the fort and the river under narrowing eyes and fashioned out of the circumstances the only reply possible: "Ed, if you give the order to run the blockade, there aren't enough guns in Texas to stop me."

2

The right hands of Wharton and Waller collided in a reach for Jeremiah's. Dr. Robinson patted his stomach with one hand and baldpate with the other, all the while suggesting that they retire to his office and drink a round in celebration. Captain Fuller eyed Jeremiah critically, as much to say he would laud him to the skies if he made it and remove his cap in memory of him if he failed. Only Austin remained silent.

From that moment Jeremiah took over. To the mate, he said, "John, you'll put the crew aboard in lazy fashion. One by one. Have everything in readiness for sailing, every man alert and sober before five o'clock. We'll let the garrison fire with the sun in its eye."

Turning to Waller, he asked if they could lay on board enough cotton bales to protect men and bulwarks.

"Capital idea!" Dr. Robinson said. "Don't you agree, Captain Fuller?"

"Plumb capital, Doc."

Jeremiah looked at Fuller and said, "Maybe you'd like to lead off."

"Who, me? Never said I'd risk it a'tall, Jerry Brown, much less sail fust."

Soon only Jeremiah and Austin were left on deck. But there was a change somewhere. The peaceful atmosphere of trade no longer dominated the scene.

Jeremiah glanced at Austin. "You didn't argue much, sir."

"No." Austin's grave countenance softened. "I seldom champion a wrong, Jerry. However, I must for policy's sake tell Lieutenant Pacho that I advised you to wait."

Jeremiah grinned, remembering Austin's politics when the law of April 6, 1830 restricted further immigration from the United States. He had persuaded the colonists that there was much good in the law even as he wrote Teran a strong letter of protest.

"Good luck, Jerry." His handclasp was strong. Then he walked away.

Around four that afternoon a gang of Waller's slaves busied themselves moving cotton bales to the wharf and placing them aboard the *Sabine's* deck amid loud grunts and occasional laughter. John Bailey shifted his cud from larboard to starboard cheek and swore the bucks would load the ship into a fifteen-degree list if left to themselves. The *Commandante* sat outside a general store, pretending conversation with enviable Latin ease as he watched the cotton go aboard.

Jeremiah supposed it was Lieutenant Pacho's silence regarding the added cargo that provoked Waller's remark: He was forced to load the ship until her decks sat level with the water in order to pay the outrageous tonnage fees.

The *Commandante's* "*Si, señor*" did nothing to relieve the tension, so Jeremiah said, "Lieutenant, I could use a pair of reliable soldiers and a scout on my journey to Anáhuac."

The very mention of Anáhuac drew a snort of disgust from Waller. He went on to say that after his protest reached General Teran in Matamoros, the whole customs outfit would be recalled for all that was due them. The *Commandante* smiled and said it was too bad that misunderstandings had to arise between friends.

Jeremiah glanced at his watch. It was a quarter to five.

A slave boy was moving toward the *Sabine* with a rawhide trunk. This would never do. All passengers had their personal effects aboard and all had been warned to fetch nothing else. Then Jeremiah saw, following the trunk, the small woman he had seen in the dining room. She stood out against the bales of cotton and boxes lining the wharf, delicately holding up the skirt of her lavender dress with one hand. Her hair fell from under a lavender bonnet, flashing golden in the sunlight against her white face. The slave placed the trunk at the gangplank when John Bailey barred the way.

They were unable to hear what was said, though a hush fell over the group outside the store. She waved her hands in protest and stamped a foot. A moment later she was staring in Jeremiah's direction.

"Señor Capitan," smiled Lieutenant Pacho, "how can you refuse such a lovely passenger?"

"If I were going anywhere, Lieutenant, I couldn't."

Jeremiah left them and entered the hotel in time to overhear his youngest sail hand giving an account of the decision aboard ship.

"S'elp me, the cap'n stood all six foot o' him and looked them cannon in the eye. Yes, sir, not a sign o' what he was thinkin' on his red face ner in his blue eyes. And everybody waitin' all keyed up fer his answer. Then he sez slow-like, 'Ed, if you tell me to run that there blockade they ain't enough soldiers in all Mexico to slow me none.' Them's his words. And the way he spoke 'em! But say, here it is close to five o'clock."

He turned and ran right into his captain. In his surprise, red eyelashes worked fast and one of the silliest grins Jeremiah had ever seen spread over his round, freckled face. Everybody laughed when the lad of fifteen said:

" 'Scuse me! Cap'n! You said five o'clock!"

"See here, Little Josh," Jeremiah said gruffly. "Didn't I say there weren't enough soldiers in America and Europe to *slow me none?*"

Little Josh's small mouth formed a perfect O before he broke and ran for the door. With his going, the crowd turned serious. A sawyer said, "Are ye going to run it, Cap'n Brown?" At Jeremiah's nod, he said, "Well, boys, let's git our blue whistlers and Kentuckys loaded."

His plans were no longer secret.

Here was sport that appealed to these men, though not to Jeremiah. When the talk calmed down, he said, "Shotguns and rifles will land you in the fort's prison, as well as give the Mexicans an excuse for making it hard on everybody. The idea right now is simply to show them we mean to abide by the Mexican laws and not Bradburn's method of robbing us."

It was past five when he finally convinced them that this phase of the show was his alone. Minutes later he was aboard ship.

Edwin Waller came on deck. "Jeremiah, Wharton and I have been talking. If you get past the fort, I want you to invest the proceeds of this cargo in a couple of cannon, complete with powder and shot. In case of hostilities, we'll be ready to return the compliment. So bring them back with you."

Aware of the stiffness of United States customs laws regarding contraband of war, Jeremiah grimaced and said nothing. Watching the shipowner depart, he smiled wryly. Waller and Wharton were growing a little ambitious to fight a war. But that was their business. His was to get under way at just the precise moment.

On deck all was in readiness. The passengers had been sent below. John Bailey winked at his captain and spat over the side. Lashings were loosed on sails. The crew squatted on deck behind cotton bales. On the dock, Waller stood lazily at the bow fastenings and Wharton aft.

"Stand by and look alive," Jeremiah said.

Now was the time to put the *Sabine* between cannon and Texas sun.

A strange feeling stole over Jeremiah, one of regret and anticipation in strong conflict; one part of him against the other; the work he was committed to versus the Jeremiah Brown he had been until this day. Such were his thoughts in that instant he stepped to the helm. Then only one purpose dominated him.

John Bailey waited, taut and alert. Watching Jeremiah, he saw his glance shift to the gangplank. He was moving to take it in when the unknown lady he had seen twice that day appeared as if out of nowhere and scampered aboard. As the slave dropped her rawhide trunk over the rail and ran, she gave Jeremiah a smile as determined as pretty.

Bailey bristled. "Shall I put her ashore?" he said.

"You just try it, bully boy!" she replied, assuming a menacing pose.

"Better get off, lady," Jeremiah ordered gruffly. "We're sailing into trouble."

"I know," she said. "I'll risk anything to get out of Texas."

Jeremiah frowned. "Does that include stopping a cannon ball, lady?"

"Sure." She tossed her head and met his gaze squarely. "Look, Captain Brown, what you're up to is no secret. The whole town knows about it."

He opened his mouth to order her ashore in no uncertain terms. Something about her stopped him. "Then get below," he ordered.

"Thank you, sir." She smiled, opened her reticule, and fished out a mirror in unhurried manner.

"Get below!" he thundered.

As she left the deck, Jeremiah cried, "Let go the mooring lines! John, hoist sail! Lively!"

The *Sabine* came to life in record time. Sailors leaped as though under the crack of a whip, Bailey and a gang at the mainsail, Little Josh on the jib sheet reaching for the downhaul. Up rose the flying jib, bellying and jerking at the bows as Waller and Wharton unloosed the fastenings fore and aft simultaneously. Jeremiah gave her helm. She trembled once and heeled, her booms straining at lashings.

Polly's voice from the wharf rose above the noise on deck. "Jerry, you wouldn't let me go! And you'd better put that yellow-head off right now! You hear me, Jerry Brown?"

"The ship's got a fores'l, ye ninnies. Up with it!" John Bailey cried. Every man gave his all as she got a way under her in keeping with the fast start they had planned. Topsails broke in the breeze, water slapped the hull and raced astern in a flashing wake to the delight of gulls; ashore, townspeople ran to the river's edge, their cheers drowned by the yells aboard ship. These things were all about Jeremiah, unreal yet as real as the fort ahead.

They were outward-bound.

3

A hundred and one thoughts flitted through Jeremiah's mind, all of them part and parcel of the one paramount aim. He was into the adventure now. He spoked the wheel and took in the weather edges of sail in perfunctory manner. Experience stood the helm as Jeremiah Brown jockeyed for position and coaxed the last ounce of speed from the schooner. In his favor were sun, wind, tide, and possibly the element of surprise. Against him were Mexican guns commanding the roadstead half around the compass.

The *Sabine* was moving under the first gun. Jeremiah was "pinching" her then, holding her too close to the wind, while tensely watching the cannon bearing on the schooner. After what seemed an eternity, she slipped out of its range.

"One gun less," Bailey shouted.

The laugh died on his lips when he saw signs of activity on the fort's mound. Lieutenant Pacho was vigorously forming his garrison. All surprise was gone.

A puff of smoke and yellow flame preceded the sound of explosion. It was followed by a screaming ball and a burst of water towering topsails high close off the larboard bow.

The deck greeted the miss with wild abandon. At the mainsail boom lashings, John Bailey raised the land with earsplitting huzzaing, which was picked up in Velasco over the quarter. It was too early for cheers, though Jeremiah joined in if only to shake the nausea of fright which the first shot evoked in him.

Following the initial salute, the garrison's small arms began peppering the water and cotton bales with more accuracy than he expected. The smooth bore of the Mexicans' blunderbusses, as Texans called their muskets, made them inferior to Kentucky rifles for sharpshooting. Just the same, an inch-thick slug struck a spoke of the wheel not a foot to Jeremiah's left.

"Compliments of Juan Pacho!" Jeremiah yelled. "There'll be more."

John Bailey rushed aft. "Look here, Cap'n," he said gruffly, "ye're the only man not behind a cotton bale. Let me at the hellum." He waited, only to receive a stern order:

"Get forward, John. And stay there."

They were passing the nose of the fort in mid-river when the battery spat fire and smoke. Detonations jarred water, sky, and ship, burst on eardrums, and vibrated through a man. Shot whined overhead. It was evident they sought to cripple the rigging and render the schooner helpless. So fast and furious was the fire, Jeremiah was beginning to think the law of averages would come to the aid of poor marksmen. He had no sooner shaped this estimate than a red-hot ball struck the foremast just above the doubling and caromed off in a sizzling streak. The topgallant mast tumbled, taking with it all topsail rigging. Spars crashed down in a tangle of halyards and sail. Then the bomb exploded in air off to leeward.

"My God!" Little Josh cried, staring at the wreckage. And John Bailey was calling the gunner a name that meant he was born on the wrong side of the blanket.

The *Sabine* was at once slowed by the loss of topsails and useless canvas blanketing the foresail. The mate was the first to leave the protection of cotton bales and go aloft. Hacking at lines and crying, "Look out below!" he seemed oblivious to all danger.

Jeremiah decided against further tacks in favor of a bold straight dash. His darting glances measured distances, took in the fairway, rigging, deck, and the fort, over and over again. All the while, the Mexicans kept up their fire. The fort was wreathed in smoke with each burst, cleared by the wind seconds later. The acrid smells of powder reached out to the *Sabine*, as if driven on tongues of yellow flame. This was the world about him, all new and fresh, as strange as exciting. He felt no fear, and yet he knew that he was afraid.

Wiping sweat with the back of his hand, he ordered heads down below cotton bales. Next he cried, "Look out! Fire bomb!"

Then it struck. A cotton bale on the larboard side amidships caught the full impact. As the bomb exploded in a sunburst, the bale seemed to jump and fall apart in a mass of flames that leaped down the larboard side. The fore and aft ratlines were on fire and deck blazes were started in a dozen places. Other bales were burning. Fortunately the fire had been thrown back from the center deck and rigging. Otherwise that one direct hit would have given Juan Pacho and Bradburn their victory.

"Fire brigade!" Bailey and Jeremiah cried in unison. Slipping a becket over a spoke of the wheel, Jeremiah ran forward to assist the crew. Every man worked at top speed, Bailey's gang forward, Jeremiah's aft. Little Josh slipped from his perch in the foreshrouds and fell yelling into the river. Cursing, Bailey fished him out and cried:

"Throw him at a blaze!"

In the excitement, the order was obeyed. He was wet enough to put it out, though he was up in a hurry, running and clutching at his steaming bottom, mouthing, "Goddam mate," over and over.

With the fire almost under control, Jeremiah ran to the wheel and turned the ship's head to starboard. The maneuver was designed to present to the fort a narrow stern target.

Although the *Sabine* was putting water and distance between her and the fort, Jeremiah realized he had yet to run the guns of the southern battery. No sooner had he put one cannon behind him than another opened up.

Water spouted ahead and over the sides, often bathing decks as red-hot balls fell close and time fuses set them off. Mere yards above his head a slug of iron ripped through the mainsail, and at the peak a ball almost took the halyard.

A great commotion back in Velasco reached the *Sabine's* deck. Captain Fuller was hoisting sail! "Well, well," John Bailey cried. "Bless his dear old heart! He's actually goin' t'run it!"

The fort loosed a volley of musket fire on Fuller even as the *Sabine* drew heavy shot from the southern battery. John Bailey was asking for permission to level a musket at the fort under the plausible excuse that it was unfair to receive all and give nothing in return. With the captain's refusal, he mouthed an opinion before tearing viciously into a cut of tobacco.

Jeremiah's next impression was one of surprise and disbelief, for there on deck behind a cotton bale stood the girl, lavender dress tinted by the low sun. She was looking squarely at him, her cerulean-blue eyes steady and defiant. As if to declare her right to remain on deck, she rubbed at the smudge on her face. He knew then that she had helped put out the fires. In that swift interchange of glances the bark of guns failed to drown the spark she struck from his imagination. There was something in her show of independence that both annoyed and attracted him, that bespoke a kinship of spirit and mutual respect, even as they bristled at each other.

"Back to the hold," Jeremiah said.

"It's more comfortable up here," she replied carelessly.

A cheer saved her the embarrassment of being carried bodily off deck. The *Sabine* was safe, beyond the range of guns. Jeremiah threw his cap into the air and lent his yells to those of the crew. Everyone laughed when John Bailey seized the girl and executed a dance between cotton bales. They laughed louder when the touch of a woman so inflamed the mate that he turned her loose as though she were a Mexican bomb.

All attention was suddenly drawn to Captain Fuller's ship, which was yawing, veering off her course. Then an answering shot was fired from her deck. Even in the twilight, they could see the Mexican atop the fort leap into the air.

"See what I mean, Cap'n?" John Bailey said with envy.

"The crazy fools!" Jeremiah exclaimed, unaware that Captain Fuller had been wounded, and that a Texan called Spencer Jack had seized his rifle to even the score. All Jeremiah could see was the folly of it.

The full significance of that single shot struck like a hammer blow; for it was the first Texas gun that had ever fired on a Mexican. The Mexican garrison ceased firing and Captain Fuller was sailing quietly on his way, though Jeremiah had a feeling that trouble lay ahead. And Captain Fuller was the cause. He alone was to blame.

These were his thoughts when the crew sent up a rousing cheer for the first man who had openly challenged Mexican tyranny by standing past their guns—"Captain Jeremiah Brown!"

Standing there with their cries ringing in his ears, he was perhaps a disappointment to them. Silent and sober, he could only agree that actually it was not Fuller but he who had committed the first overt act of resistance to Mexican authority in the colony of Texas.

However impossible it seemed to him that a man of peace could completely reverse the pattern between the breakfast and supper table, the fact remained. He felt no wave of elation or pride of accomplishment; just bewilderment as he peered into the uncertain future.

Chapter Three

CARMELA RYAN

Jeremiah thought it odd that a girl he had never seen until that day should by her very presence aboard irritate him. Perhaps it was because she seemed to watch him constantly, smiling in a manner that declared she knew his every thought. It was of small comfort that she could know nothing of what was in his mind; the intensity of her gaze proved disconcerting at a time when he was trying to figure the outcome of the *Sabine* incident.

He shaped a course for the open sea, taking a bearing on the dim point of land on one side, Quintana Island on the other. He ate with the wheel in one hand, his eyes alternately lifting to the icy January stars and falling to the balmy Gulf. Duty-bound to wait for Captain Fuller's vessel and despairing of company that would relive the excitement, he shortened sail, determined to make quick work of any celebration. The topsail schooner came on with lanterns aglow and songs rising from deck. A woman's voice gave him an idea. Here was a chance to rid his ship of the girl.

He hove to and the other craft came close. His compliments to Captain Fuller were spoken and the news of his wound relayed back. Then: "Hurrah for Captain Jerry Brown!" It came as though rehearsed. With quiet restored, Jeremiah was invited to come aboard for a drink with the skipper.

He crossed over and came upon Captain Fuller half-seas over and as inordinately proud of his wound as Jeremiah would have been showing off the schooner of his dreams. "Ah, we made history, Jerry, but why so damn glum when all the *Sabine* lost was tops'ls?" He called in Spencer Jack, a young man so overcome with praise, because he had fired the rifle, that he would not be likely to recover before the realities of life closed off his glory. Then the one woman aboard, a Mrs. Sweet, gave Jeremiah the opportunity to suggest out of chivalry that she take the lady from his schooner under her wing. There was no room aboard for another lady, said Captain Fuller, unless she shared his cabin. He thought this remark very funny until Mrs. Sweet's stern glance took effect. As Jeremiah was leaving, Captain Fuller grasped his hand and said:

"Jerry Brown, ye're a man who sails fust and gets through, one I'll follow again, give the chance." Drawing Jeremiah down to his whisper, he said, "Fact is, I didn't have the guts to lead off."

Jeremiah replied, "And I wouldn't have had the guts to follow."

Now that fine remark called for another drink, said Captain Fuller.

Jeremiah returned to the *Sabine* in better spirits; until the lavender dress caught his attention. "Make sail, Mr. Bailey. Put a man at the wheel and take over." He turned to the girl. "Young lady, I haven't the slightest idea of what to do with you. All cabins are taken and there's no room on the other vessel."

"I'll make out, Captain," she said with a toss of her head.

"Who are you, and why did you rush aboard of me?"

"Aboard of *you!* Captain! My name is Carmela Ryan and I told you why I came aboard *of you.*"

There was nothing left to say other than "Sleep on deck or in the holds," but he refrained. Her large eyes remained on him teasingly. As his gaze narrowed, her glance swept on over the side, though the saucy quirk of her mouth persisted. Between his feeling out the wind and sea and watching the progress of repairs aloft, Jeremiah ran an appraising eye over her small, slender figure. She could not stand more than five feet in her high-heeled slippers, though she carried herself proudly erect.

Suddenly she put her back to the rail. He was the subject of serious concentration. Her bright lips, no longer devilishly taut, fell apart full and red. In the yellow lantern light of deck, her curves were formed of soft shadows in daring display. And Jeremiah was wondering why he wished to be rid of such pretty baggage when she demanded:

"Why in the name of heaven do Americans come to Texas?"

"Why did you?"

"My aunt and uncle live in Texas. They raised me after mother died and father was killed in the Battle of New Orleans. But I can't stand this country. Men in buckskin, heat in winter, alligators, Mexicans, Indians, and no social life whatever."

"Where in Texas?"

"San Felipe de Austin. It isn't like Memphis."

"Give it time, girl. This country is rich in timber, cotton land, tobacco fields, and——"

"Time!" she scoffed. "I'm not thinking of a place for my great-grandchildren. Just myself. I'm tired of bewhiskered backwoodsmen trying to coax me into the bushes. One year of it is enough."

"That's just one side of Texas, young lady. We came here with ideals no different than those of the people of Memphis, Nashville, or Boston. Moses Austin was from Connecticut. Stephen F. Austin went to school at Bacon Academy in Colchester, later at Transylvania University in Kentucky. Mr. Wharton studied law in Nashville. Mr. Samuel May Williams, secretary and manager of Austin's colony, came from a New England family that produced a signer of the Declaration of Independence and a Yale College president. We publish a newspaper at San Felipe, the *Texas Gazette*. Many of our ladies are educated and refined."

He grinned and added, "The refined ladies don't go near the bushes."

"Really!" She cocked her head and folded her arms. "What a nice speech, Captain Brown. I suppose the cultured Texans who made eyes at me from front porches were counting their rosaries and listening to mission bells."

Watching her smooth down the front of her dress, blowing in the wind, Jeremiah said, "Since few Texans are crazy, I don't suppose they were."

She brought a slim hand to her hair, then leaned back with a sharp intake of breath.

"It costs a great deal to dress and live New Orleans style," he said, with intent to draw her out.

"I tutored in Memphis and I can do it again. In any case, I can pay my way to New Orleans and get along until something turns up. How much is the fare?"

"Fifteen dollars."

She compressed her lips defensively, turned her head, and treated him to a sharp, sidewise glance. Then she was invading the privacy of her bosom. Producing a small leather pouch, she extracted gold coins and extended them.

"Here's your fifteen dollars," she said defiantly.

"Keep it. I can't so much as sleep you."

Her wide eyes narrowed suspiciously. "Since I can't imagine a schoonerman carrying passengers free of charge, Captain Brown, just what's your mind?"

Grinning, he stared her down before stepping to her side and leaning on the rail. "Among other things, your age and the color of your skin underneath that chalk. Also, I'm wondering if you're just a girl dressed up for an adventure and how you would react to a man's kiss."

She eyed him with amazement. "Good heavens! Is that all?"

"One more thing, are all your dresses cut down to the waist?"

"All right, Captain Brown. I'm twenty-two. I use chalk because it's the fashion and I dress this way because it suits me. Any objections?"

"None at all," he replied. "Quite the opposite, in fact. But you haven't answered the main question."

"As to how I would react to a man's embrace, well——" Her bright red mouth took on a challenging twist. As his look held steadily to her face, she met it with more deliberate intention than he had ever seen in any woman.

She had thrown the question squarely into his face. She awaited his reply; rather imperiously, he thought, for a woman who adventured on the ragged fringes of fortune. But she was trading for a place to sleep with no mistaken ideas regarding the worth of her item of barter. Nor was he discounting values as he turned the topic of conversation and led her below.

Entering his quarters, he said, "And that's how I, the most peaceful schoonerman between Pensacola and Tampico, earned a distinction I didn't and don't relish." Watching her pause in swift appraisal of his cabin, he opened a locker. "Cognac brandy or claret wine?"

"A little brandy—to shake the chill of deck. But weren't you scared when the shooting commenced?"

He held a chair for her. "Scared? That's putting it mild." Smiling broadly, he poured and sat down. "You see, I had never been shot at before, that is except the time my brother's Kentucky went off accidentally."

He talked on, about his migration to Texas, and she listened attentively. All the while he studied her, admiring her face and easy graceful motions. He saw in her little of Polly's toughness of fiber. She was far more poised than Polly, though the latter would have slept on the deck rather than give up one iota of her independence, much less trade upon emotions.

"To whatever you want from life," he said, touching glasses.

She looked pensive. "Everything." She was studying him. "And you?"

"A nice long schooner of my own."

A slim finger touched the cleft of her chin as her mouth curved into a smile. "Now were I such a man, I'd want two, three, or four schooners, and warehouses, and a house like I once saw in Boston."

"You don't want the moonlight, just the moon," he chuckled.

"Set with rubies."

Her musical voice varied in tone just as her small mouth assumed a succession of lovely shapes. Both fascinated him, sent his mind recklessly ahead.

"Hungry?" he asked.

"I'm starving."

Soon she was attacking cold roasted fowl and cornbread dressing with more zeal than delicacy. He opened a bottle of white wine, making an occasion of it. She pushed it away and he placed it before her again, enjoying, as did she, the little duel which both recognized as a reconnoitering expedition on his part. The continual and critical inspection of each other did not end with the cook's removal of the dishes. Her blue eyes met his, swept on, returned as if in challenge.

It was getting late and he was due on deck to relieve Bailey. Right now, he told himself, might be the propitious moment to complete the conquest. He was saying she would find the "donkey mattress" softer than the deck. She arose.

"There's water in the pitcher," he said, meeting her glance. Her eyes were wide, brightly curious and expectant. He waited no longer, but reached out and swept her to him fiercely.

She came willingly. As he tilted her head back and the flood of yellow curls fell over his arm, she pressed her firm, yielding breasts eagerly against his coat. The cabin seemed filled with her scents, as freshly intoxicating as the softness of her shoulders and throat under his hands. The blue of her eyes went out as he reached for her lips, and then she was a fire burning in him and a tropical gale rushing through him. He knew only that she was responding with an astonishing passionate longing. She was breaking away, then clinging to him a moment longer.

She twisted free and stood with back to bunk post, hands behind her, eyes smoldering, though not in anger. In the shimmering light of the cabin she was all too near and fascinating, her gaze lifting and falling as though timed to the heaving of her bosom.

"Better go now." Her low voice was tremulous.

It was not in his whirling mind to leave her then. Nor would he have obeyed her had she not broken the spell by opening her pouch and tossing coins at his feet.

"I'll pay my way!" she said, the violence of her feelings breaking through her words.

As though he had plunged his head in ice water, he saw only the yellow coins. Slowly he bent to pick them up. He left her and went on deck.

A bracing Gulf wind sang through the rigging and slapped water at the ship. It came on and tore past, moving on and on. The sea ran with it, all motion and rhythm. Above and breaking the void, stars slid out of the upper clouds in a burst like tiny bombs, only to fall away as other clouds overtook them. And weaving in and out of wind, water, and sky, out of Ed Waller's order to fetch cannon, was a lavender dress. First on the wind; next in the clouds; then in the light of deck and cabin. Then suddenly gone, leaving only the empty sea and a sigh of trouble on the wind.

Chapter Four

PORT OF FILIBUSTERS

The *Sabine's* mooring lines were no sooner cast ashore in New Orleans than a small crowd gathered and placed the usual questions about weather at sea, cargo, and affairs in Texas. Jeremiah appeared on deck in time to see John Bailey proudly pointing to the jury mast on the fore.

"Aye, gents," he said. "Shot off by Mexican cannon at Velasco."

Calling Bailey aft, he said it was not their business to advertise trouble with Mexico; particularly at a time when public notice might hamper the purchase and transport of cannon to Texas.

Dismissing the matter from mind, Jeremiah walked toward Carmela.

She was poised a little forward of the gangplank, fresh and neat in pink cotton. Lines of trouble furrowed her brow. Her gaze was fixed on a street where Negro convicts with iron collars and ankle chains slopped about in the greasy black mud, making ditches to carry water off the street. Her nostrils quivered in rebellion at the swampy odors rising from garbage-littered pools and clogged drains.

She continued to survey the immediate surroundings in the manner of one trying to reconcile what met her eyes with all she had heard about this strange city. Everything in sight was enough to puzzle a newcomer. A large Negro freeman dressed in fine linen got out of a carriage and moved to a stern-wheeler. Two nuns were picking their way across the mud when a mustee appeared with a bobcat in a cage. They paused and turned about, much to the delight of a pair of cotton speculators engaged in trade with upriver planters. Fancy ladies who worked the river front ran speculative eyes over incoming oystermen before sizing up the *Sabine's* crew. All the while, United States bank notes changed hands over barrels of whisky, flour, sugar cane, molasses, and other produce.

Carmela bit her lower lip and turned a puzzled face. Jeremiah moved closer. "This is New Orleans," he said. "Care to book return passage?"

Something like a smile played across her face, though the set of her lips remained unaltered.

"That's the American section," he advised. "The most wicked place in the United States. Unless it's the section over there. It's the Vieux Carré. If there's any sin or sport or way to make merry that isn't to be found in New Orleans, I've never heard of it. But you came through here on your way to Texas, didn't you?"

"No. I got off the river boat at Natchez and went overland."

"The hard way," he said. "Well, now that you're here, don't underrate this town. A person can be abducted or killed here in a hurry and be forgotten sooner."

"I'll stay," she replied.

An hour later Jeremiah dropped her trunk inside a room of a house owned and occupied by a merchant friend and his family. Left alone with Carmela, he looked the room over, as she was doing.

It was large and high-ceilinged, furnished with a wooden bed, marble-topped dresser, two chairs, and a French wardrobe. A flowered rug lay in the center of the stained, wide-planked floor and heavy curtains closed off two small windows.

She parted the curtains and looked at flowers blooming outside. Slowly she turned and sat on the bed. Running her fingers over the cotton spread in detachment, she raised her eyes to him.

"Thank you for helping me, Captain." She seemed a little wistful.

Watching her closely, Jeremiah decided she was a brave woman on an adventure she regretted but wouldn't admit. And since he happened to be the link between her and the land of her people, his departure would leave her with nothing but her courage, and that at low ebb. On the other hand, a woman was like Texas weather, inconstant.

"What's troubling you, Carmela?"

"I was wondering if getting word to my aunt in San Felipe would inconvenience you too much." With his reply, she said, "Just tell her I'm safe and continuing the search."

His intent gaze placed a question: Was her real motive for leaving Texas to search for someone? Although it was none of his business, he blurted forth:

"A relative?"

"My fiancé."

"The devil you say! Why didn't you tell me?"

She was fingering a lock of hair. "I didn't see any reason to tell you."

As he sat down in a chair, she began slowly: "His name is Thomas M. Thompson. We met in Memphis, and on the day we were to be married, he was forced to leave hurriedly for New Orleans. Why, I don't know. Some sort of trouble. Anyhow, I haven't heard from him in eighteen months. I heard he had gone to Texas, so I followed. Then I heard he was a mate aboard a ship out of New Orleans."

"Mate? Out of New Orleans?"

She brightened. "Perhaps you know him. He's not as tall as you, rather ordinary in appearance, I suppose, and talks with a British accent."

"Rather ordinary, eh? Odd for a woman who wants the moon in a ruby setting to chase after a plain ordinary man, isn't it?"

"I'm not chasing him. It's logical to believe he'll be easier to find here than halfway up the Brazos River in Texas."

"You mean that was your excuse to your aunt?" he said.

"Now that you've mentioned it, yes."

"Then he's just an excuse to get away from Texas."

"No, I can hardly say that. Thomas and I have much in common. He's fascinating in a way. An adventurer, so very sure he's going to chance upon some windfall that he puts you under his spell. Makes you believe he will, somehow."

He folded his arms across his chest and stared at her. "Is that what you two have in common?"

"Perhaps it is."

He nodded, subjecting her to scrutiny again. "Well, don't throw yourself at him, girl. And just in case you don't find him, the old *Sabine* touches in at this port quite often."

"Thanks."

Something in her tone of voice, the slightest inflection perhaps, sounded like mockery. Search her face as he did, there was not the slightest trace of it to be found. And yet he felt it, and resented it. Rubbing his chin in thoughtful silence, he admitted to having met many women in his time, though never one who veered off her original course with a man as much as this one. She was no more the Carmela Ryan aboard the *Sabine* than Velasco was New Orleans. Which, he felt with no logical reason for it, made him the prize sucker.

Presently he got to his feet. At the door, he said, "I'll let you know if I hear of him."

Holding her eyes with his, he brought a hand out of his pocket and dropped three coins one by one to the floor. As she stared at the fifteen dollars, he stepped outside and closed the door.

2

"So much for an adventure," he thought, moving toward Canal Street in the sunset. Then he turned his mind to his mission here, guns for Edwin Waller; brass the color of Carmela's hair. She wasn't so easily put aside. And now he was asking just what sort of a man was this Thompson to run away from such a woman. However, it was none of his business. The puzzle of their lives was one thing, his job of shipping heavy guns to Velasco another.

He strongly entertained the idea of purchasing the guns outright and clearing port legally. Already he had formulated ideas in this direction. Any other method entailed risk, since United States customs officers searched ships diligently for contraband articles of war. In the past, warrants of arrest had slowed many a dream of empire emanating in this city. But New Orleans was like a woman's mind, in that what was a violation of the law one day might be considered lawful the next. At best, one would do well to lay a finger on the town's political pulse before setting a course. With this idea in mind, he decided to visit Maspero's Exchange, a popular rendezvous of international plotters and filibusters.

Without any knowledge of what had transpired during the interval between John Bailey's statement about the Velasco affair and the present, Jeremiah knocked the mud from his feet and looked at the familiar door through which he had passed many times without attracting notice.

It was like stepping out of one world into another. Under the dazzling light of Maspero's gas lamps, in a setting of polished woods, mirrors, and wineglasses, an uncomfortable sensation assailed him; for someone near the barroom door spoke his name and transformed him into an object of interest. With a hundred pairs of eyes fixed on him and "Velasco, blockade, cannon" rising above the hum of conversations, he realized that obscurity had flown. Thanks to John Bailey's indiscretion.

Unused to this sort of thing, he stepped toward the barroom only to be rescued by a Texan friend, Thomas F. McKinney of Brazoria, one of Austin's old Three Hundred, now engaged in keelboating between New Orleans and the Neches River. He jokingly addressed Jeremiah as "Lord Nelson of the Gulf." He said he was entertaining friends who were departing soon for Nacogdoches, Texas, and who would be honored to sit in the company of Captain Jerry Brown.

He moved to a table occupied by four men, two in broadcloth, one in homespun, and one in buckskin.

Adolphus Sterne, prosperous merchant of Nacogdoches, Texas, was known for his part in the Haden Edwards land scheme that resulted in the so-called Fredonian Rebellion in the middle twenties. Sterne had aided Edwards by obtaining munitions in New Orleans and secreting them in bales of dry goods and barrels of coffee. When the Mexicans discovered this, he was ordered to be shot for treason. He remained alive because he had been a Mason.

As Jeremiah grasped the hand of this small man, he was thinking of the many ways in which Sterne might aid him in the quest for cannon.

Next he was introduced to General Raguet of Ohio, John Durst, plantation owner of East Texas, and the buckskin-clad ex-governor of Tennessee, now an adopted Cherokee Indian, Samuel Houston.

General Raguet was thinking of settling in Texas. Houston's future plans were somewhat vague, though Jeremiah had heard enough to connect President Andrew Jackson, Houston, and the Indian migration to Texas into some vague pattern. All the while, Houston drank enormous quantities of whisky without showing the effect. He was a large, imposing figure of a man with an eye like an eagle's and the appetite of two men. When he stood up, his six feet and three inches and two hundred pounds in fringed buckskin drew the admiring eyes of all about them. He seemed to know and relish the fact. During the conversation when attention was turned on Jeremiah and the account of the Velasco affair, Houston revealed a look of measured combativeness that caused Jeremiah to think he resented any other's domination of man or situation.

Regarding the Mexican political revolution, McKinney, Sterne, and Houston appeared well informed. They argued the effect on Texas of the probable overthrow of Bustamante by Antonio López de Santa Anna. The latter, said Sterne, espoused the Republican cause and promised to re-establish the Constitution of 1824 in favor of states rights over a centralist form of government. Houston doubted this. What did Captain Brown think about it?

"Austin's colony believes Santa Anna will favor Texas statehood," Jeremiah replied.

"But is that what Texans want, Captain Brown?" Houston asked. "At present they don't pay any taxes. So will they vote for statehood and taxes? And will they vote to give up their slaves in keeping with the Mexican Constitution?"

Jeremiah reluctantly admitted Houston had scored a point. "But it's security we want, sir, and we're willing to make a few sacrifices for it."

Houston spoke like a judge pronouncing sentence. "Young man, you don't know your politics. The only damn thing that will help Texas is to become a part of the United States."

For an ephemeral moment Jeremiah's imagination caught and played on some gigantic empire grab that dwarfed all land speculation of the past. It vanished instantly, as if it had been but a shaft of light in Houston's eye. But he could not help thinking that the *Sabine* incident had in some way upset Houston's plans.

Jeremiah said, "Maybe I don't know politics, but I know my people. We're satisfied to be a part of Mexico. What we want are the privileges of statehood."

Houston gave him a deprecatory smile. "And you're bidding for something of small value with petty defiance. You Texans are lacking in foresight and direction when you look toward Mexico City instead of Washington."

"Did you come to Texas to preach that, Mr. Houston?"

Houston glared. "My mission has to do with Indians."

He sounded evasive, and Jeremiah took pleasure in his reply: "Maybe the Indians will listen to you."

There was no humor in Houston's twisted smile. As his face reddened with anger, McKinney adroitly turned the conversation to other channels. The tension held, however, despite the show of conviviality.

Over oysters, Jeremiah was asked if he thought the Mexicans would open fire on the *Sabine* upon her return. Though unsure about this, he saw his opportunity to broach the subject that drew him to Maspero's Exchange. His reply to the question evoked a gleam in the eyes of Adolphus Sterne and all the excitement of surprise and adventure in every other face, with the exception of Houston's.

"I'm sorely in need of a couple of pieces of hollow ware, gentlemen." Grinning, he added, "To protect us from the Indians. No offense to you, Mr. Houston."

Jeremiah boarded the *Sabine* at three in the morning and met a newspaperman who had been waiting since midnight. He asked where Captain Brown had been since leaving Maspero's at half-past eleven. With Jeremiah's reply, "None of your business," he grinned sheepishly and asked for a firsthand account of the affair at Velasco. After exacting a promise that he would neither deviate from nor enlarge upon the story, Jeremiah related the incident and turned in.

Nothing material occurred until about two o'clock next afternoon when McKinney brought company: a lawyer whom Stephen F. Austin had once worked for and a United States district judge. Jeremiah was not kept waiting. Lawyer Hawkins lowered his eyeglasses and read a document he had drawn. It had to do with the fierceness of the Texas coastal Indians known as Karankawas, who appeared to be cannibals. He read on:

"And since the honorable Austin colony in the province of Texas has by deed and enterprise shown its moral character and peaceful inclinations, any armament requested for purposes of protecting its citizens from the depredations of a destructive and abominable foe, as savage and merciless as might be found in the primeval forests of darkest Africa, should not be denied said Anglo-American Texans, who petition for same through the accredited and lawfully established militia of Brazoria."

There was more to this wordy plea for cannon, though the meat in the shell was an attempt to legalize the purchase and shipment. The judge "harrumped," looked solemn, and declared in favor of annihilating the savages.

"However," he added, fingers forking his hairy brow, "Captain Brown, I must warn you against turning these guns on the Mexican fort while aboard your ship under penalty of arrest for shipping contraband of war. That is, unless——"

"I understand, sir."

They were raising a toast to American justice when Adolphus Sterne entered with a New Orleans paper. He passed it around with a voiced hope that the last paragraph was politic enough to slow the aroused Mexican influence in New Orleans. He said:

"Captain Brown was not only wise, he was generous when he stated that Texans considered Mexican laws fair and equitable, their only objection being the enforcement of instruments deviating from the written law."

The judge pondered the whole thing and said, "Under the circumstances, Captain Brown, the Mexican consul may stir up trouble. With the Velasco encounter in public print the Indian angle begins to smell like what the fishermen throw overboard."

They waited for an unofficial ruling, which, when it came, gave Jeremiah a first and lasting lesson in international behavior: "While the law forbids the shipment of cannon, I hope you get your hollow ware past the customs.

"Also, I'll divulge something I learned long ago. Newspapers are made to read, Captain Brown, not to talk to."

Jeremiah made an embarrassed grimace. It was he, not John Bailey, who had talked out of turn. Then the full import of his error struck home: as a consequence, the law-abiding Captain Brown should be forced to smuggle contraband of war out of the United States.

3

Two weeks later the guns were aboard the *Sabine* in boxes labeled: SAWS.

Anxiously awaiting morning, Jeremiah from the schooner's deck watched dusk overtake the city. A slight chill came on the unsteady wind, relieving somewhat the oppressive humidity. The sun had dropped red over the marshes with a warning that it might rise next day with its teeth chattering. As a half moon began to brighten and struggle with the elements for a peep at water and land, Jeremiah felt the magnetic attraction of the lights of New Orleans.

He bent his gaze in the direction of the Vieux Carré, where fine wines, lovely ladies, troubadours, cockpits, cards, and pistols defined the word pleasure. Offsetting all the night held in store were morning clearance and baffling winds down to the passes. Since he could do nothing to speed the dawn and a game of running contraband, he was quick to forget these things and entertain a picture of a girl in lavender with a champagne glass in her hand—and Jeremiah H. Brown parading her against the backdrop of New Orleans.

His memory advised that he had closed the adventure upon learning of her engagement to marry a man named Thompson. True, he had done this; rather it had been a decision of the mind. But what appeared proper and wise wasn't always compatible with a man's personal desires. He knew what he wished to do, and the will to do it was stronger than any reason against it.

Carmela showed surprise at his coming. At first cool toward him, she thawed with his invitation to see the town on his last night in port.

She cost him a pretty penny that night. They crowded days into hours in their rounds of the cafés and coffeehouses after leaving the Théâtre d'Orléans. From a ball on Chartres Street, they peeped into a quadroon ballroom where in the shadows hotheaded Creole suitors touched the forbidden sword-canes in jealous threat. In the dazzle of chandeliers and in secluded nooks where one candle burned too bright, they drank champagne and laughed and forgot customs and ships and the search for an adventuring fiancé. The wealth of shimmering taffetas, velvets, and Spanish laces in an atmosphere of tropical lanquor swept Carmela out of a sane world into the dizzy realm of her dreams. He saw her staring at finery out of covetous eyes; and he knew, and didn't seem to care, that the quickest path to her heart was through the possessive touch of her fingers on these things. Nor did he experience any feeling of compunction at exposing her to the sheen of life out of his reach and hers. Instead, he got a chuckle out of holding the flame before the moth and watching the wings beat madly toward it. It was all a part of an extended adventure that would end with morning.

It was nearing the cold dawn when he helped her into a closed carriage. She fell asleep on his shoulder and upon arriving at her house, he carried her inside and placed her on the bed. When she roused and asked where they were, he said, "The *Sabine*," and laughed with enjoyment as she bolted upright and stared at him. She fell back wearily, saying:

"I had almost forgotten the fare."

Throwing a blanket over her dress, he replied, "I haven't. But I'm due aboard ship."

As she murmured something, he kissed her on the forehead and took his leave.

Outside, he turned his collar up to ward off the chill air. The carriage creaked toward the river through incoming layers of fog and he sat back reviewing the night with one part of his mind and looking ahead with rising trepidation to clearance for Texas with the other. He seemed to remember that he had not removed Carmela's high-heeled slippers. Then it didn't matter; what really mattered were the pieces of brass under layers of saws aboard the *Sabine*.

4

Day broke with weather that threatened to hold the *Sabine* to land, though by nine o'clock a freshening north wind cleared the air. With visibility good, Jeremiah presented his papers for clearance and awaited the game of hide-and-seek, his first with the United States customs.

To those less involved than he, the game on shipboard that morning promised entertainment. Besides the crew and John Bailey were Thomas F. McKinney, lawyer Hawkins, and Adolphus Sterne. Under the pretext of seeing Jeremiah off, they waited to furnish bail in case of an arrest.

Jeremiah followed the searchers into the holds and watched lids ripped from boxes. Experienced hands explored coffee beans to a convenient depth. Casks were tapped with mallets as trained ears listened for sounds at variance with the specified cargo. Dunnage was combed and scarcely a nook or cranny from bows to stern was overlooked.

Pausing before the cargo in question, the inspector remarked on the large number of saws Captain Brown was shipping to prairie land. Jeremiah reminded him of the importance of the lumber industry in Texas. The other said four boxes of saws seemed a "devil of a lot" to ship anywhere.

The inspector decided to have a look. He pried the box lid and began lifting saws one by one. Suddenly he paused in his work and shifted his sharp glance from cargo to captain. Jeremiah could almost feel the unyielding hand of a United States marshal on his shoulder. He was in trouble and he knew it. Arrest for smuggling contraband of war would mark him for life.

"Somehow, Cap'n, we suspected you might be smugglin' guns to Texas. Now I can dig more saws out of this box. However——" He squinted one eye shut and focused the other on Jeremiah.

"Why, Inspector! You know me. I've never been suspected of smuggling."

"That's what the judge said, Cap'n Brown."

Watching the inspector move off, Jeremiah sat down on the box and breathed a heavy sigh of relief. It had been a close call. But, thanks to friends and a sympathetic judge, the customs wind blew fair.

So did the north wind that put him out to sea and came on freshening over the starboard beam once he rounded the Balize into the open Gulf.

The *Sabine* reached the mouth of the Brazos in record time, only to find the north wind had so lowered the depth of water over Velasco Bar that he was forced to sit it out until the norther abated. He spent a day listening to the icy wind screaming in the rigging and watching cloud masses charging down over the Gulf like avenging gods on the loose.

On the morning of the next day a sail hove in sight out of the southeast. Unable to identify the oncoming vessel, and thinking she might be a Mexican schooner-of-war, Jeremiah passed out rifles and alerted the crew.

She hovered suspiciously on the horizon for some time. Whether slow-sailing merchantman or watchful enemy, the effect was the same. Posting lookouts, Jeremiah checked wind and currents. Although the weather had shown remarkable improvement, seas ran confused and the air was baffling. Several hours later, currents ran for shore in obedience to the Gulf winds.

Jeremiah decided to chance the bar. Under shortened sail, the *Sabine* crept in with hand lead swinging. It was touch and go. The bar lay under the incoming current with scarcely enough water to float the *Sabine*. Aft, to windward, the mysterious schooner broke the mist like a gray threat. She stood in on creeping wings, too distant for identification, too close for comfort.

"We're keel to bar, Cap'n," Bailey advised.

Jeremiah rubbed his jaw, looking ahead to the fort and astern at the schooner. "If she's armed we're between the devil and Davy Jones. Give her sail, John."

The *Sabine's* mainsail ran up and she took a step forward and slowed. Vibrations ran her length and she groaned, her keel cutting a trench in the bar. The foresail was winged out, and Jeremiah was debating the advisability of floating cargo in order to lighten her. The sails bellied full, strained at booms and hoops. She appeared grounded one moment; in the next, she began to slide.

"She clears!" Bailey cried.

Jeremiah leaped for the helm and swung it hard over. The *Sabine* heeled, grinding her larboard hull against the bar. In righting herself she slid clear and sat trembling in good fathoms.

The ship aweather had drawn closer. She flew headsails and reefed topsails on the main. Partially closed off by low flying clouds, she remained a ghostly stranger now in excellent position to veer off and greet the Sabine with a broadside. While ahead, closer now, lay the fort guarding the Velasco roadstead.

Jeremiah reached for his telescope in the binnacle box and trained it on the schooner. Sail was breaking in the wind, though it was her deck that held Jeremiah's attention. She came bows on, shrouded off in mist streamers. When at last he peered between ragged clouds and scanned her weather quarter, a broad smile lit up his face.

"John, she's Captain Fuller's tub."

With tension eased, he breathed deeply and studied Fuller's craft.

"John, come here." His eyes twinkled, and the mate approached looking curious. "Old Fuller is good at letting somebody else take the risks. He needs the daylights scared out of him as much as the *Sabine* needs protection in a run for anchorage."

Bailey's eyes narrowed and his blank look gave way to understanding. He chuckled, spat into his palms, and said, "Cap'n, 'tis amazin' how ye warms me heart at times."

When Captain Fuller cleared the bar and ran up to speak the *Sabine*, Jeremiah trumpeted out conversation while Bailey maneuvered the schooner to Fuller's larboard side. The other hadn't caught on. Even when he ran up sail he had no idea of what was happening to him. The presence of the fort caused him to whirl on his deck and stare at the *Sabine*.

"He's lowering sail," Jeremiah said, and Bailey gave the order to take in canvas. "He's hoisting sail again, John."

"Bless his heart, so am I, Cap'n."

Captain Fuller tried every trick at his command to no avail. The *Sabine* kept him between her and the fort. As the ships sailed into the range of the guns, he paced his deck and shook a fist at Jeremiah.

"A damn dirty trick, Jerry Brown!" he cried. "They'll blarst me outen the water whilst ye sail free!"

"Turnabout is fair play," Jeremiah replied.

"By God, I'll splash me anchor!"

"Under the guns, Cap'n Fuller?"

The old man's snort could be heard a cable's length to windward. Jeremiah laughed and the *Sabine's* crew joined in.

All mirth fell away as they presented a perfect target for the fort's guns. Both captains waited for the blast, watching through spyglasses. Not a Mexican had shown himself on the mound, though this was of small comfort. They realized that the garrison could form quickly and loose enough shot to sink both schooners.

"Too bad you'll catch the worst of it, Captain Fuller. But it's generous of you to lay cover for me."

No reply came. Fuller couldn't remove his eyes from the fort.

Every yard brought him closer to the guns. Even unskilled artillery-men could score direct hits at this range. The town drew nearer and the piles of the wharf were etched in sharp detail.

"Cap'n, 'tis beyond me comprehension. Not a bloody gunner in sight," Bailey said.

Jeremiah was equally puzzled. Not even a sentry walked the post. The flag waved and whipped its frayed ends like a ragged, forgotten sail. The late sun came out from behind dark clouds and flooded river and fort as the ships slid out of danger and lowered sail for the last lap to anchorage.

The mooring lines were no sooner cast ashore than Edwin Waller came aboard. Jeremiah pointed to the fort and said, "What happened to the garrison, Ed? Where's Lieutenant Pacho?"

Waller laughed. "Wait'll Captain Fuller learns the fort is without garrison or receiver."

"The devil you say! Why?"

"I'll start at the beginning. After you cleared the fort that day, Lieutenant Pacho arrested William Wharton and me, charging us with the responsibility of leadership in your scheme of defiance. He put us in the fort's prison, where Wharton argued himself free. When I refused to give an inch, he sentenced me to be sent to Mata-moros for trial. Finally, Austin and Wharton secured my release.

"Then Lieutenant Pacho presented our case to General Teran with some success."

"But why is the fort deserted?"

Waller grinned. "Just a little matter of economics, Jeremiah. When the merchants refused to sell supplies to the fort until the embargo was lifted, the Mexicans got sort of hungry. Soon Pacho and his gar-rison left for Matamoros."

Before Jeremiah could voice his surprise, Waller said, "Did you fetch the brassware?"

"You ordered them, didn't you?"

"Sure," Waller replied. He seemed disappointed as he added, "But there's not a damn thing left to shoot at."

Chapter Five

DOUBLE CHALLENGE

Almost five months after the delivery of cannon to Waller, the *Sabine* was again reaching for Velasco with cargo from New Orleans. Jeremiah stood the deck, watching the blue Gulf in detachment. The wind came on with soft, murmurous sounds, keeping alive a running chop of water across the level reaches of the sea. It bellied the weather-browned sails of the *Sabine* as she heeled and creaked to the scend of the waves. Farther on, out beyond the ship's wake, the seascape lost shape and animation and stretched on to touch the sky in a blend of azure almost without definition.

His thoughts were troubled when the lookout cried land low over the starboard bow. He could not rid his mind of the political situation at home. Following the *Sabine* incident, Stephen F. Austin had forwarded a petition to the Mexican Government urging renewal of tariff exemption for a period of five years.

For a time the outlook had been promising. Ships sailed without paying duty. Santa Anna was winning against Bustamante in Mexico, and many Texans, Jeremiah among them, thought the problem would resolve itself once he was in power. The people of Texas believed in Santa Anna, saw in his successes some permanent peace and security for Texas. When that time came Jeremiah would buy a schooner of his own.

But that was not for the present, for Colonel Bradburn had dispatched Lieutenant Colonel Ugartechea to re-establish the garrison at Velasco. The Texans liked this Mexican, even though he brought with him one hundred and twenty-five soldiers and a nine-pounder bastion swivel gun to guard the Velasco approach; despite the fact that they believed Bradburn would soon give the order to collect tonnage fees once more.

Such was the unsettled state of affairs. There seemed no end to uncertainty.

Jeremiah remained one of the few who had not joined the Wharton-Waller scheme of rising to Santa Anna's aid. Standing the deck then, he was wondering how long he could hold out against the tide at home. Even his own father and younger brother William were strong advocates of what the colony called "timely action."

As the *Sabine* entered the mouth of the Brazos, Jeremiah wondered what his people would do, what was best for them. They had accomplished much in peace. Everything he saw reflected the industry of Anglo-Americans. Other than ships lining the river shore, almost every object under the late afternoon sun was Texas-grown or Texas-made. The ideal was land, a permanent and prosperous community for men. The experiment had been a wise one. True, Mr. Cobbler's idea of raising cherries and quince wasn't proving out. Nor was John Wharton reaping anything but laughter from acres of barley and rye. But his plums were red against an orchard green. Time would tell just how much wheat could be grown on the Gulf coast. Time would declare many things.

His attention was drawn to the large group of men on the wharf ahead. Something was in the wind. He saw John and William Wharton, Waller, and Captain Fuller. And there were his father and brother William with Thomas F. McKinney and one of the Allen brothers. Then he saw Polly. She emerged out of the crowd and stood beckoning him in.

Sail was run down and the *Sabine* eased in for a broadside docking. As the lines were cast ashore, Polly rushed aboard, her brown hair streaming in the wind. In her face he saw the excitement of a child.

"Jerry!" she cried, running to him. Her arms went about his neck and, before everyone, she kissed him full on the mouth.

She had never done this before. There was a first time for everything, he supposed, but this was neither the time nor the place. He felt himself reddening from the neck up before laughter from the wharf reached his ears.

" 'Fraid of her, Captain Brown?" someone asked. "I'd give ten years of my life to be in your shoes."

Polly turned on them. "There never was any privacy in Velasco." Fixing her bright eyes on Jeremiah, she talked hurriedly. "Trouble is brewing, Jerry. They're going to collect tonnage fees. And the crowd is here for just one purpose. To get you to sail out past the guns again. Don't you do it."

Jeremiah walked away from her. She stood with eyes blazing. "Don't say I didn't warn you. Go ahead and get your fool head shot off and see if I care."

The crowd opened up a path for her as she tossed her head indignantly and moved off.

William Wharton led the group aboard and said, "Polly just about summed it up, Jerry. The order says: 'Any and all ships refusing to pay tonnage fees will do so under penalty of cannon fire.' "

Jeremiah stood still, saying nothing, his imperturbability deliberate.

"So," Wharton went on, "it seems that history is repeating itself. Eh, Jerry? Lightning hitting again in the same place." Smiling, he dropped his glance under Jeremiah's forbidding gaze, and said, "Ed, maybe you should say the rest."

"Just a moment," Jeremiah's father spoke up. Advancing, he looked up at his son, furrowed his white brow, and rubbed at a long mustache. "The idea is, son, you did it once."

Jeremiah looked them over. In his face was anything but sympathy toward their wishes. His glance paused on his brother William and he softened a little. Admiration was mutual. At twenty-seven, William appeared as poised and serious-minded as a man of forty. Not as tall as Jeremiah, he possessed the same direct blue eyes and sensitive nose. But Jeremiah knew that William carried the Brown sensitiveness to the extreme.

"Well?" Ed Waller said, as though he remembered the magic of that one word a few months earlier.

Jeremiah was unimpressed. "Ed, I believe you and Will Wharton sit around and think up schemes while I'm away." This was received with a ripple of laughter. "She's your ship, but everybody is calling her 'Schooner of Defiance.' "

In tones touched with humor, he added, "And you know what the Mexicans are calling me."

They knew the power of crowd persuasion, and they used it. Waller said he would load the ship that night if Jeremiah would sail next day. William Wharton offered to furnish a dozen slaves in support of this idea, and Thomas McKinney made a similar offer.

Jeremiah removed his cap and shook his head. "The lieutenant colonel appears to be a reasonable man. I'll try it my way this time."

2

The sun was low when Jeremiah crossed the fort's ditch and asked for an audience with the *Commandante*.

Lieutenant Colonel Ugartechea greeted him warmly. Every inch the polished gentleman, he led the way to a patio-like enclosure outside the southeast wall of the fort and ordered wine and cigars.

A man of about Jeremiah's age, Ugartechea was a student of economics as well as politics. He replied to Jeremiah's voiced hope for Anglo-American security in trade under the Mexican flag by admitting that this could hardly be realized until the Republic of Mexico found political security at home. Opposing this, he said, were men who pretended to be defenders of the Constitution of 1824 but who were in reality governed by selfish ambitions.

Jeremiah looked at a small lizard which had changed its green color to the brown of a withered banana leaf. "Political chameleons," he said. "Bradburns."

"I was thinking of Santa Anna. But since you mentioned Colonel Bradburn, I must say he is an American who thinks like a Mexican. We Latins think with our emotions. Flourish and favor often shape our political views."

"Bradburn is still wrong, Colonel."

Ugartechea smiled. "And a crow eats corn. But what are facts and sound reasoning when one is dealing in politics? What is right and just is not always compatible with one's position. For example, our consul in New Orleans calls you a pirate. While I do not agree, I would be forced to support such an opinion by my actions should it prove necessary. But forgive the illustration, *amigo*."

Jeremiah nodded understanding, even as he felt the menace of the Mexican flag above him. In the cool of the late afternoon, its shadow stretched far over the Gulf prairie. Behind him through the wall was the prison which had held Waller and Wharton.

Shifting his gaze to the lizard now puffing out its throat, Jeremiah said, "The order to collect tonnage fees is a violation of the tariff exemption. Would you uphold the law of your country or Bradburn's order?"

"It is for my superior Colonel Bradburn to interpret the law, Capitan Brown."

Before any reply could be made to this, Francisco Dulcor, port receiver for the Brazos, joined them. A stern-visaged man of short stature, he studied Jeremiah closely before moving inside for a conference with Ugartechea.

Both returned shortly, and Dulcor said, "It is just as well that you are here, Capitan Brown." He sat down and gulped wine while the *Commandante* glanced from an official-looking document to Jeremiah.

"Perhaps Capitan Brown should hear Colonel Bradburn's latest order," the receiver suggested.

Dulcor's gaze held to Jeremiah as Ugartechea read aloud:

"Expecting trouble at Anáhuac, I feel capable of defending my fort against riflemen, but not against cannon. The only two not in possession of Mexican garrisons in Texas are those Captain Brown shipped to Brazoria aboard the *Sabine*. It is therefore necessary that you get possession of these guns at all costs."

Even tight-lipped silence failed to cover Jeremiah's surprise. How the devil Bradburn had learned about the smuggled cannon was a puzzle he would give a lot to solve. Other than Bailey and the discreet friends who had helped him secure and ship the guns, only one person knew about them. Carmela.

Dulcor smiled. "Capitan Brown's presence is timely."

Ugartechea frowned. Looking up, he admitted reluctantly that this was true.

"Capitan Brown, without your aid in this emergency, as well as the tariff issue, you may force upon the Mexican Government military measures not to my liking but to the hurt and detriment of all Anglo-American Texans."

"My opinion of Bradburn hasn't changed," Jeremiah replied.

Ugartechea smiled, studying the end of his cigar. As a host, he appeared embarrassed.

Not so Dulcor, who was saying, "Perhaps Capitan Brown might save you much trouble for a consideration." He named a sum of money likely to appeal to any man.

Ugartechea responded genially, "Begging your pardon, Capitan, but Señor Dulcor suggests the extreme measure in an effort to preserve the peace."

Meeting with silence from Jeremiah, Dulcor said, "Also, I am confident that our Minister of War and Navy would entertain a recommendation from the lieutenant colonel in favor of placing Capitan Brown in command of a Mexican schooner-of-war to patrol the Texas coast."

Jeremiah glanced from one to the other with no loss of composure. Withholding any expression of insult from his face and voice, he said quietly, "I'm not interested."

As Dulcor's mouth tightened into a cruel line, Ugartechea said, "I could have told you, Francisco. A game bird has no taste for carrion."

Jeremiah got to his feet. "Thank you, Colonel. Now may I return the compliment by saying we Texans like you too much to see you open the Santa Anna-Bustamante war in Texas. Of course, you realize that's what will happen if you fire on ships refusing to pay tonnage fees."

Ugartechea arose and nodded gravely.

"In a few words, Colonel," Jeremiah said, "I'm sailing tomorrow without paying duty."

Ugartechea appeared to consider this. Then, his motions more casual than deliberate, he touched his glass to Jeremiah's as though nothing had come between them.

"To your health, Capitan Brown." Lifting his palm in a gesture akin to a shrug, he said, "What a pity that I must direct my gunners to fire upon you."

3

He had put the footbridge across the fort's ditch behind him when a movement in the path ahead drew his attention. In another moment he recognized Polly. As he reached her side, she looked up starry-eyed and sober in the moonlight.

"What happened, Jerry?"

"Nothing. Did you expect the colonel to toss me in the dungeon?"

"I don't know what I expected. Are you going to run the blockade again?"

"Perhaps," he replied absently.

Polly's hands toyed nervously with a small bow of ribbon at her waist. "The moon's mighty pretty, isn't it? Let's walk up to the bend and watch it over the Brazos."

"We're on the wrong side of the river for that, Polly."

Dropping her eyes, she said, "That's probably the way it will be always."

"Yep," Jeremiah said, "until the moon rises out of the west." He waited, suppressing a grin.

"That's very funny, Captain Brown! A sailorman must remember his geography, all right. To your way of thinking, a moon is nothing but a tide marker."

She put her back to him.

"Know where Waller and Wharton are, Polly?"

"At the hotel drinking and betting two to one you win Colonel Ugartechea over. Better hurry over there, Jerry. The moonlight isn't good for you."

"No? Turn around, Polly." When she refused, he did it for her. "I'll row you across the river. I'll look at the moon with you. But don't get any funny ideas. It's because I don't wish to sit and talk about tariff and Bradburn all night. Understand?"

"I understand. You can't get that yellow-headed woman off your mind."

"That's not so."

"Really, Jerry?" She smiled up at him. "I dare you to prove it."

"You do, eh? Well let me tell you something. The way you've been acting lately, the whole town is saying Polly Merchant is a brazen piece of baggage and I'm the cause. What'll your aunt Virginia think when she hears about the way you greeted me on deck this afternoon?"

"She heard about it, all right. She said if she could afford it I'd be packed off to an Eastern finishing school."

"I'll see if I can convince her it's a good idea."

"School wouldn't change me, Jerry. I'd still kiss you in front of God and everybody just as I did today."

Jeremiah shook his head hopelessly. "Come along. We'll see if there's a boat handy."

"There is," she said. "I saw to that."

Jeremiah said nothing as he helped her into the boat. Taking the oars, he pulled from shore. Watching her, he realized that she was entirely too forward. What she needed was something to frighten the wits out of her. Long before they reached mid-river, he had shaped a plan that might teach her a lesson.

He swung the boat toward a plantation landing. A little to the north was a peach orchard and, facing the river, a vine-covered arbor where the owner and his wife used to sit of evenings and gaze across at Velasco.

"This isn't the bend, Jerry. But it makes no difference. We're across the river and free of Mr. Waller's influence for once. Or do you ever forget he's not along?"

She talked on, about his risking his neck to save a few dollars for Edwin Waller. Soon he reached the rickety old landing and tied to.

"Golly, Jerry, it's pretty over the water."

She held his full attention. For a moment a little quake of anticipation stirred in him. The flood of moonlight intensified the darkness of her hair against a silvered face and a shining pair of dark eyes. She was long-limbed and girlishly graceful. But she wasn't Carmela.

He looked up into the sky, wondering if Carmela might be watching the same old moon, and thought to himself: "Too bad it's not you with me on the wrong side of the Brazos. What I plan to hand Polly wouldn't be play-acting with you."

He had visited Carmela on each of his many voyages to New Orleans since January. His waking hours were filled with reminders of her and nights increased the longing to hold her close. Either she was the type of woman that demanded a long conquest or he was the wrong man. On the other hand, his advances had been purposely slow. But Polly had spoken.

"Yes," he replied pensively, "it's pretty over the water."

Turning suddenly, he saw Polly the adult for the first time. The moonlight gave her an ethereal look that lends beauty to any woman. Wicked little thoughts turned on him suddenly and he felt himself go cold. When Jerry Brown robbed the cradle, the Brazos would ice over in August. That much he knew.

Less anxious to go through with what he had in mind, he walked slowly toward the arbor. She followed and caught his arm.

"Gee, it's nice of you, Jerry. You know, this is the second time I've crossed the river."

"Who took you across the first time?"

"Lieutenant Juan Pacho."

"Have a good time?" he asked.

"Yes. That is until he became too enthusiastic."

"About the moonlight?"

"Me, Jerry."

"Suppose I got that way over you, Polly?"

"I might like it." She looked up, devilishly.

He laughed.

Finding the arbor overgrown with weeds and vines, they walked back to the landing and sat on the old boards. She drew her knees up and put her head on them. Looking at him, she grew moody, talking in snatches about this and that. Her parents still ran a boardinghouse in Baltimore and she could return whenever she liked. But one kitchen and dining hall was like another. Her people had once had a little money and property, but that had been before she was born. When the British took Washington her father's store had been looted, then burned. She grew up in a boardinghouse. She didn't know anything else.

"There are good schools in those parts," he said tentatively.

"I went to school," she replied flatly. "Do I act like I didn't?"

"Schools to make a lady out of you, Polly. And hold your sharp tongue until I'm through. When I say lady, I mean a woman of refinement and culture, one schooled in behavior and speech and music and the arts, who knows her way about in polite society."

"My mother has all that and she's still running a boardinghouse. She sent me to Texas to get away from public riffraff. And look where I wound up. The bottom of the damn barrel."

She was sitting cross-legged and her hands were on her hips. He called her attention to these things, concluding with, "You're sitting like an Indian and talking like a New Orleans dockside wench. See what I mean?"

"The devil take you, Jerry Brown! If I'm so disgraceful, suppose you find yourself a society woman."

"I may at that. But it's a matter of striking one's level, Polly. You're shaping yours so that the best you can find is a man of your station in society. If you do better than that, you'll find it hard to hold him."

Silent for a time, she burst out laughing. "Golly, what a shame, Jerry."

"What's a shame?"

"All this moonlight going to waste. You could have saved that lecture for some rainy night."

"It wouldn't do any good," he said hopelessly.

Jeremiah lay on his back looking at the stars. On her side, she propped herself on elbow and toyed absently with a button of his shirt. The touch of her hand at his collar and her shadowed eyes resting on him in hungry silence sent pleasant sensations tingling up his spine. Despite all he had said, she was a woman in the flesh. A thin cloud swept toward the moon, sailed on across it, and faded away in a northern reach. Gulls caterwauled over the river. He watched and listened, enjoying the night and her company.

"Jerry," she said in low tones, "what is it you want from life?" He did not answer at once.

"A new schooner. But first the confidence in Mexico to warrant it. You know, Polly, it could be written in the stars that I'll never own that schooner."

"What else do you want?"

"I don't know. Prosperous trade, a little money, maybe a whole lot of money. A wife, someday, I guess. Four or five children. What does any man want?"

"That's what I'm asking." Her fingers touched his hair at the temple, and the warmth of her body was close.

She said wonderingly, "Four or five children." Then, "You talk sensibly for once. I'd like that, Jerry."

"*You?* I thought you weren't interested in any little schooner-men."

"I could be talked into it. Real easy, maybe."

Silence fell between them and she snuggled closer.

"You know," he began, "Ugartechea would like to favor us. He knows how popular Santa Anna is in Texas. I told him——"

Her hand covered his mouth. Then she was pressing her face to his ear, breathing warmly, softly, "Santa Anna, Ugartechea, Bradburn, Bustamante, customs, cannon. Is that all you ever think about?"

He knew only that a warm wave was splashing over and through him, that her very nearness was sapping his resolve. He managed to say with a show of indifference, "What would you like to talk about?"

She did not tell him in words. She raised her head and looked down into his face. Then she was bending to him, one hand drawing his face to hers. He saw her eyelashes quiver and fall. The next moment she was kissing him with a pressing, astonishing eagerness.

Jeremiah had never imagined her like this. The surge of her desire swept through him like a blaze, held him there, possessing him completely. Though he had planned in this direction, there seemed no remnant of organized thought left in him. Then some remote part of his brain told him that he was instinctively following the calculated plan of behavior. He was amazed at his own zeal in giving her a lesson she would not soon forget. Or was he any longer interested in that phase of it? His hand was at the fastening of her dress when she stiffened.

"Jerry!" She tried to break away. He held her fast.

"What's the matter, Polly?" he said. "Isn't this the way you wanted me to behave?"

"Hell, no, Jerry! Stop it!"

She strained with all her might to loosen his arms. Flailing him with small fists, she cried, "What the devil do you think I am?"

She was no longer trying to free herself. She seemed too frightened for that. Lying still and trembling in his grasp, she stared at him with trouble and entreaty under the amazement in her eyes.

"Do you think you can lead a man on like this?" Her mouth opened to say something, but no words came. He said, "So you might as well learn not to play with fire."

"Jerry," she said, "I didn't know. Honest!"

"Then it's time you learned."

With eyes wide, she just looked at him. "Will you marry me?" He laughed. "Marry you! Why should I?"

She gave up then, went limp in his arms, though none of the shock went out of her face. He was suddenly contrite, wondering if he had carried this thing too far. Stifled sobs escaped her, though no tears came. It was only when he moved away that they broke in a welling flood.

She sat there a long time, wiping her eyes and staring out over the river. He put his back to her and eyed the fort, dreading the guns less than another look at Polly. Then he got up and moved toward the boat. She followed, meek and silent. Neither said a word all the way across the Brazos. He tied the boat a short distance from where a crowd of blacks and whites were loading the *Sabine*.

Here they must part. Jeremiah looked grim-faced as she stood there waiting for something, some expression of his feelings.

"I'm sorry, Polly," he said. He meant it.

"You needn't be sorry," she said. Her face was taking on a fresh radiance and her hand reached for his. "I'm glad you wanted me. Glad all over. 'Cause I love you. And I wouldn't have been a bit scared, Jerry Brown, if you had said you loved me."

Then she was walking away in the direction of the hotel, leaving him standing there rubbing his chin in a state of utter bewilderment.

Chapter Six

THE PAIR OF CANNONS

Despite the fact that Edwin Waller had given him another quarter interest in the *Sabine*, Jeremiah's humor next morning was anything but pleasant. Polly had kept him awake for hours. He didn't know why, unless it was because his lesson in behavior had turned on him and presented a challenge he could not sidestep. Handling a ship in a heavy sea was easy compared to steering a course for a headstrong girl. But he was stubborn. One method failing, he would try another.

After a tasteless breakfast aboard ship, he went directly to the hotel and searched out Polly's aunt. Embarrassed but determined, he spoke his mind and spent an uncomfortable half hour in discussion. Although they were in accord regarding Polly's future, her aunt was naturally curious as to his motive. Upon leaving her, he wasn't sure that she fully understood that his interest was purely impersonal. Perhaps it did fail to make sense. Once outside the hotel, he felt strangely foolish. However, the sacrifice was worth something to his peace of mind.

Aboard ship, John Bailey approached him with curiosity strong in his face. "Cap'n, what in the devil happened when you visited the fort yesterday?"

"Plenty."

Bailey listened avidly to an account of all that transpired. When Jeremiah finished, his eyes blazed with anger.

"Why the dirty, bloomin', pepper-livered bastards! Bribin' Jerry Brown!" He spat lustily. "And you took that without roughin' yer knuckles?" After calling upon his saltiest vocabulary to voice an opinion of Mexicans in general, he said:

"But you made a mistake. Should of took the gold and bought a new schooner. Robbin' a Mex is like takin' what's yours."

Jeremiah laughed. "You sailed under Dominique You too long. But that's beside the point," he said, sobering. "Seems we'll forget the new schooner for the time being."

Bailey looked surprised.

"John, we've planned her for a long time, haven't we? Big roomy holds and cabins and tall masts stepped on a slant."

"Aye! By thunder, we have. With a spread o' sail like a United States sloop-of-war. Stop it! Ye're touchin' me weak spot, Cap'n."

"I'm sorry, John. Maybe I'm crazy, but the money I've saved to buy her is going somewhere else."

"Too bad." The mate didn't ask where the money was going, though he frowned and said he hoped Jeremiah wasn't thinking of the girl in New Orleans.

"No." The reply was touched with regret. A thoughtful silence followed. "You know, John, money has always meant a great deal more to me than I care to admit. But when Dulcor tried to bribe me, I suddenly realized that money can't buy the way a man feels about his people and all the things he believes in. So if that's how I feel, why shouldn't I risk my small capital in something I really believe in?"

The mate rubbed his jaw vigorously and looked puzzled. "Sure, Cap'n. Whatever it is, you make it sound right. That ye do. Or, like ye said, you could be crazy."

"Sure. I could be crazy as a loon. But it's the gamble that makes life interesting. Eh, John? Take what lies ahead of us today and place your own odds against the *Sabine* running safely past the guns of Velasco the second time."

The mate's reply was cut short by loud cheering from the wharf. They ran to deck and learned that Waller and a group, including the elder Brown and William, had just returned from Brazoria with a pair of cannons. The sight of the guns aboard Captain Fuller's ship had evoked the shouting.

Jeremiah looked the crowd over. Farmers, storekeepers, sailors, and trappers paraded up and down the wharf with shotguns and rifles in plain view of the garrison assembled atop the fort. Out in the river, Captain Fuller was splashing his anchor within easy range of Mexican cannon.

The leaders came aboard the *Sabine* and declared themselves ready to shout "*Viva* Santa Anna!" and open the revolution in Texas. While the brass pieces aboard ship slugged it out with Ugartechea's nine-pounder, the riflemen would work up to the fort and pick off the convict soldiers.

"You're hotheaded and crazy," Jeremiah said. "You'll lose a moral victory if you fire first. As it was in January, the idea is to defy Bradburn's order. Anything else, short of protecting ourselves, is open rebellion."

They argued that Santa Anna was winning in Mexico, that unless they acted soon, Texas would lose her opportunity to share in the victor's spoils. If Texans wanted statehood, they should make a bid for it now. And could Jeremiah name a better way of declaring for Santa Anna than by driving Bustamante's soldiers from the Brazos?

"Answer that, Jerry," William said.

"You've made a point there, men," Jeremiah replied, wanting to say their stupidity made him sick. "All you say is worthy of consideration. Yesterday Dulcor and the *Commandante* offered me money and a recommendation for command of a Mexican armed schooner to patrol the Texas coast. All I should do was influence you to pay tonnage fees and reveal the hiding place of our two cannons. And why did they want them? Because Bradburn expects trouble in Anáhuac and needs the only two guns in Texas not in possession of Mexican garrisons."

"Where's your argument, Jerry?" William said.

"Let Bradburn try and take our guns. Let him and his Mexicans make the first move. If they fire on Texan shipping today, take the fort if you can. We'll be defending our rights."

An unpopular silence gathered and held until William Wharton admitted grudgingly, "Jerry's right."

"Amen," said George Brown.

William glanced from his father to Jeremiah. Grinning sheepishly, he stepped forward and held out a hand. "Austin couldn't have said it better, Jerry. We'll hold our fire."

Jeremiah laughed. "But you're hoping they fire on me. Eh, William?"

There was no reply. Polly Merchant walked between the brothers and stood with arms folded at her bosom. Jeremiah felt the fury of her glance.

"Damn squealer!" she flared. "Traitor! So you talked my aunt into sending me off to school just because I'm not the lady to suit you! Who the devil gave you leave to shape my course with your fancy notions?"

She stamped her foot in rage, then moved a few steps away before turning on him. "I hope Ugartechea shoots both your big ears off!"

She marched straight to the hotel, not once looking back. When she disappeared inside the door, Jeremiah shook his head hopelessly, thinking that given time he might learn to think like a Mexican, but never like a woman.

Minutes later Jeremiah ordered the mooring lines taken in. Running through his mind was the thought that he had done this once before. "Make sail, John," he said.

The wind was filling out sails, calling for the helm. The fairway was ideal for the tack he was on, and the wind came in brisk and strong. Sheets and booms were hauled for the best speed in her.

Jeremiah's glance bounced from decks to bowsprit, on into the rigging and ashore. Reaching for his telescope, he eyed the fort. Ugartechea's face seemed to leap at him, steady, hard, and determined as he swung the swivel gun to bear on the *Sabine*.

"Everybody take cover!" Jeremiah cried.

Then that strange feeling of mixed nausea and expectancy began to form in his stomach. He guessed that a man would never become accustomed to being shot at.

He raised the glass again. The *Sabine* was a good five lengths out from the wharf. Now what was holding the fort's fire? Only the *Commandante*, for there was his face, as before, behind the sights of the gun.

Bailey said, moving aft, "He seems to be holdin' back to make it count."

"John, see if you can get another knot out of her."

The *Sabine* was passing the fort. Both men realized she presented the best target Ugartechea had had so far. If he waited longer, his chances of placing a crippling hit would be greatly reduced. A minute passed by, and another, in which the mate worked his cud from cheek to cheek, spat, and stared with disbelief.

"By the deep six, he's missed his big chance, Cap'n. Give me that telescope." Training it, he said, "There's the colonel, still swinging her on us. And now I see Dulcor. He looks mad as hell. Take a squint. He's tryin' to get at the gun hisself!"

Jeremiah gave the helm to Bailey. Through the glass, he saw Dulcor stalking off and Ugartechea smiling. But the swivel continued to bear on the *Sabine*. After long minutes of watchful waiting, Jeremiah lowered the telescope.

"John, he's giving us a sporting chance. He'll fire when we're hardest to hit."

"Then he ain't Mexican."

Lieutenant Colonel Ugartechea did not fire on the *Sabine*. He remained on duty until she was beyond his range.

Every man of the crew stared with puzzlement in his face. Glances alternately dropped on the distant fort and returned to their captain. Some showed disappointment, others relief, though the big question in every face was: Why hadn't the colonel fired upon them?

Jeremiah knew why. His talk with the lieutenant colonel had paid off. Ugartechea was too good a politician to open the revolution in Texas.

"John, fire a musket salute to the colonel." So saying, he loosed a rousing cheer and threw his cap far over the water.

The roar of a gun shattered the silence of deck. Seconds later the fort returned the salute, and the sounds of cheering from the wharf in Velasco rolled across the water.

2

The *Sabine* hit the open sea and cut a straight wake with the south wind brisk over the starboard beam. She was hauling abreast of Galveston Island when a tiny schooner put out as if to intercept her. Since Anáhuac lay to the north inside Galveston Bay, any craft issuing from "Bradburn's Harbor" was suspect. But as she came on and spoke the *Sabine*, Jeremiah identified her as the *Stephen F. Austin*, Captain Scott commanding.

"Was looking for you, Jerry," Scott said, drawing close by. "We're blockading Bradburn."

Thinking this was some joke, which Scott's three-man crew did nothing to annul, Jeremiah said, "Blockading? With what?"

"Nine rifles and a swivel gun," Scott replied, as proud as if he commanded the largest American sloop-of-war. "Me, the *Red Rover*, and the *Waterwitch*. We've taken two Mexican prizes already."

Upon learning that the cocky little captain was sincere, Jeremiah said, "So Bradburn is under siege."

"That's not all, Jerry. Our land forces took one of Bradburn's cavalry patrols on June tenth. Last night we drew up resolutions, one of which was to send to Brazoria for the cannon you and Waller own."

"They're yours, if you beat Bradburn and Ugartechea to them. And since I can't stay for the fun, maybe a couple of demijohns of good liquor will help."

"Help? Hell, they'll clinch it!"

As Jeremiah watched the little *Austin* bounce back toward the bay, he was keenly aware that Texan ownership of the smuggled hollow ware might decide the issue at Anáhuac. What he didn't know or imagine was that the cannon were destined to touch off the Battle of Velasco before his return to Texas.

Three weeks later the *Sabine*, loaded with supplies from New Orleans, reached Velasco a few jumps ahead of a wicked squall. Jeremiah battened down and waited for the wind and rain, which came just as his brother William boarded the ship. When the first fury of the storm had passed, they went below and opened a bottle of brandy.

Jeremiah said, "I hear you had quite a battle."

William grinned and shook his head, "I'll say we did. Too bad you missed it, Jerry.

"The citizens of Anáhuac sent for the two cannons, which were soon delivered up to the schooner *Brazoria*. Then we formed a body and visited Ugartechea for permission to sail past the fort with them. The request was refused, and we left after saying we would sail past him just the same. We put fifty riflemen aboard and set sail downriver. On the night of the twenty-fifth, the fighting began.

"Under cover of darkness, a land party worked its way close to the fort and opened fire. But we drew so much hell from the fort that by daylight we retired out of range. A heavy rain fell that morning, and we began to fight again. The Mexican nine-pounder shot our moorings away and we were floating nearer the fort. Our rifles took a toll of Mexicans who tried to man the swivel bastion. We shot at their arms and wrists. And we hit more often than we missed. After an hour of it, the gun crews wouldn't go near the swivel. By Hector, they were licked! Then——

"There stood Ugartechea at the swivel, all by himself. Well, we couldn't shoot at a man as brave as he. We wanted to cheer him."

Jeremiah could understand this.

"Around ten o'clock that morning he ran out of ammunition and raised a white flag. When he agreed to support Santa Anna, we allowed him to depart for Matamoros with his garrison. He lost seven men, nineteen wounded. We lost seven also. But we felt like free men again."

Jeremiah filled the glasses.

William said, "And to top it off, Bradburn fled Anáhuac for New Orleans the night he learned that General Teran had ordered the Nacogdoches garrison to relieve him of his command.

"So," William said conclusively, "the Texas coast belongs to Texans."

"I wonder." Jeremiah breathed out a sigh.

William frowned. Looking at his brother, he saw him studying the amber liquid in his glass. Then he heard him saying, "Seven dead. You know it's really tragic when men die to earn a victory that decides nothing."

"That decides nothing!"

Jeremiah got up, stretched his long legs and walked the floor.

"Can you say that what happened here or at Anáhuac means we can plant, cultivate, reap, and ship our produce and import the things we need with any assurance that Mexico won't send another Bradburn?"

For a moment William seemed irresolute. "We declared for Santa Anna, didn't we?"

Jeremiah appraised his brother with a look that was meditative and steady. He did not wish to tell his brother that to his way of thinking Texas and Mexico might never achieve an understanding necessary to permanent peace and security.

Chapter Seven

A LOSING CAMPAIGN

The summer of 1832 dragged its hot, humid days on into September. The Gulf Coast expected no relief from the heat for another month unless from hurricane winds. Those who could afford the cooling sea sailed aboard ships that continued to come and go without molestation. Texas was free of Mexican garrisons with the exception of Goliad and San Antonio de Bexar. In July the great Mexican ship-of-war *Santa Anna* with four hundred trained troops under General Mexia sailed up to Brazoria. Although the general and other revolutionists were suspicious of Texans' motives, Mexia departed convinced that the uprisings had been directed at the highhanded methods of Colonel Bradburn.

Along the Gulf from Matamoros to Pensacola, Texans, Americans, and the Spanish element credited the quick overthrow of Bustamante's garrisons to the foresight and daring of Captain Jeremiah Brown. Because of his initial defiance and the cannon which provoked the timely and decisive Velasco uprising, he seemed to overshadow the actual fighting. He was lauded and praised for ridding Texas of Mexican troops. It made little difference that he knew better or denied all but the train of events that made it appear so; his champions refused to listen and attributed his becoming manner to a hero's modesty.

On this September afternoon Jeremiah remained leaning against the *Sabine's* rail, watching the Baltimore square-rigger creeping toward the sea. Forgetting the bustle of lively New Orleans along the water front, he grimaced and mopped beads of perspiration from his forehead. He felt a twinge of regret at seeing Polly depart even as another side of him admitted relief at ridding his ship of her. There had been much sincerity in her entreaties and final tears, though he discounted in full her threats never to return and to marry the first man who asked her.

She had looked saucy and womanly in a stylish dress of white calico trimmed in red. With her dark hair combed back to reveal the pearl earrings he had given her, she bore little resemblance to Polly of the dining hall.

He tried to put her out of mind and think of the evening ahead with Carmela. But as he turned to go, Polly persisted.

There she was in the distance, moving away aboard the black-hulled craft. The square stern swung for a bend ahead and the gilded name *Potomac* flashed suddenly in the late afternoon sun.

He moved to his quarters and sat down staring at nothing. It seemed too quiet aboard. Then he was wondering what he might expect upon Polly's return. Perhaps under that hotel crust was a flair for music or painting. Given three years, which he might be able to afford, it was altogether possible that she might step down the gangplank a lovely, mature, and refined lady. However, such transformation was difficult to imagine.

But Polly was on her way; and that was final. On her way to a school for ladies where she belonged. What she might do to prize the institution off its dignified balance wasn't his worry. To date, he had fulfilled his part of the bargain. As he got up and dressed for an evening with Carmela, he kept telling himself that he should look upon his doing with satisfaction uppermost in his mind.

2

Jeremiah cut a fine figure in his new captain's coat of blue and gleaming brass buttons. Carmela's eyes shone with the admiration he desired on this evening of conquest as he removed a new blue and white cap and bowed in her direction. Placing her in a carriage, he named a café in the French section.

She wore lavender again, which pleased him. Her hair, like soft gold, was done up atop her head exposing small ears and a fine neck. A tiny gold chain with a cameo dipped into the gentle curves of her bosom; something for her to toy with as she took in a dimly lit courtyard in the Vieux Carré. Her eyes seemed green under the yellow lantern light, and the swell of her thigh against taffeta caught and held his attention a moment.

As a giant Negro waiter in white linens appeared with champagne, Jeremiah compared her with Polly again. Carmela was not as tall, though she was older and more challenging. For a moment he tried to balance the two women in his meager knowledge of women in general. He gave up in favor of champagne.

As she laughed at a small monkey chained to a banana tree, her amusement seemed as spontaneous and simple as a child's. Yet Jeremiah recalled how he had flamed at the touch of her aboard the *Sabine,* and wondered if he had succeeded in making it appear that he had cooled with the knowledge that she was betrothed to another man. He doubted this, however, as he realized that she no doubt read him like an open book when at times something in her stride, often the slightest movement of limb or eyelash, then again her very nearness and the aura of her warm body threatened his reserve. He was making no outward attempt to possess her. He had taken her in his arms only once. The next time he would not let her go.

As if she sensed all he was thinking, her glance fell narrowly on him. Caught thus, he said, "Is the monk better looking?"

"He's a funny little animal. Not at all dangerous."

She created an opening which he used. "You like a little danger from the right source, don't you?"

"What is the right source?" She raised a glass and sipped. As he leaned forward, studying her intently, she said, "You mean you, of course."

"Naturally," he said.

A pair of troubadours in colorful Spanish boleros and tasseled hats emerged from a corner banana tree strumming softly. They approached Jeremiah's table.

"Something lively," he said, producing a silver dollar.

Their grins revealed white teeth. "*Si, señor. Si!* We bring Lolita."

Soon the girl appeared, a slim-waisted bundle of curves and energy under hair as black as midnight. She danced, leaving little to the imagination. For an encore, she took off her full skirt, exposing a shapely pair of dancing legs. Then, using the skirt for a cape, she did the dance of a frightened matador in a mock bullfight, making graceful passes as the imaginary bull charged. Her thrusts and spasms as she was being gored were realistic. The dance ended with her writhing on the floor. Up on her feet out of a horrible death, she bowed before Jeremiah and Carmela.

"My own version of the *España Cani*. You like, no?" Her bosom rose and fell from exertion.

Jeremiah arose and placed a glass of champagne in the dancer's hand. She drank, challenging him with dark, sultry eyes. Flashing a glance at Carmela, she tossed the wineglass against the brick wall to the applause of everyone except Carmela, who made no secret of her pique.

"She's brazen!" Carmela flared.

Carmela remained silent for long moments, not taking her eyes off him. Once she touched a finger to her cheek almost wonderingly, as if he were the subject of sudden discovery. He was watching her in silent satisfaction when a man at a distant table proposed a toast to the man who drove Mexican troops out of Texas:

"Captain Jerry Brown!"

Jeremiah started. Coloring to the roots of his hair, he got to his feet. Following the warm response of the public gathering, he felt obliged to acknowledge the gesture. Raising his glass, he replied, "To the loyal friends of Texas."

Sitting down, he said, "I never will get used to this sort of thing."

"I like it. So should you," she smiled, touching his hand. "In fact, you should trade on your reputation for that schooner you once talked about." She added, with more than ordinary interest, he thought, "Never pass up an opportunity."

He regarded her critically, aware of the excitement and admiration flashing in her eyes. Shortly before she had yielded to an unguarded moment of jealousy. And this had been followed by a look of fresh appraisal. He saw these things and knew they were in his favor.

"Jerry, to think that you more than any other Texan have won the admiration of New Orleans! Can you be content plying back and forth with one small ship while the toasts of bankers and men of powerful interests ring in your ears?"

"Powerful interests? Umm."

"The man who just honored you is a West Indian sugar baron who owns the finest carriage in New Orleans. At his table are importers and bankers. Tonight you could form a syndicate. A week from now it might be too late." Her fingers closed over his and her eyes sparkled. "It's your very future calling, Jerry. And I'll help you."

"Sounds interesting," he said.

"If you'll invite the party over, I'll show you how to make them broach the subject."

Businesslike as a man she was saying: "We can convince the moneyed gentlemen of the unlimited wealth of Texas, of the future of cotton, sugar, tobacco, grain, lumber, and leather goods. If there are twenty-eight cotton gins in the Departments of Brazoria and Austin at present, within five years——"

"And where the devil did you learn that?" he broke in.

Laughing at the puzzlement in his face, she fingered the stem of her glass and looked at the far table. "I was merely demonstrating my willingness to help a handsome captain into his own countinghouse."

"Thanks!" He poured champagne, watching the bubbles rise and burst in her glass. "But how does your fiancé Mr. Thompson fit into the picture?" he inquired, glancing up. "Seems he's suddenly vanished."

She was touching the chain at her bosom between thumb and forefinger. "I saw Thomas a few weeks ago. He's quitting the sea after this voyage, to open a tavern here in New Orleans."

"A tavern?"

"Through some delay he had just received my message and was going aboard the Zachari ship *Comet* bound for Vera Cruz. He sailed that same day. But he asked me to help operate the tavern." She named a street and asked if he knew the district.

"Sure I know it. Sailors and ruffians swarm about a woman like gnats over ripe bananas. Talk about a position in society——"

"Thank you, but I've already refused it," she said icily.

"I can well imagine. But you didn't say what Thomas would be doing while we were building that shipping empire."

"You're slow, Jerry Brown," she said staring beyond him. "The men who can put ships and a business in your hands are leaving."

"What about Thomas?" he demanded.

She appeared disappointed.

"I did not break our engagement, if that's what you mean. Thomas is an adventurer who will sooner or later find what he's looking for. But he knows I have no intention of marrying a tavernkeeper."

He was quick to see it all now. Thompson's choice of a business that fell far short of her aspirations had created a breach through which he could enter. The field of conquest was thrown open and she was letting him know it, even as she jockeyed about for the best position in a race for the things she wanted. He could not censor her for this; rather he admired her obstinate courage and determination, wishing as he did so that it was possible to hand her a moon set with rubies. Then he realized that she didn't ask for this, but rather the pleasure of striving for it, the adventure of seeking, with her strings securely tied to the man who reached for the biggest star.

She had pointed to a group of schooners winging over the Gulf; a vision which, he reflected, he had for the present allowed to slip from his view.

Studying the girl seriously, he knew he had come to think a lot of her. Whether to the point of taking her for a wife was the question of debate in his mind just then. The line separating desire and love was drawn thin. Actually, they were one, he decided, though he had best think about it.

And while thinking, he might consider the idea of running a schooner fleet, with a plug beaver on his head. Whether the wine or Carmela's nearness was responsible for the idea taking hold of his mind he wasn't sure, but it was sounding better by the moment.

3

Next morning a long barkentine crept down the eastern horseshoe for anchorage. Jeremiah watched her work sluggishly inshore for the slip where J. W. Zachari ships berthed almost in the doorway of the proud and powerful Spanish house of Lizardi. Upon seeing *Comet* on her nameplate, he was curious to learn if Thomas Thompson was aboard. Giving her time to pass quarantine and customs, he dispatched a sailor to the pier with instructions to make casual inquiries.

This information was very important to him, for he had done considerable thinking since leaving Carmela. He believed her hanging in the balance, ready to lean in either direction, his or Thompson's, depending on the influence brought to bear. He had no wish to see Thompson get ahead of him with pictures of Spanish treasures at a rainbow's foot; not on the day he planned to propose marriage.

The sailor returned shortly and reported that the *Comet's* first mate was Mr. Thomas M. Thompson.

Expecting this, Jeremiah called Little Josh and directed him to hail a carriage and deliver a note to Miss Ryan and return with her.

He was checking cargo in the hold when Bailey called down to him: "The lady's below. But I'm wonderin' if this schooner is a cargo ship or a hen frigate."

Ignoring him, Jeremiah made his way to the saloon. As he opened the door, he saw her poring over his copy of Bowditch's *New American Practical Navigator*. She looked up curiously, no trace of excitement in her face, and slowly closed the book. Sitting there, quiet and patient, she reminded him of a childish possession become suddenly indispensable with the thought of losing it.

"This note," she said, making a question out of it. "You said it was very urgent."

"Is that what brought you in such a hurry?" he demanded, instead of asking if she had seen her fiancé.

"I had a piano pupil, my best paying one, and your jack tar said you were not ill or hurt."

"The lad talks too much. However, what I have to say to you will bear out my feeling of urgency."

Rising curiosity showed in her face. He sat down across the table from her, realizing his need of a strong drink and refusing it in the same thought. Then he leaned toward her and held her hand in both of his, studying a moment the crease forming between her wide-set eyes.

"I've done a great deal of thinking since I last saw you and have reached a decision, which I hope——"

Excitement instantly lit her face. "You're going after those schooners, Jerry!"

Drawing a deep breath and silently cursing the luck that set him off to a bad start, he began anew. "Hear me out and then decide if that's the most important thing. First, take me for what I am. I haven't much to offer you except the kind of future I think is right and proper. I'm half owner of the schooner *Sabine* and can't afford a new one and won't gamble on somebody else's money.

"As for all of this," he said, encompassing New Orleans with a sweep of his hand, "we can have it between voyages. I'll dress you in the finest I can afford, and I'll look at that sugar magnate's carriage that you envied and guarantee that in time I'll present you with an even finer one. Beyond that, I'll love you for keeps."

Her look held steadily to him as she seemed to shape fresh estimates of him out of the old. She rose and walked absently to a stern port and back again. "The carriage was just a symbol, Jerry."

"Was or is?" She did not answer, and he said, "It might always be the shining symbol, something high on a pedestal out of reach."

She sat still and silent, hands folded in her lap. Her steady blue eyes stared straight ahead, while the light streaming through the saloon's ports played on one side of her face and neck.

"Jerry," she said, without altering her glance, "don't underestimate me. I'm going to reach it."

Her statement was so unexpected and deliberately studied that it struck him speechless. Astonishment distorted his face and then she was looking at him, suddenly contrite. "Forgive me, Jerry. It wasn't a nice answer to a sweet proposal, was it?"

Groping for some answer to this, and finding none, he was turning from her when John Bailey announced a visitor to see Miss Ryan.

After a curious exchange of glances in which each asked in silence who knew of her presence aboard, Jeremiah opened the door and Carmela breathed an astonished word: "Thomas!"

Thompson bowed lazily in her direction before turning a pair of steady gray eyes on Jeremiah, who saw a man neither tall nor large, striking nor plain in appearance. When he smiled, which he did readily, his tanned face was instantly engaging. He offered up apologies for this intrusion with becoming ease.

Glancing at Carmela, he said, "By Jove, I was sure it was you I saw getting out of the hack."

He waited for no answer, but sharpened his glance on Jeremiah. "So you're *the* Captain Brown, and this is the defiant *Sabine*."

Jeremiah was wondering if the hint of amusement in Thompson's voice and expression was real or imagined even after the intruder's next observation. "I've known Colonel Bradburn for some time," he said. "His mistake was lack of preparedness."

Jeremiah replied, "Rather in being wrong to start with."

"Opinions differ, of course, Captain Brown." A gleam of mild hostility flickered across his face. It was gone an instant later. "I have just returned from Vera Cruz, where I was favored by an interview with Señor Rubio, who is Santa Anna's banker and general agent. He hazarded a guess that Santa Anna will in due time collect tonnage fees and halt the wholesale smuggling carried on by you Texans." He shrugged—like a Mexican, thought Jeremiah—before saying, "God knows Mexico is overlooking a juicy source of revenue there."

Jeremiah was thinking that somewhere he had met this type of man, though his memory was of no help as he tried to assess Carmela's fiancé. Long nose, overlarge ears, almost hairless brows, versus a smooth, resonant voice and suave manner, each must remain a puzzle until something more of the man put them all together. He had not long to wait.

Thompson showed no apprehension or lack of ease as he walked to Carmela and surveyed her up and down boldly. He took a chair. "I might ask just what sort of a game I'm interrupting. But I won't, since it is evident I'd gather all sorts of amusing replies."

"One of which," Jeremiah said evenly, "might be that it's none of your business."

"I expected that one, of course, Captain Brown. Now your reply, Carmela." He was lighting a cigar.

She whirled and put her back to him. "You had no business following me."

Jeremiah decided to put an end to this. "Mr. Thompson, you have my permission to leave at once. As for Carmela, it is possible that she is no more anxious to see you than she is to work in a levee tavern among ruffians and fancy ladies."

"Oh that!" Thompson got up and sauntered toward the door, appearing not in the least offended. "Since you're her champion, tell her I've decided against the tavern in favor of a commission in the Mexican Navy. My sponsor is the rich and influential Señor Rubio."

Jeremiah saw Carmela turn slowly. Her pique had miraculously vanished and in its place was puzzlement giving way now to speculation. And Thompson—as if he had eyes in the back of his head—

turned and gave her his most charming smile before addressing Jeremiah again.

"The possibilities are unlimited. In fact, only the blind and unimaginative can fail to prosper with the Gulf as a hunting ground. As Oliver Goldsmith wrote——

> *"The pictures placed for ornament and use,*
> *The twelve good rules, the royal game of goose."*

At the door, he winked at Jeremiah. Following a bow to the waist, he left them.

Jeremiah stared at the space he vacated, thinking he had never met a man who provoked so much dislike in him. Even his courtesies were overlaid with a veneer of arrogance. And the very fact that he could not fail to admire Thompson's superb calm and self-confidence further galled him.

Then he was looking at Carmela.

As her troubled glance fell under his direct gaze and she began twisting a ruffle at her collar with nervous fingers, he knew she was wavering, hanging between the one thing she seemed to want most in that moment before the interruption, and all she had in the past desired with passion.

She sank to a chair as he moved to her side. "Why did he have to come, Jerry?"

"His appearance shouldn't bother you in the least, if you love me. It's that simple."

As she glanced up at him suddenly, excitement played in her eyes. Then it fell away, like sheet lightning behind a horizon at night.

"Or if you love him," he said. "Do you?"

"No, Jerry. I don't."

"Then it's settled." He made a valiant effort to contain the flood of hope surging through him.

"No, Jerry. That doesn't settle it." She was on her feet, moving toward the door. "There are other things. Other reasons."

He stepped forward, barring her way. She stopped still before him, not looking up until his hands touched her shoulders to bring her to him.

"Don't, Jerry. I——" She broke off, staring up into his face. "I might weaken, and if I did, I might hate you for it."

He watched her go, wondering why he allowed it. As he followed her on deck and saw her step from his ship to the land, he wondered what restrained him even then. Not once did she look back, but walked on, unfaltering, until she was swallowed up by the anonymity of New Orleans. When he could no longer see her, he knew she kept on going away from him, out of his life.

Something more seemed to go out of him. The thing that filled the empty space, as something must and does, was a burning hate for the clever adventurer who had thrown another rainbow before her eyes.

Book Two

A GAME FOR SURVIVAL—1835

Chapter Eight

THE CORREO DE MEJICO

Shortly past noon of June twentieth, 1835, the lookout at the *Sabine's* masthead reported a strange sail breaking the southern horizon.

Company in these waters was suspect and Captain Brown quickly alerted his ship. He passed the wheel to Little Josh, opened the binnacle locker for his telescope and swung into the after shrouds. The ship heeled a little and he, sensitive to her every movement, glanced down at his redheaded helmsman.

"Up a spoke, sailor. Steady as you go."

With spyglass up, he scanned the seam of sky and water. In the circle of his vision was a speck of white. A sail, to be sure, though who she was or where she blew had everything to do with the course of a skipper running heavy with forbidden munitions. Visibility shortened as a rain squall crept between him and ship astern and hung like a sodden sheet of canvas from an undersea wreck before slowly passing on. Once unmasked, the stranger appeared to be making easting as against his northeasterly run. After observing her for another quarter hour, he decided she would fall away and under horizon in due time.

Just the same, he would keep an eye on her. The turn of Mexican politics demanded constant vigilance in these times.

Back in 1832 the success of Santa Anna's states-rights revolution had been assured. Having contributed to the winning cause, Texans looked to their reward and petitioned for statehood. However, their desires were not only ignored but viewed with suspicion. Undaunted, the frontier delegates had met again in 1833 and sent Stephen F. Austin to Mexico City to lobby for statehood, legal free trade, and a lifting of the immigration ban.

Austin was thrown into prison for writing an innocent letter which Santa Anna thought treasonable. From his dungeon, he wrote his people again, urging them to be patient and keep the peace. Although Texans were aroused by the injustice accorded their leader, they were influenced more by local distractions, coupled with timely economic reforms approved by shrewd Santa Anna, than Austin's pleas for peace. The anti-immigration law was repealed; Texans were given greater religious freedom, trial by jury, more representatives in the legislature of the state of Coahuila, and were allowed to write legal documents in English for the first time.

Although free trade had not been listed among the reforms, Texan schooners had run past closed customhouses and returned with Americans and American goods. Trade had been as brisk as free. These were good times. The political skies had been free of war clouds and for once the land and the sea had offered up security.

But Santa Anna had turned his back upon his states rights program which had placed him in the National Palace. In 1834 he had openly renounced republican ideals in favor of dictatorship. At the same time, he had turned his eye on Texas and approved Mexican Minister Herrera's recommendation that ships of war patrol the Texas coast for rich customs collections and the capture of smugglers.

With the death knell to free trade ringing in their ears, Texans watched security depart on the ebb tide and Mexican domination arrive on the flood tide. Early in 1835, Colonel Ugartechea appeared in San Antonio as province commander. He did not stop with a show of arms by land but employed the schooner-of-war *Moctezuma* to patrol the Texas coast as revenue cutter.

And now Jeremiah was wondering if the strange sail to the south was the *Moctezuma*.

From deck, Bailey cried to Jeremiah in the rigging, "Unless the storm chased her off course also, she ain't the *Moctezuma*."

Jeremiah would not soon forget the winds of hurricane fury that had struck him on the Matagorda approach ten days back. They kicked up snarling seas, forcing a run all the way down to the Devil's

Elbow off Padre Island. Gale winds had backed slowly. After days of becalmed seas, a welcome wind breathed over the spent Gulf. That had been only this morning. Now he was running fair for the Texas coast.

"With cargo that was due in Matagorda on the eleventh," he growled, thinking of his reputation for delivering goods on time, regardless of the elements or a Mexican revenue cutter.

Moving down to deck, he replied to Bailey, "Whether she's the *Moctezuma* or not, you know our position."

"Aye, that I does, Cap'n. On the Texas-Mexico sea lane and too damn close to the Rio Grande."

"Right, John. Now double the lookout and point her due north. Then if the sail aft continues to bear, we'll know the music we're dancing to."

"Sure. The Mexican two-step, which they'll tell ye in New Orleans Cap'n Jerry Brown is one o' the very best at."

With an eye on the southern horizon, Jeremiah moved to the weather braces. Impatient of delay, cargo nine days overdue, he began walking the deck. His hand fished a paper from his pocket and he smiled wryly before replacing it. A letter from Polly, a month old. She wrote of her progress in one sentence and accused him of making the most of her absence in the next: "So you can pursue a yellow-headed woman in lavender."

He was paying good money for such letters. And hard cash was scarce. These pages of outbursts came less often after her first year, though when they did it was like a storm wind breaking out of a letter.

His reflections were brought to an abrupt halt when the lookout cried the deck. The stranger was altering her course in the *Sabine's* direction.

Jeremiah said to Bailey, "The best defense against what might be trouble is wind in our sails."

The mate's booming commands echoed the captain's wishes. "Wing the mains'l and fores'l! Smart now. Haul, ye pelican-footed swampers! Set the fore and main tops'ls!"

Topsails broke in the breeze, cracked, and bellied. Sheets were hauled and booms were swung and lashed. The old *Sabine* dashed forward on the wing and wing, creaking and taking the chop of the Gulf in her stride.

The ship to windward came on. Tall-masted, she cascaded white sail in the wind and held her pace. An hour passed, in which she lifted her canvas up for a better view. Late that afternoon she stood all but hull up over horizon. Bailey sent dark glances at his crew and straining sails before asking if a Mexican in the Gulf could outrun Jerry Brown.

"Enemy or not, she has the speed of me." As if his one aim was to contradict this, he put the wind over the starboard beam for an easterly run.

Raising the glass, Jeremiah studied the craft. With the sun only an hour above the water, he was urgently wishing for the cover of night over the Gulf. Both ships were heeling on an easterly course, the stranger gradually eating up the distance between them. Her hull played up and down in the waves and troughs, more up than under now.

"Look, Cap'n! She's breakin' out her colors."

When the Stars and Stripes stood straight in the wind, captain and mate exchanged knowing glances. In the game of flags over the main, the enemy might resort to the colors of any nation. Moments later the ship astern hoisted an identifying naval pennant.

Jeremiah knew her then. The United States Revenue Cutter *Ingham*, Captain Ezekiel Jones commander. Wondering what prompted the chase of a Texan by an armed American, he ordered sail run down and schooner headed into the wind.

The United States ship sped toward the *Sabine*, hull black and gleaming above the last red sun flashes over the water. She took in sail and slid to within a hundred yards of the *Sabine* before the captain's gig was let go by the falls. Soon a crew of marines lay on the sweeps for a crossing.

Captain Jones wrinkled his nose and brought his small figure aboard. He had a quick, ready smile and strong handclasp for Captain Brown, who greeted him with a question: What was he doing in these waters if he wasn't searching for slavers? Instead of wincing at the mention of this worn excuse that United States ships used for cruising along foreign coasts, Captain Jones remarked on the chase the *Sabine* had given him. Below, with the finest liquor in Jeremiah's locker set before him, the testy captain said:

"You'll be damn glad I'm in Mexican waters before I finish with my story."

"I'm pleased before you begin, Captain. I thought you might be the *Moctezuma*."

"You did, eh? Well, she won't be bothering you for some time, thanks to me.

"I put in at Matagorda on the eleventh and was met by a group of hornet-mad Texans. Only that morning the *Moctezuma* seized the Texan-owned, American-registered *Martha* and ran with her for Matamoros on charges of smuggling."

Jeremiah said, astonished, "On the eleventh, you say?"

Captain Jones nodded, pausing to indulge in another courtesy of the stream before going on. "The Texans were a persistent lot, believe me. They talked as though the United States owned Texas, just because they sailed their ships under the Stars and Stripes. And there was no end of their tales regarding this outrage against the American flag.

"It being my duty to protect commerce under the flag, I put to sea after the Mexican war schooner and overtook her off the mouth of the Rio Grande on June fourteenth. She bore down on me and fired. I hoisted my American ensign, ran out my battery, and returned the compliment with a broadside. She ran for the Rio Grande and came about. I gave her another broadside. Six hours later she reached the forts and the port captain sent men to reinforce her. Then she ran aground at the harbor entrance.

"I proceeded into port and vented the wrath of the United States on the port captain, who was quick and eager to apologize and deliver up the *Martha* and her crew."

Jeremiah's grin was broad. "That's the best news I've heard since Bradburn fled. Captain, Texas owes you a vote of thanks."

"Naturally." Leaning forward, Captain Jones placed a forefinger in the middle of Jeremiah's chest. "But you Texans can't run your ships under the American flag forever and stay out of trouble."

"We've done it for some time. Maybe the Lord is watching over Texas."

"It was the United States in this instance," Captain Jones said, rising to depart. "However, I just happened along at the right time. But that's that.

"The captain of the *Moctezuma* told me he took the *Martha* in lieu of the prize he really wanted, which was you, Captain Brown."

2

The wry expression on Jeremiah's face lingered as the *Ingham* made sail and away in the night. He was thinking how Captain Jones would laugh if he knew that only a hellish Gulf storm had prevented the *Sabine's* arrival in Matagorda on the eleventh of June.

"And I was growling because cargo was overdue."

He stared out over the water, catching an occasional needle of light from the revenue cutter in the east. The sea lay dark and endless, a formless thing, impersonal to some, friendly to others. In his case, the sea had whipped up a storm that almost grounded him on a bar, where she would have battered his ship to pieces. Some men said the sea was too austere to give one a gambler's chance. Maybe so, but in this instance she had dealt him a winning hand against the Mexicans.

On such a night, after such an escape, deep water felt good under a sailing man. A little prayer of thanks was due and, looking up into the sky, he said it. In his petition, Texas was not forgotten. Never had she been out of his serious thoughts and prayers since back in 1824. But her course was perilous, like a ship lifting and falling in the hard drive of a Gulf storm. All hands must work together, as Austin said. For understanding between two races, for the things that were right. As a result of Santa Anna's promises, Texans had felt secure. And with the breaking of these promises, they had known uncertainty and insecurity as never before. And now all that was left was the struggle for the things which were right against a dictator whose ambitions had reversed his promises not only to Texans but even to the people of Mexico.

Feeling out the wind, Jeremiah crossed deck and thought of his position at sea. The *Sabine* rode the conventional sea route between Matamoros and Texan ports. It did not require a military expert to realize that Santa Anna, once he had conquered all opposition in Mexico, would turn his eye on Texas and use these very waters for the transport of his armies there. The land route was long, barren, and alive with Indians. When and if invasion threatened, only armed ships could prevent Mexican regulars from marching down gang-planks on Texas soil.

His reflections were usually serene. But now he wasn't sure, for playing about in his mind was a fleet of Texan armed ships. It was of course preposterous to think of an unrevolted province sponsoring a navy.

He went to his cabin. Throwing his cap to the table, he tried to think of other things. The thought persisted, however. The case of the *Martha* proved the need of protection for Texan shipping. United States revenue cutters couldn't and wouldn't always be handy. But who would listen to such an idea?

A host of leaders paraded before his mind's eye. Some of them had sat at a Brazoria dinner given Santa Anna's trusted Colonel Almonte during his tour of inspection in 1834. And not one hundred feet away were munitions stored by Waller, Wharton, and Jeremiah in Mrs. Jane Long's brick outhouse.

Almonte reported smuggling by Texans who should have paid duty. But was it smuggling just because Mexican laws differed from Mexican orders? Texans didn't think so. Therefore, Jeremiah reasoned, all things considered, did his idea of defense by sea differ substantially from defense by land? The only difference lay in the reception it would receive.

Further thought on the subject was interrupted by John Bailey's presence at the door.

"Pardon, Cap'n, but the lookout seen three lights over the starboard beam. Looks like three ships in company."

There was no sign of company from deck. From the lookout's perch, the picture changed suddenly from tranquil seascape to shipping lane crowded by an unknown flotilla. Jeremiah asked the lookout if there had been any noticeable change in the formation. The lad said the ship aft had been in the lead. And she appeared to be making a little westing.

"Seems we're on the same course with them, John. It might be well to fall back, then run due east once they're under horizon." Giving the lookout a nudge in the ribs, he said, "Trim a sharp eye, Little Josh," and returned to deck.

Leaving orders to keep a close watch on the ships, he went below. After recording events of the day in the logbook, he slammed it shut and went on deck again.

Through a combination of rain squall that dimmed visibility and the lookout's untimely nap in the rigging, the *Sabine* came alive three hours later to find a ship bearing toward her not a mile away. When captain and mate crowded on sail to widen the distance, they received a shot across the bows. The strange craft had worked south and was eating them out of the wind. Hastily putting the wind on the starboard quarter, Jeremiah saw himself running straight for the other two ships. He was caught between them. The next gunfire threw water on his deck.

"She's got our range, Cap'n. The only way we can run is nor'west and we're too near land for that."

Jeremiah took in seas, ships, moon, and position, and saw himself trapped. "All right, John, jettison the cargo. Let all kegs and boxes containing munitions go by the board."

Bailey stood rooted to deck. "Jerry," he said, "the proceeds o' yer last five cotton bales is in them kegs."

True, it was a loss he could ill afford. "It's a Mexican dungeon if we're caught with them."

Hove to, waiting and watching the lights of the armed ship growing larger as she came on, Jeremiah was thinking it had been his own fault. Mere hours past, Captain Jones had recited the case of the *Martha* as well as the intended victim, the *Sabine*. There was little time for regret: the other ship was bearing close, her guns run out and manned.

No sooner was the stranger within hailing distance than an officer on her decks trumpeted forth, "What ship is that?"

"The American registered schooner *Sabine*. Who asks?"

"The Mexican schooner-of-war *Correo de Mejico*."

Jeremiah felt the pounding of his heart. She was the enemy. All doubt vanished before a fact: He, the man Mexico called "pirate of 1832 and perennial smuggler," was at last caught in the precarious spot he had flirted with for years but had somehow managed to avoid. He could almost hear Captain Jones saying, "I told you so."

"So you're the *Sabine*." The gloating sound issued from the Mexican deck. "This is indeed a windfall, Captain Brown."

The voice was familiar. Jeremiah was wondering where he had heard it. Suddenly he remembered, though it was difficult to reconcile a British accent to the deck of a Mexican war vessel. But any lack of harmony in the situation was offset by the stark realization that he was in more trouble than he had bargained for.

The commander of the enemy craft was Thomas M. Thompson. Wearing the gold braid of the Mexican Navy, Lieutenant Thompson boarded the *Sabine* in company of Lieutenant Ocampo. The latter was a handsome young army officer of the Anáhuac garrison in Texas. Looking the pair over, Jeremiah was thinking he might fare better under this man than Thompson, who brought to mind other Americans in the Mexican service.

As a searching party combed the ship, Thompson carefully examined the manifest. Appearing in no hurry, he paused at intervals over items of cargo to glance up with amusement in his face. Jeremiah observed he had lost none of his easy grace or arrogance during the three years since their first and only meeting. When the officer charged with inspection of the ship reported, and his cargo list and manifest corresponded, Thompson said it was regrettable that Captain Brown shipped no contraband of war.

"But what shall we do with this man, Lieutenant Ocampo? We know his past. And we are told that he is the number one smuggler of the province."

Lieutenant Ocampo made no reply; he wasn't supposed to. Thompson studied Jeremiah under a thoughtful smile.

"Captain Brown, over a month ago, a Texan ship captain found among his passengers a courier from Captain Tenorio on his way to Colonel Ugartechea in San Antonio. Suppose you tell me what disposition this captain made of the messenger."

"He left the courier on an offshore island to live with the birds." Thompson narrowed his glance. "Why did you do this?"

Realizing the futility of denying what was public knowledge from Matamoros to Mobile, Jeremiah said, "It was purely a matter of business." After a pause, he continued.

"To save Texan shippers money. When Captain Tenorio learned that the collector at Brazoria was levying tonnage and port fees only, he sent a message to Ugartechea urging the high rates of Mexican tariff on the Brazos, in keeping with his policy."

"And by intercepting the message, your least offense was cheating the Mexican customs."

"In my opinion, I merely delayed unfair taxation."

Thompson considered this a moment. "I seem to recall your propensity for playing games."

Under Thompson's scrutiny, Jeremiah knew that his attempt in

New Orleans to separate Carmela from this man was uppermost in the other's mind. He could not entirely hide the humor in his face as he resorted to an evasion:

"As I said, it was purely a matter of business."

"Captain Brown, duty forces me to return you to Matamoros on charges of open conspiracy to defraud the Mexican customs. I must also charge you with wilfully intercepting military communications and information. The penalty for this offense could be the same as that accorded a spy."

He paused for effect, not removing his glance from Jeremiah.

"But since I am convoying the ships *Josepha* and *Ana Maria* with the Permanent Morelos Batallion to reinforce Captain Tenorio, I'll be obliged to take you to Texas first."

"Colonel Ugartechea hasn't ordered my arrest."

Thompson looked bored. "Allow me to enlighten you. I am sailing under orders of General Martin Perfecto de Cós."

Jeremiah caught the full impact of the statement. General Cós was second only to Santa Anna in the military.

"To further enlighten you, I have express orders to convoy the troopships to Matagorda and continue to Galveston in support of customs officers and strict enforcement of the revenue laws. Therefore, I seriously doubt Colonel Ugartechea's interference in your behalf."

So did Jeremiah doubt this as he played for his freedom. "You're making a big mistake, Lieutenant. Once I'm in Texan waters, the province commander has right of jurisdiction. And since you can't hide the *Sabine*, you can't hide me from Ugartechea, who knows what a hornet's nest the capture of a Texan will stir up."

Thompson laughed. "Don't take it too hard, old chap. Out of gratitude for what you have made possible for me, you will be accorded every consideration. The capture of the pirate Jeremiah Brown should not only break the back of organized smuggling in Texas but earn his captor the reward of favor in the right places as well."

Jeremiah decided it was time to play the only trump left him. His account of the *Ingham's* presence in these waters was verified by the logbook entry made prior to Thompson's arrival.

Thompson lit a cigar and frowned over the logbook. "The United States Revenue Cutter, eh? Rather unusual, isn't it, Captain?"

On deck, he ordered the lieutenant of marines to clap the prisoner in irons. Next he made a slight bow in Jeremiah's direction, and said in a voice so lightly touched with mimicry that only his choice of words made it evident:

"Purely a matter of business, Captain Brown."

3

With Captain Brown and his mate in irons below decks of the *Correo de Mejico*, and a prize crew aboard the *Sabine*, the flotilla set sail for Matagorda.

Jeremiah thought no ship's hold could be dark enough to hide the chafing iron clamps that bound a lover of freedom to an enemy hull. He was unable to reconcile this twist of fortune that resulted in trouble he had never experienced to the free sailing captain of the *Sabine*.

John Bailey recited tales he had heard about the depth and unbearable heat of Mexican dungeons. They let a man rot in the darkness until his skin turned fish-belly white, and then suddenly exposed him to the burning sun, where he went blind or roasted, or both. Some said the prison fortress of Perote was the worst, though to his way of thinking torture was torture no matter the location.

"They ain't got a goddam bit of compassion, Cap'n." He rattled his chains, cursed, and said, "Not them ill-begot bullies."

The *Correo* rolled and creaked. The bilge below them sloshed and rats scampered by squealing protest at the invasion of their world. Every sound aboard ship seemed magnified. The rush of water down the sides became a roar. And silence between captain and mate seemed to intensify the noise.

"Remember the girl Carmela Ryan, John?"

"The yeller-head? Sure. But, Cap'n, ye ain't wishin' for her now, not with both hands chained!"

"No. But have you any idea who she is?"

"I've got me own ideas, all right. But considerin' the way ye slicked up for her, I'll stow me tongue, respectful-like."

"John, she was engaged to marry Lieutenant Thompson."

Bailey's silence seemed endless before he said, "You pick out real trouble, don't ye? Now is the lootenant wise to the play ye made for his sweetheart?"

"He is."

The mate's outburst was lengthy and classic. He seemed to call up profanity so salty and fresh that he paused as if amazed at his own accomplishment before commencing anew. If the devil had a forge, he said, they were caught white-hot between hell's hammer and anvil, Satan himself whistling up brimstone and standing ready to cut them a smart dozen across their sterns with the "goddam'dest thunderbolts a mortal ever seen." Which, he added, was about as hopeful a view as he could think up offhand.

Jeremiah forgot his troubles and laughed.

"Cap'n, why did ye tell me all this?"

"I don't know, unless it's because you should know and realize it's a personal matter between Thompson and me."

The ship veered so suddenly both were thrown against the hull planking. The excited babble of Mexican troops failed to drown the shouted orders from the weather deck. Men were running about and heavy kegs were rolling across deck.

"The beat to quarters!" Jeremiah said. "Now who could be handy to give battle other than the *Ingham?* She's running for New Orleans, however. So it's probably a practice drill."

The *Correo de Mejico* lurched back on her course. All seemed quiet for long minutes. Above the normal sounds of ship in motion, a voice cried a ship's position in Spanish.

Captain and mate waited with ears strained hopefully for further excitement that might indicate a sea battle. But as minutes piled atop one another, their hopes fell. They forced conversation, but it helped little. The future seemed as dark as Bailey's expression:

"Seems Thompson's chargin' ye with enough to hang a man twice and prop him up for a firin' squad later."

He kicked at a rat, lost his balance, and fell cursing the Mexican Navy and its bilge rats.

Jeremiah did not laugh. All humor lay buried under somber reflections. Polly's education would come to a sudden end. The last slaves he had bought on borrowed money at the high price of one dollar a pound had been for his father. George Brown would lose them, unless William could earn the price aboard the tiny A. C. Allen sloop he sailed. As for himself, he would miss the Texas coast; but most of all the Velasco approach, where he always paused to thank the Lord for the land and the evidence of Texan industry. Perhaps he should regret the cause of enmity between Thompson and himself, the play for Carmela. Somehow he could not bring himself around to any feeling of contrition. He would never forget her slender figure, her graceful walk, or the parting look in her wide-set blue eyes. The vision of her swam before his eyes, and he recalled the moments when even her glance and some idle movement of her body drove him mad with desire.

Then the present seemed to leap at him. He felt his irons and heard the rattle of his chains. A sense of entrapment flooded his being. It was the total blackness of the ship's interior or the feeling of utter silence amid the noise of a man-of-war. He knew better. It was panic that assailed him. He could bear it no longer.

Slowly, Jeremiah unfolded the idea that had possessed him on deck before his capture. He spoke of armed Texan vessels to protect the coast, a Texas navy. Bailey's astonishment was equaled only by his enthusiasm, which fell away as he said, "Ye're a little late, Jerry."

"We won't think of that," Jeremiah replied, voicing a lie. "Instead, we'll believe that one of us will escape. If it's you, John, don't ever quit preaching the need of armed ships to Texans."

Chapter Nine

BANK'S ARCADE

The glow of an approaching lantern aroused Captain Brown and the mate out of their stupor. The lieutenant of marines appeared with several men and ordered the prisoners removed to deck.

On deck, Thompson stood with feet wide apart and arms folded across his chest. Beyond, far across the level stretch of water, a pale dawn was pushing up over the Gulf. In keeping with a seaman's habit, Jeremiah scanned seas and weather as well as the troopships standing to leeward under full sail. Close by, the *Sabine* seemed to be moving up on the *Correo de Mejico*. All this he grasped instantly, at the same time observing the frown of thoughtfulness on his captor's face.

There was more here than met the eye. Gunners, marines, and officers were not assembled to salute the dawn.

Thompson took a forward step and fingered his braid. "Captain Brown, I have decided to release you on a promise that you will remove yourself permanently from Texan waters."

"Evidently you don't know Texans, Lieutenant," Jeremiah replied calmly, his mind searching about for the cause of the other's strange behavior.

"Don't be difficult, old chap. Think of what I'm doing for you." He appeared to be trading for something.

The lookout's cry to deck gave him away: The Yankee to windward was coming up fast.

Jeremiah was suddenly wise to the cause of activity on deck during the night. Thompson had been so impressed by the *Sabine's* logbook account of the *Ingham's* doing that he believed the ship aft to be Captain Jones's.

Jeremiah smiled. "Yankee, the lad says. He means the United States Revenue Cutter *Ingham*, Lieutenant. But don't let that interrupt your fine speech."

Thompson retained his composure. "Captain, we'll forego pleasantries and get down to business, which compels me to place duty above personal desires. This, believe me, is the case now. For as much as I would like to parade you before Matamoros, I cannot afford to jeopardize Mexican-American relations by risking encounter with the U.S.S. *Ingham*."

"Having a captured ship of American registry wouldn't have anything to do with your decision, would it?"

"You are free to depart aboard your ship," Thompson said. He walked away, only to turn about sharply. "Perhaps we'll meet again, Captain Brown."

"That, Mr. Thompson, I can almost guarantee."

Jeremiah boarded the *Sabine*, counted heads, and watched the Mexican fleet move on to meet the rising sun. The ship aft came on, dipped her colors to the schooner, and continued on her way.

She was an American merchantman. The United States had saved Texans again.

Freedom never felt so good to Captain Jerry Brown. As the *Sabine* got a way under her, he threw his cap high, raised his leg for a resounding slap and loosed a long earsplitting yell.

John Bailey watched the cap sail away and fall in the bouncing wake before shaking his head in despair of the captain's extravagance. He was soon aware that the celebration was at an end. The Old Man, hatless, long hair blowing in the wind, used his voice for ordering all the sail she could carry and every man to look alert and lively.

"Men, luck has favored us twice. Now it's time for us to start helping the Lord and the United States take care of ourselves. We must outrun the enemy and warn Texans of the approach of Thompson."

"*Enemy*, you say, Cap'n?" Bailey was fishing for all he thought was in the schoonerman. "We ain't at war yet."

"We're on the road to war, John. And I'm not so sure it hasn't already begun. But what are you grinning at?"

"Nothin'. Nothin' a'tall, Cap'n." But Bailey was remembering the peaceful Jerry Brown whom Edwin Waller had pushed into running the blockade. The man before him now was no longer the pacifist supporter of Stephen F. Austin's ideals. Instead, he was staring at the marks of Mexican irons on his wrists with a fierceness of expression that Bailey had never seen before. And the look seemed forged out of iron into a permanent thing.

Of one thing the mate and ex-pirate was sure: The war had begun in one place. Jerry Brown was a man after his own heart.

2

The *Sabine* ran with wind in her sails and determination on her deck. She touched in at Matagorda with cargo, slipped back through Paso Caballo to the open sea a few jumps ahead of the slow Mexican flotilla, and stood up the coast in a speedy reach for Velasco. Her anchor scarcely touched Brazos mud before it was lifted. With the warning sounded, she pointed into the Gulf once more and laid down a ribbon wake for Galveston Bay. Like a seagoing Paul Revere, Captain Brown passed the news to an inbound sloop and continued his voyage to New Orleans for the purpose of warning Texan shipping there.

With their work accomplished, captain and crew celebrated the Fourth of July in New Orleans, unaware of a Texan success at Anáhuac. Several days later, Jeremiah learned that Captain Tenorio had vacated his office at the angry request of William B. Travis and his militia, for reasons of rank indiscrimination against shippers. In departing, Tenorio took his soldiers. With customhouses again closed at Galveston and Anáhuac, ships set sail from New Orleans with cargoes for the duty-free ports.

But Thompson soon put an end to this. With trade crippled, the air of summer hung electric over the province, and Texans realized that the time had come when leaders from all municipalities must take sides in an issue no longer dormant. Some argued peace while others called for open resistance and many settlers lost hope and left with their families for the safety of the United States.

The effective blockade of Texan ports by Thompson's *Correo* was felt far inland. He was meeting with success where Bradburn had failed in 1832; the guns of his war vessel spelled the difference. He boasted, "I am commander of the coast from Tampico to the Sabine." In mid-August at Nacogdoches, a resolution against Thompson and his schooner-of-war was followed by Sam Houston's request that the *ayuntamiento* of San Felipe call another convention of Texans.

The train of events seemed made to order for Jeremiah's scheme of arming ships to protect shipping. Up to this time he had been lacking a proper audience. He was looking ahead to the convention in San Felipe when a rumor issued from the secret rooms of Bank's Arcade. As the whisper grew, leaders from the various departments in Texas began moving in on New Orleans. Thomas F. McKinney, one of the few men who knew in full Captain Brown's plan, met the *Sabine* on a day in late August and said the time had arrived for Jeremiah to speak; that rumor had turned into reality:

Stephen F. Austin was in New Orleans.

Jeremiah looked at McKinney. In the face of this quiet man of thirty-four were determination and shrewdness. He was a trader who knew his way about, the number one shipper of Texas and a merchant who recognized the need for men like Jerry Brown.

McKinney said, "We're meeting tonight on the third floor of Thomas Bank's Arcade. You won't have an easy time of it, Jerry. But in your favor are Thompson and the *Correo*. Now come with me and I'll show you something."

They came to a ship lying against the wharf and stood off looking her over. Her name was *San Felipe*. "Well, what about her, Tom?" drew a slow, wise grin.

"If you can talk like you sail, Jerry, you'll learn tonight."

With no further explanation, the shipper led the way to a waterfront saloon where he raised a toast to Jeremiah's success at the "Texas convention of New Orleans" that evening.

No sooner had they moved outside than Jeremiah stopped still in his tracks and stared with disbelief at an open carriage. As it moved on, he made a step to run after it, though the other occupant caused him to halt in dismay. He pushed the cap to the back of his head and rubbed at a jaw with open palm.

"That was the Mexican consul, wasn't it?"

"Martínez in person. Why?"

Jeremiah shrugged. "I could be mistaken, but the woman with him looks like someone I know."

Jeremiah knew it was Carmela. All his buried memories and desires seemed to leap the barrier of the years as if time stood still. He wished for her now as never before. The importance of the meeting that evening was forgotten under the press of his extreme longing.

Until suddenly he remembered the company she kept. The Mexican consul! Why? Then the pattern flashed before his eyes. As the sweetheart or wife of the man who was so ably representing Mexico in the blockade of the Texas coast, what could be more natural? The ugly thought forced its nagging way through his mind. There was no relief from it until he entered the room filled with Texans that evening and stared into the pale, drawn face of Stephen F. Austin.

Then he was wondering if Carmela's presence in New Orleans was timed for Austin's arrival, or whether she was reaching for the moon in a ruby setting through the powerful Mexican consul.

3

Under the soft light of a hundred candles flooding the room, the group of frontier leaders from Texas seemed out of place. Only Austin had walked down the corridors of a palace, and only William Wharton made a pretense of elegance with his Eagle Island plantation home. But these men were not here to admire and discuss the pale blue walls or the crimson of Bank's draperies. They drank hard liquor straight and sat in plush chairs, apparently oblivious to finery. Rugged Sam Houston propped his feet on a French chair, and militant Henry Smith flicked cigar ashes on the polished floor.

Glasses clinked convivially and conversation hummed. A. C. Allen, Brazos shipowner, surprised and aroused Jeremiah's anger with his account of the *Correo's* capture of the sloop William Brown sailed. Thompson converted her into a tender for his war schooner!

Edwin Waller vowed the incident might prove unlucky for Thompson, to which McKinney and the Wharton brothers agreed. David Burnet, pacifist, remained aloof while Houston and Thomas Rusk engaged Austin in talk about the forthcoming consultation.

When Adolphus Sterne arrived, someone said he made the thirteenth. This drew a snort from Henry Smith, who strode to the door and yelled for Thomas Bank.

"Send up the blackest nigger you got, Tom." When a lanky darky entered and grinned sheepishly, Smith ordered him sit in the corner, then declared the jinx broken.

Soon Austin was talking. All merriment ceased as they eagerly awaited the important words of the most influential Texan. Whatever his feelings were, they would shape the course of Texas. He spoke softly, convincingly. He had hoped to find Texas at peace and regretted to find it threatened with immediate hostilities. Santa Anna's operations had changed him. *El Presidente* was no more republican in either form or reality than Bustamante, whom he had overthrown. But he was the idol of Mexico.

"Watch him, gentlemen. Before he dies you'll admit him to be the shrewdest politician this continent ever produced. Such a man, lacking moral integrity, breeds turbulence."

He talked on. General Cós had issued requisitions for the arrest of all involved in the Anáhuac overthrow of Tenorio, and it was known that he was coming to Texas to assume full command. Military rule was inevitable.

"In my conversation with the President, I advised that no troops should be sent to Texas, and no cruisers along the coast, that the consequence would be war. I stated that there was a sound and correct moral principle in the people of Texas, but that this moral principle could not and would not unite with any armed force sent against this country; on the contrary, it would resist and repel it, and ought to do so."

Jeremiah led the applause. With quiet restored, Austin spoke of the unnatural bonds between Mexico and his people. These bonds had to be severed.

"Hold your applause, men. I do not favor secession or any declaration of independence. The time is not ripe for throwing off the mask. It is my opinion that Texas should follow a strict observance of appearances toward Mexico at this time. As I have written from my prison cell, I see no hope for Texas without complete Americanization.

"We must and ought to become a part of the United States."

When Sam Houston said, "Amen," Jeremiah felt the influence of Andrew Jackson, President of the United States, who had made it evident that he had an eye on the most active frontier and scene of foreign oppression by sending the United States Gulf Squadron to the mouth of the Mississippi.

Austin had stated his views. His final expression, "Let the people decide what we must do in this emergency," struck as an anticlimax, since all realized that he spoke for the people.

Following a lengthy discussion, John Wharton spoke of Austin's return to Texas. It was placed in the form of a question, which evoked considerable talk. McKinney lit a cigar and made a proposal:

Austin should return to the Brazos, aboard a ship loaded with munitions.

Burnet vigorously opposed this. Such a scheme would not only hasten military action but jeopardize the safety of Mr. Austin, possibly cause him to be captured by Thompson and returned to a Mexican prison.

McKinney lifted a hand for silence. "Mr. Burnet, your thought is worthy of consideration. We cannot overlook Thompson's presence in our waters." Frowning thoughtfully, he studied the faces in the room before resting his glance upon Jeremiah.

"Captain Brown knows more about Thompson than all of us put together. Jerry, do you agree with Mr. Burnet?"

Jeremiah realized his time had come. McKinney had maneuvered well. "I agree up to a point, Tom. Mr. Burnet's concern is ours. Nothing must happen to Mr. Austin. However," he smiled, lifting his palms, "the ship could be sunk by a storm, or struck by lightning. Where there's deep water, there's risk. For that matter, life is risk. Mr. Austin gambled our desires against a prison and lost by an innocent letter.

"But about Thompson. I'll gamble any day that a ship can get past him."

"Would you try it with a load of munitions?" Houston demanded.

"Not in this case."

As Houston nudged Rusk, Jeremiah said, "I can do better than that, Mr. Houston. Since Lieutenant Thompson would like to catch me again, I can draw him off the coast and clear the way for Mr. Austin's return."

"Go on, Jerry," McKinney said.

"That's about all there is to it. Except——" Jeremiah rubbed his jaw and stared ceilingward. His glance dropped suddenly, sharply. "Mr. Houston is a military man who will agree that the easier route of Mexican invasion is by sea. That's how General Cós may arrive. Since we have no coastal defense, he could land an army on the Brazos and split Texas in two.

"And since our troubles are maritime, think what will happen if we fail to keep the sea lanes open between Texas and New Orleans, think how the blockade has already affected our source of supplies and the prices we pay for imported goods. The high cost of insurance on cargoes to Texas is still rising and that means prices on supplies will continue to soar. Mr. Rusk of inland Nacogdoches knows this. Otherwise he wouldn't have presented a resolution against Thompson and the *Correo* a little over a week ago."

Jeremiah held their full attention with facts none could dispute.

"With all the causes that brought on the American Revolution staring us in the face, we are striving to maintain our militias. But what the devil are we doing to protect ourselves where it counts—in the waters of our coast?"

Austin voiced agreement. Houston asked what Captain Brown had in mind.

"Just this," Jeremiah replied directly. "In our Texas Gulf are a few seadogs with enough daring and knowledge of water, coast, and enemy to fight like true guerillas of the sea."

"Fight with what?" Houston scoffed.

"Armed ships."

Astonishment showed in the faces of many as looks were exchanged. Following up quickly, Jeremiah said, "A semblance of a navy, gentlemen."

Sam Houston arose and shook his head in despair of Captain Brown before bending double with laughter. "A Texas navy! That's rich."

The idea did sound ludicrous in a way. As several joined Houston in open ridicule of the idea, McKinney sat composed, like a poker player in no hurry to reveal his hand. Jeremiah felt no loss of favor even when Houston bore wrathfully down on him with:

"Captain Brown, can you name an armed fleet other than pirate not sponsored by a nation? Do you actually suggest we turn back the pages to Lafitte? Giving you the benefit of doubt on this score, what can we think prompts your suggestion unless it is personal ambition?

"Gentlemen, if Captain Brown dreams of a fleet, he aspires to its command, no doubt."

Jeremiah chuckled. "Let's build a fleet first, Mr. Houston."

"Eh? Better still, Brown, let's get rid of the dam'dest pipe dream I ever heard. If and when the time comes for organized sea defense, I'll vote for a real navy man, not a badgering schoonerman."

Jeremiah walked to the huge ex-Tennessean and said with acid softness, "Mr. Houston, you're trying to brand me an adventurer. Perhaps I am. But if the adventure is for a cause that springs from the heart, then it is not a shallow one. And if there is a fleet of armed ships, you can bet your last damn dollar that Jerry Brown would like to command it."

Forestalling Houston's reply, Jeremiah said, "Now let's see how you stand on what you call piracy. Are you willing to see Mr. Austin travel to Texas aboard an unarmed ship?"

Houston turned red and appeared hesitant.

McKinney stirred then. It was time to play his hole card and he got up and waved a bill of sale before them. "McKinney and Williams is backing Captain Brown's *pipe dream* to the tune of eight thousand nine hundred and sixty-five dollars cash. Do I hear a higher bid in favor of Mr. Houston's opinions?"

Every face turned on the shipper.

"I made a cash offer for the ship *San Felipe* and the cargo of munitions she carried. The ship *will be armed*. She'll be ready to sail within a few days, in time to reach Velasco on a given date with Mr. Austin's party. In the meantime, Jerry can draw the *Correo de Mejico* off the coast."

Houston grunted for attention. "This scheme between you and Captain Brown sounds well rehearsed, Tom."

McKinney grinned. "I guess it does, Sam. All but a fixed date for the *San Felipe's* arrival at the mouth of the Brazos." Facing Jeremiah, he said, "September first suit you?"

Jeremiah's brow knit into a frown. Less than a week remained of

August. Two days to finish loading ship, two days on the open sea at best with a hurricane lurking somewhere out in the Gulf, left only two days in which to lure Thompson's *Correo* off the Texas coast in chase of the unarmed *Sabine*. He felt the need of more time and was about to add a few days to the date when he noticed that Houston appeared very observant of his uncertainty.

Suddenly he was aware of a great victory won. The first Texan ship had been armed in this room on Magazine Street. Fair wind or foul, he would celebrate the event with success in the venture ahead.

"September first," he said.

Chapter Ten

PATH OF THE WINDS

Bared to the waist, Captain Brown's skin shone like bronze under the pitiless August sun. Sweat ran down his face in rivulets, bathing neck and crop of hair on his chest as crates were slung aboard amid grunts from sailors and passed on down into steaming holds. Since sunrise he had set the pace, and at four in the afternoon he showed no signs of mercy to either himself or the grumbling men. But he was cutting his loading time in half, which meant an extra day gained for the game with Thompson.

Oblivious to any outside interest, he did not look up the first time his name was called. He was placing an estimate on unstowed cargo in terms of hours when "Captain Brown" rang musically into his conscious mind.

Looking up, he saw Carmela.

Forgetting the picture he presented, a sweating body bare to dungarees, he gave her a welcoming smile and moved toward her. Her eyes lingered a fascinated moment on his wide sun-reddened shoulders. Then she flashed him the smile he remembered and liked. Under the strong and unsettling regard between them all barriers of the past seemed to vanish.

She extended a slim hand, which he appeared reluctant to let go, and then they were resorting to conversation. She was in New Orleans for a short time only and would soon return to Vera Cruz.

A hard questioning light played in his eyes. "I saw you yesterday and would have followed you but for the company you kept."

"You saw me? Why didn't you call out? But I suppose you had reason enough, my being with—shall we say the enemy?"

"An apt definition," he replied emphatically, holding her gaze. "You're reaching high, all right. The consul's a powerful man. Or should I say you have already reached the top rung of the ladder?"

Twirling the small parasol shading her regal head, she laughed merrily. "Still reaching, Jerry." Then she glanced at her waiting carriage. "I suppose you're too busy to go for a drive."

She made music of the word Jerry. "Not if you'll give me time to look presentable."

Minutes later, he helped her into the carriage. After ordering the driver to take them through Frenchtown, he said, "Vera Cruz has been kinder to you than to most women."

"Thank you. Mexico's climate is not as bad as I thought. Summer in the mountains, and——"

"Winters on the *Correo de Mejico*," he slipped in.

"So you know about Thomas?" she said curiously.

"Firsthand. We met again about two months ago. He entertained me royally—in irons."

She showed genuine surprise. "Somehow I can't imagine you in irons, Jerry. But I'm sure political differences prompted Thomas. He's very zealous."

"Damn if he isn't! He's got Texas hot under the collar." Eying her critically, he said, "Being married to the man who is blockading our coast sort of puts you on the wrong side, doesn't it?"

"I haven't married him—yet."

Although pleased to learn this, he could not readily forget her reason for it. "So he didn't chance upon that windfall in the Gulf. Are you still engaged to him?"

"I never did break it."

"Then you're still on the wrong side."

"I wouldn't say that." She looked away, her mouth lifting in a smile. "Soon the issue will be forgotten and Mexicans and Texans will be friends again. Despite the tension, I don't consider the situation serious enough to prevent me from visiting my aunt in San Felipe."

"Is that what brought you to see me?" he said.

"Of course it isn't." She laughed. "Upon hearing you were in port,

I came to see you last night, only to find you had gone to greet Mr. Austin at Bank's Arcade."

The carriage was entering the Vieux Carré when he said, "Who told you that?"

"The lad standing anchor watch on your deck."

"Little Josh, eh?" he said, displeased. Then he was eying her. "You and Mr. Austin probably arrived aboard the same ship."

"Yes. He's a great man, Jerry. I knew him in San Felipe. His trial of imprisonment should leave him bitter toward Mexico, don't you think?"

"Austin is a peaceful man," he replied.

"He was. But do you really believe he is now, or that he will counsel peace to Texans?"

He nodded, wondering if her voyage aboard the same ship which brought Austin was a coincidence. Her position was nothing short of a spy's dream. She could gain Austin's confidence on the sea and go to Consul Martínez and on to Thompson in Texas, transporting intelligence without attracting any more notice than a bee going from flower to honeycomb.

"You sailed with him. Did he show any bitterness or give any hint of his feelings?"

"No, not really," she said curiously. "Although he did say that misunderstanding between the two races had increased alarmingly. I'm wondering, Jerry, if such a statement has any bearing on the policies he will advocate."

"Why are you so concerned?"

"My only remaining relatives live in Texas. That's why."

"Seems you're unduly alarmed." Next he said, exploringly, "So you're going to Texas. To see your people or Lieutenant Thompson?"

"My aunt, of course. Jerry, you're a friend of Mr. McKinney. Perhaps you could obtain passage for us aboard the ship he purchased yesterday."

Completely taken aback by her knowledge of matters he thought secret, he asked how she had learned of the *San Felipe*. She replied with open candor that in her search for passage the captain suggested she approach the new owner.

"You said 'get *us* aboard.' Who else?"

"Padre Alpuche."

The itinerant priest was loved by Protestants and Catholics alike. In Louisiana and Texas he baptized the young, sat by the sick, buried the dead, and performed marriages. He usually traveled on land, astride his mule.

"That's odd. The padre sailed with me here, to stay a month or so."

Her reply was a light shrug, and he was admiring the delicate arch of her brow and the full oval of her face.

"It's been a long time since we saw the Vieux Carré together." He leaned toward her. "Maybe tonight?"

"Some other time, Jerry."

He frowned, more bewildered than crestfallen. With three long years separating them and a thousand and one things to talk about, she seemed bent on parrying his every attempt at conversation designed to renew their relationship of the past.

"I know. You don't care to begin where we left off. Maybe it's for the best, but if you believe that you shouldn't have looked me up."

"I was curious, Jerry. I've wondered about you quite often since that day in 1832. Were you changed, were you married, or in love with someone who could give you the things you wanted?"

"The answer is no. I haven't changed, haven't built a schooner fleet, haven't forgotten you. But I'm as curious as you and, by your leave, will ask the question uppermost in my mind. Aren't summers in mountains about Vera Cruz a little expensive for a piano tutor?"

"Not if the señora whose daughters one tutors owns a villa."

This was logical and pleasing to his ears. His expression changed and he urged her to take the *Sabine* to Texas. He would secure passage for the padre aboard the *San Felipe*.

As though tempted and uncertain, she lowered her eyes. When she met his glance again, something of her own feelings vaguely stirred into the open, seeming to tell him she knew all he was thinking and was not at all displeased with him.

However, as he stepped from the carriage to the dock an hour later, she looked troubled, as if the thing her heart wanted most and her ambitions continued the battle inside her. Her hand reached for his and he felt the pressure of her fingers. Then eagerness showed an instant in her expression.

She said in a low husky voice, "I may sail with you after all."

"I sail at eight tomorrow morning."

He waited out the night, anxious for morning. At eight next day, he looked for her carriage. At half past eight, his searching eye masked his rising violence of feeling. Shortly after nine, he was glaring at the dock and town, making no attempt to control the tumult raging within him. She would pay for this, and pay dearly, he was saying to himself as a gruff order fell from his lips:

"Get under way, John. And show lively!"

2

At two o'clock next morning, four bells clanged harshly, and Jeremiah went on deck to relieve John Bailey. Overhead, not a star peeped through the pall. Out of the dark mass that walled off all but a tiny niche of sky a prong of lightning darted at the angry sea. The *Sabine* slid down into a trough and up, catching a rising sea on the larboard bow. She continued to rise, twisting free, her decks streaming foam and gurgling seas.

"She's going to howl, Cap'n——" Bailey's voice was drowned by a splitting peal of thunder that rolled and rumbled across the waves. "Aye! Howl like a horde o' banshees."

Jeremiah saw visibility diminishing by the moment. The binnacle lamp shone like a puffball of light. "Batten all hatches, furl tops'ls securely, reef main and fores'ls, and take up slack."

The ship stood well off the central Louisiana coast, which meant he was hours of sailing time ahead of schedule. If he was moving out to meet hurricane winds, time saved meant nothing. Although weather reports placed the storm center far south of Mobile and moving in a northeasterly direction, one never could predict the whirling monsters of the Gulf. As gusts came in stronger and the barometer continued to fall, it was evident the *Sabine* was sailing directly into this one.

Bailey cupped his hands and shouted, "Cap'n, we better turn tail and run for the Mississippi!"

Although a conn of the weather justified the mate's opinion, Jeremiah Brown remained jealous of time. Buttoning his oilskins at the neck, he felt of the weather.

Seas were mounting in size, slapping from all directions, girdling the hull and striving for a meeting across decks. Another flash of lightning revealed clouds racing raggedly atop the waves. Then the rain came on in driving gusts, first from south then from the east.

Prudence spoke: A wise seaman would waste no time in running away from a hurricane. He heeded its voice and gave the order that would send the schooner back toward the Mississippi.

"Put the wind over the starboard quarter."

Placing his weight against the helm, he called for a life line down the full lee deck, a stretch of rope for sailors to cling to while working forward and aft. Next he lashed himself to the standard of the wheel and waited for hell to break loose.

It was not long in coming. The whip of the storm bore down on the ship. A huge sea struck from astern, climbed the deck, washing Jeremiah against the wheel before reaching on to drown the forward deck. Wind tore through the rigging, driving rain before it. The slippery deck rose, scended to windward, and fell in a sudden drop that knocked men off their feet.

With an eye on the dimly lit binnacle needle, Jeremiah thought of all the perils and misfortunes written into policies insuring ships and cargoes. The underwriters gambled against storms, pirates, jettisons, detainments of all kings and princes, and more. A captain gambled his judgment and experience against loss of ship and crew. Even so, his mind stubbornly clung to notions at variance with his good judgment. All the experience and lore of the years were at work in him, weighing the weather, the slant of the wind, balancing one and the other against the storm's direction and his position at sea; jockeying them about in a daring, foolhardy desire to use this storm, to put it to work for him.

Bracing his legs against the lurch of the ship, he recalled the storm that drove him off Matagorda and prevented his capture. The sea had worked for him then. This one was working against him, joining hands with the enemy in detaining the forerunner of Austin. He was caught up in a giant whirlpool of air moving counterclockwise. It might be moving toward Mobile and then again toward the Brazos; there was no telling. Although the ship was running away from it, it still came on. The wind slant advised that he rode the northeastern edge, wind velocity nearing sixty miles per hour. Therefore, this being true, the winds below him on the right side of the circle would exceed twice that force. The *Sabine* was less than seventy-five miles off land. Thus he figured position against the unknown path of the winds.

He could run like a scared fawn on the fringe of the blow, use the wind to eat up distance—if—and only if the hurricane were moving west or northwest. The gamble was a serious one if he misjudged the direction of the circular storm and lost the fringe. The outer edge could slowly or swiftly suck him toward the storm's eye. The forfeit was destruction.

He ran on northeast, feeling for the extreme edge of the blow. An hour more and he would know if the hurricane was following him or falling away. He would gamble wisely, if at all. Then he thought of Thompson and the *Correo de Mejico* on his west and Austin and the *San Felipe* on his east. He was bellowing for John Bailey. And the mate was placing his ear in the captain's face, hearing, rebelling at the order. For Jeremiah had cried:

"I'm putting the wind over the other quarter!"

He knew as he said it that if ever a man had thrown himself into the lap of the wind gods, Jerry Brown was doing that now. He was bringing the ship's head around from northeast and safety to northwest and danger, literally gambling his all on a spin of the mighty wheel of the universe.

As the *Sabine* pointed into the storm, great seas charged in. Black waves smashed at stern and starboard side with bludgeonlike blows, poured inboard, snarling across deck, bulwarks, and clinging men, engulfing all before them. The terrific force on the weather side drove the hull alee and pushed up seas of resistance and equal fury. The *Sabine* twisted, reeled, and spun her masts in wide arcs. And still the ocean lifted to mammoth size, black and monstrous against the angered sky.

The hurricane gale was increasing in weight. A great shock of water leaped aboard. It was a warning of what was to come. Shouts rose above the wind. Jeremiah thought someone was either hurt or swept overboard. The pull of seas at his feet and the awful resistance of the helm, as well as the tossing antics of the ship, caused him to cling desperately to the wheel.

"Hang on!" The cry came just as lightning pronged the sea and lit up a giant graybeard off the larboard beam. It reared high in that instant's flash, toppling and tossing its crest ahead. Then down it came, striking the ship and shooting upward and through the rigging in a thunderous crash. Then another fork of lightning bared the scene. Men clung to anything at hand, their bodies tossed up like chips on a stream. The deck rose up, hung there before falling suddenly to windward, so violently that she seemed torn apart.

The *Sabine* could not stand much more. The last onrush had almost swamped her. Spitting salt water, Jeremiah yelled for life lines down the weather deck. He was beset with fear now, an awful fear that he had done wrong in turning back into the storm.

John Bailey made himself heard: "Ye're riskin' a brush wi' land."

Jeremiah knew this to be true, though it was a risk he had assumed. It was a part of the gamble.

The wind now exceeded whole-gale force. It seemed to veer suddenly, to come in from all directions, heavier by the moment. The reefed foresail gave before a gust. Bereft of all but forestaysail, the weary *Sabine* plunged wildly, burrowing her nose deep in seas. She staggered. There was the charging sea astern, and against the resistance forward, she could only yaw, swing on her bows like a gate on its hinges, and present her length to the oncoming surge of dark water. She was "broaching to," a term seamen spoke with a shudder, for it meant a ship was threatened with capsizing. As the *Sabine* heeled fearfully over, every man aboard was aware that his fate hung precariously in the balance, in the hands of God and Captain Brown.

But the captain recognized the limitations of mortal man and was turning to the Lord. He was praying that the Creator would remember there were things at stake other than the safety of self, men, and ship; the success of Austin's return with munitions to Texas was dependent upon the *Sabine's* safety now. The immediate future of Texas rode the storm.

With all the strength at his command, Jeremiah fought the wheel. Full right rudder must be supplemented by sail power forward. If only the storm sail held, if only a wave comparable to the hard ones taken thus far would strike at the larboard bow of the ship, she might rise and straighten. John Bailey was at his side, waiting to lay his brawn to the wheel when and if the time came to swing her over.

Then she rose, slowly, as if in agony, her stern sweep checked, but still at grips with the danger. Thrown almost over on her beam ends, she angled the seas. The rudder remained slammed hard over. Lee seas smashed high on the leaning deck, blocking the schooner's right head motion. She came up, righting her masts as if by sheer will power. Then came a lurch that almost snapped her masts. Jeremiah knew the time had come for the superhuman effort at the wheel.

"Now!" he cried at the top of his voice, hoping the rudder could withstand the strain.

The rudder gave slowly, to quarter right. Only the feel of slanting decks could guide captain and mate now. Sensitive to her every motion, they waited as on a pivot for the swing of her bows. Then it came. And in such a hurry that they realized she was in danger of throwing her starboard side to the waves.

"Hellum amidships! Heave ho! And over a quarter left." They were a team now, men against the sea.

The *Sabine* shuddered from stem to stern. Then she straightened on her course and ran west-northwest, hull taking on water, her master gambling that the hurricane was slanting more west than north, that his ship had open water between her and the land. Which would push him fast under the Texas coast toward his destination.

Morning crept over the turbulent sea, wan and sunless. Slate-gray water tossed and rolled mountains down into troughs. Ragged clouds trailed the crests and seemed to pick up flying spray for ballast. The wind diminished in force, though the onrush of seas continued to hammer at the ship. Hour after hour the ship felt the crash of waves against battered hull and decks.

Jeremiah stayed at the wheel, his every joint sore and his body taut. The exhausted mate and crew stared stonily out of bloodshot eyes. John Bailey plumbed the bilge and swore. The ship was taking on more water, which meant all hands must lay on the pumps.

"Now, Cap'n, could it be we're ridin' hard into the land?"

"John, we've ridden the outer edge of the circle from northeast to north. Which means we're too close to land for comfort."

The horizon had widened little. Gray sky and sea were united, both moving. With visibility limited, Jeremiah prudently ran with lead sounding the fathoms and lookouts posted fore and aft; and he kept to himself his probable position at sea, by dead reckoning.

He knew the Texas coast. From the Sabine River, it sloped down to the opening of Galveston Bay. Figuring sixty to seventy-five mile gale winds pushing sea and sky and ship for a given number of hours, he guessed the *Sabine* to be driving southwest under Galveston Island.

He struck eight bells noon, one day and three hours out of New

Orleans, moved to the leadsman on the starboard side and watched the red marks on the line. Suddenly he tensed. Less than fifteen feet of water lay under the schooner. She was shoaling her water fast.

The *Sabine* was instantly veered off her course. As she pointed due south, a hole opened in the pall to reveal a flat sandy beach only a few ships' lengths distant. Barely visible was a house farther on, a landmark.

John Bailey's mouth fell open in surprise. " 'Tain't possible, Cap'n. But me own eyes is lookin' at the Galveston customhouse."

There was little humor in Jeremiah's grin. Small elation showed in his eyes when Bailey spat into the scuppers and said:

"Few is them that could do it, and fewer they is who would try it. Lads, the cap'n used the storm to drive us to Texas near a day ahead o' schedule!"

Chapter Eleven

THUNDER OFF VELASCO BAR

Late in the afternoon Jeremiah risked the bar on diminishing storm winds and anchored in Velasco. He risked more, since visibility was so narrowed by confused skies that Thompson could be lurking unseen within two cable lengths. Thinking that in such weather the *Correo* was more likely snugged down in Galveston Bay, Jeremiah used the hurricane's wake for discharging cargo.

Upon learning that his brother William had escaped Thompson after the capture of the A. C. Allen sloop, he fell to the task of unloading ship.

At ten that evening he had reached that curious state of exhaustion which leaves mind and body numb and obedient only to strong purpose. At eleven he crossed the street to the hotel, picked up his mail, and went upstairs. Too tired to sleep, he sank into a chair and poured whisky.

The first letter was from Mobile. A friend urged him to accept half interest in a large schooner in the West Indian trade. From New Orleans came a demand for payment of the sum remaining on the purchase of slaves. Oddly enough, the next thing he read was an offer for the cannon, the sum almost the same as the amount he owed for the slaves. It was from Colonel Ugartechea.

He was thinking of his need for money when a timid knock sounded at his door. He admitted Polly's aunt Virginia, who apologized as she handed him a statement for Polly's expenses. Suppressing a grimace, he looked up from the paper and said as he had a dozen times before:

"Just don't let Polly know I'm putting up the money."

Alone once more, he frowned over the bills confronting him and reached for the last unopened letter. It was from Polly. Forgetting his troubles, he sat down and read:

Dear Jerry:

I think you would have been very proud of the girl who once "sat like an Indian and talked like a New Orleans dockside wench," for Lieutenant Harry Billings of the U.S.S. *Warren* asked me to lead the ball at Broadhaven, his grandfather's plantation home. I held my wine remarkably well and only once lost my temper. An old goat persisted in holding me too close and I set him on his course. Next day I rode with Harry after the hounds. As I could not take the rail fences, he dropped back and we sat by a brook and talked. He is very keen about the Mexican situation since he is of Commodore Dallas's Gulf Squadron and knew about the *Martha's* capture and release by the *Ingham*. He has heard of you, Jerry, and thinks you will run into real trouble if you persist in putting Mexican couriers on deserted islands. Harry is very handsome and polite, and is a typical Virginia gentleman. Since all the girls were vying for his attention, I decided to show them how the cow ate the cabbage. I did. At the brook, he became very attentive, and out of curiosity I sampled his kiss. It wasn't at all disappointing. . . .

Jeremiah slapped at a mosquito on his cheek harder than he realized. He was telling himself it didn't matter that she was kissing men even as he glared at the rest of the letter. It was just a waste of money on an incorrigible. He got up, crumpled the letter, and tossed it to the floor. At the window he looked out into the dark night, his mind busy drawing images of Polly dressed for the ball, Polly in riding habit, Polly a woman with enough vitality in her eyes to attract any man. Despite the fact that she was a decisive woman who could take care of herself, she had no business taking such risks. It wasn't that he was jealous, he argued silently; rather, his concern was more brotherly. That was it.

A little later he was reading his reply to her letter. Like a stern parent, he relished every word of advice he had written. It ended with:

—You can be glad your naval officer is a gentleman. I thought I had given you a lesson in playing with fire but you're either an adventuress or a virgin of short memory. At any rate, the facts of life are simple. The Lord made males and females attractive to each other. When they kiss a spark sets off the powder keg and blows reason to kingdom come. Hot blood has no conscience whatever. So remember these things before you sample the kiss of gentleman or sailor out of curiosity. Else you could wake up one day and wonder what the hell happened and why.

"By thunder, that should make her sit up and take notice," he said.

With his anger spent, he picked up her letter and read all he had overlooked before. She had taken a prize with a water-color sketch of a schooner. She sat a horse as nicely as any Southern belle, raised her voice at church with the best singers, and danced as politely as any of the young ladies. However, she detested writing poetry and, worse, listening to the horrible poems the girls penned. And at times she was ready to come home, even if it meant waiting tables again.

A hard rap at the door caused Jeremiah to put the letter away.

John Bailey entered and sat down. Sweat ran off his face and neck and his jersey was sopping wet to the waist. "She's almost belched her cargo, Cap'n. But that ain't why I'm here."

Jeremiah placed a bottle before him.

"Aye. Thanks, Jerry. As man to man, I'll say ye're as fine a skipper as ever a mate sailed of. As mate to cap'n, I'll admit ye're a fast and plumb resourceful schoonerman. But that ain't why I'm here."

"Help yourself to another drink, John."

Observing the thinning intensity of Bailey's stare, Jeremiah thought in another moment the weary mate would tell him he wasn't here for whisky.

"The skies are clearin'," Bailey said at last. "All the way to the Gulf. The reason I know, Cap'n, is why I'm here. Out past the bar I seen a white flash o' musket fire."

Jeremiah came out of his chair. "The Mexican night signal, John. Are you sure?"

"That I am."

"Then it's Thompson. He's foxier than I thought."

Jeremiah was tired clear through and aching in back and muscles. He could not think clearly and he dreaded the effort. A look at

Bailey seemed to mirror his own fatigue. In the exchange of dull glances was admission of a fact: Rest was now impossible.

"John," he said, wondering if the ship could be made ready for night embarkation, if the crew could stand the strain, "unless we can slip by Thompson before morning we'll be bottled in so tight we may never draw him off the coast.

"Drink up, John. You'll need it. We're putting to sea at once."

With three men short of a full crew, sails needing mending, the seams of the larboard hull leaking, scant food and fresh water aboard, and every man working at sails and sheets by effort of will, the *Sabine* eased away from the wharf into the black night over the Brazos. The men knew why they were sailing out to sea, for the Old Man had said: "We'll draw the Mexican in chase."

The wind came in weakening gusts. Cloud streamers ran inland on the higher air currents, and a star or two shone through, winking off and on. The ship slid forward without a light aboard. Sailing was blind. The captain knew the fairway, though no seaman could claim acquaintance with the wind. It stiffened now, promising south. It fell off, came on again slanting in from east. Ahead, somewhere out over the bar, lay the war vessel Texans from San Antonio to the Sabine cursed.

A few stars broke the gloom over the southern horizon and Jeremiah watched them closely. A mast ahead would break the skyscape for a telling instant.

The schooner crossed the bar, her hand lead sounding the depth. They were hitting the open sea when suddenly a bulk came between the *Sabine's* deck and faint stars.

Jeremiah estimated the distance separating the ships—a scant fifty yards! He caught his breath, fearing the lookout would cry the deck and give them away. A hundred and one thoughts flashed through his brain in the long minute of passing so close abreast the enemy, though each revolved about the vitally important task of running beyond the point-blank range of Thompson's guns before engaging him in pursuit.

He was sliding almost free, his stern clearing the *Correo's* bows when a cry of alert from the Mexican's deck split the night. Before the sleeping ship became aroused, the usual question rolled across the water.

"What ship is that?"

For answer, Jeremiah cried, "All sail, John! Handsome now!"

Lights flashed on the Mexican's deck, and marines ran about for stacked muskets. The sailing master bawled orders for sail and men to lay on the windlass. Then a musket flashed and a bullet sang across the *Sabine's* deck. Visible now in the lantern light was the capstan gang. Soon the anchor flukes would break water and the *Correo* would swing about for a broadside. Even now gunners were running to stations.

"We've got to outrun her anchor, lads!"

The crew responded and the schooner put her best foot forward. Heeling over, her booms swung around, and lashings and sheets tautening, the *Sabine* split waves and sent fans of spray flying from her cutwater. Close aft, Thompson's deck swarmed with lanterns, and the glow of match tubs painted the line of her decks. As yells sounded against the wind, Jeremiah considered the target he made for bow chaser or swivel, and helmed the schooner more to windward.

A gun roared, and the wild shot into the dark night was a wide miss. But the *Correo* was shaking into motion. In the glow of deck lights, the orange tints of canvas bled off into the shadowy rigging and opaque night. The wind bellied her sails and sent her surging forward with head swinging to westward.

A note of grudging admiration crept into Bailey's voice as he observed that the war vessel got under way uncommonly quick for a Mexican.

The *Sabine* ran with every rag set and drawing. She had placed wide water between her and the *Correo* when Jeremiah ordered lanterns lit. Though still within range of Thompson's fire, he was willing to gamble a light against the skill of Mexican gunners. For the game was chase, and it was unlikely that an eagle would pursue a sparrow he could not see.

Several days later the *Sabine* ran alone for the port of Velasco. All was right with the world as the last sunset of August composed sea and sky into a scene of dying day. The sunburst reached high, painting the western heavens in vivid warm colors, tinting softly the scattered clouds overhead. The whole sky was mirrored by the sea, which began nowhere and ended at the mouth of the Brazos. And Jeremiah was seeing in Nature's offering a reflection of the success of his recent adventure.

Thompson surprised and disappointed him in one sense. He had snatched the bait like a hungry tarpon and run with it. All through the first bleak morning his war vessel had fallen behind and emerged from rain squalls with remarkable speed and tenacity. The *Sabine*, unable to give Thompson a clear horizon to scan, saved her tricks for night. Under cover of midnight two days later, she sneaked south and watched the *Correo* sail by, and with morning ran the pass for Copano Bay. When the *Correo* failed to turn back, it was logical to assume she was running Padre Island down; probably in chase of another sail she thought her quarry. In any case, the effect buoyed Jeremiah's spirits, for the roadstead was free of Thompson.

Austin and the *San Felipe* could enter the Brazos tomorrow without molestation.

Grinning broadly, Jeremiah cried, "John, break out rum for the lads."

A little later every man aboard joined in the captain's favorite song of the sea. All the way to the wharf in Velasco they sang. And the town turned out to learn the cause of celebration aboard of Captain Jerry Brown.

2

The morning of September first broke insufferably hot and clammy. Not a breath of fresh air stirred over land or water. The only ripples on the Brazos emanated from the tide and sudden dives of mewing gulls in search of fish. Small craft bound upriver rode the sluggish current on anchors with sails set and hanging limp. The aftermath of the hurricane seemed an ally of the absent Thompson, since the calm would detain the *San Felipe* at sea.

While a few boatmen and teamsters went about their work as usual, most of the townspeople gathered in groups under frontier marquees to discuss the turbulent political situation. The War Party, desiring an open break with Mexico, said, "Let General Cós come to Texas with troops and we'll chase him across the Rio Grande." The pacifists said, "You warmongers forced the call for a convention rather than give up the desperadoes who drove Tenorio from

Anáhuac." Argument grew stronger each day, and the calm of the weather on this morning gave rivermen time to get in their say.

Captain Chase of the brig *Tremont* mopped sweat from his face before stalking off his ship for the hotel. He was loaded with lumber for Pensacola and "anchored by a stillborn wind." He paused in his stride for a look up the river. A cloud of smoke and the heavy thumping of an engine announced the approach of the McKinney & Williams steamboat *Laura*. Captain Chase pursed his lips. By gadfrey, she stirred up the old Brazos with a "weather-be-damned" rattle a sailing man envied. Then he turned his back on the tub which, to his way of thinking, no honorable seaman would stoop to command. However, she might tow him out to a wind. But his pride rose up in protest.

He had drunk heavily the night before with the crowd that celebrated Jerry Brown's success in luring Thompson off the Brazos approach. Seeing George Brown at the hotel door, he asked about Jeremiah and learned he was catching up on his sleep.

"Seems Jerry fetched us worse than Thompson," Captain Chase said.

"The Lord makes the weather, Captain. Man makes such as is snortin' down the river," Jeremiah's father replied dryly, turning his bearded face toward the distant *Laura*.

Captain Chase grunted and looked toward the sea. Seeing two men in a skiff waving their arms about wildly, he said, "What's the commotion about?"

Just as he and the elder Brown joined other curious citizens moving hurriedly toward the skiff, a breath of air ruffled the Brazos. As it continued to hold, light and uncertain, the *Tremont's* captain made a dash for his small brig.

George Brown moved on toward the fort. The boat was beached and its occupants were shouting and pointing toward the Gulf. What they revealed caused Brown to disengage himself from the crowd and hasten toward the hotel.

Jeremiah awoke to the banging on his door, then turned over and tried to resume his sleep. But the voice urgently sounding his name was his father's.

"Jerry, open up fast in there! Thompson's ship is outside the bar!"

It was like plunging his head in cold water. Jeremiah was never wider awake. George Brown entered and stood with crooked forefinger combing his white mustache down into the beard. His small blue eyes dug steadily and accusingly into his son's.

"I thought you said you drew him off, Jerry." Meeting with only silence and an expression that tried to reconcile a fact to what seemed an impossibility, the parent said, "It's sort of embarrassin', and it'll be a sight worse for you when the *San Felipe* hoves in sight."

Here was the gospel truth, if ever it was spoken. Jeremiah shook his head savagely and moved to a window. He felt the oppressive calm, and his eyes fell on the *Tremont* half a ship's length out from the wharf. Captain Chase was yelling to the top of his voice, "Dock her! I want none o' this Thompson!" Jeremiah made a grimace and looked away.

His glance fell on the approaching smokestack of the *Laura*. The steamboat held his attention as he listened to his father's mutterings about the responsibility of Austin's safety resting in his hands.

"So what are you going to do about it, Jerry?"

In grim silence, Jeremiah admitted he had underestimated Thompson, and in doing so, he had committed a costly blunder.

The *San Felipe* was no doubt approaching the Texas coast. He had gambled against a hurricane, risked lives and ship, had led Thompson a merry chase for days and sleepless nights in order to prepare the way for the *San Felipe*. And what was there to show for it?

"Maybe you're growing a little too sure of yourself, Jerry. Sailed in cocky, drank to celebrate a little early. Forgot the Lord, maybe. Did you say to all your friends last night you tricked Thompson, *the Lord willing?* No, you didn't."

Jeremiah looked at his father. "For the love of peace, get the lecture over with and go to Brazoria for our cannon."

A smile formed on George Brown's face. "What are you planning, Jerry?"

Jeremiah continued to stare at the steamboat. "I'm not sure," he said, "but if the sea holds calm so sailing ships can't move, the old steamboat *Laura* might come in handy." Turning slowly, he faced his father. "In fact, she's handy now. Go down there and tell Captain Grayson to tie her up and wait."

"Wait for what?"

"For something that will arouse landsmen to such anger that they'll carry the fight out to Thompson."

A half hour later the *Laura* awaited only firewood and Jeremiah's order to steam upriver for the cannon. In the *Tremont's* cabin, Jeremiah wasted no time in getting down to business. Captain Chase scoffed at the idea of putting out to sea where he would be at the mercy of Thompson and his schooner-of-war.

"Take your own ship out, Jerry," he said.

Jeremiah looked him in the eye. "How many volunteers could I muster right now to go out and fight Thompson?"

"Damn few," Captain Chase replied.

"Right. But if you or any other Texan were captured by Thompson, how many?"

The captain rubbed his leathery jaw. "I see what you mean. All right, Jerry."

The *Tremont* was raising sail in the fitful breeze when Jeremiah boarded the *Laura*.

Half an hour passed and Captain Chase stood no more than a dozen ships' lengths beyond the fort. The sentry on the mound stared idly at the craft, and gulls fluttered about her, screaming their anger at the lack of motion she stirred into her wake. Then a slow gust trembled across the Brazos and sent her down toward the bar.

Captain Grayson turned his small round face to Jeremiah, rubbed at his nose, and walked the deck. He started when Jeremiah said at last:

"Take her out in the river, Captain, so we can see what happens."

The *Laura* gave a shudder and churned out from the wharf. Townsmen in the shade of store fronts forgot politics long enough to stare after McKinney's smoke-belching curiosity. Captain Grayson yelled ashore: "Charlie, hold them mules. I'm fixin' to lay on the whistle cord."

Aboard the thumping and shaking *Laura*, Jeremiah pondered the strangeness of human nature. He was going to a lot of trouble to shake fellow Texans out of their political differences into righteous indignation.

Then he looked out beyond the bar and saw the *Correo's* guns bearing on the *Tremont*. Thompson was now capturing her.

Jeremiah watched Captain Grayson and his crew out of a corner of his eye. What he saw was his reward. Forming in their faces were the unmistakable signs of a deep and active anger that promised to be as difficult to calm as it had been to excite into the open.

3

The *Laura* almost shook herself apart as she raced for the wharf, where she slowed just enough to allow Jeremiah to leap ashore. Then she was whistling and churning for Brazoria.

Soon the streets were alive with excitement. Townsmen, rivermen, farmers, trappers, and sailors needed only a reminder from the Brown brothers that the *Laura* would need firewood, water for her boilers, hawsers for towing, and cotton bales for breastworks. Several hours later a milling throng lined the Brazos with guns loaded, powder horns, lead, and ramrods handy. The first distant whistle of the steamboat evoked yells of welcome. The answering cheers of the Brazoria volunteers sounded a half mile away. The steamboat came on and docked. The cannon were aboard.

Riflemen swarmed ashore and gathered around Jeremiah, William, and John Bailey. They were a hard, determined lot in homespun and buckskins, each anxious to have his say but more anxious to speak with their Kentuckys and blue whistlers. Jeremiah directed one group to man the big guns, which would be put ashore downriver to cannonade the becalmed *Correo*. With rafts ready, firewood and water aboard, the cotton-clad left Velasco to give battle.

The *Tremont* under a prize crew was vainly working for headway in the direction of Mexico while the *Correo* lay becalmed inshore with all sails set and hanging still.

Jeremiah raised a hand for attention. "Don't waste your fire, men. Captain Grayson, hang on her stern or you'll see blood run our deck."

Ahead, the *Correo de Mejico* cut a fine figure of a fighting ship of medium class. She gleamed like a jewel, bulwarks white, brass cannon shining, marines in full colorful attire. And she drew silent admiration as well as grudging respect, for she alone of all that Mexico had sent against Texas thus far had sustained an effective blockade. Now she was trying to swing her larboard beam around for loosing a broadside.

Jeremiah fired a signal to shore. A flare at the touchhole of the distant cannon was followed by a roar. Water leaped up near the *Correo*. The second gun on land sent a shot closer. Mexican signal flags were hoisted by Thompson, and soon the prize crew was seen abandoning the *Tremont*.

As the *Laura* churned toward the *Correo's* stern, the calm prevented Thompson from turning. As he drove his men to shift his swivel gun aft, the riflemen heard Jeremiah's order to open fire.

Small arms peppered the war vessel's deck and bulwarks. A marine threw his *escopeta*, a bell-muzzled carbine, high into the air and loosed a howl. Thompson's men lay flat until the firing slowed. Then the elements favored him with a breath of wind. The *Correo* swung slowly around and the Texans were looking straight into the muzzles of the Mexican larboard battery. A cotton bale caught the full blast of the first to roar. The next shot tore a hole in the *Laura's* funnel. The third whizzed head-high across the *Laura's* deck, missing narrowly the wheelhouse.

"Run for the *Tremont!*" Jeremiah cried.

Out of cannon range, all aboard breathed easier. There were few casualties. An Oyster Creek lad had caught the fall of the cotton bale and suffered a broken arm and collarbone. Several men sported powder burns.

The *Tremont* was taken in tow and returned to shallow inshore water beyond the range of Thompson's guns. The *Laura* was working out to the *Correo* again when a well-aimed shot from the shore battery tore through the war vessel's forward running rigging, parting stays and taking the jibs off her. As spars and lines struck the water a cheer broke on the steamboat's deck. It had scarcely died when someone pointed toward the eastern horizon.

"A sail!"

Jeremiah's heart pounded. She could be the *San Felipe*. He prayed that she was, for at this stage of the game his forces held the edge over Thompson. Captain Grayson came forward with his telescope, though all he could make out was a sail under no wind. With the decision to steam for the unidentified vessel, the volunteers sent up a protest. They had come out here to fight, not to investigate. They'd have Jerry Brown know they weren't satisfied yet.

Sweat-soaked and grimy, face blackened by powder, Jeremiah grinned broadly and walked among them. "Just be patient," he said. "You'll get more fighting than you bargained for."

As the *Laura* drew closer to the becalmed ship, the riflemen were alerted lest she turn out to be a Mexican. Not a few were disappointed when the American flag was hoisted to her peak. As they steamed on, George Brown's glances alternately shifted from the ship ahead to Jeremiah's tense face. He knew his son's mind, his hopes and prayers: if the vessel were the *San Felipe*, an error might be corrected and vindication would be complete. He waited, and at his side also watching Jeremiah were William and John Bailey.

Bailey lowered the telescope, winked at the Browns as he told Jeremiah to take a squint.

Seconds later, Jeremiah emitted a long whooping yell. "All right, boys, all together. We'll give Mr. Austin a real Texas cheer."

Jeremiah boarded the *San Felipe* while Captain Grayson and crew fashioned and secured towropes. The first man to clasp his hand was Austin. Edwin Waller, A. C. Allen, the Wharton brothers, and Thomas F. McKinney crowded about him and plied him with questions.

"Belay! You swamp me," Jeremiah laughed.

With silence restored, he told the story of Thompson's pursuit. "Last night I celebrated. This morning I awoke to find he had outfoxed me. He sat out there waiting, and I was licked by the weather. Couldn't have sailed if——" He broke off in midsentence and stared aft.

Carmela, looking small beside Padre Alpuche, stood silent, gazing at him.

"Jerry!" A note of welcome surprise invaded her voice. Then she was advancing with a hurried swish of petticoats.

Chapter Twelve

STRIKE THE COLORS

Thomas McKinney drew Jeremiah aside and bid Captain W. A. Hurd of the *San Felipe* join them. He introduced them, saying, "You two may have much in common in the days ahead."

Hurd said crisply, "We have already. Captain Brown had the pleasure of starting a scrap which I plan to finish."

Jeremiah resented Hurd's tone of voice as much as the uncalled for little speech. But he guessed an air of arrogance could be expected from a man of Hurd's appearance. His eyes were small, actively defiant, and his jutting chin was big-boned and hard.

"I'll engage Thompson and blast him out of the Gulf. The *Laura* can tow me out."

"Sure," Jeremiah replied. "Once the munitions and passengers are transferred at the bar."

"The hell you say, Captain Brown! I don't propose to wait."

"Then you'd better blow up a fine breeze, Captain Hurd. And while at it, haul your wind around to suit my riflemen. Else you'll go at it alone."

As Hurd turned and walked aft, Captain Grayson yelled, "She's tied to and ready, Jerry."

"Then make for the bar."

For the first time Jeremiah noticed the position of the sun. It was low and glaring over the still water. Smoke from the *Laura's* twisted funnel lifted in a column, so light was the air.

Waller and Wharton came to the bows and talked with him for some time before retiring to their cabins for baggage. Ahead, the *Correo* appeared in sight, now closer to the land and working anxiously for a position where she could engage the shore guns. Fresh jibs and spars were back in place and she looked as formidable as ever.

Jeremiah felt he was not alone. Faint scents of perfume told him Carmela was near. She came very close, not looking up at him as she stared into the long sun slick. Her eyes fell under the force of the mirrored sun as she spoke softly.

"I was simply unable to sail with you, Jerry."

His low laugh sounded bitter.

Her face came up, she said defensively, "Father Alpuche had already booked passage for me aboard the *San Felipe* and——"

"Forget it," he said viciously.

"As you say," she replied, looking ahead at the *Correo.*

Eying her sharply, he said, "Odd that you should come to Texas at a time when Thompson could find his windfall by taking this ship and Mr. Austin. Well, take a look at his ship and let this sink home: I'm of one mind, one aim, and determined as they come to rid the Texas coast of Lieutenant Thompson and his *Correo,* regardless of the cost."

"Even if it brings the wrath of Mexico down on your head?"

"That's nothing new to me." He put his back to the rail, his full attention upon her. "And the way I feel about my coast is the way you should feel about your life. All those crazy notions in your head. What will they get you? Trouble, a whole mess of trouble."

She gazed across the water in silence.

The *Laura* rode at the far end of the dipping hawser, seeming to gather propulsion by timed vibrations. The paddle wheel lifted water from the sheeted sea and spilled it white and sparkling.

Jeremiah asked, "Now why were you so anxious to sail aboard this ship?"

"Any ship," she corrected, almost in detachment.

"Except the *Sabine.*"

"That's really the one I wished to sail."

"Then why didn't you?"

She flung her bonnet back to hang by the neck ribbon and fished a small mirror from her reticule.

"You wouldn't understand," she said, apparently interested in all her mirror revealed. "You wouldn't even try to understand."

Then she lowered the mirror to the rail and faced him. Her hand whirled the ornamental object slowly round and round, pausing, spinning again, nervously, he thought, as she studied him.

Captain Grayson yelled from the *Laura,* "If you're signalizin' me with them flashes, I don't catch on."

Jeremiah started. Strange sensations began in his stomach and ran through him as suspicion struck. Then before he dared turn his revealing glance upon Carmela, the sounds of three muskets fired in rapid succession rolled across the water from the distant *Correo.*

A little cry of "Oh!" escaped Carmela. Turning instantly, Jeremiah saw her looking straight down over the rail into the water. "My mirror," she said. "It fell overboard."

Torn between a desire to proclaim her a confederate of Thompson then and there and an overwhelming urge to slap her face, he compromised by seizing her arm and jerking her roughly to him. "Why you damn little cheat! Done in true Mexican style, wasn't it?"

Frightened eyes riveted to his face, she stammered, "I—I don't know what you're talking about."

He enjoyed her wince as his fingernails dug into her arm. "You heliographed and Thompson fired Mexican signals in reply. Now out with it before I end your game by dragging you before Mr. Austin."

"You wouldn't!" she flared.

"By God, watch me!" He took a step with her in firm grip before she uttered a cry of protest and declared her willingness to talk.

"I'm sorry, Jerry," she began, her eyes falling before his. "Sorry it had to be you at my side when it happened." Pausing, she forced the rest. "I was sent from Mexico City—to determine Mr. Austin's course after his imprisonment. When it was learned that he was going to Texas aboard this shipload of munitions, Consul Martínez sent me to instruct Thomas to seize the ship. That's all, Jerry."

"All except your eagerness to give Thompson his big opportunity for fame and reward in Mexico. And it might have worked if the Lord hadn't sent a calm. But He did, Carmela, and I'm going to use it. As for you——" He broke off, not once removing his hard eyes from her imploring face. "I'm going to singe your pretty wings."

He pushed her aside and turned his back to her just as Captain Grayson trumpeted forth, "What about them signals, Jerry?"

Cupping his hands, Jeremiah cried back, "They mean steady as you go—vengeance ahead!"

2

Just before sundown the *San Felipe* reached the bar, where she transferred her cargo of munitions and passengers aboard the *Laura*. Before the steamboat sailed, Hurd approached Jeremiah and asked for his aid in trying to take the *Correo*. This was more civil and gentlemanly. The riflemen volunteers were asked to put it to a vote. Soon the entire band boarded the *San Felipe*.

Although night had fallen over the river and sea, the Texans knew Thompson's position. He had worked well inshore and was by now able to engage the shore guns with his nine-pounders. As the *San Felipe* sat waiting for the night wind, the *Correo* loosed a broadside that ripped through Captain Hurd's rigging and sails. Hurd swore and ordered his guns to return the compliment. An offshore breeze stirred the sails and held, like a teasing zephyr, when all expected it to die. The *San Felipe* slid forward, every eye aboard her fixed on a silhouette, the enemy ship standing against the last surge of light on the western horizon.

In the brief engagement that followed both sides scored hits. The *San Felipe's* hull and bulwarks were battered and round shot tore through the deckhouse. The *Correo* fared worse. Thompson's deck was littered with debris and wounded marines, and he resorted to the only course left to him. He gave the once proud *Correo de Mejico* all the canvas she shipped and caught the night wind for the open sea.

An hour later she was swallowed up by the black night over the Gulf.

There were times during the long vigil before dawn when only

Jeremiah and the quartermaster of the respective watch remained awake. The volunteers slept where they happened to drop their guns. One section of the deck was as hard as the next, and ship's planking differed from packed earth only by the motion of the former.

Captain Hurd appeared on deck just before dawn. "Any sign of the Mexican vessel?" he asked.

"No, but the wind is backing. She's in for another day of calms."

Hurd looked to sea, his prominent nose outlined against the first light in the east. "You know, Brown, McKinney told me about your scheme to arm ships. I'm in favor of it. And I said to McKinney, 'Tom, if this schoonerman Brown will listen to me I can teach him a thing or two about naval warfare.'"

Jeremiah forced a grin. "Now that was generous of you, Hurd."

"That's what McKinney said. He said something else that made sense. 'Before the people wake up, Texas will have to depend on privateers. Which,' he added, 'suits me.'"

"Well, it doesn't suit me," Jeremiah declared flatly.

Hurd laughed. "Coming from you, it sounds funny. That it does, since you're sitting the deck of one."

Jeremiah's face gave him away. He hadn't so much as given a thought to this aspect of coastal defense. But he was quick to realize that the lure of gain would give birth to privateers the same as a stagnant pool hatched out mosquitoes.

"So we're a couple of pirates," Jeremiah remarked dryly, pointing at a shape across the lifeless sea.

Dawn revealed the *Correo*. She lay well beyond cannon range with sails hanging uselessly. For an hour the stilled ships sat it out, the men aboard each anxious to engage in battle. Then the lookout hailed the deck with news that appealed to all.

The *Laura* was steaming toward them, with a column of smoke standing above her patched smokestack. On her deck were fresh volunteers whose rifle barrels were no brighter than the gleam of battle in their eyes. Captain Grayson trumpeted a "Good morning" and flung the towline at the *San Felipe's* bows. With the line secure, he ordered wood into the firebox and sent steam into the cylinders. The whole ship shuddered and the water wheel began to dip up the Gulf.

As the tow drew closer to the *Correo,* Captain Hurd cleared decks for action. Guns were checked for loads, cannon breechings secured, and match tubs replenished. Brazos planters became powder monkeys and Columbia trappers turned gunners and marines. Jeremiah suggested lowering away the boats hampering the guns and Hurd said he hadn't thought of that. Next he very importantly ordered Captain Brown to the "hellum," only to be told that it was his ship and "Brown's army."

Thompson's helplessness was apparent. With a wind, he held the advantage of more guns and trained men to use them; without a wind, his ship was to all appearances no better than a fishing smack.

John Bailey laughed. "We got 'im where we want 'im, Cap'n. And it's hopin' I am that he stays alive fer a dose of irons to his wrists."

Jeremiah raised the telescope. Seeing Thompson with hands on hips, legs bandaged, a set grin of defiance on his face, he said, "I wouldn't crow yet."

The *Laura* steamed to within half a cannon shot of the *Correo's* unarmed stern. At Jeremiah's signal, Captain Grayson shut off his steam and both ships slid to a halt. The *San Felipe's* larboard side faced the enemy, her guns ready to fire. Hurd trained the first cannon and fired. Following the roar, recoil, and smoke, a cheer rose from the *Laura's* deck. The *Correo's* mainmast cracked and tumbled, sending spars splintering and crashing with canvas and lines to deck.

The second cannon let go, tearing a gaping hole in the *Correo's* starboard quarter just below the weather deck. It looked like slaughter. But there at the stern was Thompson. In the circle of the spyglass, Jeremiah saw him, shirt torn and blood running down his face, grinning as though this were a picnic on the Thames. As he lifted a hand, two uniformed Mexicans jerked sailcloth revealing a ninepounder which he had moved aft in expectancy of just such an attack.

"Look out! Cannon on the stern!" Jeremiah cried.

The flame spat right into the telescope. The ugly whizzing of heavy shot was brief. The next sound was an unearthly explosion on the *San Felipe's* deck; a devil-smasher. The big mast caught the shot off-center, though pins and gear at the fife rail joined splinters like shrapnel in that instant before the shot burst open and sent deckhouse and planking shooting like mad the length and breadth of deck and high into the rigging. In a glance, it was unbelievable. The screams of splinter-stabbed riflemen were not real. Nor was the needle of wood stinging Jeremiah's ear, pierced as neatly as any pirate's wench could have done it.

But that was nothing. For death, patient and waiting, hovered over a man close and dear to him.

John Bailey lay on his side, writhing and tearing at a length of plank that had been driven through his abdomen.

Jeremiah finally shook the paralysis that rooted him to deck. He seemed to walk long miles before reaching his mate and friend. Bending down to him, he drew his lips back dry over his teeth as he wrested Bailey's hands from the piercing board.

"Easy, John. Easy. You're making it harder."

"Aye, Cap'n." Bailey's eyes darted up at his captain. They pleaded with him. Sweat bathed his face. But he managed a grin, managed to hold on to Jeremiah's glance, as if only that mattered now.

"Damn it, Jerry, I'm runnin' out on ye at the wrong time. Ye'll be needin' me." He lay quiet a moment, not breaking the glance between them. "But," he laughed, "I put one over on old Dominique You. He just laid down and died."

That was the end of John Bailey.

Jeremiah called William to him, placed an arm about his shoulder, and stood there grim and silent. Understanding flowed between them, through them. Then Jeremiah raised his ravaged face and stared across the water at the *Correo de Mejico*.

3

About an hour later Lieutenant Thompson, after a futile attempt to parley, struck his colors. He had little choice and not a Texan could accuse him of cowardly action, for he had right up to the end endured as savage an attack as any naval officer could boast of and remain alive. His guns had been dismounted by cannon fire and his decks were strewn with wounded men and debris. Masts and rigging were a shambles, and the timbers of the *Correo's* stern were so torn and chopped that more of her lumber aft floated in the still sea than ribbed her hull.

Captain Hurd and crew and Texan riflemen stared with sympathy and awe at the man who had walked from John Bailey's body to a cannon and commenced the frightful bombardment. He sustained it, going from gun to gun, pushing aside any who got in his way. He fired like a devil, saying not a word; he beat a path between the hot guns until he was so blackened by powder that only the blue of his slit eyes shone through.

Watching him board the *Correo* with Hurd, a Brazorian said, "There he goes like a stoker from hell."

Jeremiah paused on the *Correo's* deck and stared with grim satisfaction at all he saw. There was the flag, the mighty Mexican eagle, which he had taken off the main perch with his tenth shot. He looked at Thompson, who failed to cut the resplendent figure of June last. His hair was clotted with blood, and he could hardly walk, but he did, amazingly, with two wounds in each leg. And but for Bailey, Jeremiah Brown would have held out a hand to a valiant foe.

Thompson led the way to his cabin, jerked a door half on its hinges aside and bowed them in. His grace would gain him little. Inside the cabin, he produced wine, smiled as he poured, and said: "To Texans." He gulped his drink, and poured again. "Y'know, there's small shame in losing to you bloomin' fighters. Captain Brown, my compliments. Seems you've turned the tables on me."

"So it seems. Now break out your papers."

They fell to examining the packet of official orders, which called for everything from an accurate charting of the Texas coast to total blockade and capture of Texan schooners engaged in illicit trade. Jeremiah bent over one document which Thompson tried to slip into his pocket. It concerned Carmela, her motive for visiting New Orleans and Texas. Here was the written proof of all she had told him: Carmela had been dispatched to New Orleans by Mexico's new Minister of War and Navy Tornel.

As Jeremiah pocketed the paper, Thompson smiled. "Surely, Captain Brown, you're too much of a gentleman to use that."

"Don't bet on it, Lieutenant."

"Let me see it," Hurd demanded.

"There's enough here for you to see," Jeremiah replied. "In fact, everything is here but a copy of Lieutenant Thompson's commission in the Mexican Navy."

"My orders bear out my commission," Thompson spoke up confidently. "Captain Hurd will vouch for that."

"Eh? Oh, sure. Nobody can doubt that after reading these orders, Lieutenant."

Jeremiah's face broke with a grin, the first since Bailey's death. "A United States court might doubt it," he said.

Hurd turned quizzically. "What are you getting at, Brown?"

"First, Lieutenant Thompson violated the treaty between the United States and Mexico when he forced Captain Chase of the *Tremont* aboard of him with his papers. The treaty provides that the *captor* shall board the *captured* with not less than three officers."

Thompson scoffed. "The *Tremont* is as Texan as you, Captain Brown."

"But she retains her United States registry."

Hurd rubbed his nose. "Yeah. By thunder, that's right."

"You resort to petty technicalities," Thompson mocked.

In Jeremiah's mind was more than personal vengeance, a political strategy that would shoulder the United States with the full responsibility of dealing with these Mexican officers and warship, thereby relieving Texas of a situation she was not ready to cope with. And to accomplish what he had in mind, Hurd's co-operation was necessary.

"Captain Hurd," Jeremiah said slowly, "you and I must be in accord on what I have in mind. We'll call it strained logic, but the Mexicans didn't bother to think straight when they called me a pirate. Nor did Lieutenant Thompson hesitate in clapping me in irons.

"Since the *San Felipe* is an American-registered vessel, and since she was fired upon by a man who can't produce his commission, she must have been attacked by a pirate."

When a slow grin of understanding spread over Hurd's face, Jeremiah placed a hand on his shoulder. "Your position is enviable, Captain Hurd. Since you're in command of the American ship *San Felipe*, it is your privilege and duty to clap Lieutenants Thompson and Ocampo, as well as the entire Mexican complement, in irons, take them to New Orleans, and press charges of piracy on the high seas in the United States federal court."

As the sun slipped behind a cloud haze on the horizon, the flame fell away and the ball became a dying red ember. Standing out to the still sea with all sails set for the night wind, the *San Felipe* and *Correo de Mejico* seemed painted on a canvas.

Alone on the point of land, Jeremiah watched the night fall over the ships on their way to New Orleans. His shoulders sagged under the weight of the day ending. Even Thompson's last words in parting —"We'll meet again, Captain Brown"—failed to stir up any emotion. The capture of the Mexican ship, the significance of it, all fell away to nothing. Carmela, whom he thought he loved, had been revealed for what she was. And John Bailey's body had been wrapped in sailcloth and, in keeping with his wishes, committed to the deep.

The sea was cold and heartless. He turned his back on it and looked at the land. But the events of the day, the red upon the sea, continued to haunt him. Such things were . . . a board piercing the flesh, running clear through . . . an irreparable loss. Such things were . . . a woman's deceit . . . a splinter planted deep in his own heart.

Chapter Thirteen

AN ILL OMEN

Dust hung rooftop-high in New Orleans at sundown. Streamers of light filtered through millions of tiny particles in feverish colors before cooling down to evening shades. The day had been unusually warm for the last of October.

Jeremiah glanced at his watch and looked toward the foot of Canal Street. He was due to meet Thomas F. McKinney and James Bowie at nine in the big auction room of Bank's Arcade. Bowie, who had in 1818 joined forces with Lafitte in smuggling slaves into New Orleans, was an adventurer with a great following in Louisiana. Tonight at the mass meeting he would no doubt form an army of some size to fight the Mexicans in Texas.

The Texan cry for volunteers and arms and money from the United States stemmed from the surrender of the *Correo de Mejico* and the trouble that surged in its wake.

The Mexican Government was thoroughly aroused. Its Minister of Foreign Affairs protested the detention of Thompson and his men in New Orleans, and Consul Martínez officially claimed Thompson and sought his release. But the United States prosecutor ruled that a trial was necessary and the so-called pirate was held in jail. Mexican newspapers played up the outrage, and American officialdom in Washington frowned and took notice of a most embarrassing international situation in which the United States held in custody Mexican naval officers, crew, and war vessel. When the truth eventually leaked out, through Thompson, that Captain Jeremiah Brown had "hatched the scheme," New Orleans laughed at a clever joke and Mexico again placed Captain Brown high on the list of Texan offenders.

Texans continued to quarrel among themselves. The pacifists claimed with some justification that revolutions in Mexico had for years kept the military engaged at home. Others wished Texas to become a part of the United States for reasons of security. And the so-called warmongers predicted that Santa Anna's eyes were on Texas, that the big conquest would follow.

"We ought to arm ourselves," said most Texans. But little was accomplished despite the fact that with the arrival of General Cós and his regulars in San Antonio on October ninth, Texans realized they had at last fallen under the shadow of military rule.

The one thing Austin asked of his people upon his return was united action against Mexican troops on their way to Texas. They should convene and determine a course of action. The Consultation assembled at San Felipe on the sixteenth of October, but was forced to adjourn for lack of a quorum until November third because many of the delegates had joined the volunteer army.

There was no longer doubt. The only part of Mexico that had not accepted Santa Anna's dictatorship was the province of Texas. On October twelfth, Stephen F. Austin learned that he had been elected to the command of the undisciplined little army of three hundred men assembled at Gonzales. The cry for American aid issued loud from Texas.

The war had begun.

Jeremiah glanced at his watch again, mopped his face, and wished for a night wind off the Gulf. Then he looked downstream at a stern-wheeler churning the sluggish Mississippi, and on to a slave handler and overseer engaged in the grim business of herding a gang of Negroes aboard a boat, before searching the riverbank for the group of riflemen from Kentucky who had answered the Texan call for aid.

The volunteers should arrive soon. Else he'd be late in meeting McKinney.

Looking in the direction of the city, he thought again of the rumors issuing out of Vera Cruz. Minister of War and Navy Tornel was sending armed ships to Texas. Perhaps they were on their way or already there. Jeremiah had put out feelers though nothing had come of it. Montegut Joe, ex-pirate and friend of Bailey's who worked at the Arcade, was keeping a sharp ear to the grapevine.

Then Jeremiah saw the men he was looking for. There was no mistaking the Kentuckians in coonskin caps and buckskins. He was soon shaking the leader's hand.

"I'm here to take your volunteers to Texas. Schooner *Sabine*. We sail at dawn tomorrow, if there's a wind."

"Fightin' guaranteed?"

"We've won skirmishes at Gonzales and Goliad. The main army under Cós hasn't been engaged yet."

"By God, 'twill be, Cap'n!"

Jeremiah moved on to another rendezvous with volunteers from Mobile. This was his job. McKinney's was money and arms. He had been appointed financial agent by the few delegates who had met at San Felipe to contract a loan of one hundred thousand dollars in New Orleans. McKinney was due at the Consultation within three days.

It was nearing seven when Jeremiah made his way toward Magazine Street. Night was falling unnaturally still over the city. Smells of refuse and drying swamps mixed with the dust. Crickets still sang a summer's song and frogs croaked out incessant prayers for rain.

At the Arcade, several men invited him to drink. The usual courtesies done with, he followed the bulky waiter, once of Lafitte's establishment at Grande-Terre, to a private room and learned that a young Mexican connected with the Consulate was selling information in order to meet pressing gambling debts. He could be found at a house on Conde Street. But any interested party should first inquire at Countess Lillie's *maison de joie* next door. "Ask for Perfecto."

Jeremiah rubbed his jaw.

The ex-pirate gave him a wicked grin. "You can trust him, Cap'n Jerry. He knows Montegut Joe will slit his throat if he cheats any friend of mine."

"That's good enough for me," Jeremiah said.

He lost no time in searching out the place, where he rapped on the door and waited, wondering if this game of intrigue would bear fruit. A woman threw the door back and stared at him. She was the Mexican dancer who had entertained him in 1832 with the mock bullfight. A smile of recognition lit up her energetic face.

"*Muy hombre* Capitan Brown! Welcome!"

Jeremiah entered. She wore a low-necked filmy garment that exposed more than the curves of her neck. Her glance was quick and measuring, as if she were contemplating fresh conquest. Cigar smoke hanging in layers advised of the presence of another man; in the next room, small doubt, with an ear pressed to the door.

"So your lady love Señorita Ryan she turn Mexican on you, Capitan. I spit for you on her!" She was standing with hands on hips, very close, looking up at him, pivoting her torso slowly half around and back. She seemed all pepper and challenge, and but for the unseen man about, Jeremiah would have taken a devilish delight in covering her lips.

"How you learn where Lolita live?"

"I didn't. Someone said Perfecto was here."

Her glance narrowed on him, and her thin, passionate mouth twisted into a smile that could mean anything. Then she cast a furtive look at the closed door to another room and reached for his kiss. She was warm and winey. She broke away all too soon, took a backward step, and said in demanding tones, for the ears of any listener:

"What you wish with Perfecto?"

"I want to buy something."

Just before the door opened, she whispered, "If I come aboard your *Sabine* after my dance at two, you pour Lolita the amber wine?"

"By the barrel," he muttered, appraising the small handsome man who stood eying Lolita critically until she drew her gown modestly about her.

"The Capitan he wish to buy something from you," she said.

He smiled, like Juan Pacho, thought Jeremiah. "I have nothing up for sale, señor. Who sent you?"

"Montegut Joe."

"Then I patiently await your pleasure, Capitan."

"And I'll wait for your answer to this with equal pleasure, Señor Perfecto—are there any Mexican naval vessels in Texas waters?"

"That I do not know. But meet me between midnight and one o'clock and I can perhaps have the information." He named the address of a famous cockpit.

Shortly after midnight, Jeremiah stepped inside an elegant establishment in the Vieux Carré. A still fog of cigar smoke lay over the scene of pit, fighting cocks, pretty women, and fashionably attired men, dimming somewhat the soft light of the Carondelet oil lamps. Here the finest wines and liquors brought the highest prices; wagers ran into huge sums of money; and the noise preceding a feature battle was deafening; glasses touched and spilled white and red wines amid arguments and laughter.

Jeremiah remained inconspicuous on the fringe of the crowd, his eye sharpened on the sea of faces for a glimpse of Perfecto. His glance paused in study of a tall handsome Mexican of genial expression. F. Pizarro Martínez, Mexican consul, sustained with ease his position as leader of the Spanish element in New Orleans. He spent freely, entertained lavishly, and championed the rights of Mexicans with singular aggressiveness. But this suave gentleman was suddenly the Mexican eagle. And as suddenly he ceased to exist.

Carmela caused Jeremiah an inward start.

He studied her intently; hair done atop her head and shining, the curious quirk of her lips, the mauve shadows delicately formed at her neck and bosom against the bold sheen of her dress, all were striving to close his mind on the past.

He moved closer and she saw him and rose from her seat. Then she was composing her features, moving unhurriedly in his direction. Martínez looked up curiously, followed her gaze, and sat back, appearing amused. This Jeremiah saw. Anger flared up strong in him, against consul and woman.

"How is our friend Thomas faring?" he asked in a cutting voice.

She remained coolly poised. "He has a long wait in jail. His trial has been put off until January, which should please you immensely."

"You were quick to follow him here."

"Jerry, you just don't run out on a person when he's down."

Touching her sleeve, he rubbed the silk between his fingers. "Are you happy with all the pretty dresses that come out of the Mexican treasury? Or maybe they're personal gifts."

She frowned up at him. "I must appear very cheap to you."

"What would you call it when a girl turns down a decent offer of marriage for a mess of gay rags?"

"You're overdoing it, aren't you, Jerry? It wouldn't occur to you that I might be trying to find a proper way out of this adventure."

"No, it wouldn't. But what do you call proper, a complete wardrobe or a hangman's noose?"

"Just Thomas's release," she replied with a show of determination. "I refuse to desert him while he's in trouble. You more than anyone else can end this farce. He's no pirate, and you know it."

"Just what are you getting at?"

"Use your influence to withdraw the charges."

"If I promise to do that, will you tell Martínez you're through as of right now?"

When she appeared hesitant at a time when decisiveness was in order, he could not help thinking she was trying to use him, her behavior planned in the crafty minds of Thompson and Martínez.

"Forget it. I'm not interested," he said quickly.

"Jerry." Her hand closed over his. Her eyes and voice were imploring. "The day he goes free, I'll do anything you say."

"So you want to be bought. Always trading, aren't you? Never want to give, just trade. Well, I'll trade with you, but I'll dictate the terms."

He put all he was thinking in a glance so strong and unyielding that she could not escape its impact. Her lips curled with scorn in that instant before her open palm struck his cheek. Whirling, she left him, her departure timed to the announcement of the next event in the cocking main.

The presiding cockmaster held aloft an unimpressive black-feathered bird. "Sixteen months old, ladies and gentlemen, dieted and trained for running, sparring, and—drawing blood. Game and willing, from a hacienda near San Antonio de Bexar, this fine Lancashire bird with four victories on this night will compete in the main.

"The champion of Texas!"

This evoked little excitement. At this stage of the fights a cock was a cock. Each had wings trimmed to a slope and tail cut down to less than a third of its normal length. The spectators looked bored, half the house paying little or no attention to the red cock from Mexico now being shown.

"I hold here the winner of five matches, the splendid cock Antonio from San Luis Potosí, pitted against the bird from Texas in a fight to decide the main."

Bets were few. The buzz of conversation and laughter over wine and cigars threatened to let the fight go unnoticed until Carmela pointed to the red cock and spoke into the ear of Martínez. The effect was instantaneous. The consul stood and asked for the attention of all before raising his glass with a toast:

"To the red—Antonio López de Santa Anna!"

It caught fire. The ruler of Mexico versus the champion of Texas. The owners of the establishment were not blind to an opportunity provoked by accident. Betting was furious and the match was twice postponed when Texas sympathizers raised bets and the consul's party and West Indians banded together to accommodate them. The cocks were provided with long heels, spurs two inches long, and displayed in their bloodletting armor. Purses opened again in what promised to be the cocking event of the year. Men drank and hurled gibes back and forth until it seemed the game birds would turn spectators at a free-for-all fight on the Texan-Mexican issue.

In Jeremiah's mind, the scene, all its excitement, and loosed emotions, resolved itself into a simple fact: Carmela was fighting back.

He was suddenly bumped hard. "Pardon, señor," revealed Perfecto. Jeremiah followed the Mexican, who was anxious to trade a sheet of paper for money in order to place a wager on the red cock. "It is authentic, señor, from the lips of Martínez himself. I swear it!"

Jeremiah kept the bargain, pocketed the information, and joined the crowd about the pit.

A sudden hush fell over the house. The cocks were being placed in the ring. All bets were final. All eyes were drawn to a pair of fighting birds, which were no longer mere pawns of sport but gladiators carrying the battle between two races to a no-quarter decision.

What followed was sudden and decisive and gory. Carmela looked stunned. Slowly she turned until her glance met Jeremiah's. Then her head lifted proudly, disdainfully, and she laughed. The consul's party cheered. Perfecto cried, "*Viva!*" as he rushed to collect his winnings. Slowly the backers of the champion of Texas turned away, their faces unmasked and drawn with disbelief. They pondered the outcome in silence, asking, the same as Jeremiah, if this was a harbinger of things to come.

Jeremiah looked for Carmela. She was swallowed up by the breaking crowd. Frowning, he examined the scrap of paper he had paid for and read:

"Schooners-of-war *Moctezuma* and *Veracruzana* convoying troopships to Matagorda, Texas."

With a wry smile, he tore the paper to shreds. He didn't believe it, not one damn word of it, any more than he believed a simple cockfight had any bearing on the future.

Chapter Fourteen

THE VERACRUZANA

A rain squall blew in during the night. With morning weather to his liking, Jeremiah left New Orleans with Thomas McKinney, sixty volunteers and rifles, a cargo of precious munitions, and a splitting head.

The *Sabine* met tide and squall in her reach for Southwest Pass. Rain fell in blinding torrents, battering water, deck, and sails in one ceaseless roar. As the slippery deck heaved more to the motions of seas charging across the river, Jeremiah fought against nausea creeping into his stomach. Hoping to annul the feeling by detaching his mind from it, he tried to place an estimate on his new mate, William H. Leving, late of the United States Navy.

Mr. Leving knew his business. A month aboard the *Sabine* vouched for that. But what was inside this tall, erect man of fine features and easy disposition other than schooled discipline and love of adventure? True, he had been selected over men whom Jeremiah knew and trusted simply because he had naval experience. And Jeremiah was learning all he could about fighting at sea and storing it in his mind for further use.

The nausea eased somewhat, though Jeremiah's head continued to feel as if it were stuffed with canister shot. It was his own fault. Although he had told the dancing girl he would pour her amber wine by the barrel, there was no sane reason for his drinking it by that measure. His reason was, in fact, utterly insane, since there wasn't enough wine in the world to dull or sharpen his imagination into believing Lolita was Carmela. When Little Josh pounded on the door at dawn as he had been told to do, Jeremiah had rolled over and opened his eyes. The mass of black hair on the pillow had been anything but golden, and he had sent the girl away.

Mr. Leving came up, hands behind his back, and laughed. "The Kentuckians are having a time of it, sir. Sixteen at the rail at once."

Jerehiah could appreciate the humor of what was happening to the volunteers. He laughed outright when their leader staggered from the rail, swearing he'd rather face a she bear and twenty Mexicans with only his two fists than this. Seconds later the laugh died in Jeremiah. He hurriedly lashed the wheel and rushed the rail with no time to say, "Move over." A titter sounded behind him. When he looked around, Little Josh was putting his soberest face up for the captain's inspection.

"Damn little gnome," Jeremiah muttered, taking himself below.

The squall ran away from the *Sabine* that afternoon. The Gulf eased over and the wind swept in from the south with good driving force. Toward sundown a threatening dark color crept higher over the northern horizon. Seamen knew it betokened a norther. Hours later it breathed in and Jeremiah and McKinney exchanged significant glances. The latter's presence at the Consultation would probably be delayed if the blow reached as far west as the Brazos.

The weather next day proved this true. The wind howled down across the prairies and over the water through the *Sabine's* rigging. Touching in for port was impossible. Jeremiah ran the ship on through the dark night, listening to the battle of the winds.

Dawn was lifting colorless through the fog when Mr. Leving sent a boy to rouse the captain in a hurry. Jeremiah appeared on deck somewhat curious. Leving might be an old woman in his fears. Even now, he appeared more calm than self-reliant. His eternal "sir" rasped at the nerves of a man used to the informality of "Cap'n." As much as Jeremiah wished to call his mate just plain "William," he always checked himself. Such familiarity might horrify the ex-naval man.

"Sir, it seems we have company over our larboard quarter."

"Mr. Leving," Jeremiah said with strict nautical decorum, "it isn't unusual to have company while waiting for water to make over the bar."

"Perhaps, sir, but I am told you're a man who is—shall we say—particular of the company he keeps? Especially in view of the present circumstances."

Jeremiah fished to draw him out, receiving for reply, "Sir, you are high on the Mexican list for capture, and it was Mr. McKinney's *San Felipe* that robbed the enemy of superiority in the northern Gulf. Add our cargo of munitions and threescore volunteers to the aforenamed and you have the answer. I hope, sir," he added, smothering a grin, "I have passed this elementary test in simple deduction."

"Aye." Jeremiah made a grimace. "Aye, you'll do, Mr. Leving."

Peering through the fog streamers at a ghostly shape that came and departed, he was wondering just how loyal Mr. "Exact" Leving actually was. The time might come when that one virtue would have to take precedence over skill and bravery. But a commander must perforce earn and inspire loyalty. What had been good enough for John Bailey might fail to strike a spark from Leving.

"Whoever the stranger is, she's a big one and close upon us, sir. Shall I put distance between us?"

"And fast. Put her under our lee as quickly as possible."

The day lifted, the north wind still in command of the waves. The sun threatened to break through the fog, and already the stiff breeze was tearing gaping holes in the ragged streamers scudding south over the chop of water. The *Sabine* was engaged in the important business of putting the weather on her starboard quarter when the long, sleek stranger hove in sight again, this time no more than two cable lengths away. She had slanted the wind up for a better look.

Suddenly she broke out her colors. Up went the banner to her peak, where it stiffened in the wind and caught the first rays of the sun.

"Mexican!" Jeremiah exclaimed.

Leving drew in his glance and turned it on his captain, who read what he thought was in the mate's face: "Now, Mr. Schoonerman, since we're within half a cannon shot of her, what are you going to do?" He was opening his mouth to speak when the Mexican vessel sent a shot over the *Sabine's* bows.

"By thunder, she'll pick us off like a sitting duck," Jeremiah said.

McKinney rushed on deck and was soon acquainted with their perilous situation. He lit a cigar, blew smoke, and turned his back on the scene. "Jerry, get us out of this scrape and I'll see that you get the finest ship in the Texas Navy, if and when."

As Jeremiah's glance swept on to the enemy, an idea struck his brain with the suddenness of a bolt of lightning. How it came into being, a final and decisive thing to fascinate him, he could never explain even to himself.

As the man-of-war ran out her battery, he replied to McKinney, "Mr. Leving's a witness to that promise, Tom."

He said next, "Mr. Leving, hoist the American colors to the peak. Clear the decks of volunteers, but warn them to stand ready below with guns loaded.

"Josh, helm her two points west."

Amazed, Leving whirled on him. "Pardon, sir, you mean east. West will close with the enemy."

"I said west."

Leving drew himself erect in resigned manner before leaping to his orders. Jeremiah ran for his cabin, where he hurriedly removed the oilskin from the papers. Several minutes later he returned to deck with an important-looking packet under his arm.

Both the mate and McKinney stared curiously at what appeared to be the ship's papers and manifest of cargo, though neither asked the question uppermost in the mind of each.

Then McKinney said, "Better jettison the cargo of munitions."

"No time for it, Tom. Besides, ten thousand dollars in arms is worth saving."

"So are our lives."

As the *Sabine's* altered course brought her closer to the Mexican war vessel, Jeremiah surveyed the trim craft. By thunder, she was pretty! Minister of War and Navy Tornel was making good his threat. If he had others like this, Santa Anna could come by sea and anchor on the Texas coast at will.

Through Jeremiah's telescope, the gold-braided commander seemed to look puzzled as he watched the schooner bearing toward him. Marines and gunners stood alert. Now for a look at her nameplate. The sun's glare on varnish played havoc with his eyes. While waiting, Jeremiah measured her size and sailspread.

Then he seemed to come awake to what he was risking. The plan he was pursuing was bold; it was also foolish. A cold fear crept over him with the realization that he was actually sailing purposely toward possible destruction or imprisonment.

As a cloud ran across the sun, the nameplate came into the circle of his vision. The letters blurred and ran together. The mate at his side was saying, "Standing by for orders, sir." There were none, so he said, "Sir, for God's sake, what's the strategy?"

"Strategy? We didn't have a chance to run for it, Mr. Leving." Still gazing at the nameplate, he said, "In the navy book, what's the ratio of success to failure of a damn-fool hunch?"

"I wouldn't know, sir. Lord Nelson calculated his risk."

"Sure. Off Cape St. Vincent he risked a plan of action. But more to our size and situation, Mr. Leving. One bow chaser and sixty rifles against——" Jeremiah's mouth tightened into a thin line as he lowered the telescope and said scarcely above a whisper:

"*Veracruzana!*"

So Perfecto's information was accurate after all! With this discovery, he was asking if he could any longer deny that the ill-omened battle of the cocks had any bearing on the future of Texas.

Jeremiah reached for his trumpet and waved it over his head. "Dip the colors in right friendly fashion, Mr. Leving."

When the gleaming *Veracruzana* loomed up larger, her puzzled captain at a loss as to whether he should lower sail or compliment the schooner with a full broadside, Jeremiah nudged Leving.

"Pretend to take in sail, but stand by handsomely. I'm hoping to talk the gold-braided señor out of boarding us. If I do, we can come under her stern."

"I don't understand, sir."

"You will, Mr. Leving. But right now I'm praying for luck. I want her to take in sail. If she does, I can lose her while she's getting a way under her again."

McKinney said, "When she takes in sail, her starboard battery will be looking us in the eye. You know, Jerry, I believe we'd have been smart to chance a run for it even at close range."

"It's too late now, Tom. Besides, not even a Mexican gunner would have missed us that close by."

Within hailing distance, Jeremiah trumpeted forth, "*Buque aho.*" Then, holding the packet over his head, he cried, "Dispatches from Consul Martínez of New Orleans for war schooner *Veracruzana.*"

Jeremiah stood tense, Leving on one side, McKinney on the other. The latter said, "I'm not a rich man, but I'd give five thousand dollars to be just one mile away from where I am."

"Quiet, Tom," Jeremiah said. "Listen."

The Mexican captain stood out moments of silence, his black eyes in a round face darting suspiciously from Jeremiah to Lieutenant Leving and McKinney while the *Sabine*, now bereft of all but steadying sail, was sliding almost to a stop under the muzzles of six sleeping dogs, nine-pounders shotted and manned. Since they rode identical courses, both with the wind over the starboard beam, Jeremiah was fearing that his reduced speed would cause the Mexican to order him to stand by for boarding while his guns continued to bear.

Those guns looked grim to Jeremiah, who now dreaded further silence more than the expected command to bring her into the wind for a look at his papers.

"Ahoy there!" he cried again. "Dispatches out of New Orleans for the *Veracruzana!*"

The Mexican lifted a brass-rimmed trumpet. "What ship is that?"

"Schooner *Comet* of Mobile with express orders from Tornel by way of New Orleans. I am in a hurry to deliver a packet to *Moctezuma*, so must request quick dispatch."

"Stand by!" came the order.

The big war vessel came to life. Orders in Spanish were followed by sailors scampering about on deck and running aloft. She was fast bringing her head into the wind and putting sails aback. Then she was all aback and lowering a boat.

Jeremiah ordered a swing around that brought the *Sabine* down the *Veracruzana's* starboard side. He had the wind over his quarter then as against the other ship's bows pointing the weather, though he remained under the row of cannon as he slid toward her stern. With less than two hundred feet separating him from the enemy hull, he sang out an order to close with her stern. The captain of the warship saw nothing in this movement to alarm him; rather, the *"Comet"* seemed more than obliging as she lessened the distance of boating across the choppy sea.

It was touch and go to helm the *Sabine* to within scant feet of the other's stern without risking collision. The wind was an ally as he rode south for a rounding, so he came upon her gilded stern so close that he could look through the glass of her stern windows. Then he was crying in Spanish:

"No need to lower a boat, Captain. I can hit your deck from here!" So saying, he tossed the packet and drew back with pretended disgust. "Sorry," he yelled. "The wind was against me."

"*Gracias!* We'll fish it out," the other captain replied jovially.

Schooner and war vessel were beam to stern not thirty feet apart, the *Sabine* still under scant sail, when Jeremiah called out, "Where's the *Moctezuma?*"

"Off Matagorda."

Jeremiah casually waved a hand and said in low tones, "Mr. Leving, give her sail and order the helmsman not to present our stern until we put water between us." Every man aboard understood: *Sabine* was printed across her stern in big bold letters.

The schooner slid on past, pointing more into the wind and under the bore of the guns in order to hide her identity, every man tense, Jeremiah no exception. The packet was rising on a hook to the Mexican's deck. Time was short now. All sail was run up, topsails and topgallants and studdingsails loosed to the breeze. The *Sabine* swung south and leaped forward, running like a gull on the wind, her name now exposed and shining.

In her favor were headway and direction. The *Veracruzana* was a sleeping giant by comparison; she could not quickly get under way.

"By a gull's tail feathers, we made it!" Jeremiah cried.

Thomas McKinney mopped sweat from his brow and Leving scratched his ear, making no effort to hide his perplexity. It was McKinney who released his pent-up curiosity with a strong demand:

"What the devil was in that packet, Jerry?"

"Garbage from the galley."

McKinney stood with mouth open, staring unbelievably. When celebration and laughter on deck abated somewhat, Leving stuck out his hand and said more in silence to his captain than words could express. Then Jeremiah placed a question:

"Now, Mr. McKinney, what'll we name that fine Texas schooner-of-war—*if and when?*"

McKinney answered promptly, "By God, Jerry, the name she'll deserve under you, the *Invincible!*"

As Jeremiah's gaze fell on a mountain of thunderheads above the southern horizon, the name rang in his mind like the peal of a silver bell. Even the roar of guns from the outdistanced Mexican rolled across the Gulf waters like a salvo from a ship in the clouds.

Chapter Fifteen

RIVERBANK POLITICS

The Consultation did not lack a quorum on the third of November. The assembled Texans got down to business, and the people awaited the outcome while reviewing the recent victory of their troops over General Cós on the twenty-seventh of October in the Battle of Concepcion.

Jeremiah had little time to crow over a victory he knew to be minor and indecisive. Upon his arrival in Velasco, he learned to his surprise that his father and brother had marched off to join Austin's army. There was cotton to gather and no one left to supervise the slaves. Atop this, the small group that had met the first call of the Consultation, which lacked a quorum and which called itself "The Permanent Council," had issued letters of marque to privateers to relieve the coastal situation. This so angered Jeremiah that he sent the *Sabine* to sea under Leving and went upriver to save the cotton crop.

He took with him a letter from Polly. She did not begin with "Dear Jerry," but "Captain Brown, sir," and she opened fire without preamble:

> You say the facts of life are simple, the Lord made males and females attractive to each other. Amazing! Please, I knew these things at fourteen! I wrote not one word about my blood being hot, and I won't wake up one day wondering "what the hell happened and why"!!!
> Surely it is time for you and Aunt Virginia to realize that I am

neither child nor girl in her teens but a grown woman of twenty-two. Just because a backwoods boardinghouse walled me off from all freedom and adventure, am I supposed to run away from every attraction? Is being myself a perilous thing? Must I think like the servant I was brought up to be, brushing clothes and cleaning boots and wiping up molasses dripping from a trapper's beard? By thunder, *I am me!* And just you try and change me!

Furthermore, Lieutenant Harry Billings is a gentleman. He writes oftener than you—from the U.S.S. *Warren*, now in Louisiana waters, as is the whole Gulf Squadron, I hear. On account of the Mexican situation stirred up by the *Correo* affair. Did you have anything to do with the capture? Anyhow, he writes nice things, such as—"*My eyes are bandaged with love, my darling. I am intoxicated with each memory of you.*"

Jeremiah was seated on a pile of cotton in the field. He looked up as the oldest of the slaves came up, leaned on his cane, and chuckled.

"Cap'n Jerry, you looks lak yo' just et a bait of cockleburrs."

"Um-hum. *My eyes are bandaged with love, my darling.*" He grimaced. "Good God almighty!"

"Mo mail done come, Cap'n," the Negro said, handing a letter to his master.

"Know anything about women, Uncle Ben?"

"Sholy, suh." Scratching his white head, he spread big lips in a grin. "They makes yo' heart pound 'n yo' brain work. You figgers and figgers 'n it all comes out jest lak it was befo'hand."

"How was it beforehand?"

"Lak I done said a thousan' times: Figger nigger figger, but yo' never is right."

Jeremiah shrugged and gazed at the trees on the riverbank for some time before putting Polly out of mind. This letter was from Thomas F. McKinney, written from San Felipe on the tenth of November. Jeremiah read avidly, learning that the Independence Party, led by Henry Smith, went down in defeat on the seventh. Jeremiah frowned as he read:

The motion for a declaration of independence was defeated by a vote of 33 to 15, in favor of pledged loyalty to the Mexican Constitution of 1824. Sam Houston led the *nays* on the grounds that the latter plan would appeal to Mexican liberals and secure their aid in a fight against dictatorship.

Looking at the old darky, he said, "A hell of a note, Uncle Ben." There was more; McKinney wrote:

> Jerry, you will be wise to withdraw your objections to letters of marque and reprisal. Already your popularity is waning because of the strong protest of yours of the fourth. Since we cannot create a navy in a day, privateers can prevent the blockade of our coast and harass enemy shipping. They are ready bottoms and decks at our service.
>
> Captain Hurd, in pursuit of a Mexican armed vessel, went aground on Bird Island, Matagorda Bay. The *San Felipe* appears lost to us. But I am persuading our Committee on Naval Affairs to recommend purchase by the govt. the *William Robbins*, which I am buying for $3500. If you can alter your views, she's yours to command as privateer until the idea of an official navy gains the support it is lacking now.
>
> You know me, Jerry, so heed my advice and get on the popular side now if only for what it is worth to you and Texas in the future.

Jeremiah looked out over the stretching land.

"The popular side, eh? You know, Uncle Ben, that would be the easy thing to do. Tom McKinney operates in strange manner for what he thinks best for Texas."

"Yassuh, he sholy do. Yassuh!"

"Maybe I should do as he says." He got up, and the Negro rose out of deference. "Even though I believe that letters of marque and reprisal will bring nothing but harm to Texas, maybe I should take the *William Robbins*, Uncle Ben."

"Yassuh. Reckon yo' ought to."

"But I'm not."

"Naw, suh."

2

Captain Brown fastened a grasshopper on the hook, tossed the line out into the Brazos, and watched the cork. Nothing happened, so he lay flat on his back and looked into the blue November sky.

Unless a boat passed for downriver San Felipe soon, the Consultation might adjourn before he could get the message expressing his views before the body. Even with ample time his blunt opinions could easily be ignored or shelved in the parliamentary hubbub, though he felt reasonably sure that Borden, publisher of the *Telegraph*, would set his letter "To the People" in type and await his order to print it.

Feeling a tug on the line, he sat up. The cork was going under. He jerked and the hook came up minus fish and bait. He tried a worm, wondering just who would be chosen to head the Provisional Government. That was the fish he was after. If his message was directed to the wrong man, he would get nowhere. He was gambling that the delegates would not vote Sam Houston into the highest office. But fate was toying with the destinies of men; strangely, Austin the statesman and leader headed an army while Houston played a game of politics.

An hour went by. The fish weren't biting. But a boat was moving toward him. Soon it slid on downriver with two letters, one addressed to the *Telegraph*, the other to rugged Henry Smith.

Next morning, the *Laura* steamed up to Brown's Landing. Six men got off. Seeing them, Jeremiah slipped out the back and made his way unobserved to his favorite fishing spot. When Uncle Ben arrived with the group of harassed delegates, as instructed, Jeremiah raised a hand for quiet, lest his fish get away. Turning to Henry Smith, who made no effort to hide his impatience, he said:

"By thunder, Henry, he was a foot long!"

"Which, by God, don't interest me one damn bit, Jerry Brown! But this does."

As Smith produced Jeremiah's letter, John Wharton said, "Jerry, Henry Smith was elected provisional governor of Texas yesterday."

"Fine. Glad to hear it. But I still say that catfish was a foot long."

Edwin Waller and the Naval Committee, Messrs. Perry, Harris, and West, grinned, and Smith said, "Jerry, you wrote in strong language. You threatened to publish a letter to the people, so I went to Borden and read it. Hell, whose side are you on, writing up a pattern for Santa Anna to follow in invading Texas?"

"Henry—I mean, Your Excellency—"

"Goddamit to hell, Jerry, this government is confused enough without that! Publish that letter in the *Telegraph* and you'll scare half the population back to the United States. What we need now is confidence and unity, not fright, dissension, and rebellion. We've come here to offer you a privateer, and more later, if you'll destroy that letter."

"I'm not interested in a privateer." Jeremiah fastened a worm to his hook.

"Just fishing, eh? With your father and brother in the army and a Mexican warship on the coast. What the devil do you want?"

"If you gentlemen will sit down and help watch my cork, I'll tell you."

Smith smothered an oath and sat down on the clay bank, motioning the others to do likewise. Jeremiah liked and admired the fiery-eyed, hot-headed man his people had elevated to governor. His strong face and stalwart figure belied his sixty-one years the same as his caustic speech hid the man of wisdom and high ideals. Watching him, Jeremiah said:

"The first thing is something the delegates didn't want, a declaration of independence. Anything short of it is foolish, since you can expect little or no aid from the United States as long as Texas is merely a revolted province of Mexico."

"Amen! Didn't I tell you that?" Wharton said.

The Governor kicked a clod into the river.

Jeremiah said, "For thirteen days the delegates have argued the proper protection of the coast. They worked out Indian affairs and other problems, and let the coast go. A few letters of marque! Now look at it through the eyes of Americans. First a revolted province, next a bid for American privateers to do our fighting, which is economically a serious mistake, since there's not enough Mexican shipping for them to profit by. But worse, the Mexican province of Texas, through its government, mind you, advocates what Americans look upon as piracy."

"Bah! I don't believe it!" Smith declared vehemently. "Anybody can criticize, which isn't worth a fiddler's damn without a remedy. Have you one handy?"

Jeremiah laughed, "I wish I did. But I'm just a schoonerman. However, if I wanted aid from the United States I'd let Americans know that our letters of marque were an emergency of defense, and that we were backing up our eventual declaration of independence with an official Texas Navy."

Perry said, "Captain Brown has convinced me. We need a navy, if only for the sake of appearances. But as it stands, few of us have any idea of what is required, of what to recommend, how much it will cost, or how to pay for it."

Waller spoke, saying Captain Brown should have a few ideas, and Governor Smith said it would do no harm to hear them. He looked at Jeremiah, who, upon seeing his fishing line tightening, decided to let the hooked fish wait while he angled for a truly big prize. He spoke slowly, deliberately:

"I've sailed the Gulf a long time, and I know as well as any coaster that the need for a small naval force is real, that it exceeds any show we might consider staging just to convince Americans. It can mean the difference in victory or defeat on land as well as at sea. While a privateer will sail off for profit and gain, a ship of the national service will be devoted to the duty of keeping our supply routes open and our soldiers fed and armed; to the defense of our coast; to carrying the war to the enemy by effectively destroying his commerce."

"But the cost! We can't afford it," Smith said.

"You'll pay for it in the high prices of imported goods otherwise. Insurance rates will see to that. Remember the *Correo*, sir."

"Captain Brown speaks the truth," Perry said, turning now to Jeremiah. "But how many ships would we need and who would command them?"

"Mr. Perry, give us ships under men of known integrity, nautical skill, and experience. Say four schooners, two of twelve and two of six guns each. . . ."

. . . On November sixteenth, Governor Henry Smith, in his message to the General Council, said:

> Your Committee would further most earnestly represent that the establishment of a small naval force for the security of our coasts and protection of our own commerce would seem to them highly necessary and indispensible, and under that conviction would recommend the purchase, arming and equipping two schooners of twelve and two schooners of six guns each. . . .[1]

Jeremiah continued to fish. The gulf separating recommendation and decree was wide. For nine days the issue was argued back and forth, a navy versus letters of marque and reprisal. Twice Governor Smith sent for Captain Brown, only to be advised that good fishing prevented his coming.

[1]Official Correspondence of the Texas Revolution.

The days were long with the waiting. In the mornings Jeremiah's hope was high. By nightfall he had reviewed every argument men could make against a navy. So he roamed the fields by day with gun in hand or sat beside the river, seeing little of what went on about him, caring less. Work went on and cotton was shipped to Velasco. Many nights he walked the riverbank and looked at the fields and the indifferent Brazos under the pale fall of November moonlight. On such occasions he sometimes forgot politics down in San Felipe and sat by the river thinking of Carmela. He was tempted to go to her and somehow make her see eye to eye with him in all things, and only the expectancy of what could and might develop in his absence restrained him.

He had not withdrawn the letter from the *Telegraph* and Borden awaited his order to print it. The Consultation had adjourned, to meet on March 1, 1836, after electing Sam Houston to the rank of commander in chief of the "regular" army, which was non-existent, and authorizing a loan of one million dollars.

In the meantime Mexican warships *Veracruzana* and *Moctezuma* harassed the Texas coast, thereby provoking the General Council into adopting some sort of a maritime policy. The Committee of Public Safety of Matagorda purchased and armed the schooner *William Robins* and offered her to Captain Jerry Brown. When he refused the command, Captain Hurd applied for a letter of marque, received it, and became her skipper.

Jeremiah's refusal to come forward at a time when Texas needed its defiant sea dog caused much talk. In Texan ports and even New Orleans his popularity was on the decline and Hurd's was on the ascent. His many friends wrote urging him to change his views or, that being impossible, to speak up in his own defense. Smith reminded him that in a crisis of a people resistance could not be delayed in order to create laws legalizing such action; that this was as true today as in 1775 when armies formed around Boston.

Jeremiah admitted this seemed so. But he knew that if he gave up so much as an inch of ground the cause he was fighting for might suffer defeat for lack of a sponsor.

However, the time had come when he must put aside the fishing pole. He went downriver to Brazoria and Velasco only to meet with fresh disfavor, brought about by the recapture by Captain Hurd of the American schooner *Hannah Elizabeth*, laden with arms and provisions for the Texan army at San Antonio, recently captured by the *Moctezuma*. The news evoked cheers for Captain Hurd; and jeers for Captain Brown.

At heart sensitive, by nature slow to anger, Jeremiah covered up his hurt with silence. He had too long enjoyed public acclaim to know how to deal with the opposite.

On the day he decided to return to Brown's Plantation, Leving brought the *Sabine* into port. Edwin Waller appeared, saying he had reached a decision. He was going to apply for a letter of marque.

Jeremiah walked away without any reply. Even the sea had deserted him.

Mr. Leving arrived at Brown's Landing a few days later and quietly advised Jeremiah that he had refused command of the *Sabine* in favor of an uncertain future under Captain Brown.

The gladness flooding Jeremiah did not show through his dark, hostile glance. "Mr. Leving," he said, "I thought you were a man endowed with good judgment. I'm disappointed in you."

"Yes, sir," the other smiled, a light of understanding shining in his eyes.

That was on the twenty-third of November.

Three days later the *Laura* steamed to a stop where Leving and Jeremiah were fishing. Governor Smith and Thomas McKinney came ashore and Jeremiah was asking silently: What the hell could they want now? He soon learned.

Smith said, "Acting upon your suggestion, Jerry, I refused to approve letters of marque and reprisal without the following restrictions:

"Applicants must be men of skill and naval tacticians; no vessel under eighty tons burden or carrying less than four twelve-pound carronades or their equivalent in metal; cruising restricted to the Gulf of Mexico and prizes only of vessels under flag and commission of Central Government of Mexico——"

He read on and Jeremiah glared at him.

"Be it further ordained and decreed that all vessels sailing under licenses, as letters of marque and reprisal, shall carry the flag of the Republic of the United States of Mexico, and should have the figures 1, 8, 2, 4 ciphered in large Arabics on the white thereof."

"The flag," Smith said, "will symbolize what we're fighting for, the promises made in Mexico's Constitution of 1824."

He added, looking deep into Jeremiah, "Passed yesterday, November twenty-fifth. Now are you ready to sail for Texas?"

Jeremiah looked across the river, rubbing the back of his neck. Slowly he turned a ravaged face to the Governor. "If I'm licked, I'm licked. I don't believe in it, but if that's the extent of our defense by sea, give me a ship."

His Excellency the Governor nudged McKinney and said with devilish intent, "And if there had been a navy, what would you have said, Jerry Brown?"

"If you're trying to rub it in, I'll give you a real laugh, Governor —I was aspiring to the command of the Texas Navy."

"The hell you say!" Smith laughed and McKinney joined in.

Then McKinney was telling Jeremiah that the Governor had looked about for a seal of office and, finding none, had jerked a button off his sleeve in typical Henry Smith fashion and made the imprint of a star on the document.

"So the star becomes the official seal of the Texas Government, Jerry."

Smith clucked and shook his head. "Privateer Brown. Wait until the word reaches the coast."

Something seemed to snap inside Jeremiah. All the strain and hurt and disappointment and waiting demanded an outlet, and like steam it was gathering for an outburst they would long remember. He had opened his mouth to set them on their proper course when McKinney said urgently:

"Better tell him now, Governor."

A paper was placed in Jeremiah's hands. His mouth fell open and the words blurred off. But he had caught the full import in a glance:

Be it ordained and decreed . . . by the General Council of the Provisional Government of Texas, that there shall be, and there is hereby established a Navy. . . .[2]

Jeremiah sat down carefully, seeking with his hands the solid support of the Brazos riverbank as words he could scarcely believe ran together before his eyes:

. . . Two schooners of 12 guns each, two schooners of 6 guns each, with requisite number of officers, seamen and marines. . . .

[2]Gammel, *Laws of Texas*.

There was laughter all about him. Was this some final mockery? He looked up at last and saw Leving, Smith, McKinney, and aboard ship Captain Grayson and his crew, all shaking with mirth. There were too many friends here for this to be a joke. He grinned sheepishly at first, then the grin spread over his red, bony face. And he was wishing for a cap to sail high across the Brazos when he saw Leving's. And sailing it went as he loosed a yell and cried:

"There is hereby established a navy!"

Book Three

THE EAGLE'S TALON—1835–1836

Chapter Sixteen

POLLY MERCHANT

It had been a long time since Jeremiah had seen Virginia. On this late afternoon of December twentieth, 1835, he stood the deck of a small oyster pungey, staring curiously ahead at an estate in the bend of the James. Running on a chill wind, the boat made good speed for Broadhaven. Soon the handsome old brick and white-columned entrance of a Georgian-styled mansion loomed up warm and inviting.

When the boat put in at the pier and cast her warps to await his return, Jeremiah picked up a package and made his way up a path lined by dwarfed boxwood toward a brick wall on the windward side. The terraced garden seemed to begin at the private landing where deepstream ships took on hogsheads of Virginia tobacco.

He stood a moment at the entrance, looking behind him. Through the tall poplars, the James wound on in either direction, a wide ribbon symbolizing age and dignity as much as industry. Whether or not the Brazos could ever claim as much remained a matter for time to decide.

A grinning darky opened the door and Jeremiah asked to see Miss Polly Merchant.

"Step inside, suh, and I'll announce yo'all to Miss Pauline, mistuh——?"

"A man from Texas."

So she was *Pauline!* Well, he had sent her to school for a purpose. Perhaps she had found her level. Looking at the hand-carved spiral staircase, fine imported rugs, a massive chandelier glittering with enough prisms to stretch from doorway to the river, he admitted the environment would do Polly small harm. Unless, of course, this sort of thing went to her head.

"She be down soon, suh," the butler said, bowing him into a large room where a fire burned in the hearth. Placing a decanter of brandy before the guest, he said, "Season's greetings, suh."

Jeremiah was sipping his third pony when two hands covered his eyes. He grinned. "Now it couldn't be Polly, for she would have let out a whoop from the staircase. So it must be Pauline."

"Pauline?" she said before twisting his ear. "I'm just Polly. Turn around and look at me, Jerry Brown."

He got to his feet and obeyed. She remained still while he surveyed her from tip to toe, and she smiled when he arched his brows in astonishment at what he saw. There was nothing of the serving girl from the American Hotel about her. She was a lady, a very pretty one. The years had given her a dignity and a maturity of expression. The girl had grown into a woman.

Then she refuted all he saw and thought he wished to believe. She rushed to him, all impulse. With her arms about him, she said, "Damn, but I'm glad to see you!"

Her touch warmed him like brandy. She was a handsome woman, he admitted. Three years hadn't changed her curves, which appeared to be as much in the right places as in 1832.

Then she saw the package. "For me! What's in it, Jerry?"

"A Christmas present, what else? And don't open it until Christmas."

"Not until you turn your back. My but it's sweet of you! Now sit down, Jerry, and tell me everything—about you, Aunt Virginia, Texas, and——"

"Easy as you go, girl! I didn't sail all the way to Baltimore and then down here to talk about me. I'm due to meet Mr. McKinney at Fort Monroe before midnight. We're Texas-bound with a fine schooner-of-war, and I'd rather face Santa Anna's army singlehanded than tell Miss Virginia I have nothing to report on you."

"Schooner-of-war?" The girlish eagerness of old crept into her expression. "Is it really war, Jerry?"

He nodded and her face clouded over.

"Even if we win over Cós at San Antonio, war is inevitable. Santa Anna will come. Already there are rumors of his training a huge army at San Luis Potosí."

She sat out a troubled silence. He drank, watching her as the firelight played on her face. She said suddenly, "And what about you, Jerry?"

"I'm helping put the Texas Navy into the wind."

"A navy! Really? Wait till Harry hears that."

From the entrance hall came a reply. "Sorry, but I heard. Just coming in, not eavesdropping."

Jeremiah stood as Polly made introductions. Lieutenant Harry Billings was tall and striking in appearance. In his genial face was all the intensity of one man placing an estimate on another. His handclasp was strong, and he proved himself the alert host, ordering Chesapeake oysters broiled and served with chilled white Burgundy. Next he raised a toast to the company and the season.

Jeremiah could not help but compare him to his verse: "My eyes are bandaged with love, my darling. I am intoxicated with each memory of you." But the lieutenant didn't look like a poet. He was saying:

"So Texas is really launching a navy. Actually, Captain Brown, it's difficult to go along with such an idea." As Jeremiah's gaze narrowed on him, he said hurriedly, "I do not belittle, sir. I'll admit we of the *Warren* laughed when someone first mentioned it. But, Captain, at heart we're for it."

Jeremiah smiled dubiously. "Are you now?" He judged the naval man's age at twenty-five; maybe a year over or under, depending on the answer he received.

"Naturally. Commodore Dallas is waiting for one false move from your privateersmen. He may not hold the fleet off the Louisiana swamps now that Texas no longer resorts to letters of marque."

"But we do, Lieutenant Billings. We haven't a navy yet."

"Odd. There was quite a privateering scandal, I hear."

"Careful, Harry," Polly laughed. "You may step on Jerry's toes."

"Not mine, Polly. To tell the truth, as much as I deplore the scandal, I cannot deny that it gave me a great deal of personal satisfaction. You see," he got up and stood with back to fire, "I fought the privateering scheme, warned everyone concerned it would do Texas harm. My friends turned against me."

"What was it, Jerry? Anybody I know involved?"

"Well, a Captain Hurd sailed the *William Robbins* and recaptured the American schooner *Hannah Elizabeth* from the *Moctezuma*. There being no admiralty court in which to condemn the prize—if you could call a ship loaded with munitions for our own force a prize—Colonel J. W. Fannin——"

Polly interrupted. "The Fannin who sold slaves in Velasco?"

"Fresh from the Congo," Jeremiah replied. "Anyhow, Fannin smelled a profit in the deal and vowed his soldiers had virtually taken the *Hannah Elizabeth* from the Mexicans before Hurd arrived on the scene. They sold a part of the cargo to one of the captured vessel's passengers and advertised an auction on the rest of it. Their deed began to stink. Governor Smith fumed at the grand swindle and right now investigations are filling the air."

Lieutenant Billings's eyes shone. "What about the friends who turned against you, Captain Brown?"

Jeremiah's shoulders and palms lifted. "Why they said they knew I was right all along. You know how it is."

Polly stood and came to him with graceful swiftness. "Good for you, Jerry. I hope their faces are still red."

Lieutenant Billings leaned forward, elbows on knees, his gaze fixed on Jeremiah. One could hardly fail to detect a world of curiosity and admiration in his face or deny that he was staring at adventure through its symbol. Polly looked from one to the other and covered her pride with a radiant smile. Then she laughed happily and burst forth with:

"Damn! This is a wonderful Christmas!"

They laughed with her. The Negroes brought oysters and wine. Candles burned, and under the soft light sprays of holly glistened on the mantel. At his grandson's request, old Colonel Billings came down on his cane to extend his hospitality to the visitor from Texas. His interest in Texan affairs was equal to the lieutenant's. Warmed by hospitality and wine, Jeremiah stretched his long legs before the fire and talked.

Texas was truly a land of opportunity. Where else could a soldier of a regular army be assured of six hundred and forty acres of land as a bounty; and wasn't the small undisciplined army of volunteers challenging Mexico's finest troops for the possession of San Antonio de Bexar?

Polly asked about William and his father.

"My brother William designed a flag with thirteen stripes of red and white, and in a field of blue a white arm bent at the elbow, holding a blood-tipped sword that dripped gore on the shoulder. The center white stripe bore the word *Independence*."

"There's something about a flag," the Colonel said pensively. Then he started, as if he had in an unguarded moment laid bare his proud past. A little later he left them.

Lieutenant Billings appeared reluctant to depart. "Since we share the Gulf of Mexico between us, Captain Brown, we'll probably meet again."

"I hope so, Lieutenant. And may it be occasioned by a dipping of the colors."

After they drank to the Texas Navy, Billings swept Polly with a glance and a grin. "Considering the great things I've heard of you, I should be jealous."

"Hasn't she told you I'm just a big brother?"

Polly whirled and looked into the fire.

2

The big room seemed too quiet and empty with just him and Polly. "A penny for your thoughts," he said. "I haven't heard one word about you."

"There's little to tell, Jerry. I'm here for the holidays, thanks to the colonel."

"And," Jeremiah said tonelessly, "the lieutenant."

"Of course. But it's wonderful, so different from the lonely Christmas of 1832. I even tried to get a ship home. But no captain wanted a hen in the galley. I still have that fussy blue nightdress you sent me that Christmas. I save it for special occasions."

"Like what?" he said, looking shocked.

"Visits to the homes of the girls and the like. I feel as rich as the next one in it. Thank the Lord, I learned to sew. I made this dress myself, Jerry. Like it?"

He seemed as surprised as pleased.

"I study dancing under Professor Schwartz. Would you believe it, I'm helping him instruct beginners? But, of course, I'm older than most of the girls."

She looked pensive.

"At times I feel I don't belong. I rise very early, dress hurriedly, and walk as though I were going somewhere to meet someone. I don't know where I'm going, but something draws me on. Like a tree looking for its roots. Or perhaps it's because I grew up with plenty to do before breakfast." She smiled. "Then classes and out-door games and music. In the summer I tutor—but I shouldn't have told you. Aunt Virginia needn't know that I have to earn money in order to dress halfway fashionable."

"Tutor, eh?" he said, as if it were hard to imagine of Polly the frontier serving girl.

"Yes," she replied, more defiant than defensive. "And if I'm here next summer, the Billings want me to tutor their grandchildren, three girls of Harry's brother Jonathan."

"If you're here? Why the *if?*"

"I'm a Texan at heart. Do you think I could stay here if there's war?"

"Perhaps Lieutenant Billings wouldn't like that."

"I'm not married to him."

She stood with her back to the fire in study of him. "Is the yellow-headed girl still in New Orleans?"

He nodded, looked at his watch, and got up. "Time to go, Polly. We're running past Cape Henry tonight for the Atlantic, the Lord willing. And about coming to Texas, forget it. I don't want you on land to worry about when Santa Anna strikes."

She helped him into his greatcoat and went to get her wrap. He said it was cold out, and she reminded him that it would be colder inside with his going. With her arm in his, they walked toward the river. On the pier, he thought of a dozen things he had forgotten to mention. Conversation began anew; more artificial, to make parting easier. Then, as if each realized the futility of pretense, silence fell between them. Only the sounds of lapping waves against the boat's bottom, a sigh of the wind, and the footfall of a boatman taking in the lines.

With hands at her shoulders, he kissed her lightly on the forehead and stepped away. "Good luck, girl. Lots of it."

It might have been her silence at a time when some reply was expected or his own awareness of something left undone or unsaid that caused him to turn and look at her. Then he moved to her.

"What's the matter, child?"

"You know what's the matter. And a woman of twenty-two is no child."

"Twenty-one," he corrected.

"Twenty-two, by thunder! Old enough to be the mother of half a dozen webfooted little schoonermen."

He chuckled as his arms went about her. Something between a laugh and smothered sob escaped her as she looked up into his face. But she was quick to recover. She was Polly, saying:

"Jerry Brown, I thought you actually meant to leave without kissing me good-by!"

And for a long moment Jeremiah thought he had sailed two thousand miles for the express purpose of holding her close.

Chapter Seventeen

THE BALTIMORE SLAVER

Jeremiah had never seen the ship. He had the word of Thomas F. McKinney, competent judge of any craft, that she was sharp and fast enough to outsail anything in her class. She had been built for the slave trade, which demanded speed.

The ship's gig touched shore and a sailor approached saying, "Captain Brown?"

Jeremiah got into the boat, his gaze fixed on the ship.

Looking at her in the night, he saw a dim silhouette stabbed by the glow of deck lamps. Pencils of light on her varnish indicated the rake of her masts, stepped in clipper fashion. She sat the water long and sleek. However, one could build illusions, the same as if she were a woman under starlight. Admitting this was one thing, abiding by such wisdom another, for this vessel excited him as no other ever had.

If her past was shrouded in mystery, so were her present and future. And the dark picture of her in the strange waters of Chesapeake Bay on this wintry night did nothing to lift the veil from her secret. Which served to make her, again like a woman, more fascinating. In the case of the McKinney & Williams Baltimore schooner, a man could believe either of the two accounts of her past. The first, she had missed her calling; not once had she defiled herself in the game of defying the laws of nations by shipping Africans shackled to her slave deck. The other tale, she had been a notorious slaver, a veritable black joke, until her capture by an American sloop-of-war.

Supposing either to be true, it made no difference to Captain Jeremiah Brown. She was a promise of the future.

Impatient of delay in reaching her, he ordered the men to lay smart on the oars. Then he was touching her starboard timbers, her rail and deck. He was naturally curious, as much so as Tom McKinney had been aboard the *Sabine* when garbage was tossed to the enemy. The situation was reversed now; McKinney, behind a cigar, smiled noncommittally.

"What's her name?" Jeremiah said.

"You've got a short memory, Jerry." He laughed at the puzzlement this reply evoked. "Remember the morning we sat under the *Veracruzana's* guns, and I said if you got us out of——"

"I remember."

"Well here's the *Invincible*, Jerry."

So McKinney had not forgotten.

As Mr. Leving made sail and away, Jeremiah began a careful examination of the ship. He stared up into the rigging, tested the planking of holystoned deck, examined her hemp and blocks, stood forward of her, taking in all he saw from jibs, martingale, and bobstay to anchors at the catheads, her capstan, and windlass. He was aloft, then on deck moving aft, appraising a coaming, deckhouse, coils of hemp and, at last, the wheel. He nudged the steersman aside and felt of her rudder, sending her off a spoke and bringing her back as a horseman feels out his mount. He listened to the tune the wind played in the rigging, the creaking of her pulleys, and the slap of the waves at her bow and sides. Critically he eyed her, rubbing his jaw, now pausing suddenly, as if sensitive to some sound or motion at variance with her rhythmic stride.

With lantern in hand, he entered the open hatchway and descended the ladder to the slave deck. He sniffed the air for foul odors that lingered after slaves and, detecting none, searched seams and corners for lime, sprinkled regularly after cleaning "cargo" space.

After covering the ship's insides, he walked up one side of the weather deck and down the other, marking in his mind locations for mounting cannon. With a final conn of the weather over the opening sea, he joined McKinney below.

"Well, Jerry?"

Seating himself across the table from the shipowner, Jeremiah said,

"She's all you said and more. She'll mount two eighteen-pounders, two nines, and four sixes; and accommodate up to seventy men. With her speed and maneuverability, I'll venture odds she'll sprout gray hairs in Santa Anna's head."

McKinney smiled, studying the end of his cigar. "Think she's worth before fitting out the sum of $12,613.02?"

"Twelve thousand——!" Jeremiah's astonishment was quickly absorbed by his fears. "Sure—I do. But I'm not buying her. Tom, the Governor and General Council will blow sky-high."

"Not together, Jerry. What one approves, the other won't."

"Even so, when you add another five or six thousand dollars for guns and so forth, she'll cost four to five times as much as the *William Robbins*."

"*William Robbins?*" McKinney looked wise. "By the time you reach Texas, she'll be rechristened the *Liberty*. Also, Jerry, Mr. Cumings will place you in command of her, the first vessel of the Texas Navy."

"Just a moment, Tom." Jeremiah leaned forward, perplexed. "You promise me a crack ship. You name her *Invincible*, as you said. Then I get the *Liberty*. Just what sort of a game is this?"

"A very urgent one. With Texas caught between invasion and politics, can we sit out a squabble between the Governor and the Council over the high price of this one? You can outfit and arm the *Liberty*. Mr. Cumings will promise you a bigger vessel. And when and if the *Invincible* is sold, she's yours to transfer your officers and crew aboard. Then hand your brother William the *Liberty*."

"Just like that, eh?"

"Just like that."

Jeremiah shook his head hopelessly, all the while darting curious glances at the other. "So I'm to command the *Liberty*," he thought aloud. "I can understand that. But what I can't understand is how the devil you're going to hand me this ship through the government in time to intercept Tornel's navy."

McKinney turned palms up in a gesture that said he wished for the answer.

Silence fell over the cabin. Only the sounds of ship and water dominated the night as freshening winds off the Atlantic kicked up seas and sent the gallant *Invincible* heeling along with Cape Henry Light broad on the starboard beam.

2

Reaching out to sea and steady winds, instead of standing down the coast for the Gulf, the schooner made good time to New Orleans, where holiday merrymaking was in full swing. Christmas had joined the past, though the new year lay ahead. But the general agent for Texas, William Bryan, and Commissioner Thomas J. Green were celebrating something else: General Cós had surrendered to the Texans on the tenth of December. There was not an armed Mexican on Texas soil. Jubilation was high.

Jeremiah and McKinney were cheered by the good news, though lurking behind pleased expressions were thoughts not to their liking. Victory engendered complacency, and the latter slowed the effort of preparedness. Cós's evacuation would do much to popularize Santa Anna's invasion of a revolted province. Tornel was vigorously arming ships to send against a virtually unprotected coast.

There was bad news along with the good, Bryan admitted. Open hostility had arisen between Governor Smith and the General Council. The government was so paralyzed by strife that the idle army ignored Houston, commander in chief, and supported a plan calling for the invasion of Mexico and the capture of the port city of Matamoros.

All things considered, official approval of the purchase, arming, and equipping of the Baltimore ship appeared next to impossible. And still Captain Brown insisted: "There must be some way." Under the lamps of festive New Orleans on the night of December twenty-seventh he delivered such an eloquent plea for the first "schooner of twelve guns" that the general agent and commissioner opened their private purses to arm and equip her to the amount of $5000.

At first taken aback by the unselfish gesture, Jeremiah considered the possibility of private subscription on a large scale. The idea of holding public meetings in Mobile and New Orleans appealed strongly until another scheme seized and held his imagination. Perhaps he had drunk too much, or maybe there was something of the swindler in every man; at any rate, the cause was worthy of the effort, win or lose.

What Jeremiah had in mind appealed to McKinney, who on the following day ordered one of his schooner captains set sail at once with Captain Brown for the Bay of Galveston.

On a morning two days later, the McKinney schooner lay at anchor in Galveston Harbor. Why she sat idle and how long she would remain, her captain could only guess. His orders were to comply with Captain Jerry Brown's instructions to the letter and keep a closed mouth forevermore. He liked and admired Captain Brown, who was now studying through his telescope a small oyster fleet beating into the wind for a rounding of the point.

The skipper shrugged and turned away, only to hear Brown ask if he could put the schooner above Pelican Spit without attracting too much notice.

He could, and he did, reminding himself all the while that this was Saturday, that New Year's Eve came on Monday. He had marked the calendar a month back, promised the night to a buxom girl from Bayou Lafourche. And Captain Brown, rumored to be at the top of the list for command of a Texan ship-of-war, was studying common oystermen!

He had no sooner shrugged off this observation than he heard an order he could scarcely believe. He said, "How's that, Cap'n Brown?"

"Put a heavy charge in your bow chaser."

Minutes later, Captain Brown aimed at the oyster fleet and fired. When the smoke cleared, the schooner captain said in protest, "Cap'n, I know them boys ye shot at. They wouldn't scotch a flea."

"They can talk, can't they? The louder and quicker they talk, the better. One more shot and we'll run close enough for our friends to recognize the Mexican colors."

"We're flyin' the United States flag."

"As of right now, we're hoisting the Mexican eagle."

They sailed up into the bay, dropping a shot near any craft that ventured out. By nightfall, the word had reached Anáhuac, and with morning ships were crowding sail for the Brazos. The General Council must be advised and Texan shipping warned of the Mexican war vessel prowling about Galveston.

Two days later the entire Texas coast from the Sabine to the Colorado was alerted: A Mexican war vessel was firing at any and all craft around Galveston, and might be expected anywhere next.

Alarmed coastal towns sent hurried demands to the government to do something about it.

On January 5, the General Council overruled the Governor and ordered the purchase of the McKinney & Williams schooners *Liberty* and *Invincible*—the latter generously offered to the Government of Texas for the sum of $20,000—because a Mexican sloop-of-war had been reported in the Bay of Galveston. A letter of appointment was issued declaring Thomas F. McKinney commander of the twelve-gun *Invincible*, removable at the pleasure of the Governor and Council.

The Governor's protest rang loud. The treasury was empty, his councilmen were traitors to the cause. And wasn't it a strange coincidence that the sudden appearance of a Mexican war vessel was timed with McKinney's "generous" offer? Discord between the Governor and the Council had reached the showdown stage. Impeachment proceedings were under way.

On Sunday, January 27, Jeremiah wrote from Velasco:

To His Excellency Henry Smith
Gov of Texas
Dear Sir

I have the honor to inform you of the arrival off the Brazos Bar of the Government Schr. Liberty from New Orleans.

The Liberty left the Miss. on the 23d ult having under convoy four vessels laden with provisions & c. for the Government of Texas, and arrived off the Brazos Bar on the eve of the 25th. . . .

The Liberty is filled with three months provisions—manned by forty men—has three guns mounted—one medium 12 on a pivot two heavy sixes in the waist and two 12 lbs Gunnades spare.

Since my arrival Mr. T. F. McKinney has put me in charge of the Government Schr. Invincible, with order to Copeno, to which place I shall proceed this morning, having on board some volunteers for that place.

I am compelled to take from the Liberty one half her crew and put on board the Invincible she not having a man aboard.

The Invincible requires much fixing before she will be suitable for war, and I would beg leave to suggest that she be immediately ordered to the mouth of the Mississippi as soon as she returns from Copeno. . . . Her guns are not mounted (all of them) But as I have been but a moment aboard I cannot give you the particulars.

We can only get men by going to New Orleans.

Officers and crew can be obtained without difficulty or trouble by sending the vessel to the mouth of the Mis. . . . With regard to myself, I can only say that Mr. Cumings placed me in charge of the Liberty with an assurance of being given the charge of a larger vessel as soon as one could be obtained. The Invincible is the one that I desire the command of, and hope you will not consider it presumption in me to ask the same of you. You are sufficiently acquainted with me to know I merit the situation.

On my return from Copeno I shall await your orders at Velasco—until I am regularly commissioned and receive your orders I shall be at a loss what to do.

With my best wishes for the prosperity and welfare of Texas and yourself I subscribe myself your obt Svt and friend

J. Brown

P.S. Dear Sir,

In leaving the Liberty by the advice of Col. Wharton I have placed her in charge of Wm. S. Brown. Who shall be her future commander remains for you to say. Of his capacity and worth you are acquainted. I can only say I think he is deserving of notice, and hope he will not be forgotten.

Very Respectfully Yr. obt Svt[1]

J. Brown

Though the Governor had been impeached, he clung to his seal and records and defied the Council. He was still His Excellency and "By God" he would retain his seat until the Convention of March first. But he was sick of the rebellious army and the sharp-witted navy. Jerry Brown wished to command the Navy, but Jerry Brown had allied himself with McKinney in what looked to be "the dam'dest swindle" ever to grace the records of a crippled new government.

The unofficial commodore of the Texas Navy had little time for celebration. No sooner had Jeremiah received his commission and official orders than he set sail for New Orleans; Captain Brown should outfit the *Invincible*, enlist crew and full complement of officers, and take on provisions for a cruise in Mexican waters in chase of the *Moctezuma*, "real or imagined by Mr. McKinney in the Bay of Galveston."

The task of hurriedly creating a floating fort was beset with almost insurmountable odds, the worst of which was finances. Austin, William Wharton, and Archer, sent to the United States to raise money,

[1]Official Correspondence of the Texas Revolution.

described conditions accurately in their letter to Governor Smith from New Orleans on January sixteenth:

> When we arrived here, we found the cause of Texas "flat." She had not credit for 25 cents. This was produced by the opposition of certain Mercantile Houses, and Insurance Offices, who had transactions with ports of the interior of Mexico. . . . Let us urge you *again & again*, that you would use all your influence to cause the next convention, on the first day of their meeting, . . . to make an absolute Declaration of Independence. And that you despatch a *Courier* Extraordinary with the news of it to our General Agent, Wm. Bryan, in New Orleans with the instructions to publish it immediately in all the newspapers of that city. Let us assure you that on this depends the salvation of Texas. The people of the U.S. look for this, and nothing short of it will satisfy their expectations. If it is not done the sympathies, now so universally aroused in our favor, will certainly subside.[2]

In the face of this opposition a loan of $200,000 was negotiated, though demands made on this sum by the army and navy were great. Munitions and provisions under convoy to Texas must be paid for. Earlier, another item had suddenly been placed on the market. For some reason the United States Revenue Cutter *Ingham* had come up for sale. The Texans hurriedly purchased this ship and rechristened her *Independence*. And on the twenty-second, the privateer *Brutus* was purchased for the Texas Navy.

Jeremiah said to Austin and Wharton, "Seems if Texas floated the size navy she can afford, my brother William and I would row the one boat with a single rifle between us."

While Jeremiah was outfitting the *Invincible*, Mexico's Lieutenant Thompson came to trial in the federal court of New Orleans on charges of piracy. The trial attracted international attention, the United States being in the embarrassing position of holding as prisoners a naval officer and crew of a nation she was not at war with. Mexico rose to the defense of her officers and Texas forced the prosecution with all energy. Thompson claimed he was out to stop the slave traffic from Cuba. The trial was interrupted when the lawyer for defense and the United States district attorney threw inkstands and were sentenced to jail. Next day the prisoners were set free.

Upon learning that Mexico was returning Thompson to Vera Cruz

[2]Official Correspondence of the Texas Revolution.

a hero, Jeremiah grinned. "We'll meet again," he said, thinking of Carmela, who had not shown herself at the trial.

His sentiments had not changed, he admitted. He longed for Carmela as never before. She stood out in his memory as the one woman among all others. If he despised the spy, he took pity on the woman. If he swore to bring her to justice, he vowed also to bring her to his arms.

He hurried departure, hoping daily for the good word from Potter of the Naval Affairs Committee of his appointment to the command of the Navy—four ships: *Liberty*, 60 tons, 6 guns, Brown, Wm. S., Commander; *Brutus*, 125 tons, one long 18-pound swivel, 9 short guns, Hurd, William A., Commander; *Invincible*, crack ship of the fleet; and *Independence*, 125 tons, 9–11 guns, Hawkins, Charles E., Commander.

Charles Hawkins?

Jeremiah had not met this man who appeared out of nowhere with the purchase of the U.S.S. *Ingham* to impress the government with his exploits and title of "Major." Late of the Mexican Army under Colonel Mexia, Hawkins had been a midshipman in the United States Navy. Failing to receive promotion, he had followed his hero Commodore Porter, U.S.N. of *Essex* cruise fame and who then held supreme command of the Mexican Navy of 1826 operating against Spain. Hawkins had distinguished himself near Havana. Now captain of the *Independence*, he had quickly and expertly armed her ahead of the three remaining ships. According to rumor, he arrogantly boasted that given the chance he could and would use an iron hand in shaping the Texan flotilla into a fighting unit.

Despite the fact that Hawkins was as far removed as Matagorda Bay, he was like a flea under Jeremiah's skin. But so were politics and Carmela and Thompson for that matter. So Hawkins joined the things that galled Jeremiah, fell into place alongside the maze of puzzles, problems, and annoyances that he must deal with at some future date. For Captain Brown could no longer remain on land.

The *Invincible* was to raise sail for Mexican waters in chase of the armed *Moctezuma*, which had been reported prowling about the Bay of Galveston.

3

At five minutes before eight bells in the midwatch on the day of embarkation, the drum and fife roused the crew. It was nearing four in the morning and the *Invincible* lay at the Head of the Passes of the Mississippi.

With reveille, the port routine of a naval ship began. Eight bells were struck and no sooner had the reverberations rolled out into a night as black as a raven's wing than the boatswain's pipes grated against eardrums. Harsher sounded the "All hands!" and "Up all hammocks!" Alf Wate, midshipman of the watch, made his way to the wardroom and informed the officers that eight bells had sounded, for which no appreciation was given by or expected from the brass-buttoned lords of the ship. Small wonder the term "snotty" had trailed midshipmen down through the British and American navies to this experiment. Wate made his way on down to the steerage, where in the finest tradition of the service he yelled into the ears of the man who should take the deck, "Eight bells! I'll thank you to relieve me." With sadistic pleasure, he repeated it, eying the other's rump with a desire to lay a board across it smartly just to see him come alive. Then he fell flat for his wink, deaf to the grumbling of the other, who finally moved off to join sailors moving up from the berth deck with hammocks rolled and lashed. One by one the hammocks were passed up to the hammock rail where the quartermaster's mate stowed them "rip rap."

On deck the crew went to work with holystones, pails of water, and sand. The quartermaster of the watch touched his hat to Alf Wate's successor and repeated the monotonous "Eight bells," which he passed on to the officer of the deck and received, "Report it to the captain, sir."

In this manner Jeremiah was informed of the day of embarkation. A scathing reply was on the tip of his tongue when he remembered the naval reply demanded of him: "Make it so, sir, and pipe to breakfast." This was accordingly done and the midshipman reported to the officer of the deck "who made it so."

The *Invincible's* night pennant fluttered down as the jack lifted from the bowsprit. No sooner was the day officially declared than the only pleasant piping boatswain Smith was capable of, to the crew's thinking, sounded briefly and was followed by grog. A line formed quickly down the larboard side and each sailor took his turn in accepting his "tot," one of three small tin cups the purser's steward kept constantly in motion at the grog tub.

Breakfast followed and the deck signaled for a bar pilot. With his arrival, port routine left off and sea duties began. A good-omened wind blew in off the Gulf and the *Invincible* entered the Southwest Pass for the sea. The pass widened out later on and the pilot was dropped.

As the towboat's crew raised a cheer for the Texas Navy, Captain Brown appeared on deck, returned the salutes of his officers, and paused to survey decks, rigging, and weather. First Lieutenant Leving stepped forward and Mr. Kelton, the surgeon, presented a small square of white paper. The ceremony had to do with the cleanliness of the galley. But as usual the white paper, which had been carefully used to test the cook's coppers, showed not the slightest soil; and again the cook was spared the prescribed dozen lashes at the gangway.

All this was very new to the captain who aspired to the command of the fleet. All in order, he presumed, since Mr. Leving advised that it was "navy" either in the service of America or Britain. Secretly, he thought some of the formality and ceremony damn silly. However, it was a part of naval discipline and he wanted a navy.

On this eventful morning, Captain Brown in full-dress uniform of the young navy cut a fine figure: cap of blue and white with gold braid trim, flaring white collar over the neck of a blue coat adorned by shining brass buttons, and deep blue tie in double bow against a white shirt. Immaculate white bell-bottomed trousers and a sword completed the picture.

He was not ready for the boatswain to pipe the crew for evolutions. The ship herself claimed his full attention. Appearing at ease, though far from it on this momentous occasion, he lifted perfunctory glances into the rigging, let them fall from fresh hemp and brand new sailcloth against varnished masts and spars. Behind him was the struggle for all he saw now. Stubbornness, persuasion, threat, and trickery had achieved something after all. How great or shallow that something, he could not predict beyond the rightness of the cause. That was the solid foundation, the rock he and all Texans pinned their hopes to. Only that made up the past. And now he was looking beyond brass and hemp and sailcloth to a moving craft in tropical waters, looking through the smoke of his own guns and sending up a silent prayer for victory.

When the boatswain piped the crew to attention, he studied his uniformed men. The marines looked smart. The crew, warrant officers to powder monkeys, were fifty in all, twenty short of a full complement. Under the wide-brimmed, single-tasseled hats, turned up and hiding the crowns, were bearded faces and faces that could not sprout a beard. Some were tense, some seemed careless of time or future. Some were patriots, Texans, some were adventurers, and some were scoundrels, and others were risking all for six hundred and forty acres of land. Little Josh, now eighteen, gazed with adoration at the only captain he had ever sailed under. Others like him followed one man's destiny.

Captain Brown was now making his embarkation speech:

"You are a unit, as one man, engaged here for the single purpose of carrying the war to the enemy in Mexican waters. You have been advised that Texas is unprepared for war, virtually without a government, and in poor financial condition. And yet you are with me now, aboard the chosen ship of our navy, which is destined to be within a few minutes the first Texan schooner-of-war to officially raise sail in quest of the enemy.

"You have signed the articles. You know what to expect in the line of duty and what is expected of you. I urge you to be prepared for hard times as well as good. You know what will happen if you're captured by the enemy. By a decree of the Mexican Congress, all men bearing arms against Mexico are outlaws and pirates. Some of you will not live to claim the land Texas provides for volunteers. For this is war on land and sea to a decision, and only by a combination of prayer, skill, and a jockeying of the laws of chance can we hope to succeed against the new Mexican sea power."

A moment of silence ended. He removed his cap and bowed his head. All aboard did likewise, joining him in the Lord's Prayer.

Then he said, "Hoist the colors and fire a salute."

The green, white and red flag, the numerals 1824 bold against a field of white, fluttered to the peak, and the guns roared. The cheers of deck were loud and long. The order for sail, "Make sail!" rang in echo, and the *Invincible* got a way under her for the open sea.

Captain Jeremiah Brown was very proud and grateful.

Chapter Eighteen

CRUISE OF THE T.S.
INVINCIBLE

A chill morning breeze was whipping across the wide expanse of water. Riding the wind out of the northeast, low, shapeless clouds moved in to lay a vaporous blanket over the Gulf.

Running with the wind on her quarter, the *Invincible's* bows dipped and rose amid showers of spray. She held a steady pace, rolling her tall masts and decks over to larboard and back in timed motion. Mr. Abbott, sailing master, stood in oilskins, and with an eye in the rigging, he was saying, "As I calculate, Mr. Leving, we're fifty-odd mile nor'east the mouth of the Rio Grande. On the Matamoros track." As his roving glance took in the running rigging, the main top cried the deck.

"Sail ho!"

"Where away?"

"Two points off the starboard bow, sir. Two spars."

"What's her course?"

"Standing to sou'west, same as we, sir."

The lieutenant sent word to the captain, who ordered the beat to quarters. The little drummer, Gregno Dedony, who had been a drum boy in the army of Napoleon, rolled out the order with a flourish he might have shown in beating the march of Oudinot's grenadiers at Austerlitz.

Mr. Leving's glance alternately shifted from the fog clouds west to his crew. He would use this opportunity to test efficiency aboard. If the decks were not cleared for action within the allotted time he would roll sweat into the scuppers with practice drills from this day on. Now guns were being cleared and run out; breechings were secured; sand was sprinkled about the gun stations; powder boys vied with one another in fetching sand buckets, shot, and slow matches; shot rolled across deck amid the chirping of the boatswain's fife; Surgeon Kelton danced about, waving his arms for sailcloth to receive the wounded; Mr. Sevey reported to deck, and Mr. Newman, third lieutenant, rushed after him.

Turning suddenly, Leving saw Captain Brown in full uniform taking in the scene.

"Done to your satisfaction, Mr. Leving?"

"Aye, sir. And may I ask the same of you?"

"You may, sir. I am well pleased." This reply by no means expressed the feeling of assurance that a fine ship gave Jeremiah. Too long he had sailed with only a schoonerman's wits pitted against Mexican superiority.

As Lieutenants Sevey and Newman came up, he said, "I'm curious enough to lay closer to the stranger. Do I hear any objections, gentlemen?"

None forthcoming, he gave the order to alter the course slightly and stood by to call for a shot across the stranger's bows once she emerged into the open. A quarter hour and another, and the topmen reported nothing. The crew by now suspected they had been duped into further practice. A jack was saying, "For the pleasure o' the bosun probably, who I'd enjoy stuffin' the whistle twixt 'is ears and pipin' lively." A member of Franson's gun crew slapped the looping breech of a six-pounder with open palm, shifted his cud, and lowered his kerchief from nose to chin, saying, "Drop hanky to collar, Joe. All the powder smoke we'll see today I'll suck through me pipe stem." Just then a lookout cried a sail close over the starboard beam. The cannoneer almost swallowed his tobacco when the ordnance officer told him to aim and adjust the gun. Moments later, he blew sparks into the touchhole and set off the charge. As the wind drove choking smoke into his face, a sailor said, "Start suckin' it up, Cholly boy."

The strange vessel replied directly with a ball that sizzled just above deck between bows and foremast. The day looked promising indeed until Captain Brown dropped his telescope and whirled.

"Fire our signals, for God's sake! He'll shoot our ears off."

"Who, sir?" from Mr. Leving.

"He's breaking out the arm and the bloody sword—my brother William!"

The tiny *Liberty* came up, proud as a bantam cock. Captain William S. Brown made the crossing, grinned, and said that given another two minutes he would have smashed the *Invincible's* foremast. To which Mr. Leving replied, "I believe you would, sir."

"What did Jerry say, Mr. Leving?"

The lieutenant's eyes twinkled. "That in the exchange the Texas Navy wasted a couple of balls and powder charges it could ill afford, sir."

"What a closefisted admiral he would make," William laughed.

Jeremiah's expression revealed how proud he was of William. After introductions, he gave his purser a broad wink. "Mr. Wells, if we can afford it, the occasion calls for hospitality of the stream." In the officers' mess, they raised a toast to Texas, and William advised that he had been relieved of convoying merchantmen with orders to prey upon enemy shipping. He talked on:

Captain Hawkins and Hurd were thick as thieves of late and, by their remarks, were aligned against the Brown brothers. Hawkins was rumored to have said, "A fine ship like the *Invincible* in the hands of a schoonerman who came in through the hawsehole is a detriment to the service"; said it to Mr. Potter, head of Naval Affairs.

Jeremiah's brows lifted. He remembered how the tall, dashing Hawkins, as Wharton described him, had charmed Governor Smith, how all in power had taken a fancy to the cut of Hawkins's jib.

"Father joined the army again, Jerry, the moment he heard of the argument between Santa Anna and his generals."

"What argument?" Jeremiah said.

"It was learned through a reliable source that Minister Tornel and the military strongly advised Santa Anna against marching troops across one hundred and ninety leagues of barren, Indian-infested land to San Antonio. Seems he's in a hurry to avenge the defeat of Cós. Else it could be a ruse. But Colonel Wharton and Mr. McKinney think he will try to come by sea."

Jeremiah nodded. "From Matamoros." Next he said, "Did this reasoning provoke any official orders from our naval committee?"

"Why, no, Jerry."

Jeremiah blew out his cheeks hopelessly. "That's the hell of it. We should have orders to concentrate our armed ships near Matamoros in order to convince Santa Anna that the sea route is also a perilous one."

William and the *Invincible's* officers agreed, and Jeremiah got to his feet, his face brightening with discovery. "Look here, William, all of you." He sat down, placed palms on knees, and leaned toward them. "We have no orders telling us not to patrol the mouth of the Rio Grande out of Matamoros."

An atmosphere of repressed excitement fell over the group. Every man there stared at Captain Jeremiah Brown, detecting in his rather quiet face a quality that reminded them of something as intangible as the spirit of a storm at sea. Then they relaxed. William poured drinks around, lifted one, saying:

"Gentlemen, that's my brother Jerry."

It was early next morning, a time when the maze of traffic on the Rio Grande met the sea with the sun in its eyes. Standing due east of the bar four miles distant with the wind on her beam, the *Liberty* led the way. The *Invincible* approached from the southeast under light sail with about three miles of water between her and the sister ship. From the Brazos Santiago she might appear to be a heavily laden, barnacled merchantman from Vera Cruz. She was purposely sailing in lubbery fashion. The strategy was designed to draw any armed ship out past the bar in chase of the defiant Texan. Then the *Invincible* would bear down under all sail and run out her battery.

On this February morning, Captain Brown stood the deck forward, oblivious to shipboard activities. His attention was upon the *Liberty*. She glistened in the early light, her bows dipping as she breasted the light swells and cavorted a little. His face was impassive as he watched her. Soon her bowsprit would swing to the north, unless—— But William was not the kind of fool to sail under the fort's guns. Yet he kept on. He should put the wind aft. Then he looked beyond the *Liberty*, at a merchant brig putting out to sea. She was clearing port, a Mexican no doubt, her sails unfurled and cascading down until the souther snapped them full to larboard. He raised the glass and saw her pennant apeak flattened to leeward. It was not the Eagle and the Snake but the Stars and Stripes. A puff of smoke issued from the *Liberty's* bow chaser as she broke out William's colors, the

1824 flag together with private ensign, the army with the bloody sword. The brig was wearing ship hurriedly, trying to return inside the bar, and the *Liberty* was running toward her.

"Stay back!" Jeremiah cried, as if the miles separating them were mere feet.

William Brown had other ideas. He made a dash for the merchant ship and almost ran aground. He had her full under his larboard guns even as the fort awoke to find a Texan within range of its cannon. The interval of waiting seemed to stretch into an eternity on board the *Invincible*.

Then the fort opened fire.

With the ugly vomit of flame and black smoke, Mr. Leving suggested they move in to assist the *Liberty*. Captain Brown refused on the grounds that his brother was bent on taking a prize singlehanded. "Until he signals for aid, we'll abide by the plan." In silence, he added, "A plan altered by his damn impulsiveness."

But, he told himself, along the byways of the sea and through the pages of naval history such a rash maneuver was defined in terms of success or failure; either it was "blundering stupidity" or "brilliance of command." Just the same, the fort loosed salvo after salvo, jarring the very edges of the clouds as Mexican thunder clapped and rolled across the undulant reaches of the sea.

The little "pup" of the Texas Navy kept on, her flag riveted in the breeze. Then the *Liberty* was barking back at the mastiff with her little six-pounders. By God, William touched a man's admiration. He was glorious in action.

Just when Mexican guns seemed to have found the *Liberty*, they ceased fire, proving that William had put the merchant brig so close to him that the fort dare not fire for fear of damaging a neutral vessel. A half hour went by, in which Jeremiah was forced to take in canvas in order to hold his distance. At last sail was run up on the *Liberty*. As she raced for the open sea, the fort opened fire again. The little schooner bowled along on a fair following wind, seeming to dance and dodge the shot. Then she was out of range, running for the horizon. Foolhardy or daring, she was free.

Now it was the *Invincible's* turn. Sail cracked in the wind. The larboard gun crew stood in readiness. Lookouts constantly reported enemy activity by land and river. Fishing boats lined the banks, afraid to venture out. The merchant ship was working herself inside the bar; far ahead, a large ship was raising sail for Matamoros, thirty-five miles upriver.

The *Invincible* was fast closing with the land. Nearing the bar, she turned her larboard side, fluttered the 1824 flag at her peak, and further identified herself by firing a broadside at the fort. Then she dropped her anchor and took in sail casually, and sat there just beyond the range of Mexican guns for several hours.

Nothing gained, nothing lost. The crew shrugged it off, charged this strange behavior to the mysterious workings of the captain's mind.

That evening the *Liberty* flashed her signals and came alongside. Her commander and two officers boarded the *Invincible* and joined the group below. William excused his foolhardy run into the cannon fire with: "I was curious to know what was going on in Matamoros." He had boarded the American merchantman, a J. W. Zachari ship out of New Orleans. Under threat of seizure as a prize of war, her captain had divulged a little: Matamoros was excitedly making ready for several thousand Mexican troops on the march from Saltillo; it was rumored that several thousand more were moving up from Monclova, deeper in the interior, to the Rio Grande.

"Which means Santa Anna plans to invade by sea," William said.

Said Leving, "Either that or he has in mind a navy-supported supply base somewhere along the Texas coast."

"Either way," William admitted, "our work is cut out for us. The captain of the American brig grudgingly admitted that his firm was lacking enough bottoms to supply the provisions Lizardi & Company were shipping to Matamoros. And I asked what they were going to do about it. The only thing possible, he said—the same thing Tornel was doing to obtain troopships—get them from the New England of Mexico, Yucatán." He paused a moment.

"Which is where I'm sailing."

Jeremiah considered all this. It was reasonable to believe that the absence of enemy war vessels about Matamoros meant the Mexican fleet was fitting out in Vera Cruz for heavy convoy duty necessary to a seaborne invasion. "To sum it all up," he said, "I believe our action of today will give Santa Anna a slight case of seasickness.

"So, gentlemen," he spoke slowly, steeling himself for the surprise and subsequent objections of his officers, "believing that our little gesture of defiance to the enemy at Matamoros has aided our cause,

I'm in favor of repeating the performance where it will count most——

"Vera Cruz."

2

The schooner-of-war *Invincible* ran her latitude down the Mexican coast from twenty-six degrees north, crossing the Tropic of Cancer and continuing on deep into enemy waters. The roadstead to Vera Cruz lay ahead.

On this late afternoon the crew lined the starboard deck, watching the blaze of color in the heavens. The sun seemed to stand still over the distant summit of Cofre de Perote, bathing the rainswept eastern slopes in a gold that reached far out to sea. Suddenly it dropped behind the sierras and only the brilliant sky and its reflection in the water remained of the day. Low on the eastern horizon, the moon reddened in the brief twilight and threw its color down upon the quiet sea.

The crew turned to watch it climb and change from red and gold to silver. Where there are sailors there is music. A fiddler appeared and men sang and danced and laughed. The night wore on. When the moon climbed until it rode brightly overhead, only the low voices of the watch vied with the murmurous sounds of sea and wind in the rigging.

Jeremiah stood alone on the weather side, his gaze far over the water, then lifting to the maze of stars dangling in the bowl of heaven. It had been four days since William had privately nudged him with news of Carmela. And on nights like this she rose up strong and overpowering.

William had said, "By the way, I saw a golden-headed woman aboard the Zachari ship who is a dead ringer for the Miss Ryan you took out in New Orleans." Then he had laughed. "Her name is Ryan too."

Damnation! thought Jeremiah. If he had boarded the ship, he would have taken her off the brig as a man would take a prize.

The lookout cried a light winking above the southern horizon.

Turning quickly, Jeremiah's first thought was to reward the lad at the masthead, if only because he restored the captain to his ship. What appeared to be a star dipping into the sea caused him no surprise, for it was the beacon that warned of the islands and reefs on the Vera Cruz approach.

Dawn over the sea found the *Invincible* some ten miles out and standing in under scant sail, Captain Brown and Lieutenant Leving engaged in conversation. They were looking toward the most important port of Mexico and the anchorage of the Mexican fleet with full awareness of the dangers ahead. To challenge the second-best navy of the Western Hemisphere at its home base was more foolhardy than daring. The protecting castle fort San Juan de Ulúa was not called the "Gibraltar of America" without reason. Jeremiah had sailed past the gray walls of the island fortress in 1827. He knew something of the history of this Spanish stronghold over the last two hundred years. It had seen the famed silver fleets of Spain sail to sea: it had been sacked by pirates; it had seen the last Spanish flag over Mexico hauled down. It sat the blue tropical waters long, low, and flat in the distance; up close, it seemed high and majestic and commanding a range on every side with its guns.

"The fortress alone guarantees our appearance will achieve one thing, Mr. Leving—surprise. Our strategy is to scare the hell out of Vera Cruz. If we do that, the Mexican newspapers will do the rest."

"Newspapers?"

"They'll raise such a howl that Tornel will think twice before sending the bulk of his fleet to Texas."

Mr. Leving grinned his understanding. His eyes clung to Jeremiah. In them was a look that said this ex-schoonerman was not only a bold naval officer with more ability than his experience warranted but a strategist who was doing the thinking for the "Admiralty on the Brazos."

On that February morning, the *Invincible* copied the pattern set by the *Liberty* at Matamoros and ran full in the sun's eye for the island fortress. All similarity ended there.

The crew had been promised "some sport" on this occasion. Every man stood in readiness. Decks were cleared for action, doors were open to the magazine, the requisite number of tubs were at hand, and decks were sanded. The purser had orders to have his public chest and papers ready to throw overboard. In case of fire in the ship's interior, the magazine would be flooded. Boats were ready for lowering to the shelter of the starboard side and the swivel guns were pivoted to larboard, since the plan of maneuver called for a northerly run once they were close enough to present a broadside. The weather was ideal, with a fresh trade wind veering from southeast to east-southeast, some sea on. The *Invincible* nuzzled waves with her prow, gently, in no hurry.

At a distance of four miles, Captain Brown ordered the American flag hoisted. She would emulate a merchantman for another three miles, maybe more. Looking the sea around, Jeremiah's glance returned to the pile of stone atop a reef. It shone like alabaster in the sunlight, more a jewel in a blue setting than a formidable sentinel. He had been under a fort's fire before, though old Ulúa had a reputation. He was sailing against tradition now. But it didn't matter; he was not here to sack, just to defy.

Three miles more, then two. The town lay squat and white and still, fronted by ships, backed by verdant tropical growth and wooded mountains in the distance. One mile off. The fort loomed up like a giant ship with a hundred gun ports facing the sea. The crew stared, marveling at its size; Lieutenants Leving and Sevey shifted their weight from one foot to the other, darting glances at Captain Brown, as if to say, "We're under enough guns to blow us from here to the Brazos."

A pilot boat was making toward them. It was time to tack ship, though the *Invincible* ran on to meet the pilot, taking in some sail as the steam tug drew close. Then to the amazement of officers and crew, Captain Brown cried out:

"*Buenos días, señor!*"

Next, he said, "What naval ships lie at anchorage?" With the reply —*Bravo, Veracruzana, Libertador, Urrea,* the big gun brig *General Teran,* and many smaller ships—Jeremiah inquired about Lieutenant Thomas M. Thompson and learned that he was first officer under Captain Espino, of the *Bravo,* formerly the *Moctezuma.*

"Excellent. Now I'll pay you well to advise Lieutenant Thompson and his captain that Captain Brown of the Texan war schooner *Invincible* invites the *Bravo* to come out and fight."

For a second Jeremiah's glance lingered on the pilot, long enough to see the astonishment he hoped to evoke on the whole of Vera Cruz in short minutes. Then he said:

"Run down the American flag and hoist our colors. Mr. Abbott, get a way under her. Handsome now!"

The *Invincible's* graceful bows swung around and sail cracked in the wind. She took a quick forward step, her larboard side paralleling the fort. The gun crew tensed.

"Steady, steady," Jeremiah said. "Here's your chance to singe the dictator's beard. The last surprise you'll effect here, men, so aim true and bring the rubble down on their heads.

"Fire one, fire all!"

He sprinted aft where the smoke would clear first. Before he stopped, a deafening roar split the air, almost throwing him off his feet. The ship lurched and trembled, seeming to recoil like her guns. Acrid smoke choked and burned throats and nostrils, clearing fast in the wind. But Captain Brown was able to see his shot dent the walls and send stone crumbling to the water. One shot seemed to fly right into a cannon's mouth, leaving one less gun in Mexico.

While gunners worked furiously swabbing and placing powder charges for the next broadside, Jeremiah waited with telescope trained on the fort. A return of the compliment was due, though he thought the garrison was caught off guard. And who could blame the Mexicans? As for himself, ship and crew, nothing material had been accomplished. The *Invincible's* puny shot against the thick walls of San Juan de Ulúa seemed about as effective as spitting in the wind. Except for the important fact that Mexico was learning that Texas had a navy.

The garrison was forming on the fort. The *Invincible* was sliding north, still within easy range, when she let go with a pivot gun amidships. The shot cleared the wall and sailed over the parade to kick up water in front of the customhouse. Then the fort opened fire, scoring a wide miss. Calculating the range limit of the enemy's guns, Jeremiah made a mental note of it and returned the fire. The Mexican gunners were aiming truer now. Water leaped high aft, spraying the stern. Not twenty yards off the larboard beam a screaming ball exploded just above the water, showering the rigging with jagged metal. Some damage was inflicted. And now the enemy was firing grapeshot, scattering cannon balls that increased the odds of scoring a hit nine to one. Two struck home, one on the forecastle, the other tearing a gaping hole in the mainsail.

"An eye for an eye," Jeremiah said, taking over the forward swivel.

Aiming at the harbor, he fired upon shipping flying the Mexican eagle. Then he called on his gunners for the parting shot.

The battle ended as suddenly as it had begun, with no casualties and small damage. The *Invincible* ran north a few miles, wore ship into the wind for a return, where she clewed up and furled in man-of-war style just close enough to safely tease the gunners of the "Gibraltar of America" into firing round after round before giving up in disgust.

The *Invincible* sat out the day waiting for one of Tornel's ships to sail out and engage her. None came, though the obliging pilot returned with a message from Lieutenant Thompson: "Captain Espino joins me in expressing regret that the crew of our gallant ship challenged cannot be induced to fight until they are paid."

The day passed without a single merchant ship having ventured out. One Texas ship was blockading the whole Mexican Navy. Expecting one or more gun brigs would slip out under the cover of night, Jeremiah sailed into the bay of Campeche and posted a masthead watch on the Vera Cruz road.

Toward midnight, the wind veered around the compass and came in with a slow drizzle out of the north. The moon vanished and a vaporous blanket lay over the wide expanse of sea. The change in weather was relayed to Captain Brown, who assembled his officers of the wardroom and poured brandy into cups of steaming coffee. Used to his vagaries by this time, they were nevertheless so astonished at the plan he disclosed that Mr. Leving for the first time raised his voice in protest; and quiet Lieutenant Sevey sided with the first lieutenant, who was now saying:

"Sir, if you're set on it, why not send an officer and volunteer crew?"

"Mr. Leving, it's time you realize I won't send any man where I won't go myself."

"Very well, sir," Leving replied with a shrug. "But, begging your pardon, it's hardly in keeping with naval tradition."

Jeremiah smiled at the other's persuasiveness and said, "Then I'll just have to follow the tradition of a Texas schoonerman."

A little later, he raised sail for Vera Cruz again with not a light aboard.

The *Invincible* slipped silently to the very edge of the harbor without attracting notice. The beacon on the fort scarcely penetrated the drizzle, and the sleeping town and harbor showed few lights. None-theless the wardroom officers felt in their bones they were flirting with chance. Any slip meant capture. Though compared to what their commander had in mind this seemed the lesser folly; for Captain Brown continued to turn a deaf ear to entreaty. Even now he was fingering a brace of pistols at his belt and getting into the boat, his destination the inner harbor of Vera Cruz. Despairing of him, the officers stood silently by as the ship's gig slipped away from the *Invincible's* side on cushioned oars and headed for the fort.

Jeremiah sat the stern sheets with steering oar in hand. "Easy. Easy," he warned the oarsmen, lest a blade slap the water and attract attention. There were watchmen where they were going and not all of them would be asleep. A drizzle of rain continued to seep out of a sky as dark as the running sea. As the boat moved on, the fort's pale lights changed from dead ahead to their left side and then astern. The dim outlines of ships formed in the mist, and then they were close enough to see a man pacing a deck.

Jeremiah eased the steering oar over and pointed the boat's prow in that direction. Under her lee, he raised his voice, saying in Spanish, "Deck ahoy!" The watch came alive, peered over the side at a boat, and what looked to be peons. "Señor, I am sent with messages to one Capitan José Maria Espino. This is the ship, I hope. The night is a nasty one, no?"

This was the *Correo Segundo*, transport ship. The *Bravo* lay over there in the navy yard. A nasty night, indeed.

"Gracias! Gracias, señor!" And Jeremiah knew where the navy was anchored.

In the rain, he could not read the name across the stern of the first big war vessel. It didn't matter. He eased in under the overhang of her stern and gave the signal for shipping oars. Touching her rudder, he felt his way to the sternpost, then the pintle, which secured the two and formed an axis for the rudder. There was room enough for the powder charges between rudder and post. Fishing the sacks from under canvas, he examined a length of twine match and, finding it as dry as a duck's back, crammed the powder bags in from pintle up to stern overhang. Dousing the hull with oil, he brought forth a slow match from a covered tub and, shielding it with his body and hands, blew on it."

Touching it to the fuse, he said, "Shove off and pull like hell!"

The gig shot out from the vessel with all hands bending their backs to the sweeps. Jeremiah thought they had perhaps a minute, and how far a light boat could be rowed in that time depended on the occasion. They had no sooner rounded the stern of a light schooner than the night was rent by a terrific roar and flash of light.

"Easy lads," he said in muffled tones even as he hold himself they were now in the lap of the gods.

As lanterns appeared on nearby ships, Jeremiah stepped the small mast forward and hauled sail into the wind. Under way, sail drawing and men on the oars, he looked behind him. The ship's stern was burning. Beautifully! Her rudder was gone. And the flames licked up to light her name—

General Teran.

The gig had not gone far when yells rose up from the ships aft. A tugboat churned out from the customhouse pier and steamed toward them. The crack of a musket pierced the drizzle and something popped the water alongside. Puffballs of light moved hurriedly on merchantmen's decks ahead, revealing curious seamen, some leaning on the rail, others lowering boats. The idlers were quick to notice a triangular sail moving strangely in the opposite direction from the burning ship. Cries to stop the boat reached Jeremiah's ears. A gun roared from over the quarter, scattering shot into the sail. Musket fire began in earnest and the small sail jerked under the impact of bullets. One struck the gunwale, ricocheting off in a vicious screech.

The sail was a painted target in the growing firelight. Jeremiah had just unstepped the mast and lowered it to the bottom of the boat when a cry escaped one of his oarsmen. The lad flung himself forward and fell across the prow. A sailor examined him and turned away without a word.

Jeremiah stared grimly at the body.

Ahead, the guns of the fort thundered out over the bay, seeming to jar the very water. Looking up quickly from his first casualty of the cruise, he was wondering if the *Invincible* had been discovered or if the harbor excitement provoked fear of invasion.

Then some inner warning caused him to jerk his gaze aft. A small schooner was putting out in his direction. It came on, bearing down over his quarter at a clip the boat could not hope to match; and men on her deck were ordering him to stop. His men were pirates under the decree of the Mexican Congress, and a pirate's fate was death.

With no choice left, he ordered his oarsmen to abandon the boat and swim for the *Invincible*.

"It's certain death if you're caught, lads. Good luck."

The crew slipped into the dark water one by one. With the last man gone, he made ready to leap. A gun went off behind him and he felt a sting, then a searing pain in his thigh. For a moment he tottered there, half standing, half sitting, weak and unable to believe what had happened to him. He thought strangely, almost in detachment. His brain seemed to be taking bearings on the fort for the *Invincible's* position while telling him to leave the gig at once.

He would do this, he told himself, because there was no other course left to him. But first the enemy would feel his guns. He drew pistols from his belt and fired at the schooner's deck. A yell sounded. With his last shot, he threw the pistols over the side.

Then he was in the tepid water, swimming for the surface, oblivious of his wound. As his head broke the water, he touched the barnacled hull of the pursuing craft.

"I'm sure I nicked one of them. Look sharp!" The order came from the schooner's deck. "A hundred pesos to the man who discovers him!"

Jeremiah held his breath and went under. He would know that voice anywhere. It was Thompson's. When he came up again, the schooner was running off in the drizzle. He struck out for his ship, favoring the leg now, wondering if he would ever reach the *Invincible*.

He went under often. The pain of his leg was growing unbearable. Cramps seized him, stiffened the leg into a heavy weight. He worked on out into deeper water, almost wishing Thompson's schooner would come alongside. The realization that the bullet in his leg had been fired from Thompson's deck evoked little anger in his dull brain. Survival was all that mattered, though he was beginning to fear that another few minutes of agony would lessen his desire to live. A man could endure just so much. Then he could not go on. Overcome by panic, he flailed the water until the futility of what he was doing registered in his mind. He must save his energy, not expend it; must remain calm when the craving for help threatened to open his mouth with a loud cry.

He was going under when his foot touched something solid, some object out of place, surely, in the middle of the channel. But it was under him, a rock of salvation. He rested upon it, only his head above water, and tried to establish his position between fort and ships at anchor. Neither was visible in the slow rain. A faint glow and voices in the distance seemed out of direction in his mind. Then a happy thought dawned bright in him—he was on the reef, off the channel. He was amazed that he had come this far. He could only pray for the strength to carry him another quarter mile to his ship.

Lieutenant Leving and the master's mate fished him out of the water a little later. When they lifted him on board the *Invincible*, he wasn't sure he was safe. The surgeon brought him around with whisky, then took him to the sick bay and probed his wound for the Mexican slug.

He looked up at Lieutenant Leving. "Did the crew get back?"

"Two missing, sir."

Surgeon Kelton said, "Give him whisky, Lieutenant. This is going to hurt."

Jeremiah raised himself to elbows. "I can stand your worst, Doctor. What hurts is the weight of two good men on my soul. Two lives, Mr. Leving, the same as yours and mine, sacrificed to a damn-fool scheme by a commander who——"

Mr. Leving very respectfully shoved the lip of a bottle in the captain's mouth and the surgeon gouged the wound unnecessarily. Observing the broad winks the pair exchanged, Jeremiah settled back almost wonderingly.

Chapter Nineteen

AN OMEN FULFILLED

On the morning of March 19, the *Invincible's* deck stirred with anticipation. Captain Brown, officers, and crew expected momentarily the lookout's cry of land. The low delta of the Mississippi meant New Orleans and all she had to offer a weary crew after a long voyage. Jeremiah was fully aware that some of them would go ashore and fail to board ship again. New hands must be trained, over and over. Home ports caused a captain more headaches than storms at sea. Even so, he was anxious to reach New Orleans.

The ship was in need of refitting. Weather and jarring guns and peopled decks took a toll. She needed provisioning and a maze of things that would cost money. And he knew the condition of the Texas treasury. However, he was not destitute, thanks to the town on the coast of Yucatán. Recorded in the ship's official account of the voyage was this terse report:

> March 1, 1836. Following broadside and landing of marines, the citizens sent an emissary to advise that the levy of $5000 could not be met and begged a compromise of $2000, which was accepted with more readiness than we dared make known.

Here was good "hard cash." After the crew's share, a nice sum remained. He had touched in at Sisal on the third, shortly after the

Liberty had braved the shore battery and captured the schooner *Pelicano* in a boarding engagement. Her false cargo, consisting largely of munitions packed in five hundred barrels of flour, apples, and potatoes, was covered by manifests showing it to be the property of J. W. Zachari of New Orleans. Here was a legal prize of startling value to Texas, and William Brown placed a prize crew aboard and ran for Matagorda with her.

Continuing on to Campeche, Jeremiah boarded all inbound and outbound vessels without catching a prize to compare with William's. There Little Josh finished sewing the flag that now kept the 1824 ensign company. The design was copied from the banner flown by General Long in 1819 and displayed in Mrs. Long's hotel in Brazoria, where Jeremiah had seen it often—thirteen stripes of red and white, white star central in a field of red, a near copy of the United States flag except that it contained only one star. Jeremiah had made a change: the white star was placed in a field of blue. Mr. Leving grinned every time he looked up at it. His prediction, "A clever deception that might prove useful," had been fulfilled on more than one occasion when Mexican schooners had mistaken J. Brown's ensign for the American Stars and Stripes.

And now the long-awaited cry sounded: "Land ho!"

Leaning on his stick, Jeremiah moved forward of the deck, if only to be nearer the land. He was eager for news from Texas. He thought of the lamps of Bank's Arcade, of the iron lacework of the balconies, of Carmela.

The thought of Carmela brought to mind the other side of her life, the man who shot him in the thigh. The wound continued to trouble him. It pained severely at times, caused him to walk with a pronounced limp. First the chains on his wrist aboard the *Correo de Mejico*—Thompson's; next the leg that might never be the same after the bullet—Thompson's; and the woman seldom out of his mind—she had attached herself to Thompson's star. And still he hoped above all things personal that she would be in New Orleans. Nevertheless, though he knew moments of tenderness for her, he recognized the growing fierceness of his regard for an enemy spy and confederate of his mortal enemy.

But there were other things to think about. The Navy, for instance. Such an important branch of the national service called for a head, a commodore of the fleet, and he was in line for that office. Perhaps it was his even now and he didn't know it. The commissioners in New Orleans would know.

He glanced impatiently into the rigging, where all sail was working, and then at the land ahead. A smile played on his face as he adventured with the future, saying in low tones:

"Commodore Brown to see Miss Carmela Ryan."

2

Jeremiah's appearance at the Arcade that evening was an occasion for celebration. The filibustering element made much ado over the sea dog whose recent exploits in Mexican waters had preceded him here. Before William Bryan and Thomas McKinney arrived to rescue him from the host of admirers, Jeremiah learned that the Brown brothers had captured the fancy of Americans. Behind a composed expression, he listened eagerly, wondering just what sort of hero fickle New Orleans had made of him.

Newspaper accounts of his cruise had been printed in Mexico and reprinted by New Orleans papers. From Mexico City:

> The Anglo-Texan pirate Captain J. Brown, whose depredations of 1832 through 1835 are known to all, is actually blockading Vera Cruz with a single schooner-of-war. Furthermore, he shelled the fortress of San Juan de Ulúa, set fire to the gun brig *General Teran*, all under the eyes of our handsome fleet. To all appearances, this insignificant freebooter has so excited the Minister of War and Navy that any planned invasion of the province of Texas by sea has been thrown completely off its balance, for directly following the blockade of Matamoros by Captains Brown and Brown earlier in February, *El Presidente* himself marched his main army, not to Matamoros, but to San Juan Bautista on the Rio Grande, indicating a costly overland march . . .

Jeremiah drank, sat down, pleased. "So it worked," he said just above a whisper.

There was more, much more. Word had reached New Orleans of the *Pelicano's* capture. Consul Martínez had asked the Mexican minister in Washington to protest this "act of piracy" to the American State Department.

With good news ringing in his ears, he thought it odd that McKinney and Bryan appeared so glum. They were seated in a gay café in the Vieux Carré when Bryan said the latest news from Texas placed Santa Anna in San Antonio with a large army. He was besieging a small Texan force under Colonel William B. Travis at the Alamo, a fortress in Bexar.

Jeremiah frowned. His father was fighting with Travis. "How big a force, Tom?"

"About one hundred and fifty men. Reports vary. Santa Anna surprised them on February twenty-third, and they set up defenses inside the walls of the Alamo. On the twenty-fourth Travis sent out a desperate appeal for aid. Then on the third of March he sent another plea, saying the Mexicans had kept up a constant bombardment since February twenty-fifth. Actually, Jerry, his small band is all that separates the Mexican horde from our last defense at Goliad under Colonel Fannin."

"Why doesn't Fannin march to his aid?"

"General Urrea is moving toward Goliad with a thousand troops. Colonel Fannin holds the town with the biggest Texan army in the field—four hundred men, Jerry. If he moves there's nothing left to stop the Mexicans."

"How many troops under Santa Anna?"

"Four thousand, I hear."

"Which," Jeremiah said, "proves the two thousand troops in Matamoros plan to come by sea." He paused. "But where the hell is Sam Houston?"

"Give him credit for trying, Jerry. He's hamstrung. Or he was until the new government confirmed his office and fell to work. As you probably know, all the Provisional Government did was to create a navy. And but for one schoonerman——"

Jeremiah interrupted him with, "Who heads the new government?"

"Better brace yourself," McKinney said. "Our old pacifist friend David G. Burnet is President, *ad interim*." When Jeremiah slumped into his seat and shook his head hopelessly, McKinney added, "Drink one against another surprise—Burnet is a good man. So are Vice-President Zavala and the cabinet members representing State, War, Navy, Treasury, and Justice Departments. Robert Potter of the Naval Affairs Committee is Secretary of the Navy."

Jeremiah nodded thoughtfully. McKinney said:

"These men and the delegates gave Texas what she needed most, a declaration of independence. We are as of March second a nation."

Jeremiah raised his glass. Then, with a conspicuous lack of elation, he said, "God knows I hope so. But do four thousand Mexican regulars marching on us guarantee that?"

Silence between the three worried Texans merely intensified the noise all about them. McKinney passed cigars, lit one, and looked over the crowd of merrymakers. Bryan seemed preoccupied. Jeremiah drank slowly but seriously. A half-clad quadroon of fine figure was vying with a West Indian woman garbed in a few ribbons about the breasts and pelvis for the crowd's attention. A piano and stringed instruments played to the swaying of their hips, or it might have been the other way about; Jeremiah wasn't sure. He saw them and he didn't. Both women were weaving their hips with raw animal vigor, delightfully, disgustingly, depicting the tropical passions of New Orleans and Havana. The audience showed its pleasure and built its appetite in various manner, through laughter, talk, and frozen silence. Then the tempo increased. The music beat faster and the wild monotonous stamping and twisting kept pace. And Jeremiah was for a moment a spectator in the Vieux Carré and in a world apart the next. In the swirl of the dance he saw Texas caught up and rushed about in a speed too fast for her, too violent to live with in either victory or defeat; but appropriate in the passions of war.

The dancing continued. A fat man at a nearby table wiped wine from his chins and proclaimed his willingness to bet his last dollar that Santa Anna would conquer Texas before the first of May. Jeremiah eyed the man narrowly, seeing, hearing enemy guns pounding incessantly at the walls of the far-off Alamo, thinking of George Brown who had once sent up a prayer before opening fire on marauding Indians. If the Alamo fell, his father would go with it. And this man who believed Santa Anna would conquer such men as Travis and his father before May appeared more than eager to sacrifice the entire force in order to collect a wager. War was close to some, far removed from others. The dancers had warmer hearts, and he looked in their direction.

The quadroon, not to be outdone, was writhing her torso convincingly in earnest. As the crowd called for more, William H. Wharton appeared at McKinney's side. He looked beaten, though excitement showed in his troubled face. Then he sat down, poured liquor, and drank it in one gulp.

"The word has just come," he said, staring at the empty glass in his hand. "The Alamo has fallen."

"Surrender?"

Wharton shook his head sadly. "Not a man lives."

They sat there, taut and silent, staring at Wharton. Jeremiah went white. Trembling all over, unable to hide the tempest of feeling the message evoked in him, he tried to form questions. His mind and tongue failed him. Wharton had not told all. Something was left unsaid, some hope was omitted, surely. There was no pause in the blaring music, no interruption of the lewd dance. These things would end if one hundred and fifty men had died in their own blood, so there must be some mistake. But Wharton was talking now.

"One hundred and eighty-one men. Slaughtered. Santa Anna flew a blood-red flag from the church of Bexar."

Jeremiah felt shock, anger, grief, and defeat in successive waves. All fell away only to return, grief stronger than the rest. Ridges of muscles formed and moved along his jaws as mist in his eyes dimmed his vision. But there was nothing to look at other than calculated butchery and memories. A man could live with sane reflections of the past. So he probed the past and relived incidents—the first little wagon he had ever owned, with wheels of sawed pine, a parent enjoying a son's enjoyment; a first whipping and his dance to the rod and the look of hurt on his father's face; and a hundred other things. William would need him now. William was easily hurt. And he needed William. They needed each other. Their father was dead. The flag on the church of Bexar meant no quarter.

"That was on the sixth of March," Wharton went on. "The news reached Houston on the thirteenth. That night he left Gonzales in flames and began a retreat to the Colorado with about three hundred men and all the homeless women and children of the area. Rain fell in torrents and the roads were quagmires. The news reached Washington-on-the-Brazos on the seventeenth, just before President Burnet's inauguration. The convention was adjourned and the government is moving to Harrisburg. Urrea is marching on Goliad. Our people are running away from their homes.

"Texas is in a state of terror and confusion."

Jeremiah sat there, silent. No word was spoken between them. Too much had been said already. He recalled the cockfight in the Vieux Carré and tried to put the memory out of his mind. It persisted, did that ill omen of the cocks. It had been written in blood. And now— the prediction was borne out in blood.

Book Four

STAR IN THE RIGGING—1836

Chapter Twenty

REWARD FOR VALOR

A long weary week dragged itself by. Each day brought fresh reports from Texas, some true, some exaggerated, though none did anything to dispel the dark shadow of disaster falling over the land.

On this Saturday morning, Captain Brown walked the *Invincible's* deck, pausing only to look up from the watch in his hand to New Orleans across the river. Frowning out his impatience of delay, he scanned decks, masts, and rigging again, as though this inspection of freshly painted bulwarks and tarred cordage were his first during the last two hours. With Mr. Wells an hour overdue, he was trying his best not to think of the item that detained the purser.

"By thunder, Mr. Leving," he burst out, "those supplies were due aboard yesterday morning."

The first lieutenant nodded. The captain had said that twice within the last ten minutes. Now he was mumbling the rest again.

"Due to sail on Palm Sunday. That's tomorrow. No beef, no biscuits, no powder. And, by God, half a crew! Bryan and Thomas Toby said——" His words trailed off. He took a step and gave in to his leg with a painful grimace.

Mr. Leving brought his stick.

Jeremiah thanked him. "Serves me right, I guess. However, Mr. Leving, I can't get used to the extremes of human nature. Last week New Orleans met us with open arms. We could have filled our holds with champagne, and decks with fat beeves—on credit. But I was very modest. Today I'd rape warehouses."

Suddenly aware that he was to blame for the downcast look in Mr. Leving's face, he forced a broad grin. "But we're not licked yet. Eh, Lieutenant?"

A little later the purser returned from New Orleans with news that completely refuted Jeremiah's encouraging statement. Sellers wanted cash for supplies. There was no cash. The captain's and government's share of the Mexican ransom money had gone to refit the ship. Atop this, Mr. Bryan, general agent for Texas, sent a message: "Unless the merchants of Nacogdoches come to our aid again, and very soon, we will be unable to pay your officers and men."

Jeremiah shook his head hopelessly. "Gentlemen, I'm beginning to understand why a man turns pirate."

Mr. Wells handed Jeremiah two letters. The first was from Secretary of the Navy Potter. "He urges the speedy return of the *Invincible* to Matagorda to join the fleet in protecting the flank of Houston's retreating army." Jeremiah glanced at his officers. "I suppose we'll have to eat rope yarn and oakum."

The other letter was from Velasco.

Dr Jerry,
  Out of the perils which have overtaken us, politics is producing an answer to the question: who shall command our navy? Although President Burnet once opposed your warlike policies, he has spoken out for you, as have Commissioners Austin, Wharton & c. You know McKinney's mind. But Captains Hawkins and Hurd of schrs. Independence and Brutus, resp. have allied themselves against the Brown brothers, holding to the expedient of hugging the coast for purposes of political nature while the Browns carried the war to the enemy to the benefit of Texas. Such was public opinion. A week brings changes. With news of the Alamo, the delegates looked to Houston, and he is making choices right and left, even in matters foreign to army, assuming, we suppose, that he considers himself Commander-in-Chief of the combined forces in the national service. However, you have made a name for yourself and can continue to hope . . .

Jeremiah desired the office of commodore above all things. Somehow, in some way, he would provision his ship and sail for home. "Signal me a craft," he said. "I'm going after the supplies we need. And I won't return until I get them."

Before noon, Jeremiah entered the office of a chandler who in the past had gone out of his way to serve Edwin Waller and himself. His greeting was cordial enough, though the look in his eye was that of a man on guard. He listened, he was sympathetic, but he regretted the fact that he must demand cash. Jeremiah tried another angle. The commissioners would pay in land scrip. The chandler frowned, saying he could scarcely turn such a commodity after the fall of the Alamo. Jeremiah nodded, rubbed his cane, and asked if his personal credit was still good. It was, the other said politely. In fact J. H. Brown could write his own ticket. However, Captain Brown of the Texas Navy might not survive a naval engagement. Therefore, considering the risk, some security was required.

"My plantation on the Brazos," Jeremiah said. "Including fifty slaves worth a dollar a pound."

The chandler smiled and offered cigars. "Look here, Captain Brown. I'll trade with you if you can guarantee that Santa Anna hasn't taken over your plantation by this time next week."

Jeremiah walked in and out of offices and warehouses that afternoon, meeting with polite refusals. The purse strings of New Orleans were drawn tight. Discouraged and weary, not knowing which way to turn next, he entered William Bryan's office and sat down to await his return. Looking at the 1824 flag on the wall of the poorly furnished office, he thought it should be flying at half-mast. However, a flag was a synonym of hope. As old Colonel Billings had said at Broadhaven, "There's something about a flag." The thought brought Polly to mind, and she evoked a frown with the realization that he could no longer send money to her aunt for her schooling. Shrugging it off, he drew a deep breath and worked his leg into a comfortable position.

He was scanning the *Telegraph and Texas Register* when Bryan and William Wharton entered with dispatches from Texas. Their faces were grave. Little was said as they sat down and stared at the floor and ceiling. Then Wharton broke the silence.

"Jerry, brace yourself for more bad news."

"Is there any other kind?"

"Fannin has surrendered."

Both men were watching Jeremiah. They saw his face wrinkle up with an expression of disbelief. Then he lowered a troubled face in acceptance of the fact.

"On Tuesday the twenty-second," Wharton went on. "Four hundred men, the only stand of arms between Santa Anna and Houston's retreating army. Goliad is lost, and it's too late to ask why Fannin and Houston didn't join forces. Too late to hope, almost."

Wharton wiped a tear from his eye and made all sorts of grimaces in an effort to restore the composure of his swarthy face. Bryan tapped his teeth with a fingernail before saying, "President Burnet wrote Thomas Toby and Brothers to furnish Colonel Green land scrip of the government to the amount of ten thousand acres, requiring him not to dispose of it for less than the minimum price of fifty cents per acre. After Fannin's surrender becomes known here, Green can't peddle it for ten cents an acre."

"You can't get that for it now," Jeremiah said.

The silence of a wake fell over the room again. When Jeremiah could endure it no longer, he arose. "This means I've got to sail for Texas. How, remains to be seen. But I'm sailing, and with supplies and powder. Mr. Bryan, stand ready to get me out of jail."

Bryan glanced up quickly. "For what?"

"Piracy, if it takes that to get provisions."

"Sure, sure." Bryan managed a semblance of a smile. "By the way, a letter came for you. From Matagorda."

Accepting it, Jeremiah said, "Hope it's not more bad news. Probably from my brother William."

He sat down and broke the seal, wondering at his brother's reaction to their father's death at the Alamo. William put up a calm exterior to hide a deep and sensitive nature; like their mother, he reflected, who had been inclined to nurse hurt and grief.

But the letter was not from William. One brief sentence leaped at him. His eyes were glued to the page. Then he got to his feet and stalked out of the office, repeating the message over and over. At a crossing, he walked in front of an oncoming carriage, causing the driver to rein up short and swear at him. He didn't hear, he didn't care. Moments or eternities later he was rapping his stick on a bar. Whisky was placed before him. He drank, poured again, thinking he had read the impossible. Slowly, carefully, he smoothed out the crumpled sheet of paper and read again:

You are hereby ordered to join the fleet at Matagorda without delay.

That much he could understand and live with and do his utmost to obey. Obey, yes, if the message had been signed by the President or Secretary of the Navy. But the signature was neither Burnet's nor Potter's. It was instead the bold, scrawling signature of a man who had played a game of politics while he and William braved Mexican guns. The name meant nothing, what followed it did——

"*Charles E. Hawkins, Commodore Texas Navy.*"

2

Jeremiah Brown fought it out with himself that night. Bitterness and resentment followed him from café to coffeehouse to cockpit, and on. He sat at tables in gay courtyards and stared at the women on the balconies without seeing them. He drank, outwardly composed and quiet while seething inwardly, asking again and again: Why, when he or William had earned that badge of office; why, when Texas had more men and homeless women and children than she could feed and only the *Pelicano's* cargo to feed them with; why, when even Mexico admitted that the Browns had influenced the abandonment of a Mexican invasion of Texas by sea? He picked up his stick and moved to another place where he sat and asked in silence the same questions. Some inner voice, a lurking traitor, always answered: "Because Commodore Hawkins has had naval training. Perhaps it is for the best." And again he would stalk out into the street, mumbling threats, meaning all he said: He would show Burnet a thing or two, set him straight on his course. The *Invincible* could rot where she sat for all he cared. Let the commodore move her, which he would if she budged by so much as one inch, for he, Jeremiah Brown, was resigning his command. And they could lay to that! When anger reached its peak and waned, he had nothing to lean upon. Self-pity no part of him, he nursed strong resentment into a flame once more. By God, he would show them, he would let the world know how he had schemed and fought to bring the Navy into existence.

Suddenly wondering how he came to be sitting in a French coffeehouse, surrounded by gentlemen and their ladies, all listening eagerly to his account of the Vera Cruz adventure, he assumed a tight-lipped dignity and limped out of the place. The crowd watched him go in respectful silence, which was broken as he reached the door by a statement:

"There goes the man I'd like to be."

Jeremiah thought about this, deciding that since no sane man would wish to pattern his life after him the man was therefore as crazy as a landlocked pelican. At a place on Bourbon Street he came upon the Spanish dancer Lolita, who remarked on his grave manner before reminding him of her ability to cheer him.

"Sure. No doubt about it," he replied humoringly. "But this is one night that neither ships nor women interest me."

He left the place thinking perhaps Lolita was right—he *was* in a bad way.

As the night progressed he had vague memories of riding in an open carriage because the jostle was the next thing to a deck. And someone was saying it was Palm Sunday. It didn't matter. Then there was a faint recollection of his sitting in the company of well-dressed men in some remote part of the world. They talked of adventure, and a lot they knew of it, he told them, being cooped up in counting-houses, banks, and offices. He remembered enlightening them, telling them their land was won and his wasn't; that no man could possess a greater love for Texas than he, for he had watched and help her grow since 1824; if they wanted adventure, actually, and a man's life was short of fulfillment without it, they could render a service to humanity by helping him drive the Mexican Navy from the Gulf. Perhaps he imagined the rest. If so, it helped pass the time. One of the men responded by asking if the captain would consider taking him on the next cruise for the sum of fifty dollars. Which was odd, very odd, since he, Captain Brown, hadn't the slightest intention of going on a cruise.

Rather amazed at the inopportunity of the stranger's request, he was staring at him, pitying him, when suddenly he realized that he was going to sail against the Mexican fleet, that patriotism was stronger in him than any feelings of resentment and hurt. He did not voice his mind but, instead, got to his feet. He was walking away when the young man caught at his sleeve and repeated the proposition. He glared at the fellow, wanting to strike him down with his stick. Why? he didn't know. There was no reason for malice. Perhaps it hadn't happened at all, but the way it came back to him he had said, "Cash in advance." And the very fact that the other paid him, that any man could be so bereft of his senses as to pay for a berth on a naval ship, almost sobered him.

From that time on, the night seemed to take a humorous turn. He caught himself chuckling over the acquisition of hard cash and a paying member of his crew, the latter certainly something new under the sun. And he was looking about for another adventurer, and next he was searching for a printer. . . .

He awoke with sunlight streaming through a big window into his face. Now what the devil would he want with a printer? Sitting up, he shook his head and took in the surroundings.

The room was large and elegantly furnished. Over the big soft bed was a canopy in fine lace. Adjusting this to any place or event of the night was for the moment impossible. His cap and stick were atop a glossy table and his coat and trousers were carefully folded; not after the fashion of Jeremiah Brown. A woman had been in this room. Afraid she might be in the bed with him, he turned slowly. Relieved at finding himself alone, he got up. Wherever he was, he didn't belong. Water was in a pitcher, towels were laid out, and there was a razor handy. While shaving, he paused often and frowned when some event, person, or place of the night trailed by on a ragged edge of his memory and departed. In their place appeared the harsh realities of yesterday, a ship destitute of supplies, news of Fannin's surrender, the government's choice of a commodore and his reaction to this blow. All of which brought him around to the present and the realization that the *Invincible* was supposed to sail for Texas on this day.

He was dressed and writing a note to his benefactor when there came a gentle rap at the door. A moment later he opened it and found himself staring at Carmela.

His first desire was to reach out and touch her, to see if she was real. Next he was wishing she would mock his surprise with words instead of greeting him with that all-knowing look a parent gives an unruly boy. It was evident that she was thinking of last night, that she held the advantage and, womanlike, was using it. She walked inside the room, taunting him with a sidewise smile and glance in passing.

"You had quite a night, Captain Brown. But those frappés at the

Absinthe House were too much, weren't they? You hardly knew who I was."

Now it was coming back to him, but vaguely.

Standing at a window, she looked over her shoulder at the stick he carried. "You even said Lieutenant Thompson gave you the limp. And," she said turning with a light laugh, "you were a busy lad with those printed sheets."

He frowned. "I recall a printer and——"

"Then you should remember this." She drew a folded paper from a fold of her dress and handed it to him. "You were quite generous with them. They're posted all over."

As he stared at the handbill, forgotten incidents of the night returned. The one-legged printer and the smell of ink, his new friends merrily at work distributing his invitation to all venturesome gentlemen with a little hard cash:

> Persons wishing to cruise in Mexican waters and participate in the adventures of war at sea may now avail themselves of this rare opportunity at the generous price of $50 the cruise or $30 to ports of Texas, nothing guaranteed, payable in advance aboard the fast A-1 Texan Schr.-of-war *Invincible*, J. H. Brown, Commander.

He shook his head gloomily. "No man in his right mind would expect a crazy thing like that to catch a sucker."

"Which I imagine all New Orleans knows by now. However, Father Alpuche roused me at three this morning. So I went after you, brought you here, put you to bed."

"You folded my coat and trousers?"

"And tucked the Texas Navy in."

"What happened?" he asked, wondering how he could have ever let her go.

"I blew out the lamp and tiptoed out."

"Well, I'm glad of that." When she gave him a sharp, questioning glance, he said, "I want to know about it when I hold you in my arms."

Whirling, she faced the window. After a moment of silence, she said, "Have you any idea where you are?"

"Not the slightest."

"This is the Mexican Consulate, Jerry."

He wasn't prepared for this. He exclaimed, "Damnation, I slept here!" She faced him, enjoying his state of shock and perplexity until he said, "So you're still at it, eh?"

"The consul's hospitality is no secret," she said, resorting to an evasion.

"Naturally," he replied, smiling derisively. "His welcome mat is out to all who serve Santa Anna. And, I'll venture a guess, to pretty women."

She recoiled instinctively from his remarks and stood frozen. "You're way off your course, Jerry Brown, with that last remark." Her direct glance seemed to guarantee she was telling the truth.

"Then forget I said it and remember that your conduct provokes thought on the subject."

"What have I done now?"

"I can only guess. The last time I heard of you was when my brother William saw you aboard the ship at the mouth of the Rio Grande."

"I am usually well chaperoned. Father Alpuche and two sisters from the church of St. Roman in Campeche were aboard also."

"That's another puzzle, if it can be called that. The padre pops up everywhere. He's always handy, either here or in Texas."

"What are you trying to say, Jerry?"

"That the good padre travels from here to the Brazos and back, and you sail back and forth, here to Mexico. He's here when you are and then in Texas when you're gone. It takes on a meaning."

She laughed. "How could you, Jeremiah Brown! Am I to believe the mirror incident aboard the *San Felipe* has convinced you that everyone I speak to is working for Santa Anna?"

"It doesn't convince me, but it makes them suspect."

"Well, you can stop worrying about it. I've had enough. I'm quitting this business."

"Quitting? Just like that, eh? If it's that easy, you're lucky. I'd like to believe you, but your position, posing as Thompson's sweetheart, maybe his wife, seems so perfectly suited to the game of Mexican intelligence that I doubt if they'll let you quit."

"They can do little to stop me," she said on the spur of the moment.

He moved toward her, seeing her small and well-formed and looking a little fearful. "I hope you're right, Carmela. For more reasons than one. In the *San Felipe* affair you weren't in real danger because we were not openly at war with Mexico. But it's different now. You're involved in something as big and final as death. And I don't like to think of you before a firing squad."

Her eyes widened and she winced. He said, "But of course, the bigger the danger the more you're paid."

He seemed to be staring at the empty shell of the woman he still loved, then wondering if that was all he would ever see of her; and next, asking of his desire why he did not grasp the opportunity now, then leave and forget her. Then he knew why, and his face softened with the realization that hope was undying, that she was worth saving from herself, and for him. Her real need was nothing short of a strong arm to pilot her course.

His hands closed over her arms and she turned her face to him. "Maybe you're sincere and can get out of this business, and maybe you're in up to your ears. Either way, make the break and sail with me."

Thinking he saw in her face yearning to escape and willingness to accompany him, he went on. "You know what happened at the Alamo, Carmela. Slaughter that shocks the roots of your soul. You can't serve Santa Anna and fail to see blood on your hands. Do you want that?"

"No, Jerry."

Tipping her face up, he saw conflict at work in her. It was in her eyes and in the set of her lips.

"I'm sailing today," he said.

She averted her face and appeared lost in thought. Moments later her eyes sharpened into focus. As she quickly stepped away from him, her gaze fixed on the doorway, he knew they were no longer alone. Then he was looking at Martínez, who was saying:

"I trust you slept well, Captain Brown."

As Jeremiah studied the handsome consul, his alerted senses advised that he had not come here by accident. It was ludicrous to think the man who called him pirate extraordinary would go out of his way to be hospitable without a reason. But now Martínez was the very essence of politeness, suggesting they retire to the drawing room for coffee and cigars.

"Your obedient servant, sir," Jeremiah replied, giving Carmela a withering stare. He burned inwardly at her deception, reminding himself never to trust her again.

As the three entered a large room, Jeremiah knew beyond doubt that the economic downfall of Texas had been as carefully plotted here as her military conquest in Mexico's National Palace. He sat down to coffee and cigars, thinking the occasion might produce an answer to the puzzle of Carmela's participation in the over-all scheme of things.

His roving gaze took in the excellent room, noting its atmosphere of quiet majesty. The furnishings were neither superannuated nor showy, but seemed to reflect the splendid tastes of the consul. The chandeliers were of genuine cut-glass and the mirrors were from Spain. Hung directly above the sofa where Carmela sat was a portrait of His Excellency, General Santa Anna, in full military regalia. The eyes of the idol of Mexico were more mild than cruel. On either side of the wide gilt frame were tall candles that matched the color tone of the walls. There were other portraits and deep soft Turkish rugs and cabinets of polished woods. But there was something about all this that seemed cold and hard.

His appraising glance came to rest on Carmela. Comparisons were drawn. Fresh estimates brought little change in old opinions or new.

No host could have been more attentive, and few statesmen could have broached a delicate subject more adroitly than Martínez. In his voice there was no hint of gloating over a foe as he reviewed in businesslike tones the conditions which Jeremiah had met with only the day before. Nor could Jeremiah detect any note of triumph in his persuasion as he summed up facts.

"Captain Brown, one cannot deny the truth. Mexico has made it difficult for Texas to secure supplies. Her representatives here have kept an eye on you and your ship. You cannot victual her for a cruise."

Jeremiah said nothing. Though the fact was galling, it had been spoken in forthright manner. Now the consul was refilling his guest's cup.

As if to cushion the truth in the Texan's mind even as he held it up for notice, Martínez smiled engagingly and said, "But you have kept us jumping. Your tenacity is worthy of admiration. Colonel Ugartechea would enjoy hearing of your battle against such odds."

Jeremiah's expression softened. "Ugartechea and I could fight each other all day and be friends at night."

"He is representative of most of us, Captain Brown. Though it is my business to call you pirate and block you in every way possible, our differences are not of the heart. If I may say so, without being suspected of flattery, you have captured the public interest and enthusiasm of the Mexican people. There is not a captain in our navy who does not aspire to your capture. Which," he shrugged, "causes one to ponder in vain the indifference of your people."

He paused here, his intention obvious. He wanted Jeremiah to ask what he meant, and he seemed pleased when the question was placed.

"I mean, Captain Brown, your valiance has gone unnoticed by your government. The reward for valor and skill has escaped you. Commodore Hawkins occupies the position you so richly deserve. And, I make no secret of it, I am striking while this news is fresh in your memory.

"In Mexico and here, we fear and respect you. Your daring at Vera Cruz and Matamoros is exceeded only by the brilliant execution of a plan. I do not flatter when I say that your cruise in Mexican waters caused General Santa Anna to reshape his strategy. But for you Browns we might have all of Texas by now."

Jeremiah's expression remained unchanged. He sipped coffee and enjoyed the aroma of a fine cigar, all the while watching Carmela out of the corner of an eye. The consul's last pause was for effect. The brief silence ended and Martínez chose the moment for his *coup de maître*.

"Here, Captain Brown," he said, placing an official letter before Jeremiah, "is proof of Mexican sincerity. A letter from Señor Rubio of Vera Cruz, expressing the views of *El Presidente* himself."

Jeremiah read, learning that Santa Anna greatly desired the services of the man who thwarted his plans at Matamoros; that in compliance with His Excellency's wishes, Minister Tornel was ready to offer J. H. Brown the finest vessel of the Mexican Navy and to address him as Commodore of the Fleet.

Martínez smiled his appreciation of a fact. "Odd, isn't it, that the reward you so richly deserve should come from the enemy?"

"Yes," Jeremiah replied with more bitterness than he realized.

The consul had cleverly sent the thrust home. As his brows lifted in anticipation of victory, Carmela lowered her cup in surprise.

Jeremiah frowned over the letter, placed it aside once before reaching for it again. "This is quite a proposition, Señor Martínez. But how do I know that the moment I set foot in Vera Cruz I wouldn't be rushed off to the dungeons of Perote?"

The consul chuckled. "I will not be trapped into voicing a reply to a man who thrives on risk in its most exciting form. As Buffon said, 'Chance is the ruler of the universe.'"

"He was right." Jeremiah looked at Carmela. "Commodore of the 'Handsome Fleet.' How does it sound to you, Carmela?"

The excitement of old entered her face as he suggested pictures to dazzle her. Here was position and fame, her look seemed to say; here was the top of the ladder. But she was wise enough not to put these things into words as she began to eye him suspiciously. Martínez was demanding by stern look that she make a proper reply. Trapped, she said in defiance to both of them as she replied to Jeremiah:

"I don't know whether to answer the commodore of the Mexican Navy or the captain from Texas."

Jeremiah got to his feet. "The captain, Carmela."

Facing the consul, he said, "However much I desired the command of our fleet, Señor Martínez, the fact that I lost out on that score changes nothing. I could tell you of my devotion to a cause, but I won't. Instead, I'll thank you for excellent coffee and cigars and be on my way."

His glance slid on to Carmela. "Are you coming with me?"

Martínez saw the anxious look come into her face. His eyes flashed cruelly as he said politely, "Miss Ryan regrets that she must sail to meet her fiancé, whom she hopes to find enjoying position and—" he turned to Carmela "—the best of health."

She seemed to wilt under his stare.

The implied threat explained a lot of things to Jeremiah, though the fact that she had been the bait to lure him here at a time when he was beaten in spirit was by no means the greatest of these. For, looking at her now, he knew she was tangled hand and foot in a web from which she might never escape as long as she followed the star of Thompson.

3

It was past noon and he was walking toward the foot of Canal Street with his troubles. The moment he had turned his back on

Carmela every person and circumstance that had thwarted his efforts, hurt and discouraged him, seemed to leap aboard his weary mind. He could not go on thinking of Carmela, nor could he dwell on his promise to Mr. Leving—that he would not return without supplies— or the depressing news of Fannin's surrender and the elevation of Hawkins to the coveted office. He had never before known such frustration. Martínez had won at every turn. And now he should face it; Jeremiah H. Brown was thoroughly licked, ready to resign his command.

He paused and sat down on the steps of a small church to think. There were his farm and Polly and William to consider. He could not desert them. Better, he thought, to join Houston's army and fight for them. On the other side were the sea and Carmela. If only his father were alive to give him counsel. But he had done that, had quoted from the Book of James: *For that ye ought to say, if the Lord will, we shall live, and do this, or that.* God willing! Perhaps he had forgotten God.

The church was empty and he walked to the altar and got on his knees. All he asked was guidance, a way to turn. He arose and departed hurriedly, fearing the wrath of the Lord would descend upon a man who turned to heaven only as a last resort.

He was waiting for a boat to take him across the river when his purser arrived. Judging from his grin and the excitement in his face, one might think he was a bearer of good news. Jeremiah could hardly suppress a desire to order the grin stowed.

"Thank heavens we've found you, sir. Seems we'll have all supplies aboard by three o'clock. The powder is on its way now, and——"

"A moment, Mr. Wells. Just what the devil are you talking about?"

"The victuals and all, Captain. Believe me, warehouses are opening their doors for us on this day."

Somewhat exasperated by now, Jeremiah eyed the purser with more tolerance than he felt. "Now take it easy, Mr. Wells. It's only natural to get mixed up in the head once in a while. I got that way myself last night."

"Now did you, sir? If you were mixed up, how do you think we felt this morning when the first of the well-dressed gentlemen appeared on deck with your poster and forked over fifty dollars?"

"The hell you say!"

"The first of ten. That was a great stroke of genius on your part, sir. Mr. Leving and the others are still laughing. Certainly it sets a precedent in naval history, though better still, five hundred dollars and ten more men aboard are the answer to a prayer."

Jeremiah rubbed his chin thoughtfully. Providence had favored him that morning well in advance of his prayer. Perhaps the Lord anticipated the humble petitions of mortals. He looked at his ship across the river with new hope flooding his being, and then he turned his face toward New Orleans, the church and the Consulate, and tried to recall any mention of Carmela in his prayer.

Chapter Twenty-one

COMMODORE OF THE FLEET

The *Invincible* ran the pass late in the afternoon of Tuesday, March 29, and moved up the bay to Matagorda anchorage. She dipped her colors to the sister ships *Liberty*, *Brutus*, and *Independence*, and slid on to join them with the captain's single star and bars flying proudly. The "elite crew," as Mr. Leving called the recruits of Palm Sunday, were no more curious than Captain Brown, who looked ahead to a first meeting with the commodore with anticipation and dread.

Almost before the anchor splashed, his brother William sent a sailor from the *Liberty* with a letter and message advising that he would cross over shortly.

Polly's letter was a month old, written while he was in the Bay of Campeche. She was coming home to do what she could to help; perhaps it wouldn't be much but she could stay away no longer. Jeremiah decided she was probably in Velasco now. He read on:

> Harry is in the Gulf again. The U.S.S. *Warren*, you recall. He thinks highly of you, and I told him he should since he has asked me to marry him and must obtain your approval as well as Aunt Virginia's—if I should say yes. . . .

Jeremiah frowned. Odd, he had never thought about it, but he couldn't get used to her being in love.

A little later William came aboard. He had lost considerable weight. Hiding his concern, Jeremiah took his brother below and related the experiences of the past week in New Orleans, careful to put up the humorous side in an effort to draw a smile from William. The tight line about William's mouth failed to relax. He stared in a frowning, troubled way as though he had not heard, got up, and sat down again.

Jeremiah said, "So Polly is home again."

"She was. But she's caring for the sick and foraging food on the civilian retreat to Harrisburg."

"You mean Velasco is being evacuated?"

"Not on a big scale. But soon. Houston had no sooner declared his purpose to make the Colorado his line of defense than he marched down to Beason's Crossing with twelve hundred men. Then seven hundred Mexicans under Generals Sesma and Woll reached the Colorado. That was last Saturday. Know where Houston's army was on Sunday? At San Felipe on the Brazos."

Jeremiah could hardly believe this.

"It's true, Jerry. And there's mutiny in the army now. The men wished to fight the enemy. But worse than that, news just came from Velasco that Houston is going to burn the town of San Felipe."

Here was cause for alarm. The lower Brazos formed the heart of Texas, and Houston was backed up to it with Santa Anna's armies which he refused to fight on the march. Trailing the Texan force, slowing it, were hundreds of homeless women and children. This was enough to sadden William, though Jeremiah suspected something more personal was the cause.

"You've lost weight, William. What's wrong?"

"Nothing, I hope. I haven't felt the same since the Mexican cruise. Then father's death. Seems everything is happening."

"What, for instance?"

"Jerry, I'm resigning my command."

"Sure. Sure," Jeremiah smiled. "That's what I said last Saturday night. We all feel that way at times. But what prompted your decision?"

"Commodore Hawkins." William's anger was on the ascent again. He slammed fist into palm and tried to keep the overflowing mist out of his eyes. "He came here with the idea he was superior to God, thought he could run roughshod over everybody.

"Yesterday he called a meeting of his commanders, Hurd and

myself, and proceeded to rip you up one side and down the other for being in New Orleans. When I had all I cared to hear and spoke up for you, he told me to shut my 'goddam' mouth. Which I did until he opened a discussion on strategy. He solicited my opinion, mind you, and I very respectfully questioned the advisability of keeping the fleet bottled up here while Mexican supply ships were moving toward our coast. He tore into me again, and when I spoke out hotly he said I was guilty of insubordination and clapped me in irons.

"So I'm resigning."

William's indignation seemed entirely justified, and Jeremiah felt himself burning with an overwhelming desire to punish Hawkins with his bare fists. But he knew the futility of violence and he felt responsible for his brother's future in the service.

"This is no time to quit," he said. "We've got to consider what we're fighting for, not the man we're fighting under. And that's the way it's going to be."

Studying him intently, William replied, "Very well, I'll abide by that, Jerry, if you still feel the same this time tomorrow."

Several minutes later the commodore's messenger boarded the *Invincible* and presented a written order: Captain J. H. Brown should report forthwith to his superior officer. It appeared to be unduly crisp. Suspecting that William's acquaintance with the commodore's methods had prompted his conditional promise, Jeremiah realized that he must hold his own temper in the meeting ahead; for it was evident that he carried the future of the Brown brothers in the hollow of his hand.

Jeremiah made the crossing to the *Independence* with Lieutenants Leving, Sevey, and Newman, as well as his purser. Rigged out in fresh uniforms, brass buttons polished and gleaming, they boarded the flagship and awaited the commodore's pleasure. The crew lined the deck at attention, and the ship's bell struck the hour of six. The *Invincible's* officers were kept waiting.

Commodore Hawkins appeared on deck, a tall, slender man of thirty-six. He was not only handsome but dashing. His jet-black hair seemed to intensify the dark eyes, to sharpen them as he critically examined another batch of officers not of his selection. It was difficult to conceal admiration for this man of recognized physical courage even though his expression reminded Jeremiah of a judge about to pronounce sentence. He went through the formality of handshaking without saying a word, then stood apart with hand on sword, smiling derisively.

"So you finally returned," he said, staring from one to the other. "In the future any commander of this fleet will think twice before going on a pleasure cruise. For your information, I'm prepared to fashion a navy out of the material at hand. And I promise all of you, ex-coasters included, some navy discipline before I'm done with you."

His glance shifted from Jeremiah's face to the *Invincible* and back again. "Now may I ask just what you mean by flying a single star and stripes atop a ship of this fleet?" Calling up one of his lieutenants, he said, "Board the *Invincible* and bring the flag to me."

Jeremiah spoke out then. "That happens to be my personal flag."

Hawkins thrust his head forward and narrowed his eyes on Jeremiah. "You omit the 'sir.' "

"I haven't heard you call me Captain or Mr. Brown yet."

"All right, Captain Brown. You have your proper address. Though warned of what to expect from you, I gave you the benefit of doubt until reports of your dramatic and vainglorious attempt to blockade Vera Cruz proved conclusively your aspirations to quick fame in defiance to orders handed you prior to the Mexican cruise. You are not the navy, but a part of it. And the purpose of this fleet is not to play at games to glorify any individual or to shape its strategy on whims."

Jeremiah stiffened and trembled with rage. Sail hands, marines, even the powder monkeys, were witnessing his humiliation. Hawkins needed a lesson in manners, one which Jeremiah could deal out in a hurry. But Hawkins would survive that and laugh last, for he had made it plain that the resignation of the Brown brothers was the thing he wanted most.

"My apologies, sir," Jeremiah said.

"Accepted, Captain Brown, but only after you do a stint in the brig for insubordination."

The two hours of confinement were the darkest in Jeremiah's life. There had been an acceptable reason for his stay in the hold of Thompson's *Correo de Mejico*. That was the enemy. This ship was a part of the navy he had dreamed of and helped bring about and now served to the very best of his ability. Hawkins wasn't interested in the heartaches and defeats he had known in New Orleans, or in the fact that the *Invincible* almost failed to return. He did not care to establish reasons for a patriot's conduct at Vera Cruz and Matamoros. But he knew the results. The Brown brothers had rendered a service to Texas. Hawkins resented these things. He wished to rid the Navy of the Browns, to take over the crack ship *Invincible*. And this was his way of forcing their resignations.

The two hours ended and Jeremiah walked between lieutenants to the commodore's quarters, where Captains Hurd and William Brown and Commodore Hawkins awaited his presence. Hurd could not quite conceal his pleasure any more than William could hide anger and curiosity. In Hawkins's face, Jeremiah detected satisfaction and malice.

"Now, Captain Brown, before we settle down to a long awaited conference of commanders, I must ask if you have taken advantage of the privacy made possible to you by reaching any new decision regarding your future."

William looked tense, Hurd squinted an eye almost shut, and Hawkins leaned forward expectantly. Jeremiah could imagine Hurd's eagerness to inherit the *Independence* and the commodore's hopes of reshuffling his navy.

"None whatever, sir," Jeremiah replied.

William stared with disbelief and Hurd and Hawkins sat back to eye the unpredictable J. H. Brown thoughtfully. Tensions gathered and fell away.

"Very well," Hawkins said, sheathing the fire in his black eyes. "Sit down and join us, Captain Brown, while we peruse the *Invincible's* papers and reach an understanding on matters pertaining to naval conduct." After a moment in which he frowned over a stack of papers, he looked up. "This is not my idea of a good joke, Captain Brown. The solicitation of passengers aboard a Texas ship-of-war has made a laughingstock of the Texas Navy."

"With your indulgence, sir, I believe the facts will cause you to take a different view of the case."

"Proceed," Hawkins said impatiently.

Jeremiah told the story, from his efforts to secure supplies to the Mexican consul's proposition, admitting having drunk a great deal, omitting only the reason for it, that and Carmela's part in the affair. "Therefore, sir, I am inclined to believe that the joke is on Martínez."

Hawkins could not suppress an expression that seemed to declare he was shaping fresh estimates of a resourceful captain. But under his steady attention, Jeremiah thought he had found the key to the other's enmity. By their principles of action which always compelled them on, they were too much alike to ever be friends. This seemed borne out by what Hawkins said next.

"You will refund passage money to each of the ten who paid you, ship the lot back to New Orleans, and cause to be published in newspapers of that city an open apology to the service you represent."

"Yes, sir. Begging your pardon, but since I spent the money for supplies, I must ask the Navy for it."

Thwarted, Hawkins shook a finger and raised his voice. "By God, you know the money situation!"

The commodore dropped the subject in a hurry, though he peered closely for any sign of amusement in Brown's face. "Nor will there be any more ransoming of towns without express orders. This Navy is not a freebooter's paradise."

Hurd grunted. "Now, Commodore, there are times when theft is excusable. A crew must eat, sir."

"Naturally. Naturally."

And so it went for an hour. They charted enemy waters, examined the possible movements by sea of Santa Anna's supply ships, all against the rising fear that further retreat of Houston's army would force the enemy to establish supply bases at Matagorda and the mouth of the Brazos. Therefore the Navy should remain here to meet the attacking war vessels and hold the coast.

Jeremiah felt the necessity of pretense and politics. "Commodore Hawkins, as a Texan who knows every bay and inlet along the coast, I must admit you have a good plan, one likely to extend Santa Anna's line of supply until it hurts."

"Aye." Hawkins's face thawed into an expression resembling geniality. "Continue, Captain Brown."

"Thank you, sir. Now with your permission, I'll venture a guess as to what you are going to say next. I base my guess on your experience, which I envy, sir, that you plan to check any hostile naval movement by sending one of us out on patrol."

Jeremiah did not miss the look of disgust in William's face.

The commodore's eyes thinned to slits. Then he pursed his lips thoughtfully and said, "Captain Brown, as much as I hate to admit it, you are correct in your surmise. I deem it advisable to dispatch the

Invincible on a patrol cruise down the coast. You will prepare to sail by tomorrow noon at the latest."

He held out his hand. Taking it, Jeremiah glanced at his private flag hanging from a bracket. "Sir, may I have my ensign?"

Hawkins bristled and said, "Hell no!"

During the crossing to their ships, William said, "Jerry, you made me sick to my stomach with your 'yes, sir' and 'I base my guess on your experience, sir, which I envy.' *Which you envy!* The Jerry Brown I knew as my big brother wouldn't let any man spit on him, let alone rub it in."

Jeremiah sat it out. William wouldn't understand that he had swallowed a hurt for his benefit and kowtowed to the martinet of the fleet in order that at least one of the Brown brothers might continue to serve Texas on the open sea instead of riding anchor in wait for the enemy.

2

Matagorda next morning was a scene of confusion. Jeremiah was denied entrance to a store because the merchant was frantically piling goods on wagons behind his establishment. Ox wagons rolled to the water's edge and women with crying children appealed to boatmen for passage to Galveston or Louisiana. Armed citizens patrolled the streets to keep down looting during the hurried evacuation of the town. A pretty young wife with dark brown ringlets under a bonnet was begging a schoonerman to take her son aboard even if he could not find room for her. "Just as far as the Brazos, please!" The lad sniveled and his nose dripped. The seaman said his boat was overloaded. Horses and cows were herded through the mud, pointing toward the Brazos. An enterprising trader offered the owner a small sum for the cows and grinned when it was accepted. Ten minutes later he tried to sell them to Captain Hurd at a premium. The *Brutus* needed beef, and so did the army, though the trader demanded cash. Farther on, a wagon broke down and a little old woman got down from the seat and buried her face in her hands.

The word had come. General Urrea was marching fast for Matagorda. But worse news was responsible for the cries of women and children:

Colonel Fannin had surrendered at discretion, thereby placing his band of four hundred and twenty Anglo-Americans at the mercy of the Mexican Government. The people of Matagorda had known this for several days. But late last night the fate of these men had been made known. Santa Anna had ordered the execution of all prisoners, and on the morning of Palm Sunday Fannin's men were divided into three groups, marched out on the prairie, and shot. Shot legally, according to the Mexican law that said all men bearing arms against Mexico were outlaws and pirates. Thirty ran for their lives, but few escaped. The bodies were piled up and burned. The west was conquered, the road to the east was open to the dictator.

Jeremiah could not forget the morning of Palm Sunday. While Consul Martínez was offering him command of the Mexican fleet, firing squads were soaking the prairies of Goliad in blood. Fannin had asked the Mexicans not to shoot him in the head, only to be rewarded with a bullet in the brain. And Santa Anna wished to address J. H. Brown as Commodore of his fleet. These things were not imagined. They were as real as the panic he was witnessing now. A house was burning in the distance. The pretty young wife was a widow, her son an orphan since Sunday. All in the wake of the cockfight in the Vieux Carré; the Alamo and Goliad. The cattle were now moving toward a schooner and the trader was counting his money and profit. A gun went off somewhere. Everything, every sound, movement, and expression, was a part of the whole tragedy.

Jeremiah turned away, grim but determined. If experience, trouble, and humiliation had failed to condition him for the job ahead, the scenes of tragedy made up the difference. He would cut the Gulf into ribbons and foam in a war of vengeance upon Mexico and all who served her.

Chapter Twenty-two

BATTLE OF THE RIO GRANDE

At nine o'clock on the morning of April the third, there was perhaps no more peaceful setting in the Gulf of Mexico than the deck of the *Invincible*. The officer of the watch stood aft with hands behind his back while listening to a chanty rising from the men up forward. The quartermaster's mate picked up the tune and hummed it almost in Lieutenant Newman's ear. Gunner Franson held his attention, however. The waist swivel was giving him trouble in gunnery drills, forcing a reduced charge of powder on account of the recoil. If the order came to double-shot it, no sane man would wish to stand aft the damn thing. Oh well, it might be days or weeks before they engaged the enemy. On the other hand, there was no telling, since the mouth of the Rio Grande lay over the horizon.

Mr. Newman rubbed his long nose with a forefinger and thought of the day, which was Easter. Last year at this time, he was rigging out in his Sunday best to go with his wife and mother to church in Savannah. Today Captain Brown would say services and the men would lounge about enjoying freedom from drills.

He looked out over the water. The trade that whipped across the Gulf earlier in the day was backing, though the low clouds that had walled off the sunrise continued to stretch from dawn position to the zenith. Off the starboard beam at seven, the lookouts had sighted a streak of slate gray. The *Invincible* had raised Padre Island rapidly and put it down her starboard side before nine. And now a squall was running in to envelop the island and the ship was buffeting her way to windward, bows dipping spray, rising and falling to the scend of the waves in easy rhythm.

Mr. Leving came on deck smiling. "A fine Easter morning, Mr. Newman," he said, taking in the weather and top hamper. "We should be sighting the Brazos Santiago soon."

"Aye, sir. And if we know the Mexican, he'll crowd the cathedrals today instead of shaking out goosewings and loosing tops'ls."

Lieutenant Leving squinted his eyes for a search of the horizon. "Maybe yes and maybe no, Mr. Newman."

"Sail ho!" It rang down from the maintop.

"Where away?" the deck replied.

"Two points off the lee bow on the low horizon, sir."

"How does she sail?"

"Clawing offshore, sir, appearin' to be makin' little easting."

A quarter hour later the lookout called the deck: "Two of sail!" Both ships appeared to be making out from the bar at first, then all of a sudden nearly all sail was taken in. Mr. Leving whistled up a boy and sent him running with the news to Captain Brown.

The ship's bell was striking the hour of ten when Jeremiah appeared on deck in fresh white trousers and a new blue coat. He surveyed decks and weather with quick sweeping glances. The men wore their cleanest, as he had ordered for Easter, and the trade wind was veering from south to east-southeast.

"My telescope, Howell." Jeremiah swung himself handily into the shrouds and climbed. Halfway up, he crooked an arm about a tarred rope and raised the glass.

Far to the south stood two ships. In the bright fall of sunlight now touching the Mexican coast, flashes were mirrored from the larger vessel's deck. Since it was his business to suspect every vessel in these waters, he was asking if the reflection emanated from the muzzles of carronades. That being possible, the ship was an enemy fighter. All considered, he was closing with her a little too fast. Better, he thought, to move out from land in order to hold the wind advantage until the stranger was identified.

"Haul your wind," he called down. Soon the *Invincible* responded to Mr. Abbott's booming orders by bringing her head around to eastward and on the other tack. Properly harnessed, she ran on toward the brown patch of water that marked the river's mouth.

Joining his officers, he said, "We may hold Easter services over our nine- and eighteen-pounders. She could be a Mexican gun brig with ship in convoy."

He admitted it was purely a guess at this distance, though another two hours at most would decide whether or not the *Invincible* was about to engage a Mexican warship for the first time. The Lord knew how much he hoped to get at the enemy and send news of victory home to hearten Texans in their hour of distress.

"So, gentlemen, we'll be ready. It is now half-past ten. Mr. Leving, you'll clear the decks, stow all loose fittings so as not to impede action, lay out small arms, and rely on Mr. Newman to conn the weather, enemy, and any chance sail from the sea half around. Mr. Sevey, attend the magazine, see that we're prepared to keep powder and shot moving, monkey boys alert, and lay out ample langrage and grape—I want the enemy butchers to feel us. Mr. Franson, secure breechings, sand your decks, ready the gun crews, and——"

The stream of orders continued. When done, Jeremiah said:

"Maybe it's all left-handed to an old navy man like you, Mr. Leving."

The other grinned. "I believe even an Academy man who hasn't wet a foot might grasp the general idea, sir."

At a quarter-past eleven, the decks were clear. All the essentials of battle were in evidence. Captain Brown was ready to forego the old game of cat and mouse and get down to the grim business of fighting. But as yet there was no assurance that the fine ship ahead was an enemy war vessel. Topmen reported to deck constantly. The *Invincible* was opening the mouth of the Rio Grande, bringing the channel and pair of ships to bear four points on the starboard bow. The lead was sounding, the wind and weather were the same, the officers and crew waiting, watching.

As was his habit under mounting tension, Jeremiah stood apart from his officers and stared reflectively at water and sky. One thought led to another, on to Matagorda and the last letter from Polly. Written from Chocolate Bayou on the road to Harrisburg was a tale of suffering refugees fighting rain and swollen streams in their flight from the advancing Mexicans.

Jeremiah looked up quickly. The masthead was saying, "Twenty-two sail in sight up the river and no end of small boats." And Mr. Sevey voiced surprise: "That's a lot of activity for the Matamoros roadstead, isn't it?" "A devil of a lot," replied Mr. Leving with emphasis.

But Polly's letter had contained a request that cut him to the quick. She wished to see him and ask his advice on a matter important to her future, but this being impossible, she must use this method of asking his blessing on her engagement to marry Lieutenant Harry Billings in August. He remembered his reply—he wished her happiness. And though he had no objection to her making a good marriage, none whatever, his mood had matched the elements as he worked through Paso Caballo in a downpour of rain.

The ship's bell jarred the air with eight strokes noon. The last note had scarcely faded away when the forward lookout cried, "She's armed and flying the Mexican flag."

Jeremiah straightened instantly. The crew tensed and all aboard looked to him for the order to close and engage. But the captain very casually raised his glass and checked everything in sight. Then he turned and eyed Lieutenant Leving thoughtfully and said:

"There's too much traffic between here and Matamoros. And there's probably a clue in all this activity to Santa Anna's next move."

He was opposite the bar now and the enemy war vessel was inshore of him. He had the wind, the advantage, the opportunity.

"We'll stand closer in."

There was a glint of adventure in his eyes as he faced Mr. Leving. "How presentable is your American naval uniform?" With the reply, he said, "This is not an order, but I'd like to send you aboard the Mexican ship as an American officer to learn what's afoot. Under the pretext of being outraged over the changes in port regulations and the many irritations to which American Consul Smith has been subjected, you can raise considerable hell and keep your ears open."

Leving smiled his consideration of the idea. "But—how do you know these conditions exist?"

"I've never heard of the opposite in Mexican ports."

As the lieutenant stuck out his hand, Jeremiah spoke a warning: "Failure means your capture, Mr. Leving. Perhaps I'd better go."

"Sir, it's my pleasure. Besides my uniform wouldn't fit you."

The *Invincible* made a bold stand in. Flying the bunting of the United States, and resembling the former Revenue Cutter *Ingham*, her disguise seemed perfect. Within easy range of the Mexican warship a boat was lowered and Mr. Leving departed on a mission he seemed to relish.

Jeremiah looked on as the boat shoved off to the creaking of oarlocks. The blades were feathered in naval fashion at the end of each timed stroke. Leving, God bless him, was making a smart approach to the enemy. A twinge of uneasiness flashed through Jeremiah, and with it came the realization that William Leving had much in common with John Bailey——

It would be difficult to replace him on his deck or in his heart.

2

A period of tense waiting followed. Jeremiah looked at his watch anxiously. Leving had been aboard the enemy eighteen minutes. He walked forward, strode aft, and fished out his watch. Twenty-two minutes had gone by. Wincing and favoring his leg, he was about to address Mr. Kelton with a sharp complaint about his surgery when he saw a man getting into the *Invincible's* boat.

"About time," he grumbled.

He stood out a minute, debating on whether to send for his stick or go below himself. Choosing the latter, he left the deck. Once in his quarters he sat down to rest his leg and speculate on the success of Leving's mission. There was no denying that some big movement was being pushed in Matamoros with greater zeal than was common to the Mexican people. And since it was concentrated at Mexico's most northern port, it was more than likely maritime in aspect. In his mind was a picture of the Texas coast, defenseless except for the three schooners-of-war which Hawkins threatened to keep bottled up in Matagorda Bay. Texas was in enough trouble without fresh Mexican regulars——

"Who can land anywhere west of Matagorda."

Impatient of the lieutenant's return with the secret of enemy activity, he arose and moved toward the deck. He was emerging into the open when something reached his ears that caused him to stop in his tracks. The man who had left the enemy deck had not been

Leving. In the *Invincible's* gig was a Mexican officer. He was addressing Mr. Sevey while making his way to the deck:

"We lost our rudder in crossing the bar and are shipping a new one. Otherwise the *Bravo* would be standing up the coast for Texas with the *Correo Segundo* in convoy. But since we are fortunate enough to be able to serve you, Captain Espino requests the privilege of sending your officer ashore, where he may register his complaints before the proper port authorities."

The officer was now on deck. And the voice Jeremiah heard was Thomas M. Thompson's.

Jeremiah cursed his luck. As much as he desired Thompson's capture, he was the last man in the world he wanted aboard at this time. If he caught on, as he probably had already, their disguise would be blown to kingdom come and Lieutenant Leving would be caught in a trap. He was gripping his cane, and praying that Thompson had not noticed the difference in Leving's and Sevey's uniforms or the many disparities between the decks of Texan and United States naval vessels, even as he cocked an ear and waited for Mr. Sevey's reply. But Sevey, damn his slow tongue, was standing out an awkward silence. As if in answer to Jeremiah's urgent wish, the lieutenant said:

"Extend my compliments and sincere thanks to Captain Espino, and inform him of my decision to forego formal protest until I reach Matamoros."

Jeremiah heaved a sigh of relief. "Good old Sevey." His elation was brief. Sobering, he asked if this would satisfy Thompson. He had to know. If Thompson had seen through the ruse, he must not be allowed to depart; and even if he failed to reveal any knowledge of the scheme, there was no assurance that it remained their secret. With these things in mind, he stole a peep at the deck and Thompson.

The lieutenant of the *Bravo* was fingering his jaw and darting glances all about the ship. There was no longer doubt; Thompson was wise. Any other officer might have been deceived; not this one. Jeremiah could only ponder the strange workings of fate, for of all the gold braid in the Mexican Navy, he had drawn Thompson. With no choice left to him, he stepped into the open with the sad realization that he was probably trading man for man with Mexico.

Thompson showed no surprise when Jeremiah appeared on deck. He made a mock bow and smiled in his superior manner as he heard the order, "Place that man under arrest."

When Thompson failed to return, the Mexican commander naturally became suspicious. Aboard the *Invincible* growing concern for Leving's safety was felt. Any hope of effecting an exchange of lieutenants was pinned to the slim chance that Captain Espino being without rudder would be amenable to reason. The proposition was soon placed before the *Bravo's* commander, whose refusal was based on the fact that he held prisoner an enemy officer who, by act of impersonating an American, was a spy. And, since Lieutenant Thompson was merely a prisoner of war, and entitled to consideration as such, Mexico was satisfied to gain a spy in the exchange.

The game was up. The American colors were replaced by the 1824 flag above the *Invincible*, and Jeremiah promptly informed Espino of his intention to come and rescue his officer to the regret of all aboard the *Bravo* unless Lieutenant Leving reached his ship safe and sound within the quarter hour.

Captain Espino to Captain Brown: I appeal to your sense of sportsmanship. Allow me time to finish shipping my rudder.

Captain Brown to Captain Espino: I promise the same kind of fair play your military gave Texans at Goliad.

The minutes ticked by. Jeremiah looked at his crew, seeing every man at his station ready and eager. Estimating the *Bravo's* distance from the bar and her chances of running inside under the protecting guns of the fort, he ordered some sail on. The *Correo Segundo* was already crossing the bar to safety.

"Eleven minutes gone," he said. "Double-shot your swivels, Mr. Franson. Round shot."

Three minutes remained and Captain Espino showed no signs of lowering a boat. Instead he was bracing his yards around for a drive to windward. By so doing he might achieve either one of two things, make the channel inbound or eat the *Invincible* out of the wind. Though he must have a rudder to do either.

"One minute more. Bring your guns to bear. Now take good aim at her top hamper."

The *Bravo* was getting a way under her. She luffed up, headed the wind in half-board fashion, a maneuver that shot her into the wind. Gunners and sailors aboard the *Invincible* appeared taut. This was war vessel meeting war vessel, the first real engagement. Feeling the tenseness aboard, his own as well, Jeremiah ordered little Gregno Dedony to roll the drums. The Frenchman was a master at it. He played a symphony, low, higher, then faster, timing his crescendo to the end of that minute.

"Now fire!"

The guns roared in quick succession and leaped back against restraining tackles. The ship rolled to the jarring recoil. The medium eighteens had spoken fair and true. The lower sail on the *Bravo's* fore was ripped asunder.

"She's slowed but still moving," Jeremiah observed. "Sponge and reload with grape. We'll tear the last sail and spar off her." So saying, he gave the order to let go the nine-pound carronades, "Bear on her hull now!"

Quoins were jerked free and, with less elevation, the guns spurted a broadside, throwing shot horizontally across the water. All low, all falling short of their mark in an extravagant waste of precious powder and shot. "At that distance!" Jeremiah exclaimed reprovingly.

The *Invincible* was sliding gently forward, angling inshore, her starboard battery still bearing on the approaching *Bravo* when puffs of black smoke issued from the latter's deck. Round shot splashed the water fifty feet off the starboard beam.

"Excellent, Captain Espino!" Jeremiah cried, his attention now upon his sweating, black-faced gunners. The swivels were ready and waiting, though he was holding their charges of deadly grape to rake Espino's deck.

The lookouts aloft reported seas clear of sail and the leadsman droned out the mark and the deep. The water was losing fathoms, and the sailing master showed concern. But Captain Brown was timing the overheating of his guns to the moment he would put about and bring his larboard battery into action.

Then came an ugly sound no man could get used to. A Mexican ball screamed through the rigging in a sizzling streak, tearing a gaping hole in a sail on the fore, cutting halyards and shrouds like a knife. The enemy had the range of him now, and Jeremiah decided the time had come to put in and come about for the grand finale.

He gave the order. As the *Invincible's* head pointed toward the mouth of the Rio Grande, the wind on her beam sent her dashing forward in a gallant inshore charge designed to cut off the enemy's retreat and at the same time close with him at short range. Captain Espino, wise to the maneuver, hurriedly threw up his larboard side in a frantic effort to stave off the attack, but in doing so he was forced to gamble heavily by shoaling his water close by the bar. Jeremiah held his breath, hoping the *Bravo* would run aground on the north beach, where he could hammer her to pieces.

The leadsman was crying out shallow fathoms, each drawing the *Invincible* closer to the danger of grounding, when Jeremiah cried, "Now! Put the wind over the larboard quarter!"

The *Invincible* cut a scimitar wake from southeast around to north, narrowing the distance between the ships to less than two hundred yards. And Captain Espino was hemmed in between Texan guns and shallow water. The time had come. The *Bravo* had backed to the limits of safety and was taking in sail, working, working now, to keep her guns trained on the moving *Invincible*.

"Now! All together!" Jeremiah shouted. "Fire!"

The roar that followed shook every spar and plank aboard. The swivels vomited showers of deadly grape toward the *Bravo's* deck and bulwarks; the nine-pounders blasted at the rigging and the sixes at the hull. As the smoke writhed off on the wings of the wind, cheers rent the air. The *Bravo* had been raked from bow to stern. Her foremast was hanging crazily at the doubling one second, crashing down in a tangle of rigging to the deck the next. Two guns were knocked out. When the noise of celebration died down, the screams of the wounded rolled across the water. The gun brig slewed around and rocked.

"Reload!" The order rang loud and clear. There would be no mercy on this day. None asked, none given.

Mexicans lined the south beaches to watch the battle. The yard-arms of ships inside the bar were heavy with sailors. Now the excited populace was running up almost to within range of the Texan guns.

The *Invincible* took in her sails and coasted ahead of her idling wake; and the *Bravo*, to the admiration of Jeremiah and the officers, worked herself around to present her starboard guns. Then she loosed two of them, bare seconds ahead of the next Texan volley. She fired langrage, scraps of iron, glass, bolts, and nails; at close range!

The air screamed and whistled with flying metal. Aimed too high, but damaging nevertheless. The *Invincible's* top hamper was raked from forward to aft. Spars leaped up and splinters hurtled through the rigging and rained down on deck. Lieutenant Newman smothered a cry and caught at his arm. A shaft of wood had pierced his bicep. Blood gushed and Mr. Kelton leaped toward him. Two gunners had been struck by flying splinters and the quartermaster's mate by a ricocheting piece of scrap that opened a hole in his calf.

Close upon the first volley, the remaining three Mexican guns spat while the range held. Once more the deathly shriek of shot and langrage over the ocean sent shudders running up the spines of the Texans.

"Down! We're being raked!" It sounded too late. Chain and bar shot and heavy round tore across decks like a scythe. The number three gun leaped up. Thrown backward off the carriage, it pinned a sailor under it. He jerked spasmodically and threw out a hand. That was all. Wood flew and blocks fell to the deck. Pins were hurtled up and came raining down. One struck the foot of a sailor, smashing it into a bloody pulp. But not a man would ever forget the picture of the boatswain's yeoman. A heavy ball went right through him. Even with the hole in him, he remained on his feet an instant, as though trying to keep his balance. Blood ran toward the center of the deck.

Jeremiah tore his eyes from the body and yelled, "Fire!" Next he cried, "For God's sake, Mr. Abbott, swing our bows around!"

The *Invincible* fired her last four-gun broadside under the shower from aloft. The enemy gun brig caught in full down the side. Her exposed deck, hull, rail, and booms lurched with a rending of wood. The bowsprit swayed and a heavy yard crashed to her deck. Shouts and cries mingled with the sounds of cracking timbers as her bowsprit bent to the water like a splitting tree.

The battered *Bravo* had run aground and the crew was abandoning ship, taking to the boats under the shelter of her opposite side. Victory belonged to the Texans, though the item they had fought to retrieve was lost to them. Captain Espino was taking Mr. Leving with him.

Chapter Twenty-three

THE BRIG POCKET

Jeremiah had scarcely given the order to pound the *Bravo* to pieces at the water line when the lookout cried a sail breaking the eastern horizon. Whirling, he looked out over the sunlit Gulf and saw the square foreroyal of a ship of size.

"All sail!" he cried. "Lively and handsome now, or the enemy may catch us where we put the *Bravo!*"

With half the crew running the ratlines under orders to set sail in the wind, splice halyards, and rig purchases for hoisting spars, the other half clearing the decks of debris, the *Invincible* swung her head about for a dash to the open sea and a meeting with the oncoming stranger. Once she got a good way under her, the jacks hit the deck and hustled about to ready the ship for battle the second time that day.

They formed a smart crew now, Jeremiah admitted as he moved down the aisle between hot guns. He was proud of them and his pride showed in his face. If only they were all alive. But he should be thankful that his loss was small. Such admissions were necessarily brief, since the vessel he was standing out to meet had her hull up over horizon.

"Mr. Wells, order double rations of grog to every man."

He turned to look at the *Bravo* again. The picture he saw called for an artist's sketch entitled "Defeat," a picture for the eyes of Santa Anna, Tornel, and his officers. Although he had no artist aboard there was in his possession an officer of the Mexican Navy. "Mr. Newman, have our prisoner brought on deck."

Looking out over the water, he recalled Carmela's expression of defeat at the Mexican Consulate in New Orleans and his own grim realization that her bondage sprang from the fact that Martínez held Thompson's safety over her head. He remembered also his silent prayer that the future would provide a means of releasing her from this threat. And now that he held Thompson captive, she was actually free. Thompson was therefore very important to him personally. However, a week brought changes. Last Sunday he would have given a year of his life to free Thompson from any Mexican danger in order to release her, and today the accomplishment of just that very thing evoked small elation. Actually he felt cheated, tricked. Victory was in a sense mock victory, for he had traded Mr. Leving for Thompson.

Thompson was marched on deck between two marines and brought up sharp before Jeremiah. He stood at attention a moment before relaxing in a manner that emphasized his opinion of the captor and all he represented. His composure galled Jeremiah, who said nothing as he moved to the rail and pointed in the direction of the *Bravo*. If he expected surprise and alarm in Thompson's face, he was disappointed, for the prisoner's glance was lazy and brief, accompanied by a light laugh.

"Captain Brown, had I been in command here I would have damaged the enemy beyond repair." He spoke with a cool arrogance designed to infuriate. "But of course to a man lacking in naval experience——" He paused to let the inference carry itself.

Jeremiah held his temper.

Thompson produced a cigar, eyed it, then smiled up at Jeremiah. "An entertaining little game we're playing, eh, Captain? First I capture you. Next you capture me. And now you've done it again, which makes you one up on me."

"I'm way behind you, Lieutenant. Your bullet caught me in the leg at Vera Cruz. But I'll catch up."

"Really, old chap! But are we discussing war or something more personal?"

"Both. For your information, Consul Martínez is forcing Carmela to remain in this dangerous game under the threat of what he can do to you."

"Carmela, you say?" Thompson's brows lifted and he looked amused. "You mean my fiancée Miss Ryan, of course."

Jeremiah looked at Lieutenant Newman. "Take him away."

Grinning, Thompson snapped to mock attention and marched away, leaving in his wake a thoroughly aroused captor gripping a walking stick in an effort to calm his uprising anger. Back and forth Jeremiah walked, his glance lifting into the rigging and falling to water and land. His mind seethed with resentment, directed less at the man who made a Texan victory appear as shallow as a renegade's loyalties and more at the indifferent suitor who gambled a woman's safety in a game for profit.

The ship ahead gave him something else to think about. The square sails of a two-master were coming up slowly, more like a merchantman than a man-of-war. But this could be a ruse. Knowing the roar of battle had reached out to the ship, that an enemy would use every advantage, Jeremiah ran up the American flag again and sailed close-hauled in order to come up with the wind in his favor. He ran on to windward, still dubious when the Stars and Stripes were sighted above the stranger. Scanning her under his telescope, he saw she sat the water loaded to her marks and carried no guns on deck other than a small bow chaser.

The *Invincible* was two hundred yards distant when Jeremiah made a trumpet of his hands and spoke her. Laying the ship across the other's path, he ordered the 1824 flag run up and the *Invincible* brought full into the wind. The Yankee put his sails aback and answered:

"The *Pocket*, Captain Howes, out of New Orleans on March twenty-eight and bound for Matamoros. Who are you?"

"Texan schooner-of-war *Invincible*. Stand by for boarding."

The captain said he was a New Englander under the American flag and would do no business with Texan pirates. His protest ended when one of the swivels was double-shotted and brought to bear on his poop. Jeremiah ordered a boat lowered and called upon Mr. Sevey to take three men aboard of the merchantman for a look at his papers and cargo. The lieutenant made the crossing and went below. Jeremiah waited.

Ten minutes passed before Midshipman Wate appeared on the

Pocket's deck and hailed his captain. "Lieutenant Sevey requests your presence aboard, sir. Captain Howes refuses to show his papers."

"Advise the lieutenant of my coming," Jeremiah replied.

In a boat moving toward the *Pocket*, he allowed his hopes free rein. If this big ship could be claimed as a legal prize of war, Texas could perhaps arm and feed her soldiers and homeless for some time. The thought persisted as he climbed to her deck and the waiting midshipman, who eagerly escorted him below decks.

Captain Howes was a long, gaunt-faced man with dark bushy brows and a nervous pair of eyes. Mumbling an acknowledgment of the Texan's presence, he reluctantly shoved a bottle and glass before Jeremiah, who thanked him and refused. The captain stared from his chief mate to Jeremiah and said this was an American vessel and her cargo was American property.

"I'll honor and respect your word, Captain Howes. However, you know the rules of war. I must see your papers."

"Suppose I jettisoned them?"

"Then you're automatically a prize of war, sir." Turning to Lieutenant Sevey, he said, "Make a check of the cargo."

He faced the obstinate Yankee captain. "You have one minute in which to produce your papers, sir."

Mouthing strong imprecations, the captain unlocked a chest and brought forth the ship's papers. Jeremiah examined them carefully, maintaining a silence that caused Captain Howes to squirm in his chair. In due course Lieutenant Sevey returned and gave Jeremiah a significant look.

Studying the manifest, Jeremiah said, "Now it seems that cargo on shipment is by order of and charged to Rubio and Company. That is Santa Anna's banker, Captain."

"American property, just the same."

"Sure. But premium is charged them and I see here they considered the cargo at their own risk. Mr. Sevey, the cargo reads——" He went down the list—barrels and barrels of flour, potatoes, and other provisions, including blankets, clothing, and a few luxuries—before looking up at Lieutenant Sevey. "And you found this true?"

"Aye, sir. But like the *Pelicano's* cargo, hundreds of barrels and crates contain powder, shot, and muskets. The discrepancy is worthy of your personal attention, sir. You never saw so much shot mixed with apples and coffee."

"Then she's sailing with a false manifest in favor of Lizardi and Company of New Orleans." Glancing up at the *Pocket's* master, who gripped the arms of his chair, he said, "Aren't you, sir?"

"I'm shipping American goods aboard an American ship." The statement seemed well rehearsed.

"I'll have a look," Jeremiah said, rising. He left Mr. Sevey in charge and made a tour with his midshipman. Pausing to whistle his surprise at finding as much as fifty barrels of powder out of one hundred labeled coffee, he went on. When the job was done, he said, "As sure as your name is Alf Wate, lad, Texas has chanced upon an Easter windfall."

Jeremiah returned to the captain's quarters and sat down. Captain Howes waited for a verdict. "The passenger list, Mr. Sevey," Jeremiah said. The lieutenant responded with:

"First, sir, a Lieutenant Don Carlos Ocampo."

"Ocampo? Why, he was Captain Tenorio's junior officer at Anáhuac! He was aboard the *Correo de Mejico* when I was clapped in irons. You'll fetch him here and search his quarters as well as those of the other passengers and officers. But read on."

"Lieutenants Hogan and Taylor and a——"

"Lieutenants? Who are they, Captain Howes?"

"I carry passengers," came the gruff reply. "They pay passage and I don't ask questions. And I still claim my cargo is American property."

Jeremiah stared at the upset master. "Probably some more officers on their way to Tornel's rapidly expanding navy, Mr. Sevey. By the way, you may as well assemble the passengers and ship's officers in the saloon and call upon Lieutenant Newman to send a searching crew aboard."

"Aye, sir, but there's another passenger."

"Search his quarters also," Jeremiah said, cutting him short. Next he turned his glance on the *Pocket's* captain.

"Captain Howes, I have duly examined your cargo and manifest and must advise that the *Pocket* sails under false papers and that your cargo does not correspond with the manifest and papers showing your clearance from the customhouse in New Orleans.

"Also, the twenty-third article of the Treaty of 1831 between the United States and Mexico states that provided either is at war vessels belonging to the other should be provided with sea letters belonging to citizens of that country. The treaty also provides that certificates of war should be furnished so as to show that cargo is not contraband of war.

"Captain, I have found neither sea letter nor certificate aboard of you. Without such papers, a vessel may be detained and adjudged by proper tribunal a legal prize."

Captain Howes snorted and gestured wildly. He knew the law, he said. But this was American property. "Is or was?" Jeremiah said.

"That be damned, Captain Brown! This is piracy, and you'll answer for it!"

Jeremiah lifted another paper and held it before the irate skipper. "What's this, Captain, if it isn't a contract to transport Mexican troops to Texas after your arrival at Matamoros?" There was no reply to this. "We'll look further, mister, since there's no telling what else we'll find."

The examination continued. A thorough search of the cabins of passengers and officers turned up one surprise after another. Confronted with evidence, Mr. Somers, the *Pocket's* second mate, admitted to holding a commission in the Mexican Navy. Lieutenants Hogan and Taylor could not deny they had recently accepted commissions in Tornel's war fleet. However, they were quick to inform Captain Brown that they were American citizens.

"All of a sudden you're Americans," Jeremiah said, glancing at the papers Lieutenant Sevey was excitedly placing before him. His eyes fell on charts of the Texas coast. They were accurate and drawn in detail, fathoms and bars and inlets and passes, by an expert. Looking up at Hogan and Taylor, he said, "So you're spies also."

"No, sir!" Hogan protested. "Lieutenant Thompson drew those charts."

"And look here!" Mr. Sevey exclaimed. "Dispatches to Santa Anna revealing the force on each Texan vessel! And here—the best mode of attacking Texas on land!"

"Sir, believe us, we're not spies. We did not carry that information. Your officer will tell you we didn't."

"Lies! But I promise a spy's reward to the carrier," Jeremiah said. "You men know the rules of war. A firing squad is too good for Americans who serve Santa Anna with maps and information to aid in the downfall of Texas."

Lieutenant Sevey spoke up then. "Sir, in my excitement, I forgot to tell you that these papers and charts were not found in their possession."

"No! Then where the devil did you find them? But wait. We'll deal with each thing as it falls. Place these men under arrest along with Lieutenant Ocampo and the second mate of this ship. And when that's done bring in the spy."

"Aye, sir. The captain of marines is waiting for these two in the saloon."

Sevey escorted the pair out and returned. Looking up sharply, Jeremiah asked if the culprit had flown. "No, sir. But you're due for a surprise," the officer said, preparing to open the door.

"Now am I, Lieutenant? I've suspected Captain Howes from the moment he——" Jeremiah stopped in midsentence and stared out of eyes suddenly grown wide. Utterly confounded, he groped for his stick, got to his feet, and then sank slowly to the chair again.

The spy ushered in was Carmela.

2

Carmela stood before him, golden-haired, sober, lovely, and guilty, and he could not remove his glance from her face. There she stood, woman and spy, representing at once something he had long desired and something he had long despised. One pulled against the other like adverse tides running strong. It was made worse by her quiet, imploring glance. And Mr. Sevey was looking on. Jeremiah lowered his eyes only to find them scanning a message:

On an upper arm in Galveston Bay lies New Washington. Troopships can approach to within . . .

She could have written this. Maybe she had not. But she carried it to Mexico, where it would be used to aid Santa Anna and hurt Texas.

Once the Brazos is in Mexican hands the back of Texas will be broken; and when the eastern march of Gaono's army closes the gateway from the east at Nacogdoches, and the fleet controls the Bay of Galveston, the province may be considered effectively subjugated.

These things and Carmela! He lifted a ravaged face and tried to compose his mind. Then he was saying, if only to be rid of a third person here, "Mr. Sevey, send Lieutenant Newman aboard with a prize crew to take over the *Pocket* and make sail for Matagorda."

"Aye, sir." He saluted and moved to the door.

"Mr. Sevey," Jeremiah said, and the lieutenant paused and stood out a brief silence. "Under the circumstances—that is, considering the effect of such an amazing haul of information, I suggest we say nothing about intercepting documents or spies."

"I understand, sir."

"No you don't, Mr. Sevey. I don't understand myself. Not yet. Now one thing more. Transfer our prisoner from the *Invincible* to the brig of this ship. I may need him in the course of my investigation."

The door closed and he found himself with only Carmela in an atmosphere of strained silence. He said, "You may be seated."

A rustle of silk followed and he was thinking of their nights in the Vieux Carré, and saying, "Fate works in a strange manner. Not four hours ago I found the way out for you. Or so I thought."

She toyed nervously with the lace edging her collar and looked curious. "What do you mean?"

"That success is all in a man's mind and only for a short moment." He drew his long mouth into a tight dry line.

"What was the way out, Jerry?"

"I'm not ready to divulge that," he replied, a hard light coming into his eyes. "First things first." He reached for Captain Howes's whisky, poured a brimful glass, and tossed it down. Watching her, glaring at the spy, pitying the woman, he drew her attention to the incriminating evidence.

"This had to happen to me, Carmela. Before my eyes are papers that would cause even the most hardened adventurer to shudder before accepting for delivery. And yet you, a mere woman, were running them as though they were blank sheets of paper. You knew what you were carrying, knew what you were doing. Didn't you?"

"I—suppose——" She broke off, staring at him with wide troubled eyes. Then she was standing and her back was turned.

"You could have quit after the Alamo. But you didn't. Even after the Goliad massacre you kept on. You sold the lives of your own people to the Mexicans for that new dress you're wearing.

"For the goddam renegade that's using you."

She whirled and he saw naked fear and shock unconcealed on her face. But he wasn't through with her.

"Living with your aunt, you ate the bread of San Felipe. You returned as Carmela Ryan and spied and went on to New Orleans and Mexico as the sweetheart of the Thompson who blockaded our coast. How long do you think it would take a court to make up its mind and say——"

"Don't, Jerry! Please!" There was panic in her face, though it was replaced by an expression of deep anxiety as she sat down.

"Don't, you say!" He brought his stick down hard across the table, startling her. "I said don't to you for years. About letting Thompson influence you. I said it to you at the Consulate a week back. About what you were doing. And when you're caught, you say to me—don't!"

He raised a paper and said, "Listen to this. It says here—'In order to stop the flow of goods and volunteers to Texas and at the same time expose the pirate army to attack from the east, the landing of the Matamoros troops on the New Orleans side of the Bay of Galveston——' That's what you're taking to Santa Anna."

"But I wasn't. Honest, Jerry! I intended to drop all but the charts overboard. I tried, but your man stopped me."

He laughed bitterly at this weak excuse. "Perhaps you can tell me what's going on at Matamoros."

"The Mexicans are concentrating a force of two thousand men to reinforce Santa Anna's armies by sailing to Galveston. Matamoros was placed under an embargo so the information would not leak out."

"An embargo. That explains a lot. But you knew this last Sunday."

"And I would have told you then but for the sudden appearance of Señor Martínez."

"But, dammit to hell, Carmela, you didn't! Can't you see the difference it makes? I can't stand before a court and swear to your good intentions any more than I can say I sailed to Matamoros on the strength of what you failed to tell me."

Her hand reached out to his and her lips parted. "You mean—actually, you wouldn't do this for me?"

He tensed instantly and searched her face for guile. It was not there and her look was not designed to gain favor. Then he felt the gentle pressure of her hand on his. Her touch and something half hidden, half revealed, that came out of her speaking eyes, surged through him like fire. He saw the choice before him, saw and recognized it with a painful clarity.

"I mean, Carmela, I actually wouldn't."

She stared at him, unwilling to believe what she had heard. Wordless, she dropped her glance, got up, and stood a moment before turning abruptly and seeking an open port. He watched her a long time, wishing it were possible to rub all this out as though it had never happened.

Moving to the exit, he paused and, because he could not help it, placed a reassuring hand on her shoulder. She half turned to him and he saw her attempt a smile, then saw her reserve breaking. She had been able to withstand all he had thrown at her without a sound, but the merest gesture of kindness broke her endurance.

She lifted her face to him and the late afternoon sun streaming through the brig's stern window intensified her look of suffering. "Jerry," she said, burying her face in her hands, "What is going to happen to me?"

He could not answer her. His sentiments were his own, though Texas at war had first claim to a captured spy. Mexico had Leving, and he held captive a girl who had for years shaped his most private dreams. He was endowed with human traits and instincts, among them pity and desire. And these things were on the ascent and wholly at variance with duty.

He left her then, a little hurriedly, more afraid of himself than of Carmela.

Chapter Twenty-four

THE FORTUNES OF WAR

Both ships were under way and running full on a brisk following wind for Texas. Captain Brown stood the *Pocket's* quarter-deck, gazing at the dark red disk which seemed to cling mockingly to the last remnant of that Easter day. Trailing across the lower sky were cloud streamers of gold, green, crimson, and saffron, each as ragged and shapeless as his reflections. The mirroring Gulf flung the colors up and down as far as the eye could see and gave up none of its restless motion as hues diminished and fell away before the onrush of evening. The day was gone and the captain turned to survey the decks of his prize.

Looking at his watch, Jeremiah decided he had given Thompson and Carmela enough time together. "Mr. Newman," he said, "advise the lieutenant of marines to return the prisoner to the brig."

"Sir, that was done all of three quarters of an hour ago."

"But I allowed them an hour," Jeremiah said.

"Aye." Newman laughed. "However, the lady thought otherwise, sir. At exactly twelve minutes after the prisoner entered, she opened the door and said to the midshipman, 'Get this harbor scrapings out of here.' Seems she suddenly turned into a tigress."

Jeremiah grunted an answer and looked thoughtful. This could mean any number of things. Either she was through with Thompson or he had aroused her anger, possibly by his lack of sympathy when

she needed it most. However, it would come into the open soon
enough. Dismissing it from mind, he gave the lieutenant last-minute
instructions on handling the prize and asked him to signal the *Invincible* to stand by and put out a boat for his return.

"Come to think of it, Mr. Newman, I believe it wise to separate the
lady from the other prisoners. Suppose you send a boy for her baggage and advise her she's being transferred to the *Invincible*."

Jeremiah avoided Carmela during the crossing. She sat silent at the
prow and he at the stern sheets, and on board his ship she was sent
to Mr. Newman's quarters. Watching her go, her head up proudly,
Jeremiah reviewed all sorts of questions in silence before turning
away to make his rounds of the ship. He took in the weather, feeling
a change in the air, looking into the eye of the growing moon overhead, and went below.

It seemed that he had no sooner fallen asleep after hours of lying
awake than he was aroused by an urgent rapping at his door: Lieutenant Sevey requested the captain's presence on deck as soon as
possible. Thinking of the prize under convoy, he rushed to the
weather deck as the ship's bell sounded the hour of two.

"The lights of two ships low on the southern rim, sir. They appear
to be following our course."

At six bells, three in the morning, the ships came on, lights dipping
closer over and under the tossing waves. The wind was freshening
and seas drove in with increasing fury, slapping hard at the starboard
side with great sheets of spray bursting and raining down on decks.
The moon rode in and out of heavy clouds scudding before the wind.
Weather was slanting around between southeast and east, piling up
for quite a blow.

Eight bells, 4 A.M., brought two changes. The moon lay behind
mountains of clouds and the pair of lights dead astern appeared
closer. In order to force the ships to declare their intentions, Jeremiah
altered his course. When the company to windward did the same, he
knew beyond doubt the stern chase was on.

He believed the *Invincible* capable of showing any Mexican vessel
a clean pair of heels. But he was not alone. The *Pocket* was a slow
sailer heavy with valuable cargo. Knowing that only strategy could
save her, he dismissed any idea of making a protecting stand against
overwhelming odds and considered ways and means of effecting her
escape. He could double west and excite the enemy's hopes of hem-

ming him up between land and the crossfire of their guns, though in doing so he would necessarily risk the loss of sea room and maneuverability while putting up a running battle. But he could think of nothing better.

He ordered the beat to quarters. Then swinging lanterns were spelling out night signals to the *Pocket:* She should crowd on all sail for the Texas coast, showing not a light aboard; the *Invincible* would endeavor to draw off pursuit.

The ships aft were now about three miles to windward. Jeremiah ordered the course changed to due west and all prudent sail flung to the wind. This was done and the *Invincible* ran with lights aglow a full mile, drawing both enemy vessels off their courses in pursuit. Suddenly the Texan showed no lights. She was swallowed up by the night, which provoked the pair giving chase into a furious exchange of signals. The *Invincible* bore gradually to the south with her masthead eyes on Mexican lanterns.

The enemy ran on south of northwest against the *Invincible's* southwest course and came abreast not two miles east of her. The wind continued to move up the compass until it blew almost out of due east. Cross seas were running strong and the *Invincible* was reeling under too much canvas when the sky exploded with the brilliance of day. A second flare followed.

Caught thus, Jeremiah realized that his chances of getting out of this trap were slim. If he fled to the west, he would be chased aground and blown out of the water. His only escape was to the south, so he sailed south.

Dipping her bows to the gammoning, the *Invincible* lifted slowly and trembled from trucks to keelson, then twisted over and back and buried her head deep. She couldn't carry full sail in such seas. As a gang ran to relieve her, the gun crew heard the order to fire on the up roll. Then the enemy gave the Texans a surprise, an eight-gun broadside that flashed like sheet lightning above the waves.

The fire on both sides continued brisk in a running battle. Dawn found the Mexicans some three miles astern, all sails and masts intact. The 1824 ensign was hoisted and soon the gun brig aft broke out her colors. Then the lookout announced a sail breaking the horizon dead ahead. They were swarming like hornets, anxious to recover the supplies in demand by Santa Anna.

The new sail forced Jeremiah to head the wind. In doing so, he brought the larger Mexican bearing down over his quarter. The *Invincible* had lost the wind again. She had to win it back or fight three ships instead of two. It was now the *Invincible's* turn to come up on the other tack, which was accomplished at a cost. The huge gun brig bore down to within a mile of her and yawed around for a blast. Eight big eighteen-pounders let go almost at once. Only the fact that she had fired a mere second late saved the *Invincible*. Grape screamed overhead and whizzed on.

As the *Invincible* ran just east of due north, the second enemy vessel put her sails aback and waited for the Texan to come up under her guns. She was breaking out her battle flags as the distance narrowed to less than a mile, her bowsprit into the wind, her stern to the west. The *Invincible* was now a frantic mouse between a pair of waiting cats.

Jeremiah felt like the mouse. He had worked his ship into a trap in order to shake the big brig and another sail. He could not run east into the wind's eye any more than he dared a course to the west toward land. The enemy had him figured, knowing he could not avoid battle. And the gun brig aft was wearing ship for further chase.

"Mr. Sevey, the enemy ahead appears very confident."

"Aye, sir. Justifiably so. If we had open water west we might be able to run for it."

"Which the enemy is thinking we won't try," Jeremiah said, bracing his legs to the wild motions of the deck. "He's trimmed up sharp for us. So we'll put another steersman at the helm and run on. Almost on him, Mr. Sevey, we'll cut west so fast we'll either capsize or surprise the life out of him."

The ship was readied as she approached the Mexican. Only half a mile of water between them now. Then a quarter mile.

"Ready now!" Jeremiah shouted above the roar of wind. "Full rudder! Hold!" The *Invincible* reeled as the steersman sent her head around in a westward sweep to bring her up fast on the quarter and stern of the Mexican. Over went her masts and decks as she tore up acres of foam and bathed her lee decks in pushed-up seas. The Mexican loosed all her starboard guns in an effort to counter the unexpected move. The *Invincible* shuddered as a round shot smashed hard into the hull amidships.

Jeremiah warned the gun crew to hold their fire. They were two hundred yards away. He wanted half that distance when they let go with canister, grape, and langrage in a blast that would serve as a mighty equalizer.

The enemy, caught off guard, swung her bows around so fast that as she turned her stern to the weather she was momentarily out of control, too far around to deliver a broadside. With her facing west and held there, the *Invincible* threw her rudder over in a risk of collision and swept up with bowsprit driving toward the other's stern. The name was up for view now: *Veracruzana*. Seas boiled under the Texan vessel as she headed out of north to northeast and brought her larboard battery to bear.

With little more than two hundred feet separating them, the enemy rose high on a mountain of water and the *Invincible* sank into a trough. Every man braced himself for collision. Then the *Veracruzana* was falling and the *Invincible* was lifting. They were coming level when Jeremiah cried to the top of his voice:

"Fire all!"

So sudden and devastating was the blast, one might think the Mexican had exploded her magazine. Two of her cannon were unshipped by heavy shots, one rolling free down the deck, the other crashing through the rail. Forecastle, boats, and bulwarks aft leaped apart, plank from plank, in a skyrocketing mass of splinters. The main-topgallant crashed down in tearing and rending of wood, sail, and cordage. Gaping holes in her hull appeared suddenly, like blind eyes rimmed by her copper; and where her stern windows had been one moment a wide ragged mouth opened in shock the next.

The *Veracruzana* lay helpless. A long cheer went up from the *Invincible's* deck.

Jeremiah had risked collision and death, but he had sent his charge home. And now the *Invincible* was tearing on past the *Veracruzana*, running for all she was worth. The cry for "All sail!" was sounded as she made the costly mistake of coming out from cover of the beaten ship, which thus far had forced the brig astern to hold her fire.

The booming of guns had scarcely rolled across the water when above them and over the sides blinding flashes of light accompanied by the terrific roar of exploding bombs in quick succession put an end to celebration. Slugs of ragged hot metal thudded into wood, richocheted off and tore through flesh. Little Josh stared at a hand minus thumb and forefinger and Mr. Franson lay writhing under a blow from a falling block. Blood ran down the boatswain's face, and

he was touching his forehead as though he wasn't sure his head remained on his shoulders.

And then a cry sounded from the *Veracruzana:* "*Viva* Libertador!"

"So the big brig is the *Libertador,*" Jeremiah said, tearing his eyes
from his wounded. He felt a sticky substance in his left hand and
stared at it. Blood flowed in a steady trickle from a hole near his arm-
pit. Suppressing a desire to run to the surgeon, he sent his wounded
men below and waited until he had safe water between him and the
Libertador.

He was weak from loss of blood when he reached Kelton, who
pushed him flat on the officers' mess table and said, "Now brace
yourself, for this is going to hurt."

Two sailors were holding Jeremiah down. He remembered the stab
of fire just before all went black.

The next thing he saw was Carmela. She was very close and her
hands were busy with bandages. She paused as though frozen before
bringing her intense glance slowly around to meet his. Then she
obeyed an impulse and touched her mouth briefly to his.

She whirled and, to a hurried swishing of petticoats, left him in the
care of the fussy surgeon.

2

On the following evening, Jeremiah walked the moonlit deck. The
shock of battle had not departed. The stabbing pain of his wound
was less noticeable now, though lodged in his mind were problems
that defied bandages and healing balms. One had to do with duty; the
other with desire. The same nagging at his brain, the same tug of war
inside him. Carmela had kept her distance since yesterday morning.
He frowned, turned up the larboard deck, and gazed out over the
gentle sea. Sometime tomorrow, less than twenty-four hours from
now, the lookout would cry the long Texas coast. Matagorda meant
the discharge of a duty. Tonight the moon was large and the ship was
quiet. He looked aft again, hoping she would appear on deck. She
wasn't there, so he tried to think of other things.

He supposed he was very lucky to be alive and aboard a floating ship after yesterday's encounter with the Mexican war vessels. Certainly he had learned to respect the *Libertador*. His own damage could be estimated in terms great and small. But not a man was lost. Atop this, he had saved the *Pocket*. She rode broad on the starboard beam a quarter mile off, the crescents of her sails silvered in moonlight.

He went directly to his cabin. Taking a seat, he heaved a weary sigh and removed his cap. Absently, he tossed it at a hook on the bulkhead and missed. One day, he thought, he would hang the cap on the first try. Restless, he looked about for something to occupy his mind. His eyes rested on his sextant, the only piece of property worth anything left to him. It was on the table before him when someone knocked on the door.

"Come in," he boomed forth.

The door opened and Carmela came inside with a pan of steaming water and fresh white bandages. Avoiding his glance, she placed them on the table and said, "With the surgeon's permission, Captain Brown. I must have something to do or go mad."

He nodded, eying her sharply.

"Now off with your coat and shirt," she commanded, touching a finger to the water. "The marine captain has a nasty wound, so I went to him first."

"Is that so?"

She talked on while helping remove his shirt. Her hand touched his bare arm. "It's going to hurt when I remove the bandage. If you'd rather I'll have the surgeon do it."

"Hang Kelton!"

"Then suppose you lie flat in your bunk and raise the arm above your head." He obeyed and she sat down and bent to her work.

"Poor Little Josh," she said softly. "He can't get used to the missing fingers. The surgeon said he had asked every man aboard if anyone had seen his thumb and forefinger."

"Poor kid. He's sailed with me for five long years. It wouldn't do to tell him the fish fed on them."

She shuddered. "Did you have to say that?"

"You're mighty squeamish for a surgeon's mate. But I knew a doctor once who could cut off a man's leg as calm as you please and rush from the dinner table at the mention of a worm."

Jeremiah was looking at her hair in the yellow light. There was a tiredness in her face. "Ouch!" He winced and stiffened as the blood-caked cloth pulled at living flesh. Relaxing, he laughed. "If I'd done you harm, I'd swear you were getting even."

"Maybe I am." Her mouth curved up at the corners, though she failed to shape a smile. "Because you didn't pick me up and carry me bodily out of the Consulate. But hold still. I've come to the worst place."

"Then jerk like hell and get it over with."

"Bravo! Instead, I'll soften it with warm water. My way, Captain."

"You knew I wanted to take you with me that day, didn't you?"

"Of course. But hold still now."

Neither spoke for several seconds. She brushed wisps of hair from her face with the back of her hand and frowned as though it hurt her. The water soaked through the cloth. She removed it without causing him any pain, tossed it aside, and said:

"See there? My way is much better."

"I like it. And I liked the way you dismissed Thompson Sunday evening. Why did you?"

"He called me 'fool woman' for one thing, because I admitted I was asleep when I should have been tossing the documents overboard. Then he asked if I had you in the hollow of my hand. I said 'no,' and he said I'd do well to go to work on you at once. When I said that wasn't my way, he said, 'He's a man, isn't he?' Oh well, one thing led to another and I called the lieutenant of marines."

"What led to what?" he asked.

She arose and returned with a fresh cloth. "I simply told him to face the situation, that twice I'd tried to get out of the filthy business. I told him that Martínez said he could be accidentally shot if I quit. He seemed to scoff even as he said he was grateful. How grateful? I demanded. Enough to convince a Texas military court that I acted to save his neck?

"He said, 'I suppose so. But if it became known that we were engaged, it would go hard with you, and involve us both.' It was then I told him I was through with him and his kind."

Jeremiah could not withhold a question. "Through with him because he's lost his chance to make a fortune?"

"Maybe I've learned there are more important things."

Putting down the urge to say, "It's about time," he studied her with compassion in his expression. "I'm glad to hear you say that, Carmela, even though I don't like the method you took to learn it."

"Nor do I," she said meekly. "But nothing is free."

Slowly he raised himself on elbows. "You're right. It even cost you to tell Thompson off. He'll probably never help you before a court, unless——"

"Unless what?" she said quickly.

"He's forced to." He lay down again, entertaining the idea, expanding on it.

He saw mounting interest come into her eyes. As she met his glance, he could almost hear her urging him to do that very thing. Then her attention shifted to the bandage she was applying.

"He would be small help even if he were interested," she said. "But it really doesn't matter any more. I'm resigned to the worst. But whatever caused us to get off on that subject? There! You're bandaged up and I'm done with the last patient."

He sat up and caught her arm as she straightened. "You know what started all this. I could say it was when you said I should have carried you out of the Consulate. But it began aboard the *Sabine* the day I met you. January of 1832. Remember?

"Yes. I remember."

"Well, I've longed for you every day since then, loved you, taken you to sea with me, hated you, and, when I knew you were an enemy of Texas, despised you, and continued to long for you. I said you could sail free aboard of me, but you knew better. I waited for you to shake Thompson, but you didn't. He's right, you're a fool woman —for sleeping when you should have thrown the papers overboard, for tying yourself to Thompson's way of life. Right now, I'm mad enough at you for what you've done to yourself and to me to strike you a sharp dozen across your bottom."

She stared at him and he saw a little excitement in her eyes, a little eagerness stirring somewhere and expressing itself. "That was a long speech," she said.

"The longest I ever made."

She rose and stood with her back to him. "But too late to do any good. You see, Jerry, I love you too. You've known it for a long time."

At once surprised and elated, he said, "I never was sure. Maybe I'm not sure now."

She made no reply, no effort to convince him, which seemed to prove that she was not throwing herself at him. Yet doubt persisted.

"Then explain why you went on and on, following Thompson and putting me off." He was about to ask if a spy were admitting to love in order to influence the captor, but thought better of it. Then she was answering the question he asked.

"I suppose it was something I thought necessary. Perhaps it was the gambling instinct in me, or maybe I shared his belief that success lay just over the horizon. Anyhow, I had to realize the mistake myself. Too bad it came too late."

He thought about this. Thompson had been more a symbol than anything real. It was not unusual for a man to attach himself to an adventurer for better or for worse. So perhaps it wasn't so strange for a woman to follow the pattern of men. And yet it seemed very strange. Dismissing it, he thought of the rest of her admission.

Twice she had used the expression "too late." She could mean it or she could be forcing him into making promises he had no right to make.

Well, he would make no promises.

He reached for her arm and drew her to him. She sat down on the bunk beside him, and under his steady gaze she looked away, then sharply back at him, as though she had read him like an open page. And once more that hint of repressed eagerness left its mark on her face.

"What are you thinking?" he burst out.

"That I can't fight you any longer."

"Do you want to?"

"I don't know. But it makes no difference." She bit her lip and stared at the table. "I'm tired of fighting back."

"Carmela, you remember the kiss aboard the *Sabine*. You'll recall something else—I never tried to repeat it. Because I made a vow that the next time I took you in my arms I wouldn't let you go."

Her lips parted but she did not break their glance.

"You can go now or you can stay."

In her surprise, a hand instinctively lifted to her face and a curious frown dimpled her brow.

"You mean——?" She faltered.

"I'm locking the door with you on the inside or the outside."

For a moment she seemed inert, uncertain of herself, of time or place. Then she leaned toward him and the flood of feeling inside her broke. "Oh, Jerry, Jerry!" It came scarcely above a whisper as she raised her lips to his.

3

With the last stroke of eight bells midnight, Captain Jeremiah Brown appeared on deck to relieve Lieutenant Sevey. Although it was Brown's habit to be punctual, the lieutenant could remember no previous occasion when the captain strode up whistling like an apprentice in his teens. Nor could he account for what happened next.

Captain Brown made obeisance to the moon and let go with a yell before sailing his cap high out over the water.

Chapter Twenty-five

PIRATE OF THE GULF

At half-past nine on the evening of April seventh the *Invincible* was working her way cautiously inside the channel for Galveston Harbor. Every member of the crew was at his station, alert and puzzled. Since leaving Matagorda for a stand up the coast, they had seen little to remind them that Texas had ever been occupied.

And the Texas fleet had simply disappeared.

Jeremiah and Lieutenant Sevey looked ahead at bonfires burning on the island and a maze of lights at anchor off Lafitte's old fort. Schoonerman Brown knew the west-to-east channel and the island as he knew the lower Brazos. Under a waning moon, a bald prairie of sand no more than five feet above high tide curved like the blade of a scythe from San Luis Pass to the west and the bay entrance to the east. On a sea approach, it was a long smear atop the water, marked by two clumps of trees, the ruins of a fort, and, of late, a few scattered huts. McKinney & Williams had built the first dock and the old Mexican customhouse now served Texas in the same capacity. The harbor was important to both Texas and Mexico, and Jeremiah was wondering who occupied it as he made his way inside the bar with guns in readiness.

He was rounding the point when challenged. Upon declaring his identity and that of the *Pocket*, he was welcomed inside, where he learned that the fleet lay at anchor. In answer to his questions he was advised that Commodore Hawkins had established his base here in keeping with the retreat of the army, government, and civilians. Aboard the ships crowding the harbor were refugees from Brazos towns and coastal settlements as far west as Goliad. And around the island fires were more homeless Texans.

"Thanks to General Houston's aimless retreat," he was told, "it looks like the retreat of civilization."

Jeremiah was glad he had come by night. He had no desire to see by day what had happened to his people. Nor did he relish the thought of riding his anchor after the fashion of the commodore when there was much to be done at sea. He found it difficult even to imagine his government's tolerating an inactive navy at a time when Santa Anna's lengthened supply line demanded support by sea. And, he thought on, with four fifths of the Texas coast lying unprotected, and the commodore's ships snugly at rest, there was nothing to stop the flow of Mexican supplies and troops from Matamoros.

It was his duty to report to Hawkins. But he excused himself from this ordeal on the grounds that he needed men and supplies. He wished for the open sea and strong winds. Minutes later, he was addressing a letter to Colonel James Morgan, Commandant at Galveston Island.

> Sir, I beg leave to inform you that I have this moment arrived at this place with the prize Brig Pocket & Cargo which I captured off the Brazos Santiago, and understand that you are the commandant of this port and it is necessary that I proceed to sea immediately and rather short of crew you please take charge of the vessel until further orders from the Government at Harrisburg.
>
> With marked Esteem & Respect Yr. obt. svt.
>
> J. Brown
> Commdr Sch Invincible
> pr. F. T. Wells[1]

With the *Pocket* in the hands of the commandant, Jeremiah raised sail for New Orleans. Once across a bar and in deep fathoms, he went to Carmela and told her of his decision to take her to New Orleans, to keep her on board his ship until there was proof enough to charge Thompson with the crime of spying or until every means in this direction was exhausted.

[1]Official Correspondence of the Texas Revolution.

"You are not under arrest, but under guard," he told her. "Now help me get Thompson where I want him by telling me who in New Orleans can swear to his part in the spy ring."

"Jerry, Thomas didn't spy or carry information. All he did was draw the detailed charts of the Texas coast. But he was a Mexican officer at the time. So you really——"

"Hold it there! That's it, Carmela, *he drew the charts!* Now if I, Captain Brown, were caught and the Mexican military learned I had drawn charts of their coast, would I be a spy or a prisoner of war? A spy, by thunder! That's all I need to make Don Thomas more than a prisoner of war."

Under the dim light in her small cabin she listened in silence and stared almost wonderingly at her captor, then at the officer who granted her reprieve, and next at the man she had held in long embrace. She made it evident that she was trying to reconcile each to the other two, and all into one. Jeremiah could see and understand her bewilderment, for he knew himself to be all of these. Duty came first, sympathy second, and the masculine being third. Each in its proper place. But with the first and second dispensed with, he was free to be himself, to respond to what he saw deep in her eyes, a warmth, something as strong and unsettling as it had been one year or four years ago.

The thin garment she wore exposed a creamy shoulder, and the yellow light of the cabin lamp was captured by her burnished hair. Sensing the reason for the lazy excitement playing about in her face, he blew the light out, reminding himself as he did so that he had made no promises.

2

Upon his arrival in New Orleans, Jeremiah went straightway to the Texas agency and gave an account of the *Pocket's* capture and detention in Galveston to William Bryan. The agent's surprise lapsed into a grave silence which he sustained for some time.

"I'm wondering how New Orleans will react to the capture of the third American vessel."

"Two," Jeremiah said. "The *Pelicano* and *Pocket.*"

"While you were away, your brother William made a prize of the American brig *Durango*. She was laden with a contraband cargo also. The usual whitewash, Lizardi to Rubio."

"Good for William," Jeremiah replied.

"There may be repercussions. So you might be wise to refit and sail as soon as possible."

Jeremiah laughed at his fears and said he would require at least a week to put the *Invincible* in sailing order with men and provisions aboard.

That was on the ninth of April.

Two days later news of the captured Yankee brig *Pocket* caused quite a stir in official circles. In the cafés and coffeehouses there was talk of piracy, though friends of Texas laughed it off. By the thirteenth, New Orleans seemed to have forgotten the *Pocket* incident.

On the fourteenth, official dispatches arrived from Texas. Mr. Bryan admitted that he might have been unduly alarmed and a little unenthusiastic in assessing the *Pocket's* value to the Texas cause. So saying, he passed to Jeremiah a copy of President Burnet's proclamation:

Executive Dept. Harrisburg 9th April 1836
Fellow Citizens of Brasos.

It affords me much pleasure to communicate to you, the enclosed copy of the report of Captain Brown of the Schooner Invincible. The capture of the brig Pocket is not only highly beneficial to Texas by furnishing us with a large supply of provisions but by crippling the operations of the enemy, and contributing to cut off his resources and rendering it more difficult for him to obtain supplies for the future, through the same odious channels. The Government will always take pleasure in imparting to the citizens every species of intelligence on which they can rely and which is calculated to cheer and animate us in the glorious struggle.[2]

Bryan said, "The rest of the news isn't so good. The President and Cabinet sent Secretary of War Rusk to the army—*to order General Houston to fight!* Imagine that! But he still retreats, and the 'Napoleon of the West' can't get a battle out of him with even small advance columns. General Urrea is at Brazoria and Santa Anna is dashing toward Harrisburg to capture the government.

[2]Official Correspondence of the Texas Revolution.

"And—let's see. Here's an official notice addressed to all commanders of the Texas Navy—— The flag contributed by Commodore Hawkins, union blue, star central, thirteen stripes prolonged red and white, was adopted at Harrisburg on the ninth of April as the national flag for the naval service.

"Rather clever," Bryan laughed. "Enough like the American flag to fool anyone at a distance. Commodore Hawkins is to be congratulated."

He did not see Jeremiah's eyes and lips and fists as he spoke. Nor did he detect anger in his reply: "The commodore is very resourceful."

Jeremiah returned to his ship, went below, and placed a bottle on the table. Surging through him like great waves driven by a tempest was hatred for Hawkins and the circumstances that protected him from a captain's wrath. It was enough to suffer the indignities the commodore heaped upon his commanders; but to have a private flag stolen and contributed as Hawkins's own creation and then be forced to stand by and see it proclaimed the flag of the Navy seemed entirely too bitter a dose to swallow.

He walked the deck, up one side and down the other, before going to Carmela. Under her quiet gaze, anger no longer dominated him. Resentment was less strong and his hurt seemed bearable. The storm was soon gone out of him and the period of transition evoked calm observations of incongruities. It was strange, he said, that Houston the warrior would not fight, that Burnet the pacifist headed a war government, that Hawkins a harbor commodore commanded the fleet. She nodded agreement.

He liked her near him. He saw her happy at times, as now, apparently contented for the first time since he had known her. Following the *Pocket's* capture, there were days when she appeared radiant; then at times she turned moody, for nothing was certain. Often she looked at him with hope in her eyes and as often she seemed afraid. But the last week had wrought a change. She seemed to shine like a flower in the sun. This was the Carmela he had sought for years.

And now, her lips were curving in a smile. She put his bottle aside without presuming to dictate and moved to his side. "What you need, Jerry Brown, is a night in the Vieux Carré. Remember the time you were jealous of the monkey I admired?"

"Sure," he said, slipping an arm about her waist. "That was the night you didn't like the attention I gave the girl who danced the mock bullfight."

"I still don't like it," she said, eyes flashing.

He suppressed a grin. "So you think a visit to Frenchtown would do us good, eh?"

"I said it would be good for *you.*"

"Knowing when you said it, I wouldn't go without you." He studied her with narrowing eyes. "I wonder about you at times, Carmela. Suppose we did go to the cafés and you found an opportunity to escape?"

An amused smile tugged at the corners of her mouth. Then, with a finger running the line of his nose, she said, "Just why should I want to escape?"

It was a little sudden for him. He examined her for sincerity before saying, "There's a prize question. Suppose you answer it."

She slid into his lap and placed her arms about his neck. "You're a blind man, Jerry Brown," she teased. Placing her mouth temptingly close to his, she said, "Do I act like I want to run away?"

She laughed at his look of puzzlement and touched her lips to his forehead.

"What about the future?" he said.

"Hang the future! I don't think about it. Instead, I simply trust myself to your care."

"Gambling again, aren't you?"

For answer, she pressed her lips to his.

He was not prepared for this kind of trust. He had thought himself secure, his sense of duty protected against any personal desires, simply because he had promised her nothing. He felt foolish and outsmarted, for she had in one swift stroke knocked his only prop out from under him.

3

That afternoon a New Orleans paper carried a story of the *Pocket's* capture. The true facts were either missing to the writer of the piece or else he chose to ignore them and pen an account of piracy on the high seas. The American flag was pictured as a strip of bunting violated by a naval officer of a petty state creeping into existence. The same Captain Brown who in 1832 claimed the "honor" of being the first Anglo-American Texan to openly defy Mexican arms had now come forward to bite the hand that so gallantly responded to the Texan cause with money and men. The climax was reached by an appeal to Americans to protest this act of piracy and protect American rights and commerce and stamp out brutality on the high seas.

Toward sundown a growing throng of outraged citizens milled about the dock where the *Invincible* lay at her moorings. Cries and jibes were hurled at the hurriedly assembled marines on deck. The visitors wanted to look at the new Jean Lafitte of the Gulf, to spit on the man who tore the Star-Spangled Banner to shreds and flogged American seamen for the fun of it.

Jeremiah appeared on deck against the advice of his officers and stood at the rail surveying the crowd. The late sun painted his face crimson, which provoked a bold sailor into pointing at the "Red Devil of the Gulf." Cheered on, the man moved to the rail and demanded that the foreyard be loosed and braced for a lively hanging of the Texan pirate.

Knowing the people of New Orleans, Jeremiah said nothing. They were easily excited, quick to take sides, quicker to forget. What they denounced with prodigious violence one day they would defend the next. And it was the other way about. So he thought all they needed was the other side of the story, though at the moment he realized that Martínez had scored a success. He knew the clever consul had had a hand in it, for the same paper reported that in the engagement between the *Invincible* and the *Bravo*, the latter suffered only a round shot in the hull and a parting of some of her rigging.

A little later, he went below and the crowd slowly dispersed. Then William Bryan arrived and said the same kind of demonstration had trapped him at the Texas agency.

"Dammit, feeling is running high! While the devils jeered outside my office, I penned this notice to President Burnet. You won't like it but you've got to admit the logic of it."

Jeremiah read aloud:

"The result of the whole trouble will satisfy you as to the policy of invading the American flag. It would require but few such instances as that of the Pocket to turn the govt. of the U.S. against you and stop every expedition in favor of Texas."[3]

Jeremiah returned the letter. "Maybe so," he said wearily. "Maybe so."

"Hell, I know so! Do you know who forms the combine working against us? Just before the mob came, a friend from the United States District Attorney's office informed me that Lizardi and Company and the powerful Lousiana State Marine and Fire Insurance Company were not only going to court here but were sending a formal protest to the State Department in Washington."

Jeremiah scoffed. "That's a lot of talk. I know the laws of the sea and I'm certain of my stand. With all the evidence in our favor, they won't dare go to court and see it aired."

"Don't believe it. Mexico is determined to use the *Pocket* case as a means of splitting Texas and the United States for the sole purpose of stopping the flow of volunteers and supplies to Texas."

Jeremiah was glad when Bryan departed. He paced his deck a long time before giving up the idea of visiting the Vieux Carré. That could wait until tomorrow evening, he decided. By then the pendulum of popular fancy would be swinging his way again.

Morning brought a surprise, however. New Orleans did not cool off. As the day wore on, the agitators succeeded in enlisting more hotheaded Americans under their false banner. Demonstrations were held all over the city. The Texas flag of 1824 was burned before the Cabildo, and a group of citizens tried to place a Jolly Roger on the *Invincible's* bowsprit. Toward noon Jeremiah removed the ship to the other side of the river.

That afternoon he left Mr. Sevey in charge and crossed the river to speed up the delivery of supplies. Riggers and carpenters were almost done with repairs and, except for a patch or two on the starboard hull, he was ready to sail. Another day at the most, if all went well, the *Invincible* should be moving down-river.

Such were his thoughts as he stepped to land at the foot of Canal Street. But New Orleans under his feet reminded him that his officers and Carmela had tried to prevent his leaving the ship for the city. He moved on up the street without attracting any notice and made his way to the agency, entering Bryan's office at exactly four o'clock.

[3]Official Correspondence of the Texas Revolution.

He would never forget the look of utter shock in William Bryan's face. The agent swallowed hard and seemed bereft of tongue as he waved a hand and got out of his chair. Finding his voice at last, he almost shouted at Jeremiah.

"For God's sake, go back to your ship and raise sail for Galveston! The United States marshal is on his way to take the *Invincible* and arrest officers and crew. That's enough, but it's not all." He sank to his chair.

"The Louisiana State Marine and Fire Insurance Company has asked Commodore Dallas of the United States West India and Gulf Squadron to seize the *Invincible*. And I was told that the sloop-of-war *Warren* was ordered from Mobile to the mouth of the Mississippi yesterday. So if the marshal doesn't get you, the United States Navy will."

Jeremiah turned without a word and rushed into the street, oblivious to the crowd that had formed outside in the space of seconds. While pushing men aside, he was recognized. Someone cried, "That's Brown the pirate!" and another man caught at his arm. Jeremiah struck him down and ran with the crowd on his heels all the way to the river. There he eluded pursuit by running up the gangplank of a riverboat and leaping from her low deck to a steam towboat under way with a schooner tied on aft.

"Cut loose!" he said, drawing a pistol from his belt. "Get me across river at top speed if you have to blow a boiler."

The crew stared at the madman on board and responded by cutting the hawser and opening the throttle. The small craft shook and groaned into full speed ahead, her paddle wheel churning up the water, the every beat of her engine threatening to jar her apart.

"Faster!" Jeremiah ordered, looking toward the shore.

The government launch was working out into the river, and he knew her destination and purpose. Never had he imagined Jeremiah Brown running away from the United States flag. But it was so. He was being chased by that banner. The marshal's craft came on with large paddles eating up the space between them. Whether or not the marshal knew of his presence aboard the tug, the race to the *Invincible* promised to be a close one. Ahead, his ship was taking on supplies from a barge.

The tug captain shouted, "She's going to bust wide open!"

"Let her bust!" Jeremiah cried back.

Carmela crossed his mind. If he lost the race, she would not face trial. Which was small consolation when he compared her freedom to the loss of his own. And Texas needed the fleet *Invincible,* which was now less than a cable's length ahead.

With the government boat the same distance behind him, he cupped his hands and yelled to the top of his voice, *"Invincible!* Get under way at once!"

Twice he repeated the order before seeing her deck come alive. The capstan gang was "walking her round" in the double-quick. He could thank his stars for a man like James Sevey who obeyed instantly instead of waiting to ask questions. If the *Invincible* got away without him, she would be in good hands.

There was not time to weigh the anchor, and he called for a sacrifice of his hook: "Slip the cable!"

Amid a clattering of chain through the hawsehole the cable went overboard. Sail was coming up on the main. Now the fore. Jibs were loosed and she was sliding away from the astonished bargemen. He was less than fifty feet away now, and Sevey was hailing him frantically from the stern. The Jacob's ladder dropped and dangled there, close but not close enough.

"All sail!" Jeremiah cried.

He watched her gather headway and swing out into the current. Then she headed east with the wind on her beam and ran on for the lower bend of the horseshoe. A strange feeling crept over him as he suddenly realized that he had never seen her under sail from a distance; he had always been aboard when she was under way.

4

In the quiet hour before dawn next day, the *Invincible's* anchor watch sharpened their ears for some real or imagined noise at variance with the incessant songs of frogs and occasional roars of bull alligators. As the sound from upriver grew louder, Mr. Sevey was awakened. He came on deck and listened. There was no doubt about it, he said, the steam craft moving down on them was bringing either trouble or Captain Brown. He frowned as a memory of yesterday's narrow escape crossed his mind. The government boat had been close upon the captain's.

The gray light of dawn was filtering through the moss-covered trees lining the Mississippi when the towboat rattled close on the starboard side and discharged a passenger. Mr. Sevey's "Thank the Lord" was scarcely spoken before the order came to raise the anchor. Captain Brown had spoken it.

Shaking the captain's hand, Lieutenant Sevey said, "I thought the marshal had you, sir."

"He almost did. And but for the towboat's captain, he would have. Captain Pouilly hid me below. Then we started down-river, knowing you couldn't navigate after nightfall. But we'd better tie on and head for the Gulf."

The tug towed them into the wind, slipping hawsers to look around each bend in the river and let go with one blast if all was well, with two if a United States warship lay ahead. The river continued clear all the way to the Head of the Passes, where the three channels to the Gulf met. Pass à l'Outre to the east, the Southwest Pass to Texas, and the South Pass formed a bird's foot in the delta. In the wide waters, the tug moved down to survey the roads while the *Invincible* slowed her forward motion by slatting sails in the wind.

Hour after hour passed with every ear straining for the towboat's whistle from around tree-lined bends ahead. Toward midafternoon the signal they did not wish to hear sounded far down-river. Two blasts.

Jeremiah rubbed his jaw and made a wry face. "Mr. Sevey, we can't fight our way out of this. Better to lose the ship than fire on the Stars and Stripes."

The tug returned and advised that the United States sloop-of-war *Warren* stood just inside Pass à l'Outre at the Head.

With the wind out of the southwest, Jeremiah wanted that pass open. He was wondering if it was possible to lure the *Warren* out when the tug captain came aboard and said, "Reckon ye won't be needin' me, Cap'n Brown," to which Jeremiah replied, "Stick around. And I'm not holding a gun in your belly, Captain Pouilly." The tow skipper laughed, saying he was a friend of Texas all the way.

Below, Jeremiah set a bottle on the table and produced a chart of the area. "Is the *Warren* on the north or south side of the pass?" He poured for his guest when the other said, "North." Jeremiah looked pleased. "Captain Pouilly, if she sighted me in tow making for the Southwest Pass and came at me, she would be forced to sail west. Now supposing I could draw her all the way across the river, I'd have the speed of her to Pass à l'Outre while she wore around for chase, wouldn't I?"

"Right. But she could blast you outen the water whilst wearin' ship."

"Captain Pouilly, you're a fine man." Jeremiah beamed. "Take this bottle with my compliments, for, God willing, we're going to show the Lady *Warren* our heels."

The tow captain shook his head. "Cap'n, it goes to prove that you Texans is fools o' the first water."

Minutes later, the tug began to move. As the hawser tightened and curved to spank the water, the *Invincible* slid forward. Her crew heard the plan and knew their captain was right when he said, "Unless you show smart and handle sail like your life depended on it, we'll be looking at each other in a New Orleans jail."

A quarter hour passed before they caught a first glimpse of the *Warren*. She lay about a mile away almost due east under the curve that opened the Head. With the wind out of the southwest, the United States vessel could point no farther south in coming after them without making tacks for it. As the tug moved on due south with the *Invincible*, the *Warren* ran up signals ordering the Texan to identify herself and stand by. Ignoring the order, Jeremiah played his first trick by hoisting a signal calling for a Southwest Pass bar pilot.

He kept his eyes glued to the *Warren*, hoping she would respond to suit him. She could, of course, anticipate his scheme and run up just enough sail to swing her full larboard battery to bear. After long anxious minutes, a pleased grin lit up his face. She was making sail, bracing her yards up sharp for the full and by. Then she was hugging the shoal waters for a run due west. All the while her signals fluttered and, meeting with no answer, she fired a warning shot over the *Invincible's* bows.

Lieutenant Sevey said, "She means business, sir."

"Break out the wigwag," Jeremiah said. When the semaphores waited in a sailor's hands, he said, "Ask her what she means by firing on Texans rushing home to defend their land. Next, send compliments, Captain Brown to Lieutenant Billings. Too bad Harry Billings isn't her captain—but don't send that, lad."

For every foot of southing the *Invincible* made the *Warren* ran two west. Soon the American lay obliquely northeast with less than three quarters of a mile of water separating the ships. This was too close, Jeremiah admitted, though he put down impatience by reminding himself that he wanted to put the other vessel due north of him before he risked his ship and crew in a bold dash for freedom.

"Sir," the wigwag advised, "she orders you to stand by at once. Otherwise she'll greet us with a twelve-gun broadside."

"Then by all means signal that we're coming about." Taking in his deck, crew, and rigging, Jeremiah spread his lips in a broad smile before saying, "Every man look handsome now. We're putting about all right, but with a fair wind on our tail."

Every man stood at his station, alert, appearing a little awed at the captain's defiance of the greatest power on the seas, of brothers under another flag. But their brothers would place them behind bars. It was a game of winds for freedom now and they waited to jump at the captain's signal. And here it was.

Up went his hand. It hung poised above his head a moment, then dropped suddenly. "Cut loose from the tug, Mr. Newman!" he yelled. "Mr. Abbott, heads'ls! Heads'ls all!"

The still deck came alive. The hawser was scarcely cast off than jibs blossomed up white and cracked full in the breeze. Perfectly timed. Before the bowsprit felt the jerk, the helm responded to "Hard alee!" The bows swung slowly, then faster, smashing the lee sea into a surf that boiled and burst with sounds like the beat of kettledrums. As the *Invincible's* head swept around to east, a great spread of sail met the quartering wind. Spanker, staysails, and everything but the boatswain's nose rag came into play. Then the clatter of gear and high drone of wind in the rigging were silenced by a rousing cheer lifting from the throats of Texans.

Mr. Sevey shed his nautical dignity long enough to slap Captain Brown on the back. "You outfoxed her, sir! Worked her out of the pass and out of the wind!"

This was true. The *Invincible*, by pretending to reach for the sea to the southwest, had drawn the *Warren* west. Once she was there and unable to sail down into the wind, which was ideal for the *In-*

vincible, she could only fire her guns and slowly wear ship around to give chase. In response to the lieutenant's elation, Jeremiah said:

"Easy as you go, Mr. Sevey. Don't forget she ships Long Toms by the dozen."

But something in his face, perhaps the twinkle in his eye, betrayed him. Observant Sevey looked wise, knowing the captain was gambling the sentiments of Americans for their brother Texans, with whom they were not at war, that the *Warren* wouldn't open fire on the audacious Texan unless she had express orders to do so. But it was a big gamble, since they were not free.

Jeremiah looked at the *Warren* luffing up into the wind. She was coming about. And when her sails began to fill on the starboard side, Jeremiah saw her gun deck swing. She could fire now, then bear down white-winged and fleet, like an angry swan charging its prey.

But she did nothing of the kind. Instead, she politely dipped her colors, a little chagrined perhaps, in respect to the Texan who had tricked her out of Pass à l'Outre.

The *Invincible* returned the courtesy and roared on, the single star in the rigging whipping forward as she cut a foaming wake in her dash east for the open pass to the sea.

Chapter Twenty-six

GALVESTON

William Bryan wrote President Burnet, advising that the capture of the brig *Pocket* was considered by the authorities a case of piracy, and that he had been compelled to order the *Invincible* back to Galveston:

> *We presume she has escaped. Should she be detained the cause of Texas will have received the severest blow she has yet met and the agency will be involved in trouble it will be hard to evade. Our situation with all the power and wealth of New Orleans arrayed against us is one of peril and danger.*[1]

On the afternoon of April seventeenth, the *Invincible* crossed the bar and entered Galveston Harbor in a downpour of rain. As she crept on to anchorage off the old Mexican customhouse, the clouds crossed over to the mainland, leaving the island and maze of ships steaming under the hot April sun. Women and children on the decks of every size and type of craft seemed as excited over the catch of rainwater in buckets and sailcloth as their former neighbors from the Brazos or Colorado who vied with one another in dipping water from pools on the beaches.

Jeremiah's black brows drew together as he stared from the ragged

---

[1] Official Correspondence of the Texas Revolution.

and water-soaked garments of his people to makeshift dwellings. A canvas lean-to here, a square of sedge grass supported by driftwood there; dozens of one and scores of the other. Men and women and slaves of either sex and enough boys and girls to populate a settlement milled aimlessly over acres of sand. This was Texas of 1836; rather, this was practically all that was left of it.

Thinking of the great size of Texas, her millions of acres of land over miles and miles which required weeks to cross, he could scarcely believe that it had been narrowed down to this. The fact stunned the mind and saddened the heart. The fruit of the years and hopes of the future had been snatched from the people.

He took in the harbor scene, the abode of the more fortunate. Their clothing hung on stays and ropes and booms to dry, like banners for flagships of despair. Babies were tied to rails and stanchions, and mothers were staring toward the flat coast across the bay. Refuse floated in the water, drawing seagulls by the hundreds. These things were what met the eye in a sweeping glance. He did not wish to peer beneath the surface. But he knew that he must. His friends were out there.

Men and women were gathering to cheer the *Invincible*. A woman shouted, "Thank God for the *Pocket*, Captain Brown. Without her, we might have starved."

Although these frontiersmen were proud and independent, circumstances had forced them to swallow their pride. One woman asked Jerry if he could spare a little flour or corn meal. An old man needed a cut of sailcloth to cover his wife at night. Another hoped he could lend just enough whisky to "dose" a pneumonia patient, and a mother was asking for medicine to drive fever out of her baby.

Jeremiah could spare these things and more, though he advised the people that if he gave to one he must give to all; that he was reducing rations on board his ship in order to send everything possible to a central point of distribution, if such existed. He soon learned it was every man for himself. After sending supplies ashore, he asked:

"Where's Houston's army?"

"Damn old Houston!" a man cried.

A one-legged settler spoke up: "Houston was trying to retreat on the old Nacogdoches road when the army forced him to take the fork for Harrisburg. Colonel Sidney Sherman led the men. General Rusk, Colonels Lamar and Burleson backed him up. So Houston is tagging along, still in command. The last we heard the army had left Groce's. And up there somewhere is Santa Anna. We hear he's moving to the coast for supplies."

"Sounds logical," Jeremiah said.

"Nothing's logical," the man replied, limping off.

"Don't pay no 'tention to Jess, Cap'n. He ain't been the same since he set fire to his house and barn. Fact is, none of us is the same. I buried my plowshares at Fort Bend after plantin' my corn. Don't never expect to see plow ner corn agin. But a man does crazy things."

The speaker parted his whiskers and looked in the direction of the Brazos. "Damn if I wouldn't trade corn and plows for a cut of tobaccy."

A sailor tossed him a black square. "I'm grateful," he said, his eyes filling.

A short bald man worked his way through the crowd and waved. "Hi there, Jerry Brown."

"Hello, Tom. Did you burn your store?"

"Didn't have the heart. Velasco wouldn't be the same if I had of. The hotel and me still stands."

"Where's Miss Virginia?"

"Over yonder. Sort of out of her head, Jerry."

"Polly Merchant here?"

"Harrisburg last I heard." He jerked a thumb over his shoulder. "I reckon we're all glad to see a fighter twixt us and Santa Anna, Jerry. We ain't believin' what's being said about you."

"About me?" Jeremiah said, surprised.

"Yeah. They say you took a woman spy off the *Pocket.* They say she's right peart and sassy lookin'. But I says if she was the Queen of Sheba and was workin' against Texas, Jerry Brown would hang her hisself, personal."

"Thanks, Tom."

The crowd grew in size. The hum of conversation lifted with "*Invincible!* She's here!" and more and more people gathered. "It's Brown, Jerry Brown!" Cries and cheers rose, growing in volume with the rush for a look at the "fightin'" ship, and the man who had emerged victorious in the first test of the Texas Navy. The crew cheered back and pointed with pride at their captain, who forgot slanderers and their charges as something welled up inside him. The people were for him, they lauded him, made a hero out of him. Perhaps for the first and last time, he thought. But once was enough to flood the heart of any man. Unable to keep an unmoved face, he went below.

A little later he ventured on deck again. The crowd had thinned. Leaving Lieutenant Sevey in charge after sending his compliments to the commodore, Jeremiah went ashore. Besieged on every side by friends from the Brazos and coastal towns, he looked and listened. Some few avoided his direct glance and shook his hand coldly. Others said they didn't believe the gossips. A few had news for his ears:

His brother William was ready to resign; Mr. Allen's ship *Terrible*, sailing under a letter of marque, had made captures off the Mexican coast; the *Flash*, Captain Falvel, privateer, had reached the Brazos under orders from the government and removed women and children fleeing before the Mexican advance to an upper arm of Galveston Bay; there had been on board twin pieces of artillery, a gift to Texans from the citizens of Cincinnati.

Jeremiah slapped at a mosquito on his cheek and looked toward the *Liberty*. Shaking his head hopelessly, he moved on. Ahead a large square was fenced off by sand thrown up like breast-works. A rude sign read: WOMEN. Skirting this, he continued his search for Polly's aunt. On his right, a woman and a slave boy were bending over a grass pallet where a small girl writhed and moaned with high fever. The woman looked up, imploring him with her eyes to do something. He tried to move on, but couldn't. Then he was holding the child in his arms and moving toward the *Invincible*, the mother and slave boy trailing after him.

She was a pretty little girl with long brown curls. Her face was flushed and she was very warm to his hands and arms. "Where are you from, ma'am?" he asked of the mother.

"All the way from Goliad, sir. We made it to Lynchburg before I learned about Homer. That's her papa. He was, I mean."

"Goliad?"

"The Alamo."

"What's her name?" he asked.

"Sally."

That was all that was said between them. On deck, he sent for his surgeon and said, "Take care of her and the mother, Mr. Kelton."

Back on the beach, he saw the Negro boy at his side. Under his stern glance, the lad said, "I stays by yo' all, Cap'n." The grin and show of white teeth disarmed Jeremiah, who trudged on. Everywhere he paused, the boy drew up also.

"What's your name, boy?"

"Sodom Brown."

"Brown!" Jeremiah glared.

Just then a messenger from the flagship appeared before Jeremiah with a sealed letter. "The Commodore's compliments to Captain Brown, sir."

Jeremiah broke the seal and read the order: Captain Brown should without delay ship and mount two six-pounders aboard the steamboat *Yellowstone,* Captain Grayson, and patrol the western arm of Galveston Bay as far as New Washington.

Which, Jeremiah thought suspiciously, was too closely timed to his arrival. However, the commodore could not arrest Carmela without a formal charge from the *Invincible's* captain. Or would Hawkins allow recognized methods of procedure to stand in his way? With these things in mind, he returned to his ship and advised his purser and first lieutenant of the order. He could trust them to watch over the ship.

Captain Grayson awaited him with open arms. The little steamboat owner had already received orders from the commodore and he gave the weather-beaten craft steam at once. Leaving a pilot at the wheel, he took Jeremiah below and fished out of his locker a bottle of imported whisky. They talked of old times and lived again the episode of the *Laura* and the taking of the *Correo.* "Aye! Those were better days, Jerry. But you've gone a long way since then." Then they went on deck and supervised the mounting of the six-pounders. By sunset they were well into the bay.

Jeremiah remained on deck that night to scan the shore for lights of a Mexican encampment, to think, to stare up at the stars hanging low and bright in the spring sky. The heavens were at peace, indifferent to the tragedy of the land. The pale night masked the muddy waters rushing down from the swollen Trinity River, and Saturn and Mars twinkled atop the northwestern horizon like bivouac fires on the shore before dipping under. Astern, the glow of fires on Galveston Island reminded Jeremiah of the suffering of war. But the heavens moved on while the land waited tense and quiet for morning.

Dawn was not far off when a flickering light was reported off the larboard bow. Raising his glass, Jeremiah saw a glow from fires on shore many miles ahead. Curious, he ordered more firewood under the boiler and speculated on whether the light emanated from friend or foe.

Daylight revealed nothing, and the *Yellowstone* crept farther up into the bay under morning showers and hot sun.

Toward midafternoon a schooner was sighted far ahead. She was anchored well offshore, due to the gradual shoaling of the water, though close enough to treat with the shore.

Raising his telescope, Captain Grayson said, "By the devil's grandson, there's something strange about this! Look at the boats and barges tied up on the shore. Why half the small craft of the bay, and Buffalo Bayou to boot, are assembled for some big movement by water."

"Maybe it's Houston," Jeremiah replied, fixing his glass on the scene ahead. "It wouldn't come as any surprise if he planned to retreat across the bay."

"On second thought, Jerry, it would. I know Colonel Sidney Sherman. I don't believe he'll go on retreating."

"Supposing then it isn't Houston ahead?" Jeremiah said.

"It's either our people trying to escape to Galveston or it's Santa Anna's army."

Jeremiah fingered a jaw absently. "You know, General Gaines of the United States Army is vigorously seeking recruits in New Orleans and St. Louis. He has let it be known that his government considers the Neches River the true boundary between Mexico and the United States instead of the Sabine. So it could be possible that Houston, a friend of President Andrew Jackson, is trying to draw Santa Anna across the Neches—into American territory. Know what that would mean?"

"A windfall."

"Look beyond that. Since Old Hickory has a congress controlled by abolitionists, he can't even think about annexing Texas. But if Santa Anna crossed the Neches, he could take it by conquest under the pretext that the United States had been invaded."

"You think too deep for me, Jerry."

"Which, if that's the scheme, makes Houston a traitor. A criminal who has sacrificed towns and homes and farms and lives to further a foreign cause."

"You don't like Houston, I gather."

"I wouldn't say that," Jeremiah replied. "I admire him in a way, but I don't trust any man who is against any situation, person, or principle he cannot dominate from A to Z."

"Maybe so," the steamboat man said, training his glass ahead. "But I've seen that schooner somewhere. Now I remember where. She's the German who sat over in East Bay for days. But pipe this, will you, there's some activity on shore."

Jeremiah looked and saw the red- and gold-trimmed uniforms of Mexican officers. A longboat was putting out for the schooner. Dragoons pushed and poled and caught up oars. While on the beach a flag-bearer and a line of troops were shouldering muskets and standing at attention.

"Seems someone of importance is in that boat," Jeremiah said. "Can we get another knot out of this teakettle, Tom?"

"She's glory-bound if we do. Besides, we can reach the schooner ahead of the oars."

His prediction was borne out with time to spare. As the *Yellowstone* ran between the schooner and shore, the boat turned back in hasty retreat. If there was excitement aboard the German and on the land, there was equally as much in evidence on the steamboat's deck. For Jeremiah had recognized the famous Almonte, trusted aide to Santa Anna.

"Move for the land!" he cried. "Full speed!"

Captain Grayson couldn't believe they had chanced upon such big game. Another fact claimed his attention. The schooner would make a run for it in a good wind if he took the *Yellowstone* closer inshore. But his orders were to obey Captain Brown, and he did so reluctantly.

All the while Jeremiah's telescope was trained on the boatload of Mexicans. At the stern sheets with his back to the pursuit sat a small man with gold epaulets and braided stiff collar. Then he turned to stare at the steamboat, now running up the one star and stripes. The energetic, thin-featured face caused Jeremiah a start, for it was the same he had seen in the portrait hanging in the Mexican Consulate in New Orleans.

"Santa Anna!"

To capture him! What he wouldn't give to take *El Presidente* captive. By a suffering gull, he might do it! He cried for more steam and ignored all talk of running aground. The prize was all that mattered. Here was the idol and the soul of Mexico, the spark that set off guns and deployed armies in one gesture, that dictated laws to Mexico's millions in another. Here was the butcher of the Alamo and Goliad, the embodiment of strength and power that staggered one's imagination.

Impatient of delay, Jeremiah exhorted the crew into superhuman effort. The steamboat was giving her all, gaining fast. She was also shoaling her water fast. Dragoons were forming on shore to repel the Texans with musket fire, and a cannon was showing itself.

These things were small and unimportant to Jeremiah, who saw only the dictator and realized that few men in all history had been favored with an opportunity comparable to this. And he was yelling and probably making a fool of himself, caring little, as he demanded the impossible of crew and overworked steamboat. Unmindful of the musket fire from shore that fell just short of his deck, he clenched his fists and urged the craft on. The destinies of thousands of Texans rode the *Yellowstone* now. Almost within his grasp was something armies in the field could not hope for. Not a cable's length ahead. Success here meant the end of hostilities, possibly the freedom of Texas, perhaps the future freedom of the downtrodden people of Mexico.

Then it happened. Fate had flung the lure only to jerk it away. The *Yellowstone* shuddered and groaned from stem to stern. Her bottom was grinding the shoals off Cloppers Point. And astern, the German schooner was raising sail in a reach for the eastern arm of the bay.

Jeremiah gripped the rail and held his balance as others were thrown off their feet. Then he stood as though paralyzed, his shoulders slumped. For long seconds he said nothing, just stood gazing at the boat that was moving on away from him. Then he rallied and looked about him. The *Yellowstone* was racing her paddle astern and her crew to the last man were running for poling spars.

The best Jeremiah could hope for now was a direct hit. Accordingly, he shotted the cannon, took aim, fired. The ball fell short, though the "Napoleon of the West" was drenched by water thrown into the boat. He leaped over the side and waded in water up to his thighs for the beach. A second shot tore up sand on the beach.

The greatest prize of the war and the time was lost to Captain Jerry Brown. Angry, beaten, he turned a haggard face on the schooner and ordered the starboard gun around. Two shots brought her to, and an hour later the steamboat worked off the shoal. Then they steamed for the German and boarded her.

The schoonerman's affected ignorance of the English language was quickly corrected when a line suspended from the foreyard was tied into a hangman's knot. Fat Hans admitted to having no interest whatever in a war that did not concern him other than the opportunity it presented for making a little money. So when the Mexicans contracted with him to ship a gentleman extraordinary to Vera Cruz, he had agreed to do so. Why not? He shrugged and turned palms up. When asked why all the boats and barges were concentrated here, he said they were intended to carry troops to Galveston. Amazed at the importance of all he had uncovered, Jeremiah asked the German if he knew the identity of the passenger he had just lost, only to meet with the same gestures of indifference.

"He was the President of Mexico."

"*Nein!*" the other exclaimed with fictitious surprise.

"*Ya!*" Jeremiah replied. "Seems you've scratched for a penny and found the fires of hell, *mein* friend. While my guns blast the last boat and barge into kindling wood, I'll set the torch to you."

2

The *Yellowstone* reached Galveston early on the twentieth. She had not ridden her anchor an hour before the island buzzed with Captain Jerry Brown's achievement. He had almost captured Santa Anna and had prevented the Mexican horde from descending upon the island. Before Captain Grayson and his crew had finished their varied accounts of the Cloppers Point incident, Commodore Hawkins received Captain Brown aboard the *Independence*.

In the privacy of his quarters, Hawkins refrained from comment until he heard his subordinate out. Drawing a deep breath, he began to fan his temper into a blaze. In the first place, he said, he should have gone himself instead of trusting so important a task to a man who placed impulse over reason. Properly handled, the mission would have netted Santa Anna and given the Navy an opportunity to rout the whole force of enemy land troops, to cut them off perhaps and prevent the sack of Harrisburg.

"How so, sir?" Jeremiah replied with restraint.

"You should have hastened back with the news."

"One doesn't hasten aboard the *Yellowstone*, Commodore. Nor did I have an opportunity to persuade Santa Anna to wait for you."

"Captain Brown!" With face burning red, Hawkins struck the table with the flat of his palm. "I won't tolerate your goddam sarcasm!"

Jeremiah rose. "And I've got a bellyful of your kind of talk—sir."

After an astonished moment, Hawkins chose to smile. He had the faculty of losing none of his menace by a change of expression. "Since your illustrious brother feels the same way, Mr. Brown, why don't you make a double ceremony in presenting your resignations?"

"I'm not about to resign." He added, "Sir," then said, "Nor is Captain William S. Brown if I can prevent it. You should know me by now."

"Then between us lads," Hawkins leaned forward and said in devilish low tones, "it will be my pleasure to break you and watch little brother tag after you. Oh, it can be done, Captain Brown, so don't hide behind your *gallant service to Texas* and defy me. Public opinion would not sustain you one day, not after I disclosed a few facts. First, you're expensive, too damn costly to the service. Second, you have convinced Americans that we are pirates. Third, you are harboring an enemy of Texas. I hear she has a nicely turned leg."

He paused for effect, daring Jeremiah on with arched brows and accusing smile. Then he got to his feet and thrust his head forward. "And fourth, I hope, for what I'm expecting at any moment. Strike me and speed your departure from the fleet."

So strong was Jeremiah's desire to oblige him that he almost gave in to it. Then he was gripping his hands behind him until they ached. He was glad when Hawkins resumed his seat.

"Well, Captain Brown, for once you didn't obey an impulse. My congratulations." He studied Jeremiah closely before reaching for a paper in his desk.

"Now down to cases, Captain Brown. On the third of April you captured aboard the brig *Pocket* a woman who held in her possession charts and information of value to and en route to the enemy. You did not and have not arrested this agent of Mexico, and you have not given reasons to me or to the Secretary of Navy for this breach of duty and conduct as an officer. Furthermore, after leaving the *Pocket* here, you sailed to New Orleans without orders to do so. Therefore, knowing me as you do, may I out of curiosity ask why you deliberately played the damn fool by giving me an opportunity to punish you?"

"I was trying to catch another spy with this one, sir. And I had no time to offer explanations which you or others could hardly understand. Only the proof in the person of the other spy could verify and substantiate my motive."

"Have you this proof now?"

"No. I had intended to settle the matter on the afternoon you sent me into the bay."

Hawkins reappraised Jeremiah with a look that was meditative. "I am inclined to think you are telling the truth, since you could have left a pretty leg to the safety of New Orleans, and because you played right into a court-martial, knowing I'd gladly see you broken. However, I won't press the charge against you unless you force it, because I wish to spare the service the disgrace which your conduct, if aired, would heap upon it."

Taken aback by the first sensible speech he had ever heard from the commodore, Jeremiah was quick to realize that Hawkins had not started the gossip campaign against him.

"So," Hawkins said, rising, "unless you bring in the woman to absolve you and the naval service of blame within the next forty-eight hours, I must place you under arrest. That is all, Captain Brown."

3

That morning the *Flash*, which had arrived in Galveston the day before, disgorged the refugees who had escaped Harrisburg. Women and children, the President, Vice-President, Cabinet, and their families marched down the gangplank to join the homeless without roofs over their head. Soon every person on land and aboard ships in the harbor knew the terrible story. The government had barely escaped on the fifteenth. Next day Harrisburg was in flames. When an express rider for the Cabinet returned without learning the whereabouts of Houston's army, Burnet ordered everyone aboard the *Flash*. Even this escape was a narrow one. A detachment of dragoons rushed the shore before the *Flash* could get away and only the chivalry of Colonel Almonte prevented them from opening fire on the women and children in the boats. Next day the *Flash* rescued President Burnet from a small open boat between Cloppers Point and Red Fish Bars.

This news struck Jeremiah a hammer blow before he reached the *Invincible*. Excepting the Nacogdoches area, only the island belonged to Texas, and only the Navy stood between this barren strip of sand and the butcher of the Alamo and Goliad. And against all this there was small hope that the lost army of Texas could or would even try to turn back the Mexican tide.

His heart was heavy as he glanced at the flag above his ship and wondered how low the star of Texas could fall without dropping permanently under the horizon.

He watched the *Flash* under Captain Falvel move to Fort Point to defend the island in case of an attack by sea, and then he moved after the refugees into the city that boasted of one house on the sand.

The sea of ragged color and poverty stretching in every direction was given animation by a human tide. And over this lay a shimmering heat haze. The wind off the land made it hotter and brought mosquitoes in great swarms. Each person or setting seemed subordinated by the entire scene of hopelessness. Then again, the whole terrible episode of war and retreat was written into each face or crude shelter. Santa Anna would gloat if he could see this, Jeremiah admitted.

A shadow sped over the island and big drops of rain fell here and there. The sky came on gray and heavy and dumped water over everything. Then the sun came out and under its warmth, the smells of wet clothing filled the still air.

He looked from the masts in the harbor to the *Invincible* under a convoy of gulls, and felt himself drawn to ship and Carmela. He was moving toward them, or away from the things that pained him, when he saw something that stopped him.

Polly.

A wave of elation crept over him. Moving toward her, he was

beset with memories that reached back into the years, ending with a picture of her on the pier at Broadhaven on the James. She had been a grown woman then. And now he knew she was even more matured. She could not be otherwise. The civilian retreat had aged even the children. She was holding a sick child in her arms, cradling it gently, and singing in a low voice. Her face was smudged and her dress was ragged, the left sleeve torn from the shoulder, though her hair was groomed and shining.

Suddenly she frowned and held the child away from her. "Now why did you do that?" she said, looking down at her dress. "First the rain and now you."

Jeremiah spoke up. "Ungrateful little brat, isn't he?"

"She's not a boy," Polly said, not looking up. Then she turned her drawn face to him and stared as though unable to believe what she saw. With a visible effort, she swallowed, and slowly lowered the child to a crate, not once taking her eyes off Jeremiah. She was rushing to him, crying "Jerry!" when she stopped still and looked down at her dress.

"Jerry Brown, why the devil don't you give a woman a chance to tidy up before barging in? Look at me!"

"All right. Suppose you go to your room and change."

A bright smile took over her countenance as she threw her arms about his neck and pressed her cheek to his. "Golly gee, I'm glad to see you!" Holding him at arm's length, she appraised him from cap to boots. "The hero of Vera Cruz, Matamoros, and Galveston Bay. Jerry, you've done right well for a Brazos schoonerman."

"A webfooted one at that," he laughed.

The pride and joy had gone out of her face and she was looking at him almost wonderingly. Her large dark eyes dropped as she said, "But you had to go and ruin it all."

His smile held. "Because I caught you like this or because I failed to catch Santa Anna?"

"I'm serious, Jerry. I was so proud of you. Then I overheard something."

Her hands fell to her hips. She spread her feet wide apart and raised a face so alive with reckless anger that he was caught off guard. "Why in the name of hell did you have to undo all the good by carrying that yellow-headed spy around with you?"

As he reached for her arm, she shook him off and took a backward step. Eyes blazing, she told him the gossip had reached Harrisburg. "The people continue to believe in you. They think you have a good reason. Knowing about you and that golden piece of baggage, I can't agree. But one thing I'm telling you, and I mean it, don't you let them down!"

He was no longer grinning at her. "I had a good reason, all right. And——"

"A personal one!" she retorted.

He tensed and a fierce light played in his eyes. "You're like everyone else, won't listen because you'd rather believe the worst."

"I'm not far wrong. And you know it. And I don't like it."

"Right or wrong, what difference does my personal life make to you? You asked my blessing on your engagement to marry Harry Billings in August. I gave it to you, didn't I?"

"You silly fool! That was to make you jealous. And after I read your letter I was so mad I threw a rock at Joe Turner's mule."

"Angry, not mad," he corrected, glaring at her.

"Mad, I said! Ask the mule."

"All right—mad! But sending you off to school was a mistake. You haven't changed one damn bit."

"But I'm not a spy to disgrace you! No, siree, I'm not. I could claw your eyes out when I think of your doing this after all you've done in the Navy. And now they say the United States fleet is looking for *pirate* Brown."

He shook his head hopelessly. "Seems I tackled a wildcat." Glancing sharply at her, he said, "So you're not engaged to marry Lieutenant Billings?"

"No. But as soon as I can find a scrap of paper to write on, I will be."

It was then he saw her aunt Virginia sitting cross-legged on the ground, staring at him with no sign of recognition in her eyes. "Polly, we've got to get her aboard ship. You're coming too."

"We're contented here, thank you."

"Don't be a fool, Polly."

"I'm just being considerate. You have a guest on board."

"Very well. I'll send food and blankets."

"I'll send them back."

He turned away and walked toward his ship.

She ran after him. "Jerry," she cried, hurt breaking through, "I'm going to stick by you through this mess. All the way, even if you do love that woman."

He looked down into her wide appealing eyes and wiped a tear from her cheek.

"Good girl," he teased. "Now I'll send paper so you can write Lieutenant Harry Billings. Send my compliments and gratitude. The *Warren* tried to intercept me, Polly."

She listened eagerly to his account of the incident. "Jerry," she said when he had finished, "I'm glad for you, glad you got away. Now arrest that spy and everything will be all right."

"I know what I'm doing, Polly. And nobody or no amount of talk is going to influence me."

She shook her head. "And I threw a rock at a right sensible mule."

Making his way to the *Invincible*, he recalled his feelings just before finding Polly. Carmela had hastened his steps in her direction then. And now it would be difficult to look at her in silks without seeing Polly's ragged dress.

4

That night he sent Lieutenant Sevey and two marines ashore for the commandant's permission to transfer the prisoner Thompson to the *Invincible*. While awaiting their return, he was surprised by a visit from William. Seconds later he was wishing his brother had gone elsewhere, for William lashed him up one side and down the other. Secretary of the Navy Potter had sent for William that afternoon for the express purpose of gathering a few facts regarding the source of gossip involving Captain J. H. Brown before calling the latter to account. Caught unprepared, William had no defense other than his faith in his brother's integrity. Which, William stormed, sounded weak. When his anger subsided, he asked Jeremiah to get rid of the woman.

Stubborn and defiant, Jeremiah told him in no uncertain terms that he would stand on his own two legs. "But what's between you and Hawkins, who tells me you wish to resign?"

"The same old bone—you."

"Better quit defending me or you'll become his permanent boarder in irons."

"I'm ahead of you, Jerry. I've already quit. And only because I believe for the first time in my life my brother is wrong."

He left this for Jeremiah to think about, to file with the lectures preceding his; the commodore's and Polly's. Potter was next, and after that only the Lord knew who else. The net was drawing tight; this much Jeremiah realized. And the more he thought about it, the more importance he attached to the outcome of his forthcoming interview with Thompson.

He met Lieutenant Thompson as a fellow officer, setting the finest liquor on board in front of him, and discussed the war situation in all its phases. Eager for news of recent happenings, Thompson listened avidly as Jeremiah gave an account of Santa Anna's near capture, and said at the conclusion:

"By Jove, that would have been one for the records. But we do or don't succeed."

"You ought to know. For nearly four years you have pursued the royal game of goose under the Mexican eagle."

"True enough, old chap." Thompson smiled easily. "But a gambler over the main as well as over the table learns the art of losing gracefully. Tonight you're up and I'm down. It may be my turn tomorrow. *Quién sabe?*"

"Sure. Who knows? But you display a remarkable patience for a man in your position."

"One learns not to expect quick voyages or special favors, Captain. Take the present for example. Your grog is excellent and your conversation is preferable to confinement below decks. In fact, I'm quite content to sit here while you go on beating about the bush."

"Then I'll come to the point. It's about Carmela."

"Naturally," Thompson replied.

"She will stand trial and face a probable death sentence."

"She played the game and lost." The reply was so casual that Jeremiah showed surprise.

"She played your game, Lieutenant. You are morally responsible for her."

"Come now, Captain Brown," Thompson mocked. "She was well paid, but never satisfied."

"I maintain you're responsible. If there's a spark of decency in you, you'll help her out of this."

"I? How?"

"Don't pretend, Lieutenant Thompson. Shortly after the engagement with the *Bravo*, I told you Carmela tried to quit this business, but Martínez held your safety over her head."

"Really, old fellow, I find that hard to swallow. Carmela didn't convince me. Therefore, I'm still inclined to believe the two of you are pulling my leg."

"Knowing the trouble she's in, you seem to be evading the issue. You're the only man who can come forward and convince a court that you are actually to blame for all she's done."

Thompson said, "You know as well as I do that Texans wouldn't shoot a woman."

"We're talking about a spy," Jeremiah said, folding his arms and glaring at the other. "Now will you co-operate or not?"

Thompson shrugged, lit a cigar, and sat back. Looking up sharply from the glowing tip, he said, "Captain, I don't recall your offering any inducement whatever other than risk on my part. Surely you didn't call me here without something to appeal to my trading instinct."

Jeremiah eyed him steadily. "I have that something, all right. But it isn't what you're thinking. Even if it were possible to trade you back to Mexico for Lieutenant Leving, I could no more do that than I could grant you title to Galveston. So forget about freedom or escape."

"Too bad," Thompson said. "Carmela is a charming woman."

Jeremiah realized that he had failed up to this point. He rose and walked to the door. Opening it, he motioned Lieutenant Sevey, Mr. Wells, and the captain of marines inside. Closing the door, he turned to Thompson again.

"Is your mind made up, Lieutenant?"

"Quite, old chap."

Jeremiah held Thompson's glance while fishing a gold coin from a pocket and flipping it to the ceiling. It fell, ringing on the table top. "That's a lot of wealth for a Texan these days, but I'll gamble it all that your mind isn't made up."

Thompson responded quickly to the challenge. Lacking money, he placed his watch and diamond-set fob on the table without breaking the glance between them.

"This says I have made up my mind."

"Maybe you'll change it when I tell you that Lieutenants Ocampo, Hogan, and Taylor have admitted that the charts of the Texas coast seized aboard the *Pocket* were drawn by you. Do you deny this, or that they were on their way to you and destined for use by the Mexican Navy?"

"No denial," Thompson replied in lazy fashion.

"One more question," Jeremiah said. "Did you chart the Texas coast while aboard the *Correo de Mejico* last summer?"

"Correct."

"Then since you could not produce your commission in the Mexican Navy at the time, as the records will bear out, the charts were drawn by a pirate and spy."

For the first time Thompson showed concern.

"Therefore," Jeremiah said, "I charge you with the crime of gathering information for the enemy and causing it to be transported to Mexico for the purpose of hurting the cause of Texas, and direct that you be held aboard this ship to await orders regarding your confinement until trial."

After a moment's pause, he said, "And that's the way it stands unless you've changed your mind, Lieutenant. You have one minute to think it over."

Thompson used up the allotted time. The furrow between his brows deepened and he stared thoughtfully at his fingers as they drummed the table. When Jeremiah said the time was up, Thompson raised his face and very nonchalantly picked up his watch and the gold coin.

Rising, he said, "Captain, you've failed to convince me."

Chapter Twenty-seven

AN EYE FOR AN EYE

The morning of the twenty-first broke clear, though the wind whipping down the bay lowered the depth of water over the bar and landlocked ships trying to clear for New Orleans. As the island came to life and everyone turned anxiously toward the mainland, Secretary of the Navy Potter boarded the *Invincible* and asked to see Captain Brown.

Colonel Robert Potter greeted the commander of his most active war vessel warmly and came to the point. Jeremiah knew more about this rugged North Carolinian's past than the colonel realized or might have appreciated. His claim to the post in the Cabinet emanated from a boast that he had been a midshipman in the United States Navy. And it was rumored that this signer of the Texas declaration of independence had been expelled from the legislature of North Carolina for cheating at cards. But he was a strong man in the Cabinet and took pride in the laurels the Brown brothers won for his branch of the service. Therefore, he said with the humor of a politician, he could condone a man's interest in a charming woman as long as nobody was hurt. But what about this pretty spy who threatened the good name of the Navy?

Jeremiah told his story, admitting his great admiration for Carmela since 1832. He pleaded her case on the grounds that she was forced to carry information for the enemy because Consul Martínez of New

Orleans had threatened to do harm to her fiancé if she refused. Potter appeared sympathetic and Jeremiah went on to tell of his interview with the prisoner Thompson last evening. Then he exploded a bombshell that shook the colonel then as it did the Cabinet later in the day:

He had taken the liberty of charging Lieutenant Thompson with the crime of spying for the enemy.

Potter frowned over this. "So you're applying Mexican logic to the situation. Can you make it stick, Captain?"

"I'm going to try my damdest, sir."

The Secretary tossed off three glasses of whisky and departed with a promise to use his influence with President Burnet in the lady's behalf.

The day had an auspicious beginning. However, the showdown was yet to come. President Burnet would decide the issue.

Toward noon the *Independence* ran up alert signals. Pennants fluttered and messenger boys moved from ship to ship. The blue peter broke in the breeze at the peak of the *Brutus*, then the *Liberty*. The sudden activity of the fleet caused much excitement on the beaches. As the curious throng increased along the dock and shouted questions, Jeremiah called for his trumpet. He was soon telling them, and wishing it were true, there was no cause for worry or fear, that the fleet was merely being repositioned in the harbor.

Hawkins's message would have created a panic on shore, for he advised that three sails had been sighted near San Luis Pass. He ordered his commanders to prepare for an attack by sea. Under normal conditions this news would have been welcomed aboard each ship with cheers. But on this day the wind was off the land and there was scant water over the bar. Hawkins could not put a ship to sea in defense of the island.

The harbor craft cleared a way as the naval formation was reshuffled, the *Independence* close by the shore, the *Brutus* next, the *Liberty* farther out in the harbor, and the *Invincible* commanding the inner roadstead between the island and Bolivar Point.

As the hours went by with no sign of the enemy, Jeremiah paced the deck forward and aft. Carefully laid plans threatened to blow up in his face all because the alert completely annulled a meeting in private with the President.

The lookout spoke the deck: a small boat under lugsail was moving down from the upper bay. Almost at the same time the square sail of a brig was sighted to the south. The latter was running for the bar. The lugger drew alongside with news from the mainland:

The armies of Houston and Santa Anna were nearing each other in the vicinity of the mouths of the San Jacinto and Buffalo Bayou. Although the information was days old, it constituted the first news of the whereabouts of Houston's army since the twelfth.

Jeremiah looked toward the sea again. The brig was unable to cross the bar, and a longboat was putting out for shore, probably with mail from New Orleans. He watched the boat—she was having a devil of a time of it in the surf—and then turned to stare up into the hazy reaches of the Bay of Galveston. Somewhere up there a decision was probably in the making.

A second later his thoughts were scattered as though blown to bits by an exploding shell. The lookout forward bawled excitedly, "The enemy! The enemy!"

Whirling for a sweep of the southern horizon, Jeremiah cried, "Where away?"

"The island! Marching in from the west!"

Since the topman's warning coincided with the expected attack announced in the alert, it was logical to believe that the enemy had boated San Luis Pass and landed marines on the west side of the island. Jeremiah ordered warning signals fired in quick succession and pennants hoisted to the fore signal yard.

The boom of the *Invincible's* guns split the air over the harbor and land. Gray-black smoke was instantly snatched from the muzzles by the wind and dissolved alee as signal flags broke in the breeze and flattened like boards.

"Shall I clear for action, sir?" Sevey called from aft.

"Aye, sir. Bring her starboard battery to bear. Masthead there! How goes the wind aloft?" The drummer boy was beating to quarters, and the sailing master's voice was giving the drum admirable competition as the crew jumped to make sail aft and swing her stern on the quartermaster's helm. While aboard the *Liberty* and *Brutus*, "what-the-hell?" flags, as Mr. Abbott called them, were breaking out, and the *Liberty* was placing her semaphore jack in the chains. Ahead, the *Independence* had opened her signal locker and bent pennants to a halyard. They snapped at the masthead, and the wigwag astraddle a yardarm was repeating, his semaphore flags almost touching above his head: "Do not understand."

When the signal officer cried the reply, Jeremiah, halfway up to the lookout's perch, shouted back, "The devil you say! He's almost on the scene. So point the enemy out to him with a blast from Long Tom! Fire high and over the *Independence!*"

As he reached the maintop and looked in the direction Little Josh pointed, he saw a moving mass of red and blue interspersed with white. His telescope came up and hung there for a long moment before slowly dropping to his side. The Long Tom spoke and a round shot screamed on a foolish mission over Galveston.

With face red and eyes snapping, he turned on Little Josh. "Boy, it's the brig for you. Maybe a whole month on bread and water."

"But, sir! What's wrong, sir?"

"Look through the glass, you blundering ape, and tell me what's wrong. Why old Hawkins and the government are saying Jerry Brown is drunk."

The lad looked and swallowed hard as he turned a chalky green, for the enemy advancing on Galveston was nothing more than the refugees' morning wash whipping in the wind.

On deck Jeremiah brought all activity to a halt and, under the curious glances of his crew, admitted his embarrassment. When they made all sorts of grimaces in an effort to suppress smiles and outright laughter, he said, "Go ahead and laugh, boys. As for me, I'm going to hang up my spyglass and secure for squalls."

The flat red face of the sailing master was the first to burst open with a guffaw that was heard aboard the *Liberty*. That set them off, and every man aboard save the culprit who "couldn't tell a petticoat from a marine" joined in. Even the captain shed his official manner and bent double with the rest of them.

The incident broke the mounting tension aboard ship and on the land and served as a tonic to chase away depressing thoughts and memories that came with the approach of evening.

2

With the sunset came a battle of the weak winds. Night pennants broke in the uncertain air and bent first south then all around until the Gulf wind freshened on a light squall. The rain continued inland, leaving cordage dripping and stars hanging in the darkening sky against the network of rigging. Between the *Invincible* and the island, the mirrored lights of *Liberty* and *Brutus* shone in the jet waters of the harbor like long daggers of flame.

The tide was sucking lazily up the beaches and swirling about the barnacled piles of the dock when Jeremiah's gig touched shore. Silhouettes appeared against fires, and in the direction of the custom-house a fiddler began to saw away with more zeal than ability. Farther on a group of darkies lent pleasing harmony to an old spiritual.

A man collided with Jeremiah and apologized. He was Thomas McKinney on his way to see President Burnet. With the same destination in mind, they threaded the crowd toward the lee side of the customhouse. The shipowner said he was in need of cash, having financed the government to the tune of more than one hundred thousand dollars. Creditors were breathing down his neck. Just before his turn to see the President, he said:

"Jerry, better stay out of New Orleans. And it wouldn't be a bad idea to nudge Mr. Burnet into doing something about declaring the *Pocket* a legal prize of war. You can take this for what it's worth, but Hawkins said he saw no reason to get excited about creating a court to judge the *Pocket*."

Jeremiah's brows joined. Hawkins of all people knew that the penalty for failure of the Texas Government to comply with the laws of nations in dealing with a seized vessel was in effect an admission of piracy. The *Invincible* and her crew would be forfeited.

The flap of the executive tent opened, and McKinney said, "Good luck," a moment before the soldier-guard cried, "Captain J. H. Brown."

Jeremiah entered the tent with cap in hand. Two lanterns at each end of the oblong enclosure, a ship's mess table and benches constituted the furnishings of the presidency. At one end of the table sat the Secretary of State and a visitor. The President and his secretary occupied the far table end. Mr. Burnet arose wearily and greeted Captain Brown, seated himself, and motioned his visitor to do likewise.

His eyes brightened as Jeremiah extended a package which he opened. "Cognac brandy and Holland gin! Captain, how did you know my favorites?"

"I read my cargo lists, sir."

"My undying thanks. Under the strain of escape and all, the gift will come in handy. Or," the President said with humor, "is this a bribe?"

Next he extended congratulations and the thanks of Texans to the man who had done more than any other to prevent a seaborne invasion of the homeland. Jeremiah was then asked to state his business. When he complied, the President called for a copy of his letter addressed to Mr. Collinsworth, whom he had asked to accept the office of district judge to determine upon the character of captures, notably the case of the *Pocket*. Collinsworth had not accepted. However, Captain Brown could rest assured that as soon as the confusion of retreat allowed, a judge would be found.

"In the meantime, Your Excellency, we are being treated as pirates in the States. You are acquainted with my narrow escape from the U.S.S. *Warren*. Next time I might not be so fortunate. If I may suggest, sir, an admiralty court might be set up here at once. Also the payment of freight and demurrage to Captain Howes would have a good effect in the United States."

The President was very much in sympathy with the captain's views and would counsel with Commodore Hawkins at his earliest convenience. Now as to the other matter Captain Brown wished to discuss——

Jeremiah asked if Colonel Potter had talked with him that day about the spy. Mr. Burnet admitted that the Secretary of the Navy had admirably presented the case. Taking hope, Jeremiah repeated the story given Potter earlier, of his acquaintance with Carmela over the years and the influence of Thompson on her behavior as far back as 1832. He told of the meeting at the Mexican Consulate on Palm Sunday, and concluded with a request that Thompson be held as a spy and that the charge against Carmela be reduced to accomplice to the act.

"Captain Brown, I admire your chivalry and stubborn courage in this affair. You have walked dangerously in the face of opposition that could break you. But there's more to it. Personalities and sentiments must not blind our eyes to the light of proper justice.

"In the case of Lieutenant Thompson, we must remember that we are not Mexicans, and cannot therefore shape the evidence you gathered into any honorable pattern of justice. He was captured in uniform and held as a prisoner of war. According to the laws of nations, which you urge upon me in the case of the brig *Pocket*, he cannot be charged as you desire."

Jeremiah checked the torrent of his feelings in order to say politely, "Mr. President, I still believe in an eye for an eye."

"So do I, though conformable to the rules of war and the society of men."

Jeremiah was projecting his anxious thoughts ahead to the President's decision regarding Carmela.

"Sir," Jeremiah began, "I beg to remind you again that Miss Ryan was guided by compassion for her fiancé, whose safety she was led to believe rested entirely in her hands. I firmly believe that under the circumstances she merits the consideration if not the intervention of the government and yourself before she is arrested and formally charged."

The President lowered his head and massaged the lines of weariness at his forehead with thumb and forefinger.

He fished among his papers a moment before finding what he searched for. "This afternoon the brig across the bar boated in mail. There was a letter from Mr. Bryan of New Orleans. In his message is an item which has a direct bearing on the case. It is also of unusual interest to you, since in this instance eye-for-an-eye justice conforms to the rules of war."

Extending the paper, he said, "Read it, Captain Brown."

Slowly Jeremiah lowered his gaze from the face before him to the letter and followed it to a sentence well down the page:

> Through an official report which came into my hands while writing this, I am grieved to report that on the 14th of April at the Adobe prison of Matamoros a firing squad ended the life of Lt. Wm. H. Leving of the schooner-of-war Invincible.

The President said, "Captain Brown, do you still ask clemency for a spy?"

After a long silence, Jeremiah replied, "No, sir."

Accepting the hand of the President, Jeremiah turned and walked out of the tent into the night.

Chapter Twenty-eight

THE CRUEL HARBOR

On board ship, Jeremiah went below and sent for Lieutenant Sevey and Fleming Wells.

Their entry was marked by a significant exchange of glances after a look at the captain's face. A burning light in his eyes advised of a tempest at work inside him. He stood tall and straight, looking beyond them as he said, "I've just come from the President's office."

Slowly, deliberately, he told them what had happened, of his defeat on both counts. "Gentlemen, you know my sentiments regarding the spy and the woman. I had hopes of forcing Thompson into absolving Miss Ryan of blame. Now that is denied me."

Mr. Wells pinched his chin between working thumb and forefinger, and the lieutenant sat tense. Looking from one to the other as he paused in his slow stride, Jeremiah said:

"Order the guard to bring Lieutenant Thompson here, Mr. Sevey."

"Aye, sir."

With the officer's departure, the purser said cautiously, "Sir, I hope you have carefully weighed any course of action you may pursue."

"Mr. Wells, there comes a time when the course shapes the man."

"Sir, may I ask what the devil you're talking about?"

"You'll learn in due time. Now do me the honor of setting out the finest whisky and inviting Mr. Kelton to join us."

The purser was not long in attending to these things and returning.

As he entered, Jeremiah said, "Mr. Wells, if anything of a final nature should overtake me tonight, please see that my full back pay goes to Miss Polly Merchant of Velasco."

Mr. Sevey and Lieutenant Thompson entered. A moment later the fat little surgeon arrived and stared in displeased manner over the rim of his spectacles. When Jeremiah bid them sit, the prisoner shrugged and said:

"Seems we're enjoying quite a social fling of late, Captain. What now?"

"One to end them all, Lieutenant," Jeremiah replied, standing before the seated quartet with hands behind his back. "But first, it's the duty of the host to bring his guest up to date on the latest developments. So help yourselves to drinks.

"Gentlemen," Jeremiah said, "tonight the President of Texas informed me of a tragedy. On the fourteenth, Mr. Leving fell before a firing squad in Matamoros."

Mr. Sevey looked stunned, then angry, and the purser and surgeon sent menacing glances toward Thompson, who started a trifle before composing himself and meeting the cold glint of Jeremiah's gaze.

"I went to the President to plead the case of a lady who has endeared herself to all aboard the *Invincible*. Mr. Burnet was unable to interfere in her behalf. In fact, it was in answer to my plea that he disclosed the fate of Mr. Leving."

Mr. Kelton's round face turned red. "Rank injustice!" he burst out. "Why that little woman was a victim of circumstance, nothing more."

"And our friend Thompson," Jeremiah added.

Thompson frowned and fingered a jaw, darting glances from purser to surgeon and on to Jeremiah, who was saying: "I had another reason for visiting our President. It was to urge upon him the prosecution of charges I pressed against Mr. Thompson, namely, pirate and spy. I felt that such charges were actually justified."

"Amen!" said Kelton. "Did they stick?"

As Lieutenant Sevey leaned forward expectantly, and Thompson's eyes narrowed to mere slits, Jeremiah said, "President Burnet said we must remember that we are not Mexicans, that we could not shape the evidence I gathered into any honorable pattern of justice. The prisoner was captured in uniform and, according to the laws of nations, he must remain a prisoner of war."

Thompson's face slowly assumed the expression of a man suddenly enjoying the very best of luck.

"So we must surrender our lady of the *Invincible* to the misfortunes brought about by Mr. Thompson, the same as we have given Mr. Leving's life in exchange for the protected prisoner of war Thompson. Seems the laws of society have for once failed to mete out proper justice. I find it difficult to agree with the verdict, and cannot therefore pursue my normal course in a happy frame of mind without demanding personal satisfaction."

He stepped to Thompson's chair and said, "Will the prisoner please stand?"

Thompson stood.

"In view of what I have in mind, Lieutenant Thompson, I must grant you a brief parole."

So saying, he threw down the glove in traditional manner by slapping Thompson's face.

The invitation to a duel evoked a stiff nod from the challenged man. "Your servant, sir."

Jeremiah looked at Thompson. "Pistols at ten paces suit you? We can row to the mainland and light lanterns."

Thompson smiled superciliously. "By Jove, this is quite a novelty, a Texan resorting to the dueling practice of polite society. Now, Captain, I have in mind something more in keeping with your character. Perhaps you've heard of the unique method employed by certain pirates on the Spanish Main. Two men, each armed with a knife, go overboard. Tied to the ankle of each is the end of a six foot length of rope. In the middle, to carry them under and keep them together, is a heavy chain weight. Two go down, and the name of this duel, *Uno Viene Arriba*, tells the rest——

"One comes up."

Wells, Kelton, and Sevey were instantly on their feet in protest of this procedure. As their voices ran together in discord, Jeremiah called for silence and gave Thompson a caustic smile.

"My apologies, Lieutenant Thompson, for expecting a pirate to emerge from the New Orleans jail a gentleman." Turning to his men, he said, "So we'll conduct the duel in pirate fashion."

The time for talk was at an end. Jeremiah changed his naval uniform for sailor's togs. On deck, the officer and members of the watch looked on curiously as the captain, resembling a fisherman, got into the boat with surgeon, top brass, and the prisoner.

In the boat, not a word was spoken. The oars lifted, fell, rose again in a swish of water. Waves slapped gently at the sides, occasionally splashing over the gunwales. Patches of light appeared and bounced on to the motions of the choppy surface. The surgeon tossed the hand lead to the prow and drew it up at the stern sheets, all in silence. At his side were a lantern, which he would light at the proper time, and two knives fashioned after the pattern made famous by the late James Bowie. At his feet were a small coil of rope and a length of chain.

Jeremiah shipped his oar. "How deep is it here, Mr. Kelton?"

"Lacking three fathoms. The current is strong."

"Then tie the weight to the anchor before we go overboard. That should keep us from sweeping out to sea." Next he asked the surgeon, whom he had chosen for his second, to secure the rope end to his ankle.

"Aye," Kelton growled. "Though it's an honorable duel, you're risking too much for too little, Captain. But it's your grave, and I'll remember you as the stubbornest captain I ever sailed of."

With both men's ankles tied by the same rope length and the weight affixed, the surgeon lit the lantern, and Mr. Sevey said, "Now when I count up to three, you will go over the side."

Jeremiah tensed and looked at Thompson. In the lantern-light, his knife flashed. Then the purser was saying, "One—two——" And after an eternity, "Three!"

Though only one step separated them from the water, it was like stepping out of the world. They took it together, and the jerk at their ankles was so sudden that their bodies were thrown together almost before they splashed. The weight swept them down and under, striking the mud without sound. There was no light, no sound other than the roaring in their ears. This was blind fighting, as final and dark as death. It would last until one of them used up a lungful of air or ceased to breathe altogether.

Something touched Jeremiah's shoulder. Instinctively, he stabbed out. Meeting only water, he pulled himself down on his haunches until his hands touched the weight in the mud. His head collided with a solid object. When he felt for it, it was no longer there. Then he realized that Thompson had the same plan in mind, which was to come up from the floor of the bay with knife slashing. His groping hand touched Thompson's leg. A frantic movement took Thompson beyond his reach.

In rising, Jeremiah was seized by a cramp in the leg. The pain was terrific, and worse it rendered him inactive. In another moment he felt a line of metal moving across his arm. The searing of salt water advised that Thompson had drawn first blood. He jerked himself up, thinking the cramps would depart only to learn that he could rise just so far. He was caught between Thompson and the cramps. The knife arm continued to explore in arcs as vicious as the undersea would allow.

He made a desperate grab at the rope and contacted the weight. Beyond it, he tugged again. Thompson came with it, and Jeremiah was clinging to the other's leg with his left hand, when fingers slid down his knife arm to his wrist and closed like a vise over it. A frantic jerk and backward movement brought Thompson closer, still grasping his wrist. Thompson was inside his arm now pushing it outward as his legs touched in, his knife free and searching. He had not far to explore, and Jeremiah knew this as his left hand extended out defensively, moving and feeling about for the hand that held the blade. Unable to find it, he lunged up and in, drawing his arm about Thompson's waist and on in a violent effort to grasp the other's right arm before it stabbed him in the neck or back.

He found it just as the point of the Bowie knife pricked the skin at his chest. It continued to press in, slowly, even as Jeremiah's hand closed over Thompson's wrist and held the blade in check. It was a matter of strength now. They were at grips, floating in upright position with no footing under them. Unable to lunge or bring the muscles of legs or lower back into play, they could only sway and heave at their moorings in a test of endurance.

Slowly Thompson's knife arm bent, though Jeremiah wondered if it was intentional, when the hand holding his weapon out of play jerked downward so suddenly that he was thrown off guard. He straightened and his hand slipped off Thompson's. As if propelled by coiled springs, Thompson's blade lashed out, the point streaking just under the skin across his chest.

Doubling up, Jeremiah grabbed the rope in order to escape the second sweep of the knife and, feeling an advantage, drove his foot toward the hand at his wrist, tearing it loose. Free now, confidence surging through him, he placed a foot on the weight and sprang upward. The line burned into his ankle as he was brought up short. Once more, he reached for the line that secured Thompson and gave it a jerk.

It came to him, empty. Thompson had cut loose from the weight.

2

The *Invincible*'s boats combed the surface of the bay for hours before Jeremiah gave up the search. He was not alone in his opinion that the current had carried Thompson out to the bar and beyond. However, the fact remained that Thompson had escaped.

It was past midnight and the ship had quieted down. With Jeremiah's wounds dressed, officers looked at their watches and suppressed yawns. The last half hour had been reminiscent of a wake over the captain's loss. He simply sat and stared at nothing, his mind far away even as they departed one by one. He sat up to find himself alone, then eased into position again, thinking:

Hawkins's howls would fill the air, and there would be talk of a spy's success in securing her sweetheart Thompson's release through Jerry Brown.

He was in the same position when the midshipman rapped at his door and announced eight bells. "Oh!" he said, rousing. "Make it so, sir, and pipe to breakfast."

As the morning advanced the ordeal ahead was like a weight hanging over him. Carmela's sublime trust in him seemed to emphasize his failure. The fact that she had served the enemy, that he was right and she was wrong, appeared both impersonal and foreign to their relationship as man and woman.

On the other hand, duty was clear and demanding. At a quarter to nine, he knocked at her door and looked at Lieutenant Sevey and the marine guard who would wait outside for his order. A moment later she bid him enter.

"Good morning, Jerry," she smiled up from her mirror. "You're just in time to join me in a promenade of the deck."

She looked fresh and cool in checked gingham with puffed sleeves.

Her small waist seemed tiny against the sweep of her bosom and curving hips, and her skin glowed in soft rose tones. As her hair caught and held any number of yellow and golden tints, he found her more entrancing than ever.

She was reaching for a matching bonnet, saying, "I waited up for you until midnight. But with all the noise and clatter of decks and lowering of boats, I supposed some drill was detaining you."

"I wish it had been a drill. Lieutenant Thompson escaped last night."

She looked up quickly, her full attention on him. "You're joking."

"No."

"How could anyone escape from the ship's brig, Jerry?"

"I challenged him to a duel and he got away."

"Duel! Are you serious?" She stared at him as though despairing of his sanity. "What good would he be to us dead?"

"As much as if he were alive." He gave a brief account of his meeting with Thompson two nights before. "So when he refused to become involved, I pressed fresh charges against him, pirate and spy, thinking he would be glad to defend you after thinking it over. But he was riding the wings of lady luck last night. President Burnet dismissed the charges."

Her glance was strong and accusing, then questioning. Swinging her bonnet by the ribbon strings, she said with noticeable vexation, "This is certainly not the news I was expecting from you, Jerry."

"What were you expecting?"

"That I was absolved of any blame and the whole silly matter had been dropped." She moved to the open port and stared out. "Where did you make your mistake?" she said, not facing him.

She seemed very demanding, though he knew she was upset.

"Thompson simply outguessed me. And the President had just received word that Lieutenant Leving had been shot in Matamoros as pirate and spy."

She turned a puzzled face and said, a little indignant, "Do you mean to tell me that this backwoods lawyer you call President refused to hold Thomas a spy after Mexico shot a Texan for that very thing? Seems he's rather inconsistent."

"No, Carmela. In Thompson's case, the President overruled me in favor of honorable justice as prescribed by the laws of nations. He said we must remember that we are not Mexicans."

Perplexed, she lifted her shoulders with marked annoyance. "It doesn't make sense to me."

"Thompson was captured as a prisoner of war. The charges I tried to bring against him were not sufficiently strong to change the picture. Mr. Burnet acted as he saw best."

"Certainly this Burnet is not lacking a champion," she scoffed. "I'm beginning to wonder whose side you're on." Facing him, she said, "What are you going to do now, send me to New Orleans until this blows over? Or do you expect Santa Anna to dissolve the mighty government of Texas at any moment?"

"Neither," he said crisply, causing her to dart a surprised glance at him. Under her look of curious watchfulness, he said, "The same rules of war that protected Thompson fail to protect others. Mr. Burnet refused to sanction my views in another matter."

"What do you mean, Jerry?"

"I told you of Mr. Leving's fate," he said.

Defiance went out of her face, and in its place he saw growing consternation. She bit her lip and frowned. "What has Mr. Leving's fate got to do with us? That was Mexico and this is Texas."

"A spy is a spy in Mexico, France, England, and Texas, Carmela. The law dealing with a spy is universal."

"I won't believe it. You're trying to frighten me, in order to cover up your poor game of politics in my behalf. Jerry——" She broke off. Her uneasiness was fast turning into panic. "Say something, Jerry. Don't just stand there."

He had neither the courage nor the words to meet her demand. She could endure silence and doubt no longer and she rushed to him, her only refuge. "Jerry! Hold me in your arms and say nothing else about it."

Her hands were at his shoulders, and in her face was naked fear mixed with appeal for his protection. His arms went about her and he held her close. Former passions did not rise with her nearness; instead, his sympathetic heart went out to her. She trembled under his touch, clinging to him, her eyes beseeching him to annul all her fears in a word or gesture. When this was not forthcoming, she reminded him of their love and the tender moments they had known.

He couldn't stand this kind of punishment. His hands held her at arm's length. Then he broke from her and threw the door open.

"Mr. Sevey," he said, "arrest Miss Ryan and take her to the commodore."

Carmela backed a step, her slim fingers pressing against her cheeks. She stared at him with more shock in her expression than he had ever seen in any woman. Then her lips curled with scorn and a laugh escaped her.

"What a fool I turned out to be! Arrested by a gang of rebels! I've been through many adventures, but this is my first with a blundering schoonerman."

Jeremiah knew that hurting him was the most important thing in her mind then. She laughed derisively and said for the ears of his officers and marines:

"You look almost as foolish as the time you proposed to me, Jerry. But not quite." Then she faced Mr. Sevey. "Get me out of here, Lieutenant."

Jeremiah did not follow her on deck, but remained still for long minutes before stepping to the port. He saw her in the boat moving away from him, going out of his life as she had done on that day in New Orleans four years in the past. He seemed to know that it was final this time. He did not take his eyes off her until the boat became a tiny object nearing the side of the *Independence.* Then he turned away and picked up a dress she had left behind. The cabin was filled with her perfume, as his mind and heart were overflowing with memories. He could not believe she had meant all she had said. It was just her way of meeting with trouble. But her scorn persisted and the hurt commenced anew.

Then he gazed out over the water. The running waves had long since covered the track of her departure, and the harbor under the sun and wind seemed indifferent to the fortunes of mortals.

Chapter Twenty-nine

SAN JACINTO

It was early evening of April twenty-eighth.

On this night, Jeremiah paced the deck, pausing often to glance toward the island, the sea, the mainland, and up into the bay. Like a tiger in a cage, he moved on only to stop again and stare at the same things.

There had been no change in the scenes of harbor and land during the last five days; no news of the little army. The only visible change was the attitude of his friends since Carmela's arrest. Polly had consented to his placing her aunt Virginia under the surgeon's care and both had moved to the ship. William was once again the brother, and Hawkins, though silent and watchful, breathed easier now that the naval service was no longer a target for gossip. But Jeremiah realized that someone was at work against him. Though he could not put his finger on the person or the mode of attack, he felt it as one feels an undertow, believing it had to do with his defense of an enemy of the State. It lay behind Hurd's eyes and Hawkins's abnormally quiet face, in the reserve of Vice-President Zavala and members of the Cabinet. All in silence, which to a man of action was a terrible weapon since there was no way of coming to grips with it.

He shook his head in an endeavor to dispel the picture, and moved on up the larboard side to the bows. The fires on shore cast a yellow pencil of light down the jib boom and bowsprit, pointing to the spot where he and Thompson had gone down to the undersea. The game of One Comes Up had backfired. Two came up. Jeremiah's face burned as he thought of Thompson's escape.

Looking over the side, he saw a boat nearing the ship. Mr. Sevey replied to the challenge of the watch, came on deck, and said: "Sir, Miss Ryan accepted her belongings and sent her love. Mockingly, I regret to report."

"Where is she now?"

"In a tent near the customhouse. Two of the commodore's marines are on guard at all times."

"Devilishly odd, isn't it? Hawkins knows how easily public feeling can get out of hand. The rowdy element on land might be glad to get their hands on a spy."

From aloft came the lookout's cry: "A boat under sail!"

"Where away?"

"The bay side, sir. A man is shouting something."

The ship had swung on her anchor with the run of the ebb tide and her bows pointed into the bay. Jeremiah and Lieutenant Sevey rushed forward and strained their ears for some sound. It came faint against the wind, sounding like, "He's one," over and over. Then Jeremiah heard his name called:

"Jerry Brown? It's me, Caulder!"

"This is Brown, the *Invincible*. Come on!" To Mr. Sevey: "Lower my gig with all speed, sir. Caulder's from the mainland."

"Jerry! We've won! We've won!" The cry came from the boat.

"Good!" In lower voice, he said, "Mr. Wate, call the surgeon. Caulder is probably out of his head."

With six strong men at the oars, Jeremiah at the stern sheets, the gig came upon two men in an open boat rigged by a jury mast with an old army blanket up for a sail. Caulder and Benjamin C. Franklin. The former was still crying the news. "We've won, Jerry, old boy! Victory is ours!"

Franklin verified this. "Captain Brown, we won the battle of Buffalo Bayou, all right. We routed Santa Anna on the twenty-first, took nearly six hundred prisoners, one cannon, and no end of muskets. Santa Anna escaped."

Jeremiah cleared his throat. "You boys feel all right?"

"Hell, yes, Jerry!" exclaimed Caulder. "Outside of sleeping cold and living on what we could for five days, we feel all right. I could drink a gallon of whisky and——"

Franklin said, "We left on the twenty-third without provisions. We're bearing the official dispatch from General Rusk to President Burnet. Here it is, signed and sealed."

"All right, lads. Bend to the sweeps," Jeremiah said. "We've got some celebrating to do aboard ship." When under way, he said, "So Houston decided to fight."

"After Colonel Sidney Sherman paraded the men before his tent and said they were going to attack. Now did old Sam want to come along? Houston looked like he was drunk and said if that's the way the men felt about it, he would get on his horse and go with them. The Mexicans were taking their siesta. We slaughtered them. General Houston was wounded."

"So we won. Men, that's the best news in the world," Jeremiah said. "Maybe Houston intended to fight after all."

"No, he didn't. The proof is there, Jerry. If he had, he would have done it on the twentieth, before General Cós arrived with reinforcements that brought Santa Anna's forces up to fifteen hundred men, twice our strength. He knew Cós was on the way."

"Then my hat's off to Sherman. And so Santa Anna is somewhere up on Arroya del Bufalo without an army, right?"

"Right! Deaf Smith found his horse in a bog at Vince's Bayou, got him out, and said he was sure Santa Anna wasn't far off."

The glorious news filled Jeremiah to running over. This was his victory, every patriot's triumph. For over four years he had dedicated himself to the fulfillment of this moment, which meant, by the grace of God and the wisdom of the people in handling the peace, that once more the Brazos approach would meet the sea with freemen's cotton, corn, tobacco, and orchards. It meant a schooner with large roomy cabins and slanting masts. It meant security.

On board ship, he shouted the glad tidings, then ordered the long swivel amidships charged. He fired three salutes over the harbor, threw his cap high over the water, and loosed a yell that carried as far as the *Brutus*.

"Hold on, boys," he said after the third gun, "or old Hawkins will clap me in irons again."

Though the Long Tom was silenced, nothing could have stopped the celebration on board. Sailors scrambled up from the berth decks, shouting to the top of their voices. "Hip hip hooray!" and "Grog!" were on every tongue. Wild yells of abandon rolled across the harbor, causing lantern wigwags to appear on sister ships, and musket signals to break from their decks. From the commodore down to the last powder monkey on the *Independence*, they were saying Jerry Brown was drunk, was probably drawing pictures of another Mexican army out of petticoats. But it didn't matter to Captain Brown, who roused out the purser's steward and said, "Give the lads grog. And let them do the dipping." The order was carried out. As Jeremiah led the messengers of victory below for the finest liquor aboard, the fiddler appeared on deck. Fortified with repeated "tods" from the grog tub, he struck up a tune. Sailor grabbed sailor, and the deck under their feet soon rumbled like a giant bass drum. The drummer boy struck the fiddler's rhythm, and soon someone made a rhyme to suit the chord:

> *"Old Santa Anna got his reward*
> *When us Texas lads caught 'im off guard;*
> *Once old Santa Anna was pow'ful and rich,*
> *But now, we're gonna hang the . . . ."*

"Lanterns!" cried the sailors. "One on every yard 'n line to light up the old *Invinc'ble!*"

"Aye! Cholly boy, we'll wet the sails down wi' grog. Hoo-ray fer Sam Houston! Hoo-ray fer President Smith!"

"Smith ain't President, Jim. You're drunk."

Sailor Jim giggled. "Who the hell cares? We'll 'lect Cap'n Brown. Hey you there, Mister Midshippy, you fer President Brown?"

"Aye!" Alf Wate cried.

The sailor pawed over the midshipman; Alf might be a "brass-bound snotty" but he was a fine fellow also, and any man who said it wasn't so would have a fight on his hands.

The bedlam of decks drew only a smile from Jeremiah. When Rusk's couriers were "primed to bustin," he escorted them to the flagship *Independence*, where Hawkins ordered up the finest food on board before cannonading the heavens with a thirteen-gun salute. "Thirteen for the stripes in the ensign!" he cried. The word had been passed to the *Liberty* and on to the *Brutus*. Every sailor in the Texas Navy was now celebrating victory. Hawkins quickly sent word to all captains of the fleet to hold crews aboard ships. He was a little late. Sailors emptied on the beaches of Galveston by the boatload and began a disorderly march toward the customhouse, taking everything that would burn, canvas, tents, poles, and firewood, in order to build a bonfire. Refugees heard the news, let out cheers, and joined the sailors. Men and women danced, kissed friends or strangers of the opposite sex, danced about and yelled until breathless, then moved on with the crowd. Some talked of rushing home to till the land, others paused to send up prayers of thanks, while others shed tears of happiness.

When Caulder and Franklin had eaten their fill, Hawkins suggested that they had better report to President Burnet. With some difficulty, he got them under way, and he found it quite a task to assemble as many as six marines to open up the crowd for the messengers, himself, and Captain Brown. By the time they reached the executive mansion, as the people called Burnet's many-patched tent, the crowd of merrymakers were threatening even that. Guards were throwing their guns high in the air and the President was sticking his head out in an effort to learn what was going on. Upon hearing the news, his expression was one of instant shock and disbelief. As it underwent a change and his face seemed to shed its weariness, he said with noticeable vexation:

"It appears odd that everybody on the island knew about the glorious victory before I did."

There was little sleep in the vicinity of Galveston that night. While the government went into hurried session in Burnet's tent to plan its return to the mainland and establish an orderly and safe program for the refugees who were already clamoring for passage to their homes, sailors and civilians continued to look for ways in which to turn their long-pent gloom into a celebration they would remember. Before midnight a huge dancing party was in full swing. Liquor had miraculously appeared from out of nowhere and fiddlers had bunched on the sand. Slaves scraped on any piece of metal at hand, and here and there a few performed on the clevis and sang a favorite chorus:

> *"O git up gals in de mawnin'*
> *O git up gals in de mawnin'*
> *O git up gals in de mawnin'*
> *Jes at de break ob day——"*

Men bent to their ladies and pranced backward and forward, their backs as stiff as their toes were nimble. The fiddlers kept at it, and by two in the morning all were playing the same tune. Bystanders kept time by hand clapping. The girls swung out, heads moving saucily, eyes roving. A settler laughed. "They say Texas is a heaven for men and dogs, but a hell for women and oxen. Can't speak for the oxen tonight, but, Lordy Lord, look at the women!"

Criers followed the flagship's boatswain and drummer. "All sailors of the Navy return to your ships! By order of the commodore. All sailors of the——"

Jeers lifted: "Tell the commodore to strike his bell eight! Give the commodore me regards, bosun boy! Tell the commodore to go sit on the capstan!"

A spirited girl rolled her eyes at the boatswain and swept him into a dance. Bewilderment left his face in favor of a puzzled grin as he put motion into his legs.

But the scene was not all revelry. Between torchbearers a preacher stood praising the Lord before a gathering that shouted "Amen!" following his every statement. Farther apart from the dancers, Negroes raised their voices to heaven with old spirituals and prayers of thanks.

The stars wheeled on in their courses, lifting in the east as others seemed to dip reluctantly under the western horizon. The sea breeze came on, cool and damp. One by one, the dancers turned away from the circle. A pale band of light appeared on the eastern horizon. It pushed higher, taking on the pink tints of a sea shell. The rolling sea and the quiet depths of the bay emerged out of slate gray to accept the color. Ships sat still in the water, their hulls and masts mirrored under them. Lanterns still hung in their rigging, with no hands aboard to put out the lights of victory. Few noticed them, fewer cared.

Stragglers moved aimlessly over the prairie of sand where hundreds of tired refugees slept. A man pointed to an empty boat with *Brutus* on its stern drifting into the current. The surf curled white for the shore, and clouds on the wings of the sea wind lost their soft lavender tints as the sun lifted suddenly above the rim of earth and sky and set them afire.

Jeremiah was turning away from the scene of morning when a boat from the *Independence* brought a message:

"Commodore Hawkins requests the immediate presence of Captain Brown aboard the flagship. Carmela Ryan has escaped."

2

At half-past twelve, Jeremiah returned to the *Invincible* with Hawkins's accusations still ringing in his ears.

Below, he paced the length of his small cabin, back and forth, slamming a fist into a palm as he glared at the bulkheads and thought of the fresh indignities heaped upon him. Hawkins wanted to know where he had been since leaving the President's tent shortly after nine last evening. So did the government, he said. Now was Captain Brown sure that he had not seized upon the excitement of victory to free his sweetheart?

Further thought was interrupted by a three-gun salute from the *Liberty*. Minutes later, William Brown rushed aboard the *Invincible* and threw his arms around Jeremiah and began dancing about in a most undignified manner.

"Jerry, loose a salvo!" he cried. "Santa Anna has been captured!"

There was more. Sam Houston sent word that three Mexican generals had been killed, that General Cós had been taken alive.

"Jerry, it's incredible," William said. "An act of God. *El Presidente* has ordered the armies of Filisola and Urrea back to the Rio Grande. Texas is free!"

Clinging to Jeremiah, he went on. "The Navy cut the Mexican supply line and sent the dictator reaching for the Gulf. He was going to Galveston to meet his fleet, which we kept away, and it was his intention to capture the government there. Jerry, the army may have won the battle, but the Navy won the war!"

Something of William's enthusiasm surged through Jeremiah. The truth was up for the notice of the world. The Texas star flew high and proud.

From down by the island, the guns of the *Independence* spoke again. The smoke had no sooner disappeared than her signal flags broke in the wind: The commanders of the fleet should repair at once to the flagship. William and Jeremiah made the crossing together, and joined Hurd, Hawkins, and President Burnet. The latter had a word for the valiant men of his floating service.

While it was an accepted rule of warfare that a general or head of government lost all authority the moment he was captured by an enemy, Texas would gamble on Santa Anna's political control of Mexico to put an end to hostilities and secure Texas's formal independence. But regardless of success on this score, the Navy was indispensable, for without maritime supremacy, which the Navy had won and sustained in the recent campaign, Texans could know little future security.

Though the victory at San Jacinto overshadowed guns over the waves, all Texas knew that its little navy had done more than prevent a seaborne invasion.

"Gentlemen," Burnet said, his glance falling on Jeremiah, "you literally starved Santa Anna into a desperate reach for his supply ships in the Gulf."

With the President's departure, Hawkins proceeded to bring forth a bottle and glasses. "Gentlemen, we'll raise a toast to the future. Then we'll forget rank and enjoy ourselves as men should after a victory." He added with almost casual menace, "Aye, even though at least one of you will start damning old Hawkins all over again before this day ends."

At eight that evening Jeremiah boarded his ship again and went below. He was frowning over the purser's inventory of victuals aboard when a rap at the door drew his attention. A moment later the appearance of a lavender skirt in the doorway gave him a start. Then he saw Polly. She curtsied, said, "Captain Brown," like a lady, her large eyes alert to his humor.

Though surprised and aware of her deception—she wore Carmela's dress—he could not deny that she was ravishing.

His frown deepened. "What the devil are you doing in that dress?"

"Why, I thought you'd like to see me dressed up for a change. Now in polite society a gentleman extends a compliment whether he means it or not and the lady smiles because she wishes to believe him sincere."

"In this case there's too much lady for the container, a fact which polite society would verify with lifted brows."

"Maybe you mean the wrong lady is in it."

He surveyed her curiously, a stern light in his eye.

"I'm sorry," she said. "It fit fine in the waist. I lowered the hem line and let out seams under the arms, but it was impossible to make enough room in places. Aunt Virginia said I'd better not sneeze."

"She's right. You'd pop right out of it. Now go take it off."

"Why, Jerry Brown! If my memory serves me right, lavender is your favorite color."

"Just where did you get that dress?"

"I traded for it."

His eyes narrowed accusingly. "And what did you give in return?" he demanded.

"Value received," she replied, moving with a swish of taffeta to a chair. "However, we won't go into that. Instead——"

"*You're* telling *me* we won't go into that? Look here, Polly Merchant, what do you know about Carmela's escape? They're saying I set her free."

"You!" she smiled. "Well, here's one person who doesn't believe you did it."

She laughed when he stared at her in speechless amazement, then said, "Aunt Virginia talked a lot when she was delirious, Jerry. Kept saying, 'Jeremiah, it's costing you a great deal to keep her up there.' I wonder what she meant."

"Go ask her."

"I did. And I finally got an answer."

He squirmed a little. "That's neither here nor there. What I'm interested in——"

"You paid my way, Jeremiah Brown."

"Maybe I'm not the first person who gambled on the impossible."

"And won," she put in quickly. "I am a lady, and you're the one person I want to hear say it."

"If you call it ladylike to help a spy escape, you're wrong."

"Why, Jerry, how can you sit there and accuse me of trying to get her as far away from you as possible?"

He sat up and took notice. "So you did it, eh?"

"I'll never admit it. If I had set her free it would have been for you. With her near, all you could think of would be borrowing money to pay lawyers to defend her, worrying and forgetting duty. And all the time she would be making a fool of you. I'm glad she's gone!"

"So you had it all figured out. How did you go about freeing her?"

"Don't be silly. In all the confusion of celebrating a victory, she just walked off. Besides, it wouldn't have done any good to call for her guards. They left when a man with a British accent appeared saying President Burnet wanted them at once."

"Thompson!" Jeremiah exclaimed, rising.

"She called him Thomas. What's more, she threw her arms about him."

He stared fiercely, then shook his head with disbelief. "She was just anxious to escape, that's all."

"Like hell she was!" Polly said, eyes flashing. "Jerry Brown, you're a big, blind, stupid idiot." She got to her feet in defiant pose.

He looked at her then. "What did she say to Thompson, Polly?"

There was no reply. She stood still and silent a long moment. Then she was gone. Which wasn't like Polly, he mused. She could be expected to take the dress off right in front of him, fling it at him, say something like, "Go fill it up with yellow-headed trash!" and rush out with petticoats rustling. He gave a slight shrug.

Moving toward the window, he muttered, "So Carmela left with Thompson——"

Several minutes later, he admitted a messenger from the flagship bearing sealed orders. Still thinking of Carmela, frowning at the thought of her arms about Thompson, he broke the commodore's seal absently. Then he was reading the order:

Captain J. H. Brown, Sir

You will at your earliest convenience raise sail for New Orleans for refitting the *Invincible* & return for patrol duty along the coast to prevent any Mexican retaliation by sea. I sincerely & anxiously hope that you & your brother officers will so comport yourselves during your absence *on duty* as to return me the vessel in first rate order & discipline.

The order appeared innocent enough; the *Invincible* was actually in need of refitting and revictualing. But Hawkins had not written into the order an opinion he had given the government weeks back: He saw no reason to get excited about condemning the brig *Pocket* as a prize of war. And his reason for this statement then had been the same that caused him now to order the *Invincible* to New Orleans; for since the government had done nothing about creating a court to judge the *Pocket*, the United States accepted the Texan attitude of indifference as an admission of piracy.

Jeremiah's jaw muscles knotted in hard ridges. The commodore's words of the afternoon rang in his ears—— "At least one of you will start damning old Hawkins all over again before this day ends." And now, couched in polite language, was his determination to break Jeremiah Brown, even if it cost him the *Invincible* to do it. For sailing to New Orleans was like a bird flying toward a hawk. His ship and crew would be seized and held for trial.

Hawkins had presented another quality one could either admire or despise. It was patience. He had played the game with a sharp eye open for his opportunity and, finding it, had slammed his trump to the table.

Jeremiah felt a surge of animosity rising up in him, and he knew that henceforth their relationship was stripped of all pretense.

But there remained the practical side. Orders were orders, Jeremiah admitted. He must obey them. But while at it he should not allow his burning hatred for Hawkins to get in the way of the one purpose that dominated him now; and that was to turn what appeared to be an ill-fated cruise into a complete vindication of Texas, himself, and crew in the capture of the *Pocket*.

A little later, Jeremiah advised his officers that they would sail with the tide next day. Toward trouble, he told them, probable arrest and confinement. As he watched their faces, his own expression softened in appreciation of stanch loyalties that not even Hawkins could snatch away from him.

When he appeared on deck and watched the blue peter break in the wind to advise of his departure, he thought of Polly and her aunt. This was not a voyage for women. So he must find a place for them, and at once. He mentioned this to Mr. Sevey, who replied:

"Sir, I thought you knew. Miss Merchant and her aunt boarded the *Laura* for New Washington."

Staring at the distant *Laura*, he recalled his regret while watching Polly depart for school back in 1832. Fresh in his memory were her letters. Even remotely, she had touched some spot in his heart and mind. Then there were a hundred and one little things that up to this night seemed unimportant.

With the squally morning, he sailed out into the worsening weather over the Gulf with pictures of Polly parading before him. Watching the bows taking on long charging seas and rolling them aft into the scuppers and sails filling like great white cavities, he bent to the pitch of decks, still seeing the woman, the lady. It was all rather surprising to him, like suddenly discovering a pouch of pure gold that had been under his feet for years.

Chapter Thirty

A SQUARING OF ACCOUNTS

The dawn of May first broke with stiff winds and heavy seas. All that morning the *Invincible* wallowed under storm canvas toward the delta of the Mississippi, with her decks running seas into the scuppers and the muzzles of her lee guns dipping in and out of the waves. Before noon the wind backed and the Gulf charged in with less fury. There was still some sea on, though Jeremiah was thinking a ship might open the pass before nightfall.

He was standing aft with a hand in the weather braces, taking in gray seas and scudding clouds while figuring his position. The heavy pall of morning sky which had shut off a view of the *Brutus*, in company since Galveston on the twenty-ninth, was thinning fast. Twice during the last half hour he had warned the lookouts to trim a sharp eye for any sail, since the weather that closed off the *Brutus* could be hiding him from the very thing Commodore Hawkins wanted him to meet, a United States sloop-of-war.

As the horizon continued to widen, revealing Hurd's ship a mile west and a smear of land far to the north, it appeared that the Texans had the roadstead to themselves. At two, the mouth of the pass lay only a few miles over the larboard bow. At a quarter to three, the flag on the signal yard was breaking for a pilot when to windward a mountain of sail bore down on the *Invincible*.

The sighting of a huge sailer dipping and streaming water as she

heeled and split the foam was suddenly a cause for alarm. The Stars
and Stripes broke wildly at her peak and minutes later she laid a shot
across the *Invincible's* bows.

With her sudden appearance out of the clouds still low inside the
horizon, all sail was crowded on the Texan. The bark of the gun
caused Jeremiah to take in sail and signal the *Brutus* to close in fast
and stand alee. As Hurd cracked on canvas, he fluttered imprudent
signals:

Shall we give the American battle?

Jeremiah shouted, "Answer him fast—hell no!" before looking at
his decks. Officers and crew stood as if paralyzed, awaiting his command. They flew into action as he cried an order to helm her across
the American's course in an endeavor to race for the open Gulf.

"She's the *Warren!*" cried Mr. Newman, lowering his glass.

Soon the two ships were separated by only a mile of water and
running converging courses. Less than a mile astern, Captain Hurd
was driving up with every rag he could muster, his yards and masts
slanting alee. Jeremiah thought he was bearing in with more zeal
than was necessary. Frowning over the possibility that Hawkins
might have sent Hurd along to guarantee trouble for the *Invincible*,
he said:

"Advise Captain Hurd that I will sink him if he brings his guns to
bear on the American."

Hurd read the signals and soon bore a point north, proving that he
had been anxious to loose a broadside. Jeremiah shuddered as he
thought of the effect in the United States of a Texan gun turned on
an American war vessel. Then he was wondering if Hawkins would
stop at anything. But Mr. Sevey was tugging at his sleeve, saying
excitedly:

"The *Warren*, sir! She's luffing up!"

Jeremiah turned quickly. "For a broadside!" he said, seeing her
gun ports triced up and larboard battery bearing full on the *Invincible*.

Suddenly a great billow of smoke enveloped the *Warren*. Her sails
and yards shook as ship met the recoil. A roar hammered across the
sea and the *Invincible* staggered under a rain of iron. Gaping holes
appeared in sails, and blocks were hurtled through the air. Lines
snapped, flattening to decks ahead of broken spars and splinters as
rope ends dangled in the wind in a futile reach for fastenings. The

upper foremast tottered, held its balance a moment, then tore a swath through sail and cordage in a rending crash to leeward.

Unable to look away from the rubble of deck, Jeremiah said, "She's not the same *Warren* we ran from at the Head of the Passes."

"An avenging devil," Sevey replied.

Little Josh looked aloft. "Cap'n," he said, "you mean the Newnited States done that to us?"

This was difficult to believe. Jeremiah shook his head slowly and trained his glance on the American vessel again before giving a heartbreaking order:

"Strike the colors!"

He removed his cap and others did likewise. He watched the single star and stripes, his own ensign, flutter down in surrender for the first time. With the mist in his eyes came anger. The old malice surged through him stronger than ever in the past as he realized that Hawkins had willingly submitted the flag to dishonor in order to break Jeremiah Brown.

"He won't get away with it," Jeremiah said under his breath. Then he was surveying his crew and visualizing forty-six of his men behind bars in New Orleans. His officers were gathering about him now, and the *Brutus* was standing to leeward. Seeing the *Warren's* boats putting out with officers and prize crew, Jeremiah addressed his men:

"The game is up, lads. You'll be placed in jail to await trial for piracy. Submit to this and conduct yourselves as gentlemen. While Mr. Sevey attends to the formalities of surrender, I will swim for the *Brutus*. My escape will leave me free to get all of you out of jail and clear your names." Pausing, he looked at them. "I'm counting on you as I would in battle."

A minute later he dropped into the water and struck out for Hurd's ship.

2

Jeremiah reached New Orleans and went into hiding in a house on Canal Street. William Bryan and the lawyers engaged to defend the

"Pirates of the *Invincible*" came by night and worked with Jeremiah. The case opened on the fourth of May and when the prosecution failed to produce witnesses it was postponed. Two days later, three officers of the *Warren* were examined in the United States district court, where they testified that they had taken the *Invincible* on charges preferred by the Louisiana State Marine and Fire Insurance Company, because she had detained an American vessel on the high seas.

On the eighth, the defense based its case on laws in effect and proved beyond doubt that Captain Brown had observed them to the letter. The court ruled that since no criminal act had been committed by the prisoners, as it had been shown that the *Pocket* contained contraband articles of war intended for the Mexican Army, there was not enough evidence to justify trial by jury.

The prisoners were discharged. They were no longer pirates, but heroes, and fickle New Orleans paraded the *Invincible's* crew in a body to a feast in their honor before sending them to the Théâtre d'Orléans.

Jeremiah met the news with a feeling of uneasiness. He came out of hiding only to be arrested and released. Somehow, he thought victory had been too easily won.

"It's very strange," he said to Bryan, "that after the insurance company went to all the trouble to have my ship taken by the *Warren* they failed to put up a fight in court. Didn't even mention the fact that Texas has failed to condemn the *Pocket* before a legal admiralty court."

Bryan came forth with something else: "Despite the ruling of the court that the insurers would not be obliged to pay a cent of insurance if they could prove that the *Pocket's* cargo was contraband of war, I hear that Lizardi and Company collected its eight thousand dollars."

But nothing happened. The Spanish element seemed indifferent to a Texan victory in the United States courts. Day after day the quiet held, and Jeremiah pushed the refitting of his ship. The New Orleans *Bee* continued its tirade against Texans who insulted the American flag, though Consul Martínez, Lizardi, and the insurance company appeared disinterested. In the meantime, Texas paid the outrageous price of $35,000 for the *Pocket* in order to appease public feeling in America. And while this was in process Texas lost the schooner-of-war *Liberty* because the treasury could not meet the repair bill due on her. And William, who had resigned from the Navy, continued to lose weight and appear more dispirited.

Tense, anxious to sail, Jeremiah waited for the day his ship would be ready. It was on the morning of the twentieth that the strategy of the Spanish element and the insurance company broke into the open. The United States marshal appeared on board the *Invincible* and took Jeremiah into custody. Although Jeremiah had expected something in the way of retaliation, he was amazed to learn that the Louisiana State Marine and Fire had instituted suit against him personally for $8,000, the amount of the premium paid to Lizardi and Company for the cargo of the *Pocket*.

He was marched before his friend Judge Harper of the United States federal court, who ordered him held to bail in the sum of $9,000. He was released that morning after succeeding in having the trial postponed until December.

He returned to his ship in a state of fury. He had exonerated Texas and his crew, had erased the stigma of pirates from their names, only to find himself once more embroiled in the same defense. Martínez and the insurance company had foreseen public disfavor in prosecuting forty-six Americans under the Texas banner, and no loss in their endeavors to widen the split between Texas and the United States in singling out Captain J. H. Brown for prosecution. But worse —and Jeremiah's wrath soared—they had been aided by the government of Texas, which had listened to Hawkins and failed to declare the *Pocket* a prize of war.

That night his brother William came aboard with a letter addressed to Jeremiah through the Texas agency. After long minutes William asked why he didn't open it.

"I'm almost afraid to," Jeremiah admitted.

"It carries the seal of the government."

"Which could mean I'm kicked out of the Navy, charged with anything from rape to barratry, or ordered to put the *Invincible* in ordinary. But I'm sure of one thing, William—if it isn't trouble it's addressed to the wrong man."

William laughed for the first time in days. Watching his brother tap the letter against his fingertips, he said, "I'm glad to be free of old Hawkins."

Jeremiah broke the seal. "It's from President Burnet." He read avidly, then said, "And it's trouble. The army versus the government."

The restless Texas army, continuously swelled by volunteers from the States, had united to oppose the government's attitude of bargaining with Santa Anna, on the grounds that he should be punished for his crimes. The army charged that the Treaty of Velasco, signed on the fourteenth, which stipulated that Texas should return Santa Anna to his homeland, was in effect setting a tyrant and butcher free.

"Since the fourteenth, the army has been in a virtual state of mutiny! A hell of a note."

"Read on, Jerry."

"Burnet says: 'Navy Secretary Potter has apparently been won over to the opposition sponsored by the army. By treaty, we have agreed to send Santa Anna to Vera Cruz, which calls for the formality of protection aboard a Texan war vessel.' Now listen to this, William——

"The President advises that Potter has to all appearances won the commodore and Hurd over to the opposition sponsored by the army——"

William came out of his chair.

" 'In this emergency of State,' the President goes on to say, 'only Brown of the *Invincible* is left for the Government to appeal to. Therefore, I earnestly hope that you will serve Texas now as in the past, regardless of personal views on the subject of justice due Santa Anna, by proceeding in all haste to Velasco where you will take on board the *Invincible* Santa Anna, his suite and the commissioners of Texas, who will voyage to guarantee his safe debarkation at Vera Cruz.' "

Jeremiah drew a deep breath and exhaled noisily. William sat down, saying, "Santa Anna killed father, Jerry. He ought to hang."

"Hang him and we annul the victory at San Jacinto in the eyes of all civilized people. But worse, our government would be overthrown and we would be at the mercy of Mexico again. It won't do, William."

William broke the silence that followed with, "Well, your trouble is cut out for you, Jerry."

"Trouble?" Jeremiah was grinning. "This is going to be a pleasure."

"You always did talk in riddles, Jerry."

"Yes, sir, a real pleasure," Jeremiah said. "For the whole thing has narrowed down to a personal matter between the commodore and me."

3

Next day, the *Invincible* made hurried departure from New Orleans. Once in the Gulf, she ran under all sail until heavy seas and a May storm off Galveston sent her far off course, delaying her arrival in Velasco by four days.

President Burnet came aboard shortly after the ship anchored in the stream, grasped Jeremiah's hand in appreciation of his loyalty and said it was gratifying to learn that the naval service had not deserted him to the embarrassment of the government and Texas. Then he advised that Santa Anna's departure had been scheduled for June first.

Hurd's *Brutus* lay at anchorage, though the *Independence* was missing. The President said Hawkins was in Galveston, that the army had drawn up a resolution demanding that Santa Anna be held until a new government was formed to deal with him.

"The situation is very alarming, Captain Brown."

"So was my position in New Orleans, sir. You recall my plea for a court to judge the *Pocket*. But somebody was against that for some reason."

As their glances met, Burnet realized that Jeremiah was opening his eyes to Hawkins's part in the New Orleans affair even as he made a silent bid for the office of commodore.

Burnet accepted his favorite brandy, sipped, and resorted to what seemed an evasion:

"Our navy must remain intact, prepared to repel an enemy. In confidence, I'll tell you that the Mexican Government has said any treaty with Santa Anna isn't worth the paper it's written on. We're gambling that it is. The Lord knows we have enough troubles without looking for another invasion. Why even our own people are forcing deception in high places."

Jeremiah listened as Burnet admitted to having executed two treaties with Santa Anna, one very severe, drawn to pacify a demanding public, the other a secret one, in which Santa Anna was to prepare the way in Mexico for the reception of a Texas mission to negotiate a treaty.

"So let us hope, Captain Brown. Once we pass this crisis, time will effect proper changes—in the proper places."

"To that day, sir," Jeremiah replied.

When the President departed, Jeremiah went ashore. He searched out Polly's aunt Virginia and learned that Polly had gone upriver to Brazoria to look for work; she wanted money in order to return to Broadhaven and tutor. Polly was hurt, she said, hurt deep. And Jeremiah should know Polly Merchant—when she said she was through, she meant it; and Polly meant to pay back every cent he had spent for her schooling.

"She's just plain stubborn," Jeremiah said. "I'll find her and set her on her course."

"I doubt that, Jeremiah."

Next day, Jeremiah let it be known in Velasco that he was here to transport Santa Anna to Mexico. Upon seeing one of Hurd's lieutenants leave hurriedly for the *Brutus*, he knew that Hawkins would soon learn of it. The trap was baited and he thought the commodore would spring it.

Two days later, he boarded a steamboat for Brazoria. Upon his arrival he learned that Polly had quit her job as tutor after saying she was going to Pensacola. Jeremiah was far from pleased at hearing this, for Pensacola was the base of the United States Gulf Squadron and therefore the address of Lieutenant Harry Billings. Impatient, jealous, and determined to find Polly even if it meant a delay in Santa Anna's departure, he took the first boat downriver and arrived in Velasco shortly after sunrise on the first day of June.

He had scarcely set foot on the pier when one of his marines saluted and delivered letters from his ship. As he read them his expression underwent many changes. Polly was forgotten.

The contents of the letters were not only sensational and unexpected but most gratifying. Properly documented and signed, here was all the proof he needed to convince anyone that Commodore Charles Hawkins had overstepped himself by siding actively with the army in an attempt to prevent the government's sending Santa Anna to Mexico:

Schr Invincible May 30th 1836

Dear Sir——

I have the honor to inform you that on last evening we saw a vessel in the offing, showing a flash of a musket which we took to be a bright light; (Knowing it to be a Mexican Signal) we got under weigh. After running down and signalizing we knew it to be the Brutus——

The Brutus captn must have known by our signals that we were the Invincible—— If so ignorant not to know and thinking we were an enemy—why should he run from us, if knowing that it was the Invincible why fire into us—that Sir is a question I hope will be investigated—& why did Captn or Commodore Hawkins hail the gun which was fired at us—this information I received from Captn Hurd—also he told me that Ct. Hawkins wished to fire a broad side into us—being in haste and more information wanted every officer & men are willing to testify that we have acted with prudence & discretion during your absence——

Most Respectfully Yr Obt & Obt Servts
Seward P. Morse
Q. Master

To J. Brown Esq. Commander
Read before and approved by the whole crew of the Invincible[1]

Then Jeremiah read his first lieutenant's letter, which told of all that had transpired back at anchorage: Hurd had boarded the *Invincible* and admitted that Hawkins had elevated the big gun and ordered him to fire a broadside at the *Invincible*. Then Hawkins had sent for the lieutenant——

. . . Commodore Hawkins asked me several questions in relation to Capt. Brown's proceedings while in command of the Invincible and at the same time Capt. Hurd requested Commodore Hawkins have the Invincible got under weigh and carried up to Galveston. Upon which I told them the thing would not do and requested them not to attempt it. They informed me that they had come down to take the Invincible from Capt. Brown as he would be broke. They told me to take a decided stand, that I would be discharged from the Invincible and that Capt. Brown had brought with him from New Orleans a man to take my place. . . .[2]

[1]Official Correspondence of the Texas Revolution.
[2]Official Correspondence of the Texas Revolution.

Jeremiah said, "And I thought Hawkins would try to take Santa Anna at sea. But what a windfall this is!" Hawkins had done everything else to rid the Navy of him and, failing, he had fired on the *Invincible*. And now Jeremiah knew the time had come to very politely call for a showdown. After boarding his ship and calling a consultation of his officers, he wrote the following:

Velasco June 1st 1836

To His Excellency David G. Burnet
  From a feeling of duty to my officers and crew I submit to your consideration the foregoing statements and in addition thereto it may be as well to state that Captain Hurd informed me I was to be dismissed from the command of my vessel. If so I would like to know what are the charges alleged against me—I will never shrink from an investigation of my official conduct.

Very Respectfully Yr. Obedient Servant
J. Brown[3]

Assembling his officers, Jeremiah lowered away his gig. They appeared before the President in a body and Jeremiah presented the letters. As Burnet read them the furrows of his brow deepened and his face reddened. When he looked up at last, there was conflict in his face, and Jeremiah knew he was caught between policy and desire. The President admitted that the event was inexcusable and deplorable, but assured Jeremiah that his dismissal was the furthest thing from his mind. Also he would deal with the matter at the proper time.

Jeremiah said, "Sir, may I suggest that now is the proper time?"

"Captain Brown, Santa Anna will be coming aboard of you soon."

"If I may be so bold, sir, it is the fondest wish of my entire crew that Santa Anna remain where he is until the commodore and Captain Hurd are officially reprimanded before my officers."

The President felt the pressure of the moment. Though politely phrased, here was a threat. Jerry Brown, sole hope on this day, had him over the hip, so he temporized by admitting that upon thinking it over he saw no reason to postpone the matter. With this, he dispatched a brief order to the offenders to appear before him as quickly as possible.

Soon Hawkins and Hurd entered the President's office and stood

[3]Official Correspondence of the Texas Revolution.

at attention. Upon seeing the *Invincible's* officers in the room, they looked uneasy. They listened to the formal complaints and said nothing, holding themselves erect and staring straight ahead as Burnet dressed them up one side and down the other. Such conduct, he said, addressing the commodore, was not only unbecoming to an officer and man but was a disgrace to the service Hawkins headed; the rights of his brother officers had been trampled in the dust; their view of him was justified for he had turned on his government and used force to prevent the departure of Santa Anna in accordance with the Treaty of Velasco, and to break Captain Brown. But he had failed, and it was only fitting and proper that the perpetrator of such acts should be stripped of his insigne before the eyes of the entire fleet and drummed out of the service.

"And but for two reasons, I would order it done, Commodore Hawkins. The same applies to you, Captain Hurd. Although you have gone over to the mutinous army in defiance of your government, I have enough worries without throwing before my people a scandal at a time when feeling is high. The other reason is this. The Navy is very important to our security. Yesterday your government learned that a rumor issuing out of Mexico was based on fact.

"The huge new Mexican gun brig *Vencedor del Alamo* is said to be sailing for our coast on a mission of vengeance."

Every man in the room showed by one sign or another his surprise and concern.

"So in conclusion, Commodore Hawkins, for the time being you will remain in charge of the fleet, but with limited powers of office. You will sail today for New Orleans for refitting your ship, leaving Captain Brown to serve Texas in her need now as he has so valiantly done in the past." He stood then. "That is all, gentlemen."

Hawkins's face burned red and his eyes flashed as he brought his arm up in a crisp salute. Then he left the room.

When all but Jeremiah had gone, Burnet said, "You understand, Captain Brown. Now put Santa Anna aboard and get him home in a hurry. Else we're threatened with invasion again."

As Jeremiah turned away, he could not put down a feeling that he would soon command the fleet.

On the other side of the door, Hawkins met Jeremiah with all the animosity he could muster into his expression. But his hand was extended and he was saying, "Congratulations."

Jeremiah eyed him, ignoring the hand. He had waited a long time for this moment.

"You forget the 'sir,' Commodore. But that's to be expected from an old navy man who has lost so much salt that he allows the army to dominate him."

"But I'm still in command of the fleet, Captain Brown."

Jeremiah grinned. "Then it's still your privilege to ride a safe anchor while I engage the *Vencedor del Alamo*, sir."

So saying, he bowed and turned his back on the angry commodore.

Chapter Thirty-one

TWILIGHT STAR

The red and gold dawn of the mid-August morning broke with a cry from the masthead.

For nearly six weeks now, Jeremiah had chased, maneuvered, and used every ruse at his command to draw the pride of the Mexican Navy into battle; had even sat at the front door of her Vera Cruz anchorage, inviting her to an engagement. For the last week she had ridden anchor under the guns of the fort at Campeche. And now she was moving handily for so large a battle wagon up over the horizon of the bay. Even at her distance, there was no mistaking her identity. She was a majestic thing in the water.

The Vencedor del Alamo.

Jeremiah held her in the circle of his telescope, watching, admiring great sails in a cascading of white. They poured down from her yards and bellied like gilded crescents as the first rays of the sun burst through the clouds. The trade wind blew a fine breeze and the long Yucatán coast lay thin on the edge of the blue water. Seascapes went unnoticed. The naval officer was sizing up wind, distance, maneuverability, and guns, a fact made known by his ringing command:

"Beat to quarters!"

Turning abruptly on Lieutenant Sevey, Jeremiah said, "Had we the weather gauge, I'd run for a stern approach. Instead, we'll see if it's possible to work between her and the land and force her to fight."

All about him were noise and action. The clearing of decks and the tacking of ship. Sailors swarmed the rigging and yards came around sharp. Lines burned through palms as the wind jerked at this sail and that, cannonading each full.

"Deck ahoy!" the lookout forward cried. "She's altering course to north."

"So ho!" Jeremiah scoffed into Mr. Newman's ear. "She won't give up her wind. So we'll close for battle and give her leeward run she'll not soon forget."

Again the tack, the wearing of ship, and the bowsprit pointing north. Done handsomely. Soon the five miles of water between ships had narrowed down to three. The heavy gun brig loomed up an awesome sight, her white and red and black gleaming, her gun ports triced up.

The decks were trimmed for battle. As Jeremiah walked the aisle between guns, pausing to grin at this lad and touch that one reassuringly on the back, he missed nothing of the preparation for battle. For once, he offered no suggestion but moved on to the bows and stood alone.

Aft, Lieutenants Sevey and Newman studied the captain intently before exchanging significant glances. In the mind of each was the single sentence of a letter they had kept from their commander. Now, with battle ahead, they were debating on the wisdom of advising him of his brother William's death in New Orleans several weeks earlier. They decided it wasn't the time, even as, forward, Jeremiah was telling himself that William would be up and ready for another ship of the fleet by the time he returned. Aye, now that Hawkins had been put in his proper place.

The departure of Hawkins from Velasco on that day of June first was worth almost the disappointment of what followed. But was it? He would never forget the arrival of Santa Anna aboard the *Invincible,* any more than the storm that forced him back to Velasco that same day; any more than what happened on the third of June. Santa Anna had distributed a brief farewell address to Texans on the first—"My friends!" Santa Anna had the temerity to say in opening his letter of promises and gratitude. Then the arrival of the volunteers from New Orleans bolstered the army into full mutiny. Aboard ship while the angry crowd gathered on shore were President Burnet and

Santa Anna. Burnet made a speech imploring them to withdraw the order for the dictator's removal from the *Invincible*. He had said:

"Patriotism is emphatically a moral sentiment, and the citizen soldier who has no veneration for the moral character of his country may be brave and enterprising, and may render a good service in the field, but he can never meet the illustrious title of a patriot."[1]

The army was in no mood for flowery speeches; an unyielding thing with the growl of mutiny against its President in its voice. Jeremiah had looked over the sea of faces and said so all could hear him, "Mr. President, all the men here cannot take Santa Anna from this vessel and shall not without your order."

All as clear and fresh in his memory as the picture of the fine Mexican warship moving toward him now—Santa Anna broke and required much opium when President Burnet signed the order releasing him to the custody of the Texan army to prevent bloodshed. It was a sad day for the government. Jeremiah had ordered his flag at half-mast in a gesture of rebuke to an army that didn't know how to deal with peace. And the star of Texas had dropped like the star of day.

But it would rise again, and he, Jeremiah Brown, would keep pace with it. Hawkins was in disfavor, and the time might be drawing near when the *Invincible* would be the flagship of the fleet, J. H. Brown the commodore. And victory here on this day would almost guarantee that.

Further reflection was brought to an end. The *Vencedor del Alamo* thundered a broadside. It fell short, and crew and officers and commander breathed sighs of relief.

Jeremiah said, "We'll let the enemy come closer before feeling our metal. We don't have shot to waste."

A long half hour went by. Closer and closer the ships drew to one another, each tacking, jockeying for position, hoping to send a crippling shot home. The *Vencedor del Alamo's* great size made her heavier in the water and slower to respond to sail. Which fact, Jeremiah told his officers, so evened the laws of chance that he planned to use his speed against it to the enemy's everlasting regret.

The water between them was narrowing constantly. The great *Vencedor* refused to be eaten out of the wind, though she played the game warily, now holding her fire as the Texan was doing. They

[1] Official Correspondence of the Texas Revolution.

were almost at a standstill, sail lifting and falling, toying, testing, nearly locked in battle. Then the ships sat parallel to each other six hundred yards apart.

"Bring your guns to bear on her decks."

A second and another passed. Then, "Fire!"

The *Invincible's* full larboard battery hurled shot across the water. Before the smoke was jerked away by the wind, the order sounded to close in on the enemy's wake.

The neat spread of canvas on the *Vencedor's* mizzen a moment before now dragged the water. A yard had crashed on her deck. She was·vulnerable now. The arrow had struck the heel of Achilles! If she had lain heavy and slow on the turn before the hit, the loss of her after sails would increase the drag on her stern to an amazing degree. Another hit like this and she would lie at their mercy. And the *Invincible* was moving under full sail for her sluggish stern.

"Now! Drive into her wake!" Jeremiah gripped the rail, jubilant. "Close in fast and damn her fire!"

From the *Vencedor's* deck twelve guns barked almost in unison. So great was the blast, the thunder seemed to smash down the waves. Her decks and masts and bowsprit and sails writhed under the mighty concussion. Just as the *Invincible's* second salvo was loosed in a belch of flame that threw guns backward in a savage thrust against their breechings, the awful hail of Mexican iron struck the *Invincible*.

The world seemed to blow up in Jeremiah's face. There was a sudden blinding light, and a scream above what seemed a thousand explosions all about him. He was on his hands and knees, trying to rise, trying to think, shaking his head savagely. Red colored his vision, dripped off his nose, and men were handling him. Then the light went out and a great quiet spread over a scene of timeless space without beginning or end.

2

Jeremiah stirred.

The voice was familiar, Kelton's to be sure. "Mr. Kelton, what's the noise out there? Thunder? Order storm sail and tell them to batten down."

"Aye, Cap'n. She's going to blow, all right."

Another voice, urgent: "She's hulling us!"

Jeremiah sat up, throwing off the restraining arms. "Mr. Sevey! Are we winning?"

"No, sir. The *Vencedor* met our drive for her stern with a full broadside. We were badly out-gunned."

"Are we severely damaged?"

"Aye, sir. She shot away our main-topgallant mast. She's trying to close in for boarding and Commodore López is demanding that we strike our colors."

"Strike our colors!" Jeremiah struggled up. The surgeon and Little Josh pushed him back, but not before he cried:

"Beat out of range! Cripple her masts and rigging. Do you hear? Rally the crew and——"

He was swimming off again, hearing his own guns run out. The rattle of musket fire, the whine of tackles, all blended into one thunderous roar.

Carmela with the golden hair was sailing off into space with him, her lavender dress flowing in the breeze, accepting the many changeable colors of taffeta. Her finger was on his cheek and she was smiling. "Why should I want to escape, Jerry?" And her eyes were drowsy and longing, her full breasts pressing against him. Suddenly the scene of space was filled with charging dark clouds. Carmela ran with a stab of lightning that illuminated her, pointing at him—a fool! "You look almost as foolish as the time you proposed to me, Jerry. But not quite." All lavender and gold, tinsel . . .

As Mr. Kelton worked over him, the ship gave to a concussion and shuddered and groaned down to her keelson. Then she heeled so suddenly that the surgeon was sent reeling off balance. Falling flat on his back, he swore. "By God, it's my last voyage aboard this infernal ship!"

When he got up, Captain Brown was saying in rational voice, "Mr. Kelton, you're a boozy little old liar."

"Bless me! Am I now? So you've decided to live!"

The surgeon paused over another patient. A bloody rag in his hand drew his thoughtful gaze. "Take him away, boys. It's too late.

'Pon my word, too damn much violence turns even the Lord's stummick."

Jeremiah said quietly, "A violence for freedom, Mr. Kelton. A life dedicated to something."

Then he was trying to leave the officers' mess table. As he fell back, Kelton said gruffly, "Stay down or they'll be saying the same about you."

"Perhaps," Jeremiah said. "It's not for us to say, Mr. Kelton. A man goes the way God wants him to go. That's the way I felt on deck. Once I was scared. Today I felt fear. But you know—it's different when you give the Lord a free hand to do with you what He will. It puts you in His hands, trusting Him to see you through."

The surgeon paused in his work and nodded his head slowly.

The peal of cannon and whine of shot gradually fell away. The choking sulphur smoke was cleared by the wind. With the silence of the ship's guns, the wake of battle fell over the *Invincible*. Groans of the wounded mingled with the noises of clearing the decks of rubble. Lieutenant Sevey appeared in haste, and soon Messrs. Newman and Wells were standing quietly with concern in their faces as they looked at their commander.

"He's hard to kill," the surgeon growled.

Jeremiah propped himself up on elbows and said, "Now how long must I wait for news of the battle?"

"We gave as good as we received, sir," Mr. Sevey said.

"Is that all?" A moment of reflection. "Then we didn't win?"

"No, sir."

"So we didn't." Though frowning and wincing, he appeared more thoughtful than in pain. "Just so the flag waves up there."

"Yes, sir."

Jeremiah was tired, very tired. He turned his head and watched sailors removing the body of a shipmate, seeing in blood and death a hollow symbol of the glories of the *Invincible* of the Gulf. On her decks he had fought the *Bravo, Libertador, Veracruzana,* and the mighty *Vencedor del Alamo*. Only he of the Navy had engaged the enemy in battle. And what was the reward? He was penniless and worn-out. He needed Polly now, for she and only she could give him victory over the years and over a man's errors.

Polly. A pensive smile spread over his face as the memory of their last meeting came to mind. . . .

Only a few hours after the army took Santa Anna off his ship, Aunt Virginia had sent word that Polly was at the hotel. He remembered rushing to her room and throwing the door open, looking at her as she glared at him——

"Jerry Brown! Who gave you the liberty to barge in on a lady?" As he stood there admiring her every line and curve and hair in her head, she said, "What do you want here?"

"What I've wanted for years and didn't know it."

She turned to her trunk and continued her packing. "Where's the Ryan woman?"

"Gone and forgotten."

"I'll bet! Well, it makes no difference to me. I'm leaving for Pensacola."

"What for?" he demanded.

"To marry a gentleman." She busied herself without turning to him. "I recall a certain schoonerman's advice back when I was nineteen—it was all a matter of striking one's level."

"When you were *eighteen*."

"Nineteen. I'm twenty-three now."

• "You're twenty-two. And you're not going to Pensacola. You're going to marry me."

"Marry you, Jerry Brown! Brazos thunder and damnation! Are you daft? You awaiting trial in New Orleans. Branded a pirate in the United States. With Hawkins out to clip your wings, and Sam Houston, who doesn't like you two cents worth, slated for the next President, where do you stand?"

Her face taut with anger, hands on hips, she was moving toward him. Backing a step, he said:

"All right, Polly. I was just thinking that maybe we could get a little schooner of our own when peace comes."

"There isn't going to be any peace. Not with Mexico preparing to conquer Texas again. You and Texas court trouble, find it! Besides, you've talked about a new schooner since back in thirty-one. Even wasted good schooner money by sending me off to learn how to be a lady. Why I wouldn't marry you under any circumstances——"

"Not in this dress."

She rushed to his arms, laughing and crying. Looking up at him, she said, "I knew I'd get you. Since I was fifteen, I've known it. But don't stand there looking like you'd just been captured by a Mexican, Jerry Brown! Do something!"

And he was holding her close, telling her they would have a schooner and a home and many little webfooted schoonermen, when the President's messenger arrived with word that he should put to sea at once—the *Vencedor* had reached the Texas coast. . . .

3

There was a commotion on deck. As Sevey ran from the room, the surgeon bawled out, "Now what?" Then the drum rolled and pipes sounded. The beat to quarters! Jeremiah raised himself slowly and felt the surge of blood in his veins. It no longer mattered that all Polly had said was true, about war, his trial in New Orleans, and Sam Houston's dislike of him—the fact that she awaited his return filled him with fresh hope and purpose. The light of battle shone in his eyes again. He was on his feet, staggering toward the deck. He would make it and direct the battle himself. By God, he would make it.

He did.

There she was, the *Vencedor del Alamo*. He had the wind of her now, had her right where he wanted her. His mouth spread into a grin and he was wishing for a cap on his head. A cap in his hand.

He would throw it high, aim it at the ensign whipping proudly, defiantly, in the trade wind, the star in the rigging.

BY GARLAND ROARK

NEW NOVEL— Texas Novelist Garland Roark will have his eighth book published this week. The author of "Wake of the Red Witch," "Fair Wind to Java," "Rainbow in the Royals," "Slant of the Wild Wind," "The Wreck of the Running Gale," and two Westerns under a pseudonym, has taken a thrilling tale of true naval history, that of the almost forgotten Texas Navy, for his subject in his new novel "Star in the Rigging" to be published by Doubleday Thursday. Oddly enough, this story has been under the eyes of novelists for over 100 years and this is the first time it has ever been told in novel form.

Star in the Rigging

BY GARLAND ROARK

Tension in 1832 between Mexico and her arrogant progeny, Texas, was mounting fast. Mexico placed an embargo on all Texas shipping. Outraged shipowners sent up a storm of protest. Finally Captain Jeremiah H. Brown of the schooner *Sabine*, urged by the people of Texas, sailed past the roaring guns in Velasco Harbor in a dash for New Orleans. This first act of open defiance was to touch off the Texas war for independence.

Captain Jerry matched his wits and cunning against the powerful Navy of Mexico. He brought the fight to Mexico's front door by committing sabotage in the harbor of her largest port, Vera Cruz. But he was torn between patriotism and his love for a treacherous woman who had turned her back on her country for the wealth and glitter of Mexico.

This is the story of a country paralyzed by strife told against a background of the Alamo, the surrender of Colonel Fannin's army, Samuel Houston's retreat, and the eventual triumph of Texas. Garland Roark has written the unforgettable and little-known history of the Texas Navy and the part it played in winning freedom for the Lone Star Republic.

United States

Nacogdoches

SABINE R.

RED R.

TRINITY R

MISSISSIPPI R.

San Jacinto R.

Anáhuac

n Felipe

Harrisburg   Galveston

Velasco

Brazoria

Matagorda

HURRICANE

Mobile

New Orleans

PASS À L'OUTRE

S. W. PASS

GULF OF MEXICO

R628

BAY OF CAMPECHE

Vera Cruz

Las Arcas

Sisal

Campeche

YUCATÁN

96   94   92   90   88   86

32   30   28   26   24   22   20   18